Resilience in Love

by Lynne Hunter

Michael Terence Publishing

First published in paperback by
Michael Terence Publishing in 2020
www.mtp.agency

Copyright © 2020 Lynne Hunter

Lynne Hunter has asserted the right to be identified as
the author of this work in accordance with the
Copyright, Designs and Patents Act 1988

ISBN 9781913653729

No part of this publication may be reproduced, stored
in a retrieval system, or transmitted, in any form or
by any means, electronic, mechanical, photocopying,
recording or otherwise, without the prior
permission of the publisher

Cover image
Copyright © Mihai Andritoiu
www.123rf.com

Cover design
Copyright © 2020 Michael Terence Publishing

To my Aunty Tina, cherishing all the wonderful memories you have left us with and miss sharing your special coffee & biscuits.

Prologue

Sara laid curled up on the filthy cold floor of the barn, in excruciating pain. Concentrating on her breathing until the pain subsided again. She had no idea where she was or how long she had been there, the only thing clear, was that it would all end soon. Her plan had worked, Bruce and little Ava had gotten out, they had escaped.

Sara reflected on her life. She had packed so much into her 23 short years. All her hopes, her plans and her dreams for the future were to be snatched away, violently.

A sharp sting, sprang to her eyes and a huge lump rose in her throat, making swallowing difficult. She refused to let any tears fall, that would show weakness and she would not leave this world and give that evil bastard any satisfaction.

This was but a short reprieve between the savage beatings, just long enough for him to knock back another whiskey and get his breath back. Her fears were magnified as she realised, she was staring directly into the face of her own mortality.

'Please God, let me peacefully slip away before he returns,' she pleaded.

She let her mind drift and thought of Bruce, the night of the Wrap Party, the very special nights in her hotel, and all the ways they found to love each other, and their very understated visit to Coney Island, just the two of them. How long ago was that? It seemed like time had slowed down and the world had disappeared.

Life was so cruel. To have experienced such a life-altering connection with love once in a lifetime, but to be given that chance twice, and have it end tragically short both times, made her belief in fate a mockery, and a far greater suffering than the physical pain she was enduring.

Her mind drifted on to thoughts of her parents and she sent them a heartfelt farewell:

Mum, you were always there for me with a loving smile and staunch encouragement for Cameron and me to do better and succeed. I am so sorry to leave first.

Dad, forever the Jekyll & Hyde, the generous sole one moment, and nasty the next, with a vicious temper, I hope one day you will acknowledge your depression and seek help, please give mum the support she will need in the coming days and weeks.

Cameron, my wonderful big brother, I would never have achieved all that I did without you, always by my side, guiding me and sharing my hopes and dreams, thank you. For the love you have for me, please give Bruce the support I know you are so good at giving.

I carry all your love in my heart and I send you mine, please take care of each other, until we meet again. I'll be waiting.

Last but by no means least, Bruce. We had such a short time together, but what an incredible time it was. I take all those wonderful memories with me. Even in these darkest moments, the thought of you makes me smile, thank you for showing me how to love again. I love you and it hurts so much to never know what might have been, remember me with a smile, you carry the remainder of my heart with you.

Her mind drifted again in a kaleidoscopic haze of wonderful memories, especially the day she first met Bruce …

One

London - November 1986

Sara fidgeted in the makeup chair, her heart beating a strong staccato rhythm, her breathing, stalling every time the door to the make-up trailer opened. The first day of shooting on her latest film 'The 2nd Son', a period drama set in 1815. 'Why did the first scene have to be an intimate one,' she thought. There was only one other profession, where you meet someone, say hello, then jump into bed and get down to business.

She endeavoured to calm herself by concentrating on her breathing in to a count of 5 and out to a count of 5, whilst having a conversation with her inner voice or conscience or - *Nagy*, as she had named her, well they seemed to have so many conversations, it seemed only right to give her a name, a therapist, many of her American friends had one, would probably have a field day trying to analyse *that* one.

Today, Nagy was on usual form, '*Get a grip you idiot, do you want to bumble through your first scene, relax and for God's sake, breathe. You can melt into a pathetic puddle later.*' That was Nagy's umpteenth reprimand since waking this morning. Her thoughts were congested of meeting *him*, *again* and her stomach was still doing multiple somersault's. Breakfast had been totally out of the question and it was now starting to make embarrassing, loud, growling noises, perfect!!

The hair and makeup team started transforming her into her character. Tania, her make-up assistant, picked up one of the magazines from the usual pile left on the coffee table.

'Have you seen this recent article in, 'Compute IT', about Bruce and his equally gorgeous Business Partner, Jack Mason?' Tania asked, Sara shook her head, 'It says they are starting to make quite a name for themselves in the computer world with their Company iByte.'

Sara's eyes widened in surprise, 'He owns *that* Company?' she asked.

'Co-owns,' Tania corrected, whilst flicking through the magazine to the article in question and handing it to Sara to read. Sara's interest slammed into overdrive, whilst *attempting,* to give the impression of vague interest.

Bruce Bailey, was the main lead in this film, as he was, the 2nd son.' He seemed to be a success in everything he touches. *'Probably with an ego to match and a nightmare to work with,'* Nagy whispered. Thanks, Nagy, that's not helping. Why the hell did I agree to this, it's going to be the longest five months of my life, Sara thought to herself. She endeavoured to give the impression that she may as well read it, there was little else to do for the next hour, but secretly, she was riveted.

She read how Bruce and Jack met at a Rock festival. Bruce describing his interest in the Bands and the music and Jack saying he was, 'There for the alcohol and women.' Sara read on through the article, occasionally laughing at the banter between the two men and felt the camaraderie that came across between them. According to Jack, 'Bruce is the brains.' 'And Jack is the showman, with the ideas and drive behind the company, always pushing it forward, getting the company noticed,' countered Bruce.

Sara finished reading and put the magazine down, as the stylist took over to create an intricate style for her character. Sara let her mind wander back to last week and the night out with, *the girls,* her three closest friends Samantha *Sami,* Olivia *Livy* and Alexa *Lexi,* another girl had recently joined their group, Mia. She instantly fit in with the complexity of personalities of the group. It was Mia who suggested going to see the recently released film 'Goose Green' starring Bruce. It was a biographical account of the Falklands Conflict, for which Bruce was being nominated for both a BAFTA and Oscar for the lead role.

Sami, Livy & Lexi were instantly aware of how this film would affect Sara. She was still mourning Matias. They all were. Was it already sixteen months since he died?

Sara and Matias had celebrated their engagement only a month before it happened. Matias Moreno was Argentinian. A young man, having just finished his National Service in his country, six months before. Matias was visiting his family before commencing a long contract in a new Broadway show, just as the conflict was announced. His departure was officially refused and he was subsequently, conscripted and fought at Goose Green.

As Sara watched the film, she found it difficult. Matias had fought in this Conflict. The realisation of that reality was difficult to rationalize. As a British person she should be routing for the British soldiers, but after having loved Matias and his family, she found her allegiance … conflicted. Neutrality was the only way to get through watching the film.

Bruce played a British soldier severely wounded at Goose Green, with a heart-rendering scene when he was airlifted to safety, learning that his long-time school friend, whom he joined up with hadn't survived. It was being hailed as the most heart-breaking scene in a film, in the last decade, reducing many audiences to tears. It included flashbacks to some hilarious antics they got up to, before joining up and after, whilst on leave, the girls they met and loved. Also, the shower scene with his fiancée when he returned home and recovered, was being hailed as the most, sexiest. It was reported that Bruce's fan base had quadrupled overnight after the films' premiere in Leicester Square. Sara had to admit, the shower scene was definitely sizzling hot and that body of his …

Sara endeavoured again, to relax in the makeup chair and formulate a plan of action, to improve on her reaction towards him, for their second meeting, at the first she felt she showed herself to be a complete nervous, novice and she was a professional – wasn't she? This being the only make-up trailer and their first scene being imminent, this meeting was going to happen at any moment.

Sara closed her eyes as Tania finished on her eye makeup and thought back to her first meeting with Bruce the almighty beautiful, that's what her friends had started calling him, after seeing that film, it was at the read-through.

Sara had arrived at the studio offices and was shown to the room they were to use. As the secretary opened the door to show her in, she saw him and froze, as there he was in the flesh, looking impossibly gorgeous. He looked up from the script and straight at her as Producer, Carl Davis, famous for many successful period pieces, made the introductions.

Sara took her fill of him, from his thick, rich, sable wavy hair. that curled up over the collar of his snug-fitting deep blue shirt, casually opened at the neck, which intensified and darkened the blue of his eyes, they were framed by the thickest black eyelashes women the world over would kill for, his Romanesque nose and his sexy, sensual, full pillowy lips.

As he strode across the room to place the script on the table, Sara was transfixed by the way his body filled his clothes, his fitted shirt was almost at bursting capacity, stretching across his broad shoulders and how his muscles moved under his shirt. He sauntered towards her holding his hand out in greeting, he positively towered over her 5'3 frame by at least a foot, she would barely reach his shoulder in bare feet, thank God, for high heels or she would have to raise her chin a fair way to meet his gaze.

Sara felt her heartbeat so fast in her chest as she stood immobile, unable to breathe, bug-eyed and drop-jawed - must have made *such* a lovely sight! *'At least close your mouth dear, before you catch a fly or start to dribble,'* she heard Nagy reprimand her as usual. Sara immediately, snapped her jaw shut and raised her hand and placed it in his, she instantly felt a frisson, like an electrical current travelling up her arm and through her whole body, settling into an over-heated glow at her womanly core, making her clench the muscles between her legs as her heartbeat an ever faster rhythm.

'Hi, I'm Bruce, it's lovely to meet you.' Sara searched her scrambled brain for a response, all she could think of was, *this is Bruce Bailey*, for crying out loud and he was smiling that beautiful, bright, white smile that lit up his whole face, reaching his eyes, *this is Bruce Bailey*, she screeched in her brain. *'Ok, let me try and locate that intelligent part of your brain,'* Nagy whispered.

Since accepting this film, Sara read avidly about Bruce, buying all the newspapers and magazines that had a story about him, no shortage of reading material there!! A former Kick-Boxing champion which he had started doing when he was very young, his trainer recognised a real talent and started entering him into competitions. At the age of just 20, Bruce had to retire from the sport, due to a serious leg injury, his trainer ordered him to take some rest time to heal and let the dust settle, before making any life-altering decisions.

The publicity surrounding the fight went worldwide in the Sports world. Bruce's opponent, Mel Forbes, lost his temper and ignored the rules. The fight had to be stopped, but not before each had sustained serious injuries.

Following the fight, there were discussions between Bruce and The Sporting Federation with an agreement reached to offer Mel a concession, for his lapse in adhering to the rules of the competition. If he agreed to drop a level and work his way back to attaining his title. Mel refused, saying it was unfair for him to be penalised, as it was Bruce's fault for making the first illegal move, he had only retaliated. This was refuted by all the Judges. Mel was summarily disqualified, fined and told never to return to the sport.

Although Bruce also received lacerations to his face, just seemed to add to his appeal and he was inundated with many lucrative advertising and modelling assignments, they liked the tough, rugged look. Bruce did this whilst gaining his BSc Hons Degree at University and it helped pay his fees and living costs. Towards the end of his time at University, he formed his band 'Turbulence' which he was the lead singer and lead guitarist, playing gigs on Campus and around local pubs, which is where they were spotted and offered a recording contract. Upon the release of their first album and trying to break into the American market, Bruce attended a music festival in New York, which is where he met Jack Mason.

Sara loved the band, had bought every one of their singles and albums, knew all the words to their songs and went to their concerts, at every opportunity. The more she read about Bruce the more she was impressed by his humble beginnings and his self-motivation to better himself, but it could also lead to arrogance, only by getting to know him would she be able to judge which way his attitude had led.

Sara wondered what other talents Bruce had, she couldn't help the quick glance down at his tight-fitting trouser area, as they shook hands.

His smile broadened, and did she detect a spark of hunger in his eyes?

Oh God, did he notice where I just glanced, Sara you slut, stop ogling him, if he stared at your breasts you wouldn't like it, she told herself.

'*Liar,*' sniggered Nagy.

Probably has this effect on all his leading ladies, Sara thought to herself. '*Ok, we need to unscramble this brain and make like a conversation - immediately. I'm working overtime here,*' Nagy shouted at her. Sara took a deep breath, but it still sounded breathless when she replied, 'It's incredible to meet you too.' '*So not cool,*' Nagy, whispered, this time.

'I mean, pleased to meet you too,' Sara corrected.

Bruce smiled and gestured towards the table and chairs and said, 'Shall we?'

Cripps!! He's even more gorgeous up close?

For the next two hours, they read through some of the scenes and discussed their characters, Sara all too aware of her faux pau and kicking herself for allowing him to unsettle her, *incredible to meet you?* That was stoking his ego with a great big shovel.

Suddenly brought back to the present by her embarrassment of the memory, Sara leaned forward in her chair and involuntarily groaned aloud, covering her face with her hands, jogging Tania who was working on her lip makeup.

'Oh Sara, now you have a clowns grin,' Tania exclaimed and started to remove the smudge.

'Sorry, I was distracted and thinking of something,' Sara said.

It was precisely at that moment Bruce walked into the makeup trailer with Davy Philips, the Director, Bruce charmingly greeted everyone, Sara noticed the various reactions he was creating, women started to subconsciously preen themselves by either flicking their hair, straightening their clothing or standing seductively, Sara rolled her eyes at this. The men tried to act cool and greet him with an 'Alright Bruce' and pretend to carry on with what they were doing, but Sara caught them eyeing him in the mirror, some were discreetly scowling, probably because of the effect he was having on the women or seductively if they fancied him. Sara rolled her eyes again as she thought, how typical, bet he gets this reaction wherever he goes and probably fully expects it too.

Sara tried to stop looking at him because he seemed to be ignoring her and that annoyed her, why was everyone else getting his attention and not her, she was his leading lady after all and should have been the first one greeted, not the last. *'Oh, for God's sake, what are you? – 10? grow up!!'* Thanks Nagy, always making me feel *so* much better!! Sara responded to herself.

Then he turned around, caught and held her gaze in the mirror and slowly the corners of his mouth lifted and he gave her that full-on dazzling white smile, with a deep rich timbre to his voice as he said, 'Good morning,' Sara's heart immediately slammed against her chest and beat even fast and much louder, she swore everyone could hear, her breath caught in her throat and she could feel the heat, creeping up her neck and across her face.

Dear God, he really is beautiful, he certainly does not disappoint when meeting him in person, unlike some film stars, Sara thought. *'Bet he knows it too,'* Nagy advised. You're probably right, Mr Charmer and knows it, personified, thinks he can charm his way into every girl's knickers, well not mine, I will not be his next used and discarded conquest. Sara lifted her chin, held his gaze and gave him one of her brightest smiles and replied, 'Good morning,' let's see who's playing who, she thought.

Two

As Bruce wandered into the makeup trailer, talking to Davy about some changes to one of the scenes, he caught his breath, sitting in one of the makeup chairs and looking radiant and utterly beautiful was Sara Kaye, it was as if all the lights in the makeup trailer suddenly increased by 10,000 watts. She looked directly at him through the mirror, he quickly looked away and greeted all in the trailer, aware of how nervous he was, he felt like a green adolescent, whenever in her presence.

Get it together, before you talk to her, he scolded himself. He received the usual response from all around him, which he still found unnerving, he never thought himself anything special.

After greeting the last person, he turned and caught her gaze in the mirror and was captured in that moment, he stared at all that beautiful wavy long blond hair that reached halfway down her back and was being pinned up, he had never seen so much hair, it was beautiful and his fingers itched to reach out and touch the golden, silky tresses, he clenched his hands into fists and held them by his side to stifle the temptation. Those huge chocolate brown eyes he felt like drowning in and knew so well, framed by unbelievably long eyelashes, her lips reminded him of sweet, succulent strawberries, that he was so tempted to taste, triggered thoughts of the numerous tantalizing fantasies he had had of this beautiful and sexy lady, whilst alone in his bed.

It created a delightful shiver to run down his body stirring and awakening his manhood. Bruce smiled while taking a deep breath and gave himself a swift talking too, '*do not*, make an arse of yourself, not here, not now, with loads of intimate scenes, there will inevitably be times ahead for that.'

She gave him a breath-taking smile and when she replied, 'Good morning,' he felt like he would never tire of hearing her softly spoken voice. Never had such an everyday, ordinary and mundane exchange felt so extra-ordinary. It was as though his world had suddenly tilted on its axis and was about to completely change - he certainly hoped so.

Yesterday had been his first day of shooting and today he was getting ready for his first scene with Sara and it was an intimate one. Bruce endeavoured to keep his nervousness in check. Everyone thought he was so cool and oozed confidence, or so he was frequently told in interviews and read in the tabloids - so it must be true, right?!!! But he was a common nobody, an escapee from a brutal London council estate, and when the few successful films he'd made and the spotlight fades, which it will eventually, they will all wonder what it was they saw in him. Therefore, he thought he would reap the benefits while it lasted, the profits from all this helped start his and Jack's company iByte and he was determined that when this was all over, their company would succeed.

He remembered something his mother once said, 'Promise me you will always be genuine, my little Brucie, in thought and deed.' He didn't understand what that meant, as he was only eight at the time and when he asked, his mother replied, 'That means, always be kind in your thoughts and show kindness in what you do, treat people with respect, you never know when you will need help and people *always* respond to kindness. Never become a false charmer like your father, no one knows what goes on behind closed doors, they only see what's in front of them and think it happens all the time, down the pub, everyone loves your father, but we know differently don't we?' He made that promise to her, endeavouring to honour it as he grew up. He would not become a false charmer and be anything like his father.

Bruce greeted his makeup assistant Marie and sat in the chair she indicated, acutely aware of Sara's presence and close proximity to him. He relaxed and closed his eyes and relived their first meeting two days ago.

Whilst he waited for her arrival and doing a walkthrough on his own from one of the scenes they were to do together. Bruce looked up from his script at the sound of the door opening and froze - framed in the doorway was an ethereal vision of beauty wearing a low-cut wispy white lacey creation exposing a glimpse of the top of her rounded breasts, producing an instant reaction from one very hot-blooded males' anatomy. Bruce forgot to breathe.

As Sara walked past him as they sat to do a read-through of one of their scenes, his gaze was drawn to her cute behind and swaying hips, which were tucked into tight-fitting bright red trousers, which outlined those amazing legs he had seen in an almost obscene flesh coloured catsuit, she wore in one of her shows he went to. The incredible grace and style of her dancing, performing amazing acrobatics, that defied gravity, so daring, he had been utterly and completely, mesmerised.

Bruce had been dragged along to the show that night as a surprise birthday present for their mum from him, his brothers Blake and Brett and sister Brooke, who chose the show. Bruce didn't really mind, their mum had always enjoyed live shows and dancing and tried to watch them on TV, but only if their father was out, as he controlled the TV. It made his heart swell to see his mum all dressed up on a night out to the theatre in the centre of London with a broad smile on her face, a sparkle in her eyes and the way she clapped and cheered, oohed and ahhed at the death-defying choreography, singing along and tapping her feet in time to the music, thoroughly enjoying herself. She so deserved this, after all the misery their father had put the family through.

Since finally leaving their father she had come off her 'nerve tablets', quit smoking and went regularly to the local swimming pool and learnt to swim and seemed so much more relaxed and enjoying her life. Making new friends and finally able to meet up with old friends she was forced to lose touch with, and now able to have her many brothers and sisters visit whenever they chose. Their father never liked visitors, discouraged them at every opportunity, their mother came from a big happy and very close family, seven sisters and four brothers. Her family had to make appointments, no turning up at the door because they were passing, that was a definite no-no, as far as their father was concerned.

Mum was always smiling now and had many hobbies. When she was with their father and suggested going to evening classes, their fathers' reply was, 'What do you want to do painting for, do you think yourself a Picasso or something, you can't sell the rubbish you'll paint, what's the point, waste of bloody money, *my* bloody hard-earned money,' he would shout and if she argued any more then there would be an almighty row and he would slam out of the house and disappear down the pub for hours, returning blinding drunk and the shouting, then the beatings would start.

Bruce shuddered as a flood of horrific memories threatened to swamp him, the numerous and frequent beatings he and his brothers endured at the hands of their drunken father. These thoughts had a periodic habit of escaping and he always fought to tamper them down.

His youngest memory was seeing his older brothers kicking, punching and screaming at their father trying to pull him off their Mum. He was maybe two or three at the time. As he grew older, he joined his brothers in taking turns in receiving beatings, to deflect their fathers' anger away from their mum and, later, their little sister, their father hated the sound of her crying, she was only a baby and that's what babies did. He and his brothers were scared that if their father used his full strength on their mother and sister – he would kill them.

Steadying his breathing, he brought himself back to the present. Bruce absorbed the sound of musical laughter and light giggles next to him. It made him think of summer rain and birdsong, brightening the darkest of all moods, like casting rays of warm sunshine on his face.

He sat patiently letting the very talented Marie create her masterpiece, applying scars to his body for the character he was portraying and the intimate scene ahead. Bruce's first scene, the previous day, had been his character returning home, having suffered numerous injuries in the battle of Waterloo and arguing with his brother, a Duke, in his study, after his brothers' accusation of, 'going off and playing soldiers,' whilst he had to stay home and assume his duties after their father's death and it was high time he remained at home and helped him.

Bruce enjoyed this scene as he got to raise his voice and shout, 'Playing Soldiers? Playing Soldiers, I was defending this country with my life and the lives of my men in my Regiment, against enemies who want to invade, keeping *you* safe so you can sleep at night, so don't you dare accuse me *ever again* of Playing Soldiers', then storming out of the room and slamming the door.

Bruce was still relatively new to the filming industry and found it difficult to work his way around the thought process of filming scenes out of sequence, one minute it was intimate scenes with Sara with all the scars of his character which was later in the film, then the cementing of his relationship with his brother, when he sees the scars he has sustained from the war to the next scene with Sara, at his regiments camp at the beginning of the film where he has no scars, Sara plays his brothers' fiancé, although, in that scene he doesn't know who she is, she comes to his camp in Brussels before they march towards Waterloo. Bruce is shirtless whilst shaving and she is enquiring if he can spare a man to escort her and her maid part of the way as they try and get passage back to England.

A period drama was a step away from Bruce's usual genre up to now, and he had tried to reason with his new agent of 4 months, Aidan Proctor, who had begged, even pleaded with Bruce to accept this part, convincing him that it would serve him well to broaden his repertoire as an actor.

Bruce respected Aidan's honesty when he told him that it was the first time a film company had contacted *him,* without having the hard work he usually had of pushing for auditions for the rather small list of actors he represented, and having Bruce on his books had been the biggest boon in fifteen years of hard graft, frequent knock backs and next to no commission.

The studios wanted Bruce, which meant he was able to negotiate an insane fee, because of the millions of fans Bruce had in his fan club and the complete sell-out tours with his band, Turbulence, and box office smash hits of his latest three films, it was for this reason Bruce had made it a condition of his contract that Sara plays his leading lady, never in a million years did he believe it would be his good fortune that she would accept.

Three

It was now a month into the shoot, it had been a long day filming a rather intricately choreographed intimate scene, leaving Bruce exhausted, frustrated and extremely horny, he was definitely getting laid tonight.

He met up with his four closest mates Dom, Jamie, Max and Flynn, starting at The Dog and Duck in Soho, then joining up with twenty of their mates, in various pubs around Soho, they had known each other since school and kept in touch by celebrating their birthdays with a pub crawl in a location chosen by the birthday boy, and they would all make a weekend of it. This time it was Dom's 28th Birthday, there was a month between them in age and as Bruce had been away on promotional work for his birthday, tonight was a combined celebration. With various location shoots, it would be a while before Bruce could enjoy nights out like this with his mates, therefore, they all intended to get totally hammered tonight.

Bruce was ribbed mercilessly, when after one drink too many, he mentioned his current sexually frustrated state, after simulating sex all day, he was subjected to ceaseless innuendos, with girls blatantly throwing themselves at him. Two of the girls in particular, eagerly and suggestively, whispered explicitly how they could discretely *and not so discretely*, satisfy him.

As the alcohol flowed, his mates made the mistake of suggesting how he should ask the sexy Sara out. Naming 'places to do it' or just to bring her to the next gathering for her to have a pick at the best pack of 'prime males'. Bruce managed to keep his temper - just. The comments were getting lewder as the night wore on. Bruce could endure no more. Olly made the biggest mistake, he was standing at the bar a few feet away from Bruce and shouted a rude comment followed by a suggestive hand gesture, making all around him throw their heads back howling with laughter.

Without warning, Bruce lunged forward, grabbed Olly by the collar and held him up against the wall, drew back his fist and said through gritted teeth, 'Don't you ever use her name in a sentence like that again, she deserves better than to have a pack of depraved bastards like you panting after her.'

The look on Olly's face was pure shock, he instantly held his hands up in surrender saying, 'Take it easy Bruce, didn't mean anything by it, too much drink, I just got carried away, I didn't realise you had feelings for her, honest.'

There had been a sudden surge of several friends surrounding the two of them, many of them trying to hold Bruce back, telling him to calm down, that Olly meant nothing by it, and neither did any of them. They were all apologising for their comments, very few people saw this side of Bruce and those that did, didn't come out of it looking very pretty.

Bruce closed his eyes briefly, took a deep breath and loosened his grip, then slowly let Olly down. As he calmed his rage and forced his heart rate to slow down, he looked around and saw all eyes were on him, with sudden realisation, this was Olly, one of the good guys who treated his girlfriends with care and respect and maybe, just maybe, he had overreacted. Bruce started to back off and smooth the clothes down on Olly's collar and said, 'Just watch your mouth, ok?'

'Ok', Olly replied and moved away to give Bruce some space.

Olly had never been on the receiving end when Bruce reacted like that, and it scared the shit out of him. He also felt ashamed, for making such degrading comments about women, this was not his usual happy go lucky self and decided too much drink and letting the atmosphere have too much influence on him, he should never have rolled with it. He would let Bruce calm down and then go over and apologise, he certainly didn't want to permanently fall out with him, this was Bruce, he had far too much respect for him, after all, he had done for him.

Olly had been bullied first by his father and then at school. The leader of the bullies targeted him because of his small stature, but Bruce befriended him and included him in his circle of friends and slowly the bullying subsided. A few years later, he had a sudden growth spurt, no longer the shortest in class. Bruce invited him to work out in the gym with him, and one day he faced his bullies and silenced their taunts, never again did they bully him.

Bruce led by example, making it cool to listen to their teachers and do the homework, pass exams and eventually achieve a better way of life, Olly was now an architect, earning good money in a large firm in a good part of London and had a massive flat in a respected neighbourhood, not sure if he would have had all this, if Bruce hadn't befriended him and he will never forget that, *ever*.

Bruce was joined by his four close friends, who all looked at him wearily before Dom said, 'Where did that come from mate? Never seen you turn on Olly like that – ever.' Bruce looked down at his beer that Max had handed him and said, 'I have no idea.'

'That reaction was very intense, maybe you have strong feelings for this Sara and not ready to admit it to yourself yet? added Jamie.

'I have a rule of not dating people I work with, whilst working with them, it gets complicated, I'll see how I feel when the shoot is finished.' He was not about to admit, even to his closest friends, that he had fancied Sara from afar for many years, how pathetic did that sound!!! 'I'll have this beer and go over and talk to Olly and apologize,' Bruce said.

Jamie Allen, Bruce Bailey, Dominic *Dom* Carey, Max Devereux and Flynn Ewen, were the closest of friends, they had so much in common, came from the same tough council estate, all, except Max, had drunken fathers, only Bruce and Max were the lucky ones, with loving mothers who cooked proper meals each day. Max was the envy of them all, his parents were French, worked really hard in a local restaurant and didn't mind them being around, and Max's Dad loved his family and never laid a finger on Max or his brothers, Bruce, Jamie, Dom and Flynn were not so fortunate. It was always Max's Dad they turned to when they needed fatherly advice. They never had any money, but occasionally they would pick flowers for the mums and maybe sometimes these would come from someone's front garden, Bruce's mum told him not to do this, Bruce would agree, but added that they would only do this on special occasions then, giving her a cheeky smile.

They would alternate between Bruce's and Max's house, their mums would always have something for each of them to eat, maybe just a small meal and a drink, it was all they could afford and the boys loved them for it, both the mums would talk to them and be interested in them, and through the boys, their mums had even become close friends, Bruce's mum didn't have many friends because of his father's unpredictable and demanding temperament. Jamie, Dom and Flynn's mothers never seemed interested in them, they were either high on drugs, passed out through alcohol or in a rage from withdrawal.

They knew each other from the first day at school, seated together alphabetically, on the first day for the register by the teacher, and then by their own choice. They formed a close friendship, always together at playtimes and sitting next to each other, they became inseparable.

When they moved up to Junior school, thought it rather clever when they gave their little group, *for a short while*, the name 'The Alpha Betas', not just because of their surnames, they also took turns proclaiming to be the Alpha, for that particular day's adventure and the others were the Betas and had to follow orders. It made them feel important, and like a band of brothers in arms, they looked out for each other, when one had taken a beating from their father, the others would rally round because they all understood what that felt like.

They got up to all sorts of mischief and trouble, but there was also a lot of fun, going fishing or swimming, playing all sorts of games in derelict houses that were earmarked to be demolished, feeding the odd cat and kitten wherever they found them, clubbing together to buy a bottle of milk for this reason.

Moving up to secondary school, they dropped the group name, it used to sound cool when they were younger, but when they had discovered girls, it sounded … childish.

Four

During their first month of filming Sara found it difficult to concentrate on maintaining a professional façade. Every morning, she endeavoured to keep to her routine of rising early to fit in, at least, an hour's fitness, varying her exercise routines and swimming multiple lengths of whichever pool was closest to her. She followed this by making and drinking a fruit and protein drink, many of which, she had devised herself as they were delicious. She found most hotels to be very accommodating to make these shakes if she made friends with the Chefs. She would always take the time and make the effort to compliment the Chefs on delicious dishes, as she was always interested in learning new recipes, and would try them out when she got home. Sara loved to give positive feedback, credit where credit was due, had always been one of her motto's.

After her protein drink, she would then take a shower before leaving for her days' work and it always made her feel awake, alert and ready, she hated keeping people waiting and letting anyone down. She had worked with many so-called 'professionals', who just seemed to roll out of bed, after a late-night and it took them ages to be ready for the first scene, and they invariable oozed an unsavoury odour, which made working with them rather unpleasant. Bruce, on the other hand, always seemed to be as ready as she was whenever they worked together, whatever the time of day, always looking good, she would breathe him in and become intoxicated by his scent with a temptation to press her nose to his neck to smell him, lick him, taste him – *what was wrong with her!*

It had been a very long day, filming an intimate scene that took *all* day, and as much as she was not complaining about spending a whole day semi-naked, with a close to fully naked Bruce, it did leave her feeling a little sexually frustrated. Usually, Sara would head back to her hotel to sort herself out, but tonight she felt like company and rang some of her friends and asked if they wanted to try some new places in London, as usual, it was Sami, who was always the most outrageous of the group, to choose Soho, Sara had never been out and around Soho in the evenings for drinks and was therefore exhilarated and excited.

They all met in the bar of the hotel Sara was staying, to have dinner in the restaurant, afterwards they all headed into Soho on the underground. Sara wore a black baseball cap over her loose hair, knee-high black boots over her tight-fitting black jeans, a black and red leather jacket and a red shimmering top, deciding to keep her makeup natural and neutral, except for the bright red lipstick.

They toured a few pubs, then stumbled across one that sounded quite lively, they walked in and ordered a round of drinks at the bar, it was quite full of raucous men, celebrating something. As usual, it was Sami who got talking to two blokes whilst waiting for their drinks, as Sara and Lexi commandeered a recently vacated table. Livy went to help Sami carry the drinks over, Sami invited the blokes to join them, they soon found out that it was a duel birthday celebration, they introduced themselves as Jamie, Max and Flynn, then pointed over to another who was in the middle of a, 'drink a yard of ale' competition, which was in the shape of a large glass boot, that held a yard of ale, a novel idea introduced by the present owners of the pub as they had recently renamed the pub, The Jug & Boot, Dom was surrounded by a crowd who were cheering and yelling their support, whilst timing him.

Jamie, Max and Flynn shouted their encouragement and congratulations as Dom seemed to have won the competition, and they beckoned him over, as he reached his friends, wiping his mouth with the back of his hand and wiping it on his trousers, he was introduced to the ladies and shook their hands, and as ever the charmer of the group, he kissed the back of each of their hands, 'How charming and old fashioned,' commented Sami, very obviously smitten by the look she gave Dom, smiling and staring at him longer than was necessary, thought Sara.

'This is Dom one of the birthday boys,' Flynn said to the party of ladies, 'where is Bruce?' he asked Dom. Sara froze, could it possibly be *her* Bruce – oh my God, what was she thinking, when did he become *her Bruce*. Sara could feel the familiar heated blush rising up her neck and would be full-blown and all over her face in seconds, Sara excused herself, saying she needed the ladies and quickly disappeared.

'Not sure,' Dom shrugged, 'probably busy receiving a birthday pressie from the look those two girls were giving him,' he nudged Flynn and Max with a conspiring smile and raised eyebrows, 'anyway, I'm not complaining, if he had been with me in that competition, I wouldn't have won, he can drink faster than me, I won seventy-five quid' Addressing the whole table he said, 'Ladies, what can I get you?' They gave him their order and Sami went with Dom to help with the drinks.

Sara asked at the bar where the ladies was and made her way through an archway that looked like a closed restaurant area, she could see some people occupying one of the tables near the back. Sara hurried through to the ladies.

On her way back, she heard female giggling and realised it was the occupiers of the table she spotted earlier and started to make her way through to the bar, when she heard a male voice, that was familiar saying, 'Take it slower,' which produced more giggling from the females.

A prickly sensation travelled through Sara's body, as she turned, she saw Bruce, sitting over in one of the booths with one arm laying relaxed across the back of the booth seat, one of the girls was under the table, Sara could see the top of her head bobbing up and down, the other was kissing Bruce and he had her breast in his hand, Sara let out an involuntary audible gasp, then embarrassed that she had let her presence known. Comprehending what was going on, she immediately clamped her hand to her mouth, turned around and ran out to the bar area, finding her friends she told them she needed to leave, then ran out of the bar without waiting for an answer.

Bruce heard the gasp, pulled away from the girl who had been kissing him, caught Sara's eyes for a split second before she turned and ran. He quickly disengaged himself, pushed the girls away from him, getting up he tucked himself into his trousers and quickly made his way into the bar, finding his friends, he asked if they saw a girl rushing through.

Jamie answered, 'Yeah, Sara rushed through and left, what did you do Bruce?'

He ran out of the bar, looked around and caught sight of her blond hair in the distance, she was running down the street, he ran fast to catch up with her, all the while the image of what she had seen went through his head and he didn't like her thinking badly of him, although he wasn't sure why. What he did, and with whom was none of her concern, he was a single, unattached male with a healthy sexual appetite, but for some reason, he thought of Sara as – pure, innocent, and the thought of her with another man brought out a possessive reaction he scarcely recognised in himself, and the word *mine*, came to mind, *Sara is mine. What the fuck was wrong with him*, one month working on a period drama was getting to him more than he realised. He needed to get his head back into the current century.

He was gaining on her, but decided not to call out in case she stumbled and fell, instead, he doubled his efforts and caught up with her and grabbed her arm while he said, 'Sara, please stop, please, let me explain.' As she turned and faced him, she backed up against the wall behind her and he saw that she had been crying, her mascara was a mess, she had tried to wipe her tears and the sight of her being upset, tore at his heart, but he was confused as to why she had been crying. Tentatively, he asked, 'Why are you upset?'

'I have absolutely no idea,' Sara sobbed, 'I have no right to be, and totally confused with misplaced jealousy, I just want to forget what I saw and get out of here.' With that, she ran towards the main road, hailed a taxi, got in and was gone.

Bruce felt bewildered by her reaction, but also captivated by her complete honesty, she didn't try to cover it up and blame it on something else, it was about what she saw, what she saw those girls and he were doing, *misplaced jealousy*, she said, could she have feelings for him? she must have, he thought.

The corners of his mouth slowly creased upwards, forming a slow satisfying, smug smile. He walked back to the pub, taking his time, thinking of Sara and her sweet tear-stained face. He started formulating in his mind what he would say to her, he would make sure to seek her out tomorrow, they had no scenes together, but they would be in the same location. He had a very physically demanding shoot ahead of him, the battle of waterloo, this would require travelling to various locations and Davy, the Director wanted to do this over the next three weeks.

As he walked back into the pub Sara's friends asked if she was ok, he told them he saw her get a cab, but left out the conversation they had, as Sara said she was embarrassed, it would be up to her what she told her friends.

Five

Bruce never got the chance to speak with Sara the next day, the closeups on set, for the battle scenes took up the whole day and they would be travelling to their first location shoot that evening. Carl and Davy had received special permission to shoot some of the scenes on the actual Battlefield of Waterloo and the whole crew were extremely excited.

Bruce felt hollow leaving things the way they were between them, he knew the hotel Sara was staying at and decided before he left for the airport, he would visit her and try and explain, although he was still a little unsure what he would explain, it was pretty conclusive what he had been doing and how was he going to apologise for that, it happened, there was no changing it, he could only apologise for her having seen it and maybe he should have picked a less public place and blame the drink? – how lame did that sound?

Bruce arrived at Sara's hotel, he had found out where she was staying by asking Carl's assistant, Kelly, as to her room number, saying he wanted to discuss some script issues he had before he caught his flight, he knew the hotel wouldn't give him her room number, Kelly informed him that Sara was also about to depart for a different location shoot and he may be lucky enough to just catch her.

He ascended the stairs and found her room, he rapped on the door and waited, but there was no answer. He went back to the reception and enquired if Sara was still occupying the room, only to be told she had checked out earlier. Damn, he wouldn't be able to see her for at least the next three weeks, until they both returned for the last bit of shooting in England before leaving for America.

Bruce cursed, shocking the receptionist, he apologised and dragged himself out to the front of the hotel and asked the doorman to get him a taxi to the airport, his hotel was sending his suitcases directly to the airport.

Sara took her seat on her flight to Prague which was doubling for Brussels as her character was returning to England. She thought back over the last twenty-four hours and winced with embarrassment. How stupid she was to have gotten so upset over seeing Bruce with those women, she had no right, this being the one phrase that kept going through her mind most of the night when she wasn't punching the pillow and telling herself, what an idiot she was.

God, how he must be laughing at her right now, and she had stoked his ego with an even bigger shovel than when they first met. When the hell, was she going to learn that men in this profession were only after one thing, *after sex*, was to inflate their ego, and boy, had she done that last night. Well, the only thing for it was to face it, pretend nothing had happened and keep the hell away from Bruce, she had no intention of telling her friends, they would only rib her mercilessly for being such a prude and what did she expect, did she think he lived the life of a Monk? no understanding there, how could there be, she didn't understand her reaction herself.

For the next three weeks, she concentrated on her work, travelled to her various locations and tried to keep Bruce out of her thoughts, but when alone at night, he always crept in and invaded her dreams.

Sara was on her flight back to England and was apprehensive about the scenes she had with Bruce ahead, thankful that all the intimate scenes between them had all been shot out of sequence and all done, after that night at the pub, she was not sure she was that good an actress.

The next morning Sara walked on set, got dressed and made up into character, deciding to be prepared for when she came face to face with Bruce again. She could not help the sharp intake of breath and the pounding of her heart when she saw him.

God, he looked handsome, Sara thought, she stole a moment, looking down and fussing with her costume, to gain a few moments to compose herself, and appear unaffected by his appearance, she had to admit they certainly knew how to dress in the 18th Century.

Bruce was in a black, fitted rich tapestry cutaway tailcoat, black full-length trouser, with a white waistcoat with silver embroidery and white shirt and a fancy creative knot in his cravat with a diamond pin in the centre. His black buckled shoes were highly shined, his hair was the very height of styles for the period and encouraged his own dark curls to be shown off to great advantage, he looked every bit the leading man and simply took Sara's breath away. The black outfit seemed to deepen the blue of his eyes and they certainly caught everyone's attention, if the whispers from the cast and crew Sara overheard were anything to go by.

Sara fidgeted constantly with her costume and impatient to get the scene started and finished, so she could avoid the inevitable conversation with Bruce, as he was striding across the set towards her.

Bruce found it difficult to concentrate on Davy's instruction for the next scene, as they walked across the set, his attention was riveted on Sara as she fiddled and fretted with her costume and avoiding eye contact with him, did she want to avoid talking about that night? How was he going to start *that* conversation and he did feel it was up to him, he had been feeling guilty and needing to apologise, this was definitely a new arena for him, but tackle it, he would. He decided it would have to wait until they wrapped for the day.

Bruce held back till Sara had finished, he didn't change out of costume just in case he missed her. As soon as she started walking towards her trailer, Bruce placed himself in front of her, she stepped back in surprise with her hand going to her breast, which drew his attention to the area and the low cut of her costume, how on earth did men concentrate on anything in those days with women's fashion being as it was, he would definitely, have been going around with a permanent *cock stand* as that era called it.

'Sara, please we need to …'

Sara held her hand up and stopped him from continuing, 'We have nothing to say, I had no right to react the way I did, can we please just leave it at that, I am embarrassed by my behaviour,' she then turned and walked away.

'Sara, please,' Bruce called after her, but she just kept walking. She must have a very low opinion of me, she can barely look at me, he thought.

Over the next few weeks, Bruce sent Sara flowers with little messages. *Sorry, you witnessed my public and depraved behaviour. Please do not think that I always behave in this manner. I was very drunk that night.*

Bruce talked to his friends, who had kept in touch with Sara's friends, and with their help, Sara finally agreed to meet with Bruce at the restaurant in Sara's hotel, and it would be just the two of them.

As the waitress left with their order, Bruce decided to address the subject head-on, 'Sara – I'm so sorry …' Bruce started, but Sara again held her hand up to stop him.

'You don't have anything to apologise for Bruce,' how he loved her voice with his name on her lips. Sara picked up the napkin, twiddling nervously with it through her fingers. 'I had no right to react the way I did … I have a suggestion.'

'O … kay …' Bruce said cautiously, he was hoping she wasn't about to say they ignore each other or go their separate ways after the film was finished, he didn't want that. He wanted more and he wanted Sara. His body ached for her and that hadn't happened in a very long time. He didn't want any other and hadn't been with another woman since that night, all his thoughts had been consumed with her, which for him was unbelievable. If any of his mates knew, they would be having a field day at his expense.

'Can we - start over and forget that night ever happened? I am so embarrassed and I really don't want to talk about it, I still feel so stupid, I couldn't even tell my friends.'

'Deal,' Bruce immediately agreed with a hefty sigh of relief, he held out his hand and they shook to seal the deal. Sara gave him a full bright smile, which made his heart stutter.

The rest of the evening they ate, drank and laughed about antics of the cast and crew on set, the evening slipped by, far too quickly. As the restaurant started emptying, they realised it was quite late and they both had early starts in the morning.

Bruce signalled for the bill and they made their way out to the reception area. Sara faced Bruce and thanked him for such a lovely evening, then leaned forward and gave him a buzz kiss on the cheek, then turned and walked toward the lifts and disappeared into one.

Bruce could still feel that sweet chaste kiss on his cheek and his gaze was riveted on her behind, as he watched her walk away, and enter the lift. He slowly made his way to the exit and took a taxi to his hotel. He felt like it was the first night, at the start of something new in his life, and he couldn't wait for tomorrows dawn.

Six

It was New Year's Eve. The Production Company took a break from filming over Christmas and New Year. Bruce had spent the break partying with his mates, spending Christmas day with his mother at her new flat with his brothers and sister, it had been one of his happiest Christmases.

Two months ago, Bruce had completed on his second property, an impressive mansion on the Isle of Dogs in London, he hadn't had time to furnish it, as he had just started work on 'The 2nd Son'. He only brought the basics for himself on the occasional times he visited. As soon as he had the time, he would get an interior designer to remodel and redecorate the whole property. It had seven bedrooms, he had no idea why he bought such a large property, other than because he could.

His first investment was a large three-bedroom flat in Belgravia, his main residence at the moment. It gave Bruce such a buzz, to take his bike out for a ride around London, knowing that he had been able to buy the properties and his bike outright, and he intended to build a portfolio of lucrative properties, he believed property was a secure investment, his future plan, along with the computer company with Jack, for when this *fame*, was all over. He smiled to himself when he thought back to the day, he first rode his bike into the garage and played with the automatic doors, just like a child with a toy.

As the house was empty, it seemed the ideal time to have a wild party and New Year's Eve the perfect reason and timing, he wouldn't worry if the place got trashed, he was celebrating and life was good.

The party organisers had just left after doing a fantastic job, decking out his sparse house with all that was needed for a party, from the plates and glasses to tables and chairs, even bringing large arrangements of artificial planters, to make the colossal expanse of space, more homelike, the caterers were imminently due with the food, and to stock and serve at the bar. Tables were scattered around and there would be food on huge buffet tables, for those who wanted it.

It was a clear, but cold night. The garden had been decorated with hundreds of small multi-coloured lanterns, adding to the ambience. He had no idea how much would be seen of the London Fireworks from here, through the backdrop of the Canary Wharf skyline, but additional tables and chairs had been placed outside to watch them anyway. The extensive gardens sloped gently down to the Thames, as it lapped and glistened in the moonlight, there was a docking area for a boat, which Bruce intended to get as soon as he finished this project and take a well-earned extended holiday, it felt like he had worked non-stop since leaving University.

Bruce wandered leisurely through the rooms, marvelling at the sheer size of his newest investment, imagining making it his home one day, hopefully with a family of his own, a far-fetched, out of reach dream maybe, but one that he instantly felt when he first viewed the house. With its dark oak wood flooring and sheer white voiles cascading around the windows, the high ceilings, and ornate coving and central rosaries anchoring, elaborate, delicate chandeliers.

He couldn't suppress the swell of pride in his chest with the realisation, *this* was all his. To come from where he did, to owning such a large property. *Now*, his father had reason to be jealous, of his sons.

That was something his eldest brother Blake, once said, 'Let him rant, he's just jealous,' while he comforted Bruce after he had received a beating for having all his homework over the dining room table. He had been building a Galleon ship, which was stuck on thick card, covered with Polyfilla that would have been painted to represent a choppy sea. It was a school project, he had been building it in his bedroom for weeks, but on this day, he had just come in from school and needed to finish an intricate and delicate part of the ship, and thought to use the dining room table as it was easier and the light was better, intending to get it all cleared away before his father came home from the pub, but he got so absorbed in his work, he forgot the time. When his father walked in and saw all the items spread across the table, he instantly lost his temper, he wanted his dinner.

As he took his belt off, Bruce instinctively ran for the door, but his father caught him and held him by the back of his collar, he remembered apologising over and over again, 'I'm sorry Dad, I'll clear it up, I'm sorry,' but his father wasn't listening and continued hitting him with the belt. As Bruce laid crumpled on the floor, his mother was begging and pleading for him to stop, his father walked over to the ship Bruce had spent weeks patiently making, and slammed his fist down on it and smashed the Galleon to pieces, then picked it up and threw it across the room.

Bruce was seven years old and began to cry, which enraged his father more and earned him further straps from the belt. His brothers took him upstairs and bathed his wounds, his mother was forbidden to go upstairs after him and told not to *pamper a weakling*, his father wanted his dinner. Later, when he went out to the pub again, his mother rushed upstairs and held Bruce in her arms, telling him it was a fine ship he had made and should be proud.

How could his father be jealous of them, he had always called Bruce, stupid, or an idiot, that he would never amount to anything, it always felt like he hated them, him in particular as he seemed to be the target of his father's anger most of the time, he never even seemed to notice their sister, Brooke.

They had all worked hard and achieved so much, Blake was a Senior Registrar at St Thomas', Brett was a Lawyer in one of London's top law firms and his little sister Brooke, had just got her first placement with a large Accounting firm in Central London.

As soon as they were able to afford it, they collectively bought, a luxury ground floor, two-bedroom flat for their mother, in Hyde Park Gardens, she loved the parks and she had the largest in London just outside her door to enjoy. They got her out of the dingy council flat around the corner from their father, who even after they had divorced, bombarded her with abusive drunken visits.

Bruce walked through to the kitchen with its glossy white units and black granite worktops, opened the fridge door and grabbed himself a beer, swigging from the bottle, he meandered through the dining room and looked out over the gardens towards the Thames, from the floor to ceiling patio windows, that opened onto the terrace that expanded the width of the property, which led onto the gardens and the fiesta view of London beyond, all lit up. This was his quiet moment before his guests arrived.

He thought of Sara's beautiful smiling face, as he seemed to be doing more and more lately, she was never far from his thoughts and dreams. Bruce felt tense and restless, one whole week away from her had seemed like a torturous eternity and he couldn't wait to see her. Tonight, he felt good and tempted to break his rule of not dating anyone he worked with, this abstinence was driving him crazy, he needed sexual release, but every time he thought of being with another woman, the damnedest thing, it felt like he was cheating on Sara, which made absolutely no sense, as they weren't even dating, but aside from that, other women paled into insignificance compared to Sara, he was lost, he had it bad.

Finishing his beer, he returned the bottle to the kitchen then rushed upstairs to get ready, he wanted to look good for her, *fuck,* what was happening to him, what was she doing to him.

Seven

Sara treated herself to an unusual lie-in, and luxuriated in a deep, steaming hot bath, that released the sweet aromas of the most exotic oils, her generous brother had bought her for Christmas, as she immersed herself in the water she thought of her brother.

Cameron always had the most exquisite taste in all things female, the next best thing to having a sister was having a gay brother. In fact, it was better. No one to borrow and ruin your clothes and she could talk to him about *almost* everything, *he drew the line at female body functions though*. There was no jealousy, only encouragement and she always lapped up his praise and took heed to all his careful criticism's.

If she ever had any boyfriend problems, Cameron was there, on the one hand, giving the best advice from a male perspective, but annoyingly, on the other, telling her how typically confusing the female mind was, using a brother's prerogative. If she was unsure about what to wear out on a date, Cameron was there to give an opinion and was the best clothes shopping companion, better than her friends, *sometimes*.

It was because of Cameron's good taste, that Sara agreed to go into partnership with him and they were about to launch their own fashion label. The name was a result of an evening consisting of lots of wine and laughter and surrounded by hundreds of scraps of discarded ridiculous names they had scribbled, they eventually agreed on a simplistic 'K' based on their name, Kaye. They envisioned a large backlit blue K for men's fashions and a pink K for the women's selection.

Sara got out of the bath as the water became tepid, and her skin started to resemble a prune. She put on her dressing gown just as there was a loud knocking at her front door, Sara rolled her eyes to the ceiling, her friends had arrived early and she was hoping for a little more pampering time on her own. As she ran down the stairs at the impatient, persistent knocking, she opened the door expecting to give her friends an admonishment, instead, it was her brother Cameron, her mood softened instantly, 'I was just thinking about … you,' Sara said, but the last word fading as she saw his face swollen and discolouring around the cheek and left eye. 'Dad.' A statement, not a question. She opened the door wide and Cameron walked past her and made his way into the lounge.

'He is such a fucking close-minded bigot.' Cameron paced back and forth from the window, wringing both his hands through his hair in exasperation, stopped mid-pace, looked at Sara and said, 'I could do with a drink.'

Sara was standing by her drinks cabinet and held up a bottle. 'Whiskey?' she said with a knowing smile.

Cameron visibly relaxed and returned the smile, 'Perfect, make mine a double, straight.'

'What happened?'

'He found out I'm gay and confronted me.'

'How? ... Cameron, I never told him ...'

'I know Sara when you make a promise you always keep it.' He took the drink Sara handed him and sat heavily into one of the leather armchairs letting out a huge sigh and swore, then knocked back his drink in one, Sara poured him another measure.

'What happened,' she repeated.

'I popped in to see mum, I'm through ever talking to him and I certainly don't go there to visit *him*, if mum ever left him, he would never see me again, this ...' pointing to his slowly swelling eye. 'Is the last straw, no more chances, I'm done with him.'

Let me get some ice to put on that', she left the room and returned with a bag of frozen peas.

'Dad went down the pub last night, *what a surprise*,' Cameron said sarcastically, 'a gay son of one of his cronies told Dad how I hit on him in a club last week and how he & I ... you know, his friend accepts his son being gay, even Dad accepts him, it turns out this Darren ...'

Before she had time to think it was out of her mouth, 'Darren is gay? Did Dad know this?' She didn't know Darren personally, but their Dad had regaled many stories to them of his friend and his son and what a *great bloke* and *good for a laugh* Darren was. Cameron shot her a disbelieving look, 'Sorry, didn't mean to interrupt, but if Dad knew he was gay, why did he turn on you?'

'Because he's a fucking hypocrite. His friend is ok with his son being gay, but not the Great Glenn Kaye, all my life he's given me a hard time, today he told me why, apparently I was never the son he wanted, too soft he said coz I liked drawing, gymnastics, dancing, he started pushing me and shouting, saying how much I disgusted him being a *Nancy boy*, mum was trying to calm him, but he just lost it and punched me, then kicked me to the floor and kept punching and kicking me. I should have punched him back, instead, I just tried to deflect the blows because he's my father. How pathetic is that, anyone else and I would have given worse. I managed to push him off and got up, asking him why his friends gay son didn't disgust him, but I did, he said that his friends family was none of his business, but *I was,* his business, and how could he hold his head up in the pub with a son who was as *bent as a nine bob note.*' Cameron downed his drink and rested his head back against the chair, holding the bag of peas to his eye.

Sara recalled the day she finally gathered the courage to ask her brother if he was gay, he immediately denied it. Over the next six months, Sara endeavoured to get him to admit it. Then one day, Cameron asked her how she would feel about him if - hypothetically, he were to admit he was gay, she told him she would still love him, he would still be her annoying big brother and it changed nothing, she just wanted him to be honest with her, then he could get on with being who he was, with no secrets between them. That was when she promised him, she would never tell anyone, it was his decision, that included their parents. She remembered how he looked at her in astonishment and told her that she was an incredible sister and he was lucky to have her, then he admitted to her he was gay.

From that day on, she felt closer than ever before to her brother, a gay brother was definitely so much better than a sister. Cameron was not an obvious gay man, without knowing, you would never guess unless you knew him really well. He was discreet by his own choice, he once told Sara that it was none of anyone's business what he got up to and with whom, he never felt the need to shout it from the rooftops. This was the '80s and a lot of gay people were being discriminated against, and he didn't want to be one of them. Cameron was so popular because of his personality and had many straight male friends, in fact, it was Cameron who introduced Sara to Matias.

Dad never noticed *either* of them, let alone congratulate them on their achievements, the pub was all that seemed to interest him. When he was home, they all wished he was out, as the atmosphere was like waiting for a bomb to go off, and when he walked out the door, there was always a huge sigh of relief and they could enjoy the evening, agreeing between the three of them what they would watch on TV. Aunty Valentina lived up the road, had never married and was mum's saviour, visiting virtually every day, she was like a second mother to Cameron and Sara.

Unfortunately, each enjoyable evening would end in the drunken return of their father, and he would pick a row with their sweet kind-hearted mother who just wanted a quiet life. Sara remembered the misery their father caused their mum, but she refused to leave him and neither of them could work out why, not until they got older and noticed that she was petrified of poverty. Holding onto the house was so important to her and why she put up with Dads mood swings. Mum grew up in Italy during the war. Nonno and Nonna had a small farm, but there was never enough food, let alone decent clothing, another reason why they noticed the joy she showed when given new clothes as presents.

Mum told them of one time when she was young, and she was looking after the goats and a friend visited and had some bread with her, which was a real treat, mum milked the goat and they enjoyed the sweet taste of the bread dipped in the milk, later she overheard Nonna complaining that she couldn't understand why the goats had not produced very much milk that day, and how guilty she felt, but happy that her tummy was full.

Sara remembered their dad's moods only got worse when he moved jobs from the buses to the railway and they had a social club just up the road from where they lived. He now had a social club that was closer to home and as a member, the drinks were subsidised, this pleased Dad, no end.

It was their mother Sofia that they turned to who always helped them, working so hard with a house full of students offering bed and breakfast, working hard was in her Italian nature and the reason that they both spoke fluent Italian, much to their Dad's annoyance, whenever they spoke it, therefore they quickly learnt from a very young age, not to speak Italian in front of him, but when he wasn't around they spoke nothing but, between the three of them, and they loved it, when they could converse with their grandparents, when they visited, as Nonna Athena was born in Athens they were also taught Greek, their mother spoke both languages to them.

Having already mastered two languages, it was no surprise that they both found learning other languages easy, Sara could speak eleven languages, Cameron was happy with the six he could speak.

Sara remembered how Cameron found an easier way for them to learn French, Spanish and German together by sticking pieces of paper all around the house, writing the words for objects in different colours for each language, French words were in Blue, Spanish words were in Red and German words were in Black, as they got better in each language, they would write sentences using the objects as clues, that way they could also read and write in each language, which made the travelling they did now, far more enjoyable.

Ever since they could walk, they would be tumbling about, never able to walk along the street on their feet, their mum was getting exasperated with them, until one day, they were walking home after picking Cameron up from school, and as usual Sara was trying to copy Cameron, he was walking on his hands, as Sara attempted it, she fell over near the kerb and nearly got run over and suffered a cut to her forehead, a small scar she still had. It had bled profusely and it scared mum and Cameron, a cut to the head it probably looked far worse than it actually was, they rushed Sara to the hospital where she had a few stitches, it was then that mum agreed to let them have gymnastic lessons, with a solemn promise from Cameron that they would get it out of their systems during lessons and walk along the road like 'normal children', seeing Sara bleed like that had scared him and he instantly, agreed.

It was during entry into a small local competition, they were spotted by an ex-Olympic champion who saw their potential and wanted to train them, so eager was she that it came at no cost to their parents. They were quickly entered into mainstream competitions and their mum worked even harder, taking on a part-time job and keeping some money from the students hidden from their father, to pay for their Gymnastic expenses.

After a few years, they were selected to be part of the Olympic team, and each won a gold medal, which would have taken pride of place on the mantlepiece. Mum explained because of Dad's unpredictable temperament it would be best if they kept them in their bedrooms. Although hidden, they were never to think for one moment, that she would forget the pride she felt when both *her babies* had won such a prize, she took them to work at the factory, showing and telling all her friends and keeping all the newspaper clippings, even carrying one in her purse.

It was Cameron who thought it best not to return to defend their titles with the possibility of losing, and to leave whilst at the top at their grand ages of thirteen and fifteen. He begged mum for the chance to train in dance, as he believed gymnastics had a short career life anyway, and there were fewer options open after they were too old to compete. Sara as always, followed her brother and they both gained entry, after rigorous auditions and again it was their talent that shone through and won them boarded placements at a very prestigious London Dance School.

They missed their mum and called her every night, but it was not possible for her to commute from Brighton where they lived to London every day and their father was useless, he loved his drink too much and couldn't be relied on to stay sober, how he drove buses each day without a crash made them shudder.

Sara looked at her brother, comically still holding the bag of peas to his eye, dwarfing the armchair he was sitting in with his 6'2 taut and defined frame most male dancers had, his blond curling hair damp and darker on one side where the peas were defrosting. Cameron was now a much-in-demand choreographer for some of the biggest West End shows. Sara went over to him and removed the peas and asked what his plans were for tonight, as it was New Year's Eve.

Cameron opened his good eye as the other was closing up a little. 'Not sure, don't think any good clubs will let me in looking like this,' he motioned to his eye.

'Well the girls are coming over to get ready and we are going to a party at Bruce's new house, do you want to come?'

'Do you think he'd mind you bringing along your brawling big brother?'

'More the merrier, not sure one more will make a difference, we can always practice our make-up techniques on you to conceal your shiner, you know Mia would love to spend some time with you up close.'

'Does she not yet know that she is sniffing around the wrong tree?'

'Well, you're not an obvious gay are you, maybe if you camp it up a bit, she will get the message, if you don't want to tell her directly, it's your decision to tell people, as it stands right now, I don't think she does know.'

It was now early afternoon and Livvy was the first to arrive and suggested a liquid lunch to start, holding up a chinking bag full of different bottles of wines, explaining she had trouble choosing which ones were best as a really attractive shop assistant in the Off-Licence was very distracting, so she bought the lot.

Cameron held up his glass and said, 'Beat you to it, already started,' followed by telling her what had happened when she asked about his eye, and adding that tonight, everyone will ask and he had better find an abbreviated version. Sami, Lexi and Mia arrived shortly after Livvy, and the afternoon breezed past in a flurry of clothes strewn everywhere and the air heavy with various perfumes and make-up on every surface.

By seven o'clock, they were all ready, in a variety of colours. Sara wore a bright emerald green satin shift dress with three different silk chiffon layers, each lighter than the other and cut away in the front to show off the shift below, a deep loose V shape at the neck, no sleeves and her only jewellery was a green choker necklace and matching bracelet, with matching shoes to complete the look, her make-up she kept natural with her hair in a simple French twist.

Eight

Bruce was trying to calm himself, and not look at his watch every few seconds, he was unsure if Sara would turn up, what if she had other plans or got distracted with all the other New Year's Eve events going on. This was ridiculous, he needed to get a grip, stop thinking about her and start enjoying the party, but she kept creeping into his thoughts and his head snapped round every time he heard new arrivals. He went to the bar and got himself a Brandy and walked over to join Dom, Jamie, Max and Flynn who had just arrived.

The party was in full swing and getting quite crowded. Bruce didn't see Felicia arrive and make a beeline for him, he was standing in the doorway of the dining room leaning casually with one shoulder against the door frame, drink in hand. She appeared in front of him, ignoring everyone, put her hands on his chest, leaned in and pushed him into the corner, knocking him off balance, he had little choice in going with the momentum, by this time he had had quite a few Brandy's and his balance was not so good. She had him trapped against the wall and was pressing her body against him and leaning in for a kiss on the lips, but Bruce turned his head to one side with her kiss landing on his cheek.

'Felicia, what are you doing?'

'Wishing you a very Happy New Year, darling. New year, new beginnings, we should be together,' she said seductively, pouting and fluttering her eyelashes.

As she raised herself up on her toes, to give him another kiss, this time Bruce had a little room to move his head back, and with his free hand, managed to push her back by the shoulder, but Felicia was always very insistent and determined to get what she wanted, she managed to push him back and land a kiss fully on his lips, even trying to deepen the kiss. Max came to his rescue, *partially*, he took his drink. This enabled Bruce to place both his hands on her shoulders and push her back with a little more force, and end the kiss, but Felicia stepped forward again and placed her hand on his chest.

'Felicia, stop this, we are not getting back together.'

'Bruce, I want you, and you know when I want something, I don't stop till I get it.'

'Well, when you put it like that - no chance.'

'Bruce, your guest has arrived,' Dom interrupted.

'Who is your guest Bruce?' Felicia said with a frown and a tinge of annoyance in her voice. Ignoring Felicia and moving quickly out of the corner, now Felicia was distracted, he asked Dom, 'Where did she go?'

'Bruce, don't ignore me and who is your *female* guest that has your full attention?' Felicia almost spat the words.

'Felicia - I don't owe you any explanations, now either enjoy the party or leave,' with that Felicia stormed out of the room, whether she left or went to another room, Bruce didn't care. He turned to Dom and asked, 'When did she arrive.'

'About 10 minutes ago and um Buddy … she saw you and Felicia,' Bruce growled. He couldn't believe that Felicia had come to the party, he certainly didn't invite her and now, somehow, he had to explain it to Sara. Bruce went hunting for her.

Sara had arrived at the party full of excitement and anticipation in seeing Bruce again, being reminded by Nagy, to act with restraint in both her manner and behaviour, she took a deep breath to steady herself as she stepped into the front hall, then had to take another, at the sheer breathtaking view of the central sweeping staircase. All the way over, Livvy and Sammy had insisted on stopping at various pubs, 'It was never good to show up early to a party.' Sara couldn't care about etiquette or playing it cool, she just wanted to get to the party and see Bruce.

Her crowd decided they needed yet more alcohol and disappeared in search of the bar. Sara went with them, not because she wanted a drink, but to have something to do with her hands, she was beginning to feel a little nervous at meeting Bruce, which was ridiculous considering all the intimate scenes they had shot.

She saw Lexi, Livvy and Sami talking to a couple of really good-looking men and a very pretty woman and there was a similarity between them, probably related? As Sara got her drink and joined them, Lexi introduced them as Bruce's brothers Blake and Brett and sister Brooke, they all had the same dark curling hair, but hazel eyes, whereas Bruce had the most beautiful blue eyes, that Sara had the good fortune of staring into on many long occasions, *even if it were only in a professional capacity.*

As the group dispersed, Brooke remained to talk to Sara, asking about her work, telling her they had taken their mum to one of her shows and were awestruck by her dancing and acrobatic abilities, Sara flushed at the barrage of compliments, saying she was glad they enjoyed the show. They talked about what they had been given for Christmas, Brooke told her that all three of her brothers gave her the best collective present she could ever wish for.

'They paid off all my study debts.'

'What were you studying towards becoming?' Sara asked.

'I recently qualified as a Chartered Accountant and got my first placement with a large prestigious accounting firm in Kensington. We all went over to mum's for Christmas and they presented me with a big box that turned out to be a box within a box within a box, each getting smaller and I told them that if the last one was empty, they will be for it. With three older brothers, I learnt to give so much more than I got, therefore not an idle empty threat. The last box contained a card, it was specially made with such beautiful wording saying 'congratulations you are now certifiable' which was crossed out and 'qualified' printed in its place, typical of my brothers not to keep it all sentimental. Inside they had put a photocopy of a handful of cheques that had paid off all my debts, they had each written in it about how proud they were of me.' Brooke started laughing but said at the time she was crying.

'That is really lovely.'

'Yeah, my brothers are the most annoying at times, treating me like a child, but when they go and do something like this, I realise just how lucky I am to have them and wouldn't change them for the world, at the bottom of that last box was another box with this beautiful necklace.' Brooke caressed the emerald and diamond necklace she had on.

'My God, that is really beautiful,' Sara exclaimed, 'it suits you and matches your eyes.'

'It's my favourite stone and they said it was my graduation present as if paying my debts off wasn't enough, apparently, it was Bruce's idea, which is typical of him, such a softy, but don't tell him I told you, he hates compliments, doesn't know how to take them. Now insults, well he's used to them, I blame our Dad, always took his anger out mostly on Bruce, ... Umm, sorry, too much info and way too much drink.'

Sara rather liked Brooke's openness and honesty and showed Bruce in a different light, he looked out for his sister and Sara liked that aspect of his personality, she had always seen him as a little cold, detached maybe, like he wasn't listening as he didn't talk ten to the dozen like some people, just let people talk, then gave his opinion to the conversation in one or two sentences - had she got him wrong?!! After hearing what he had done for his sister, he was obviously generous, but then she was family and people reacted differently towards their family, either good or bad, this was definitely good.

'How about you, do you have any siblings?' Brooke asked, interrupting Sara's stray thoughts.

'Yes, a brother, but just one and that is enough thank you very much, can't imagine having three of Cameron, don't know how you cope with that.'

Sara was really enjoying her conversation with Brooke. She seemed so down to earth, friendly and funny, they promised to meet up at some point for coffee, and Brooke gave Sara her business card to get in contact. Sara replenished her drink and went in search of Bruce, just to say Hi, she told Nagy.

Liar.

Sara told herself to walk around slowly and chatted to a few people she knew, endeavouring to look casually, probably failing as she searched around for Bruce. She wandered into the Dining Room and spotted him, in the corner with Felicia glued to him, body and lips.

Sara just stood there, heart racing, forgetting to breathe with her eyes open wide and her mouth gaping, then he put his hands on her shoulders as they came up for air and Felicia stepped back slightly, then leaned in with her hand on his chest, they looked very cosy. Sara turned and walked away with her eyes stinging and threatening tears, she decided to escape the heat of the party or maybe it was her inflamed embarrassment, did anyone notice her gawping at Bruce and Felicia, *God, she hoped not.*

How could she have been so naïve to think that when she turned up at the party, he would be so pleased to see her, that he would leave his friends and wrap her in a tight embrace and tell her he had been waiting for her.

Well that's what you get when you have a totally wonky mind,' Sara berated herself, but it hurt all the same and when was she going to learn that Bruce was just not interested.

She grabbed her coat and went outside, spotting her friends at the end of the garden, she immediately swiped the drink from her brother's hands and knocked it back, asking if anyone was in the mood to get refills, Sara didn't want to return to the house.

It was Mia who said, 'You go, girl, we are here to parrrrrtyyyyyy,' then raised her drink, as a salute, then knocked it back, copying Sara, then set off up the garden on her drinks mission.

Sami said she would go with her and get some of the *yummy* food she spotted on the way in.

The music was loud in the garden, through special speakers and there was a patio area near the water's edge, ideal for dancing. Sara grabbed Cameron as one of her favourite songs came on.

'Come on, big bruv, show me some of those amazing moves you've been telling me about,' whilst pulling him towards the outdoor dance floor, where other couples were dancing.

Sara decided she was going to enjoy herself, it was New Year's Eve, after all, she giggled and laughed as Cameron tried some outrageous moves, he said he had been experimenting with new choreography for their show and twirled Sara around and lifting her. Sara could always rely on her brother to make her feel better by making her laugh, lifting her mood and forget her problems for a while.

Sara remained outside with her brother and friends, shortly joined by many others as it approached midnight, then the countdown began, as they heard Big Ben ring in 1986, followed by huge cheers. She joined in singing Auld Lang Syne, then fireworks began. She hugged her friends, then turned to Cameron and told him that it was a New Year, and the start of new things to come, and a lifetime of him being himself. If their father chose not to accept him and whomever he chose to love, then it was his loss, Cameron would always have her love and that of their mothers, who also knew he was gay, and it had never mattered to her. Cameron turned to her with his eyes wide in astonishment saying, 'When did mum find out I'm gay? I've never told her.'

'She told me. Just before I asked you and spent the following six months trying to convince you to confide in me, I came home one day and mum was asking me about you, how were you feeling, had you said anything to me, those kinds of things. When we were sitting having a cup of tea, mum started asking me if you had any girlfriends, I said I wasn't sure, then she said, 'I think he might like boys.' I can tell you, I nearly choked on my tea and sprayed it all over myself. At that point, I evaded and changed the subject, but it got me thinking, for the next week I thought about nothing else, it was driving me mad, I decided to ask you, the rest you know. Promise me, in fact, vow to me, you will enjoy your life, Cameron, don't fester on what Dad thinks, know that you are loved by me and mum, she loves you no matter what and without asking any questions, she doesn't need to hear the answers. I've had friends, who have been rejected by their family, and they took their own lives and I couldn't bear it, if you ever felt like that, always know you can talk to me about anything, and I will always listen and help, however I can.'

Cameron cupped her face in both his hands as he looked at her and said, 'You are a bloody amazing sister, and we have one truly wonderful mother, as long as I have the two of you in my life, I can handle anything and yes, I vow, I will come and *bug* you, whenever I have boyfriend problems, I think you owe me big time in that department, little sis, don't think mum would want details.'

'I don't think *I* want details either, a short, severely edited, recap will suffice.' They both laughed, Cameron kissed her on the cheek, then they wished each other a Happy New Year. Cameron hugged Sara close and told her, 'I love you.'

'I love you too,' then Sara rested her head in his shoulder and they turned around arm in arm, to watch the rest of the fireworks.

Nine

After leaving the dining room, Bruce skirted the parameter of the rooms, searching, being stopped periodically by friends commenting on the beautiful house, how great the party was and the delicious food, he nodded politely and excused himself quickly. She wasn't in the house. He grabbed his coat and a drink and went outside to the gardens and there at the end of the garden on the patio dance floor, he spotted her in the arms of a man who was twirling her around, she was laughing and looked so happy with him. Bruce's heart pounded in his chest, he tried to calm his anger at this unknown man who dared lift her in his arms and hold her so close, they both looked so relaxed with each other.

Bruce was finding it hard to breathe, he was clenching his fist, then he knocked back the drink he was holding and slammed it down on the table near him, almost breaking the glass. He then marched off descending the steps from the terrace onto the garden towards Sara, to tell this man to take his hands off her.

As he made his way towards the patio, the countdown began, then as he heard Big Ben, there was a massive cheer and everyone was hugging and wishing each other a Happy New Year. Bruce was caught up in the melee, almost losing sight of Sara. As the fireworks began, he saw them, as the man turned and cupped Sara's face in both his hands and they looked like they were having a very private conversation.

Bruce moved closer as if drawn by a magnet, unable to take his eyes off the couple who seemed to only have eyes for each other, as if all the noise around them, didn't exist. Bruce was feeling sick, he had lost his chance with Sara over his stupid, stupid rule of not dating anyone he worked with, whilst working with them, look where that had got him.

They probably arrived together as he didn't know this man, maybe they have been dating for some time and the magic of the evening had now cemented their relationship. He didn't feel he could interrupt their moment. Felicia was to blame for this, damn her, if she hadn't tried to kiss him and if Sara hadn't arrived at that moment, maybe she wouldn't be with this man now. 'Damn you, Felicia,' Bruce muttered.

As Bruce stood there unable to move, he saw them hug and although he couldn't hear above all the noise around him, the three simple words 'I love you' was not hard to lip read and Sara returned the sentiment. It was like someone had just reached into his chest and ripped out his heart.

As Sara and this man, turned their backs to him, arm in arm watching the fireworks. Bruce whispered, 'Happy New Year, Sara', then turned, and walked back up the garden, and disappeared into his house.

Ten

They all returned to work in the new year and filming resumed. There were endless episodes of laughing and joking during filming, forgetting their lines, a horse not doing what it should, props or scenery mishaps. It was a fun set to work on and everyone enjoyed numerous nights out, with Bruce and Sara enduring endless good-humoured innuendoes from everyone, about the blatant chemistry, between them.

Sara smiled and played along, what else could she do? but the chemistry was purely professional, how she wished it played out in real life, but she couldn't let on how she felt, her traitorous mind kept creating images of Bruce and Felicia, together.

Even her dreams betrayed her, when she fantasised of herself being with Bruce, her face would morph into Felicia's and she would wake and punch her pillow in frustration. Unable to return to sleep, she would get up, put music on, exercise in an effort to exorcise the thoughts of *them* together, out of her mind.

Sara once again decided to throw herself into her work, ensuring she was always ready for whatever scene they were about to shoot. Increasing her workout with her trainer, whenever the filming schedule allowed, finding every distraction she could find to stop herself thinking of Bruce. She rarely succeeded.

Especially as they decided to re-write a scene. Her character was delayed in returning to England with her maid, due to the impending Battle of Waterloo.

She had to nurse Bruce's character's injuries after the battle. His character was supposed to be naked, under the cover he was given due to a fever, and she was to raise the cover and give him a bed bath. Usually, actors wore a modesty pouch, but Bruce decided to *actually* be naked, and cause a reaction, the infuriating man. When they filmed the scene, Sara caught her breath and only managed to mutter, 'Oh my,' when she got an eyeful of his manhood. It was not the correct line, but they kept it in and Davy said it was better than the line that was written. When the scene was finished, she smacked Bruce on the arm for his devilry, as her blushes were profuse, and his body was magnificent, with all that close-up attention she had to give it. That night her dreams of him were even more vivid.

As the weeks passed and they approached the end of January, it was reported that whilst leaving for her tour of the States and before embarking on a world tour, Felicia had dedicated her new release to Bruce, as the song, was the inspiration of their relationship and left the question hanging, when a reporter asked if they were back together, Felicia only gave a cryptic answer. 'What do you think,' then winking as she left to board her plane.

Sara was livid when she read that particular tabloid. The next day at work she felt like she had to draw on every ounce of acting experience to enable her to portray a woman in love, they were filming an emotional scene, where her character tells Bruce's character that she loves him, scars and all and didn't care that he was the second son and not the Duke, titles meant nothing to her, followed by lots of close-up shots of them kissing, there were lots of takes and lots of kissing Bruce.

Sara loved and loathed it in equal measure, it felt so good to be kissing him, to be in his arms and hear the words of love as he said his lines, but to feel the emptiness knowing that none of it was real, *she would give anything, for it to be real*, how pathetic was she becoming.

Every day on set, was becoming torturous and Bruce was getting more gorgeous, but she couldn't have him, he was someone else's, Sara was convinced of this as he moved away at the end of every scene, he wasn't smiling, chatty or charming with her anymore around the set, not like he was before Christmas. The only thing that had changed, was his steamy kiss with Felicia, they were obviously back together. He gave no clue as to how he felt after Felicia's dedication to him, he worked on, after every take he would release Sara from their embrace, and look awkward whilst they waited as the Director took a quick look at the 'rushes,' and decide whether to go for another take or to move on to the next scene.

Bruce looked so dashing and handsome in the full red British army officers' uniform, with his sword dangling from his hip and searched around her brain for something to say. As they awaited Davy's decision and before her brain had time to engage, her mouth was in action, 'It was nice to have a song dedicated to you.'

'What the hell is wrong with you?' shouted Nagy.

Oh God, please, please, please, don't answer that, forget I said it, pretend you didn't hear it, she desperately thought to herself.

He had heard though, he stopped from turning away and turned back to face her, looked her straight in the eye and said, 'I suppose it is regarded by some, as rather flattering,' then gave her a humourless smile.

Sara needed to get away and whispered, 'Excuse me,' and called for ten minutes, then made her way to her trailer. Trying to control her breathing and fight the sting of tears, as one escaped and rolled down her cheek, she increased her speed almost breaking into a run, aware that he may be watching her, she steeled herself to slow her pace a little, and reached her trailer. With every fibre of her control, took rapid deep breaths and willed herself not to cry, there would be too many people to explain the mess of her makeup and hold everyone up, and *that,* she would not do.

Her assistant on the set knocked on the door, Sara willed her self-control and bade her come in, Shelley opened the door but didn't go in, just said from outside that the Director was happy with the last take and they would be moving on to the next scene, which required Sara to change costume and her hair would need to be redone, make-up and costume would be ready for her in half an hour. Sara was immensely relieved to get a small break. Suddenly Sara could hold it in no longer and allowed herself the release she craved, the tears flowed uncontrollably, make-up will fix her face.

Through her tears, she whispered, 'Oh Bruce, I so wish I were the lucky one to have you, instead it is Felicia.'

Sara grabbed the towel in the bathroom and held it to her face as she broke down, at least it muffled her crying, a little. She then washed her face and gave herself another five minutes before making her way to the make-up trailer.

The next scene didn't involve Bruce, she was about to tell her fiancé, the Duke that she loved his brother and to release her from their engagement. She could at least spend the rest of the day without facing Bruce, he was doing a different scene with the second unit on location nearby.

That night when she got home, exhausted from keeping her emotions in check, it was Friday and she had the day off tomorrow, before starting some night shoots in the evening, at a Stately home. She called up her friends and asked if they fancied a girl's night in, with popcorn and a movie, thankfully they were all up for it, and Sara sat in her pyjamas and slippers as her friends poured the wine and emptied the popcorn into bowls.

Sara took a moment to look round with contented pride at her friends, as they chatted lively about getting the wine and snacks ready, they really cared for each other, Sara knew that if she ever needed them they would drop everything to be with her, like tonight, they didn't need to ask any questions, they would leave it up to Sara to tell them, when and if she wanted to, unless it was serious, then they were her Rottweilers, persistent and fierce in their protection.

Sami was Sara's oldest friend, they had known each other since infant school, the liveliest and most outrageous of the group with her long, silky straight raven hair and dark eyes, who worked as a hairstylist at a busy salon on Bond Street, with ambitions to one day own her own salon.

Livvy, originally from Edinburgh, who wasn't far behind Sami in being outrageous with her masses of beautiful fiery red curly hair and grey eyes, was a Staff Nurse in A&E at St Thomas' Hospital, Sammy and Sara had known her since Junior school.

Lexi was always the most outrageous in the way she looked, no-one knew her natural hair colour, she was always dyeing it different colours and changing her hairstyles and up do's, Sami, Livvy and Sara met her whilst at Secondary school, she was always getting bullied, just because she wanted to experiment with her hair and her own fashion. They befriended her and defended her and she got through school, got herself an apprenticeship and was now a really good Graphic Designer working for a large firm and getting promotions.

Mia was the newest addition to the group having met the group less than a year ago in a club and fitted in well with the group's personalities, her brunette hair with beautiful natural reds and golds that caught the sunlight or club lights, was neatly styled in a shoulder-length Bob cut. Mia was the kindest hearted person Sara had ever met, and she worked for Barnardo's as a Fund Raiser.

Sara put on the videotape Sami had rented for the evening, she had chosen 'St Elmo's Fire' which they all couldn't wait to see, they had missed it when it came out at the cinema. Sara joined her friends on the large squishy sofa and relaxed as the film started, answering questions if she had ever met or worked with the many dishy men in the film, Sara answered that she had met them and knew a few of them, but hadn't worked with any of them. The evening was exactly what Sara needed, a good film with her best mates and an endless flow of good wine.

Eleven

Bruce was out pub crawling with his mates on the last night in England before he was due to fly out the following morning with the second unit. Sara, due to join them in a week, after finishing filming some night shoots at a Stately home.

He had spent weeks dodging reporters, eager to get any details they could of his relationship with Felicia and when they couldn't get the truth, they made it up. Dedicating her new song to him, along with her stunt at the airport before embarking on her US tour, had helped push her single to No 1, it seemed the less he said, the more interest, it generated.

Bruce just couldn't get the image of Sara dancing with another man at the New Year's Eve party, out of his head and was finding it difficult to connect with her the same way he did before that night. Lip-reading her say 'I love you' to someone else, felt like a punch to the gut, he wanted it to be him on the receiving end of those words. Onset, hearing her speak her lines of love to him, he so wanted it to be for real, but she loved another. Tonight, Bruce was going to enjoy the night with his mates and let whatever happens, happen.

As the drinks flowed, they started attracting a lot of attention from women, Bruce was aware earlier in the evening he was drinking a lot, but as the night wore on, he lost that awareness and was finding it hard to walk straight. Two of the women were either side of him, holding him up, one had short copper colour hair and introduced herself as Victoria, the other had long blond hair and reminded Bruce of Sara, she introduced herself as Zoe.

As they stumbled outside of the pub, he heard Dom ask if they needed a hand with him, but they assured him they could get him home safely. As they got into a taxi, they asked him which hotel he was staying at and relayed that to the taxi driver.

In the lift on the way up to his suite, they took turns kissing Bruce and he didn't object, *she loves another, kept going through his head like a mantra, on constant repeat*. In fact, he very much participated in the kisses he was receiving, *she loves another*, he hadn't had sex in months, under the deluded belief that when the film was finished, he would ask Sara for a date, how misguided was he, to think she would wait, be available, my God, he was so stupid … now someone else was with her, doing things to her that he wanted to do.

The lift arrived on the fifth floor and he was asked which was his suite. Maybe tonight he would be able to stop thinking of her for a short while and have some fun. As they entered his rooms Victoria and Zoe, wasted no time or subtleties in showing him exactly what they wanted. While one of them was kissing him, the other was stripping him of his clothes. They all stumbled into the bedroom, Bruce still had his trousers and socks on as he fell or was pushed onto the bed. Victoria had swiped a bottle of brandy from the lounge area. Bruce smiled and said, 'Haven't you had enough tonight?'

'There are other things I might like to do with this, than drink it', Victoria suggestively replied. She then took a swig from the bottle as she kneeled on the bed beside Bruce and then tipped a little of the Brandy onto his chest and bent down and started to lick it off. Then he could feel Zoe remove his shoes and socks before starting to remove his trousers, then they both removed their clothes, till they were all naked.

The next morning when Bruce woke, he was alone and he was thankful that they had left, it had just been sex, a welcome and gratifying release, but a torturous reminder, whenever Zoe took him into her mouth, because of her blond hair, he kept visualizing Sara doing that to him, every time he suckled on Victoria's breasts, he would close his eyes and imagine they were Sara's. This was insanity and again the mantra returned *she loves another*. Bruce got showered, packed, went down to reception and checked out, then made his way to the airport.

Twelve

Sara found the whole week of night shoots difficult, and it seemed to drag. For the last month, it had been difficult to face Bruce each day, she looked forward to them and dreaded them at the same time. Now he wasn't around it was like someone had turned a light off, and everything seemed dimmer, and she didn't feel as alive as when he was around, even if the atmosphere between them had changed dramatically, since New Year's Eve.

Her mind kept flashing images of Felicia plastering her body to Bruce that night. Experiencing pure, unadulterated jealousy was a new emotion for Sara, and she didn't know how to handle it, telling herself Bruce could see whomever he liked and do whatever he liked, she had no right, was not helping. Every time she heard Felicia's music her mood darkened, with a desperate need to smash something. A few times the radio sufficed, but it didn't have the desired effect, especially as she had to clear up the mess and *replace* the radio.

At times of sheer stress or boredom, Sara would immerse herself in composing music on her guitar, that she took everywhere with her, but when at home she preferred the piano. Over the years she and Cameron were constantly writing, choreographing and designing costumes for new numbers for their shows, to keep it alive both for audiences and performers, so that it never became bland and predictable, it was probably the reason the shows were always sell-outs, that, and because it helped to raise funds for various charities.

With all the accomplishments in her life, she still felt she was lacking, her stomach would be tied in knots before a live performance and first days on new film sets, she always thought everyone else looked so confident and she envied them that. Felicia had exuberant confidence, was more voluptuous and sensuous, maybe that was what Bruce liked and found missing in Sara, hence the flirting had stopped, their exchanges were of professional courtesy towards each other and she wanted, yearned for so much more.

No matter, he was with *her* now, all the tabloids were reporting that they were back together and although Sara knew from experience with the Paparazzi, this could be exaggerated, she never heard Bruce deny them, maybe they *were* true.

Sara had a one-night stopover at home, to replenish her wardrobe and wanted one last night out with her friends before flying out to join Bruce on location in Prague, maybe she could ask him outright when she saw him if they were back together, and congratulate him – *absolutely not, no way, what was she thinking.*

It felt like a special evening and Sara was looking forward to it. They were going to a new club that had just opened up and they were all dressing daringly and outrageously, Sara had got all their names onto the VIP listing, and the evening started with Champagne flowing and a sumptuous buffet. Her friends were so lively and there was so much laughter, music and photographs being taken, they were on a real high when the taxi arrived to take them to the club.

They were shown to their VIP area, and opening a tab for their drinks, they immediately hit the dance floor. Some while later, as they left the dance floor, excited, exhausted and in need of their drinks, Mia said to Sara, 'I hope you don't mind me saying, and I know I haven't known you for as long as the others, but you don't seem as sparkly this evening.' She raised her two first fingers as in a speech mark mime as she said this. 'As you usually do, is everything ok?'

'Sparkly, am I?' Sara laughed.

'Yes, you are always happy, smiling and laughing and you always make us all feel happier when we are with you, we have all commented on how you don't seem to be the same. Please don't take this as prying, we are all concerned.'

Sara was really touched by their concern and was again reminded how lucky she was to have such good friends like Sami, Livvy, Lexi and Mia, they always looked out for each other. She cared about each one of them, but how could she explain, that she spent her nights crying into her pillow or punching it, and in her temper visualizing it was Felicia's face. Jealousy was a side of her personality she didn't recognise, didn't like and had never experienced before. She had missed her chance with Bruce, he was now with Felicia and she was angry and frustrated with herself. Letting her friends know how she was feeling would sound *really*, pathetic.

'I'm fine, just a little tired, night shoots are never easy, they mess with your body clock, anyway I'm off to Prague in the morning, thankfully it's not an early flight, tonight, I intend to have a really good time. Come on let's have some drinks and then show this place how to dance. '

They danced to all their favourite songs and kept the DJ busy with constant requests, with Sara leading the way with some dance moves, that others quickly copied, everyone in her close proximity was having such a great time, and they were creating quite a stir, as Sara got recognised and some celebrities joined in on some of the latest dance crazes, in particular a friend of one of the celebrities, Jake, was paying a lot of attention to Sara, she didn't mind, she was having such a great time and she thought he was good looking, very easy going and they laughed a lot.

One by one all of Sara's friends seemed to have found a date for the night, they would usually get a taxi home together with several drop-offs, it was clear her friends wanted to stay with their dates. Jake offered to escort Sara home. During the journey, Sara considered if she should invite Jake in for a coffee and let whatever, develop between them, she couldn't live her life like a hermit, *Bruce was now with Felicia*.

Sara never had first night, one-night stands, maybe she was a snob and although she never judged anyone else for sleeping with someone on a first date, it was just a code of morals she had set for herself, she didn't want men to think she was 'easy'. All her sexual experiences had developed into relationships, some for a short time, and others not long enough. She thought of Matias and her eyes stung and a huge lump formed in her throat, which she quickly blinked to stop them from escaping and cleared her throat.

The taxi was pulling up outside her house, Sara thought about it again, but her heart just wasn't in it, and therefore turned to Jake and said, 'Jake, I would invite you in, but I have an early flight tomorrow and a heavy schedule, thank you for seeing me home, maybe I will see you again when I am *next* home?' This was her way of letting him down gently.

'That's a shame, Sara, I was hoping you might invite me in for coffee,' he said with a cheeky grin. 'But I understand, next time, definitely,' then he leaned across and kissed her on the cheek goodnight.

Sara got out of the taxi and thought how things may have been different if she wasn't so obsessed with Bruce, and with that sudden nostalgic memory of Matias. Jake was really lovely, and she would have been tempted under different circumstances.

She let herself in, took her shoes off from her aching feet and headed into the kitchen to make her favourite bedtime drink of hot chocolate, it was a ritual from her childhood, they would sit on the sofa, just the three of them.

They would talk or their mum would regale them with stories of old Italy from when she was young and how she would have loved to go to the local dances, but Nonna was so strict so she would sit up and listen to the music that could be heard from the village. Her parents had a small farm during the war, she told them of the Sundays she enjoyed attending Church, but they had to do their work first, she and Aunty Valentina were the eldest of five, she said she would ask Aunty Valentina if she would finish the work as she was never all that keen on Church, but she would run away towards the village before Aunty Valentina could refuse and be left with the goats.

They loved hearing about their mum's earlier life. When they finished their drinks, they would brush their teeth and their mum would tuck them into bed and kiss them good night.

It was always their mum who did that, their father was nearly always down the pub and they would never see him until the next day, and that would be for a short while after he came home from work, ate his dinner and headed off to the pub, returning after they had gone to bed. If he returned too drunk, he would start an argument with their mum, when this happened, Cameron would come into her room and they would cuddle up together as the argument downstairs was sometimes so loud and occasionally they could hear things being smashed, they were always fearful that their Dad would come into their room, but Cameron would always cuddle Sara close and they would sing nursery rhymes or he would tell her a story, she always felt safe as long as she was with, her big brother.

Sara smiled at the fond memories of her mum and brother, but there were very few she could recall with her Dad, they were more of him shouting or promising things and always breaking them.

She poured the hot milk into her mug and took a sip of the velvety smooth drink and went upstairs. As she finished her drink and removed her makeup and got ready for bed, Bruce popped into her head again, she would be seeing him again soon and that made her stomach flip and then plummet, *he was with her*. Sara got into bed and read her book till she could no longer keep her eyes open, turned off the light, punched the pillow a few times, but thankfully, fell asleep.

Thirteen

Prague was stunning and a perfect substitute as a location for old France, they were filming some of the scenes where Bruce's character was a spy for the British Crown on a dangerous mission to gain vital information on Napoleon Bonaparte's plans, these scenes precede the Battle of Waterloo which had already been shot.

Bruce was enjoying all the power play of his character. The plot and conspiracies in the story and all the times his character was nearly discovered, with a lot of sword fighting scenes, which he spent every morning with experts, choreographing the moves which were looking realistic, he had seen the rushes each day and Davy and Carl seemed pleased.

As the days had passed relatively quickly, with Sara arriving tomorrow, and the start of filming the wedding for their characters and the intimate wedding night scenes. It was the only intimate scenes left to be shot and will require all of the limited acting abilities that Bruce had, to not be affected and embarrass himself.

He had accidentally fallen into acting, had never been to drama school, it was his looks that got him to where he was today, after all the interest from his kickboxing days, that led to modelling jobs, followed by film offers, he was even nominated for an Oscar and Bafta next month for his last film 'Goose Green.'

It was ridiculous, and soon everyone will notice and accuse him of being a fraud, there were so many better actors than him. He was winging it and soon, everyone will be saying it and the only reason he was investing heavily into property and his Company with Jack, was in preparation for the day this 'fame' and the money stopped.

Businesses had always interested Bruce as another means to invest, and as his friends had various ambitions, it seemed a good setup for Bruce to invest into their businesses as a partner, he financed it and they did the hard work, this arrangement was working well for everyone.

His closest mate was Dom, he was the charmer of the group, with the same dark hair as Bruce, they instantly stood out whereas Bruce had blue eyes, Dom had Hazel eyes, and soon after he qualified as a Solicitor, he was offered a position in the same firm as Bruce's brother Brett.

Max had worked his way up in a restaurant from washing dishes to now being a fully trained Chef, it made sense for him to want his own French cuisine restaurant, he spoke the language fluently, as his parents had encouraged Max and his brothers from birth to be bilingual. It had become a family run business for Max, his parents took care of all the ordering and bookkeeping as they had worked in the restaurant business all their lives and they worked hard, even Max's brothers were waiters and barmen. Having the whole family to run the business had its advantages, it seemed to cause a stir, with Max and his brothers looking so alike with their curly brown hair with red and copper natural tints, that caught the light, and their amber eyes that all the female clientele seemed to fall for.

Six months ago, they had a grand opening of their first restaurant in Mayfair. Bruce invited all his celebrity friends and alerted the media. Sometimes this celebrity status worked wonders and the business quickly surpassed their expectations, turning over an amazing profit, getting more and more popular due to the rave reviews, it wouldn't be long before they would attain the Michelin Stars Max was working towards, his standards were extremely high. 'It certainly helps having a great mate with fantastic contacts,' Max said to Bruce on the opening night.

'Just keep creating those delicious dishes and it can only get busier, and in no time, we will be opening the second, start thinking of locations buddy, hope you are up for some really hard work and long hours.' Bruce replied.

'You bet mate. I know you never want any praise or thanks, but I am going to say it, and you are going to listen. You are the best mate ever, and I want to thank you for believing in me, I am not going to let *us* down.'

'Stop it, please, you'll have me blushing like a girl,' Bruce replied with a big grin and slapped Max on the back. 'Where's that Cognac of ours you promised me would be ready for the launch tonight, after two years distilling it, and how is that cocktail side-line coming along?'

'It is, and yes, we have a display area next to the cocktail bar for tonight, come and have a look.'

They had opted for a central island display for the bar, with versatile bright coloured lighting to allow for lively cocktail party events, or subtle lighting for more romantic ones, there were even large room dividers, that could be pulled across the centre of the restaurant, to allow two separate events to be held at the same time, or opened up to cater for larger special events such as wedding receptions.

As they walked around the bar, both of Max's parents were putting the final touches to the display and Bruce greeted each of them in the traditional French style with a kiss on each cheek. Bruce commented on how impressed he was by the display and congratulating Max's mum, on the artistic and distinctive labelling in black and gold for the cognac.

Max's Dad stepped forward reached up and placed his hand on Bruce's shoulder and said, 'You have made my whole family very happy, thank you, Bruce,' he said in his distinctive French accent.

'It is I, who would like to thank you, Mr Devereux, if not for you I would have thought all fathers were bad, I think all of us would,' Bruce said gesturing towards where Dom, Jamie and Flynn were standing. Max's mum then enquired if his mum had arrived yet, Bruce told her his brothers were picking her up and would be arriving shortly.

This had always been Max's dream, so they had called it Devereux Cognac, the pathetic huge grin on Max's face when Bruce suggested it, was priceless and he enjoyed inflicting the barrage of good-humoured abuse, Max took it well, he had no choice, Bruce was merciless.

Jamie was in Construction, he had started as a labourer when leaving school, having no idea what he wanted to do, with the help of a foreman he worked for on one of the sites in London, he put Jamie on a bricklaying course releasing him one day a week to attend. Jamie never forgot that, and now employed him as his foreman, he was so grateful for all the help he had been given when he was younger. Bruce financed the business, but through Jamie's drive, ambition and shrewd business acumen, having enrolled in evening school to learn the business side, of running the company, it was now a large company, with a multi-million-pound turnover.

Construction seemed to suit Jamie, with his blond hair and blue eyes, he really enjoyed working outdoors and getting all the attention he received from women, especially in summer with his muscled body on display. Jamie's ambitions included building high spec properties and not only build them but also employ interior designers for the houses and blocks of flats, wanting them to be in prime locations all over England, their mate Olly was their Architect. They had recently moved on to building indoor shopping centres.

Flynn was the most noticeable of Bruce's mates, all of them were over six foot, Flynn being the tallest at 6'4, born in Edinburgh, he spoke with a soft Gallic lilt, which women were attracted to and found sexy. Having moved to London the day before his first day at school, he had always been targeted by the bullies because of his accent and for his thick, curly and always slightly overlong red hair and green eyes.

He had always dreamed of having his own Pub with whiskey theme nights, all the different whiskeys and cocktails and to blend his own whiskey brand, that ambition was due to be fulfilled and ready by the summer with the plan to launch it in June or July, they were going to call it 'Ewen' and the bottle would have the coat of arms of his family name. Not in honour of his father, but his Grandfather, as he had always been his inspiration, he had worked in the Whiskey industry all his life.

Flynn spent so much time with his grandfather when he was young, even being taken to work with him, he was heartbroken when his father moved the whole family to London, work was his reason, but Flynn found out at his Grandfathers funeral many years later, that his father had a falling out about money, which he apparently had asked for and been given on many occasions, but this time, his Grandfather had refused to loan him anymore as it always went on booze and never his family.

Although this was Flynn's dream, he was the most reserved drinker of the whole group, he enjoyed a good Whiskey, but never overindulged, a remnant of seeing both his mother and father, drunk or stoned on drugs, turned him in the opposite direction.

Bruce and Flynn found premises on the South Bank in London for their first venture, and it had an outdoor area right next to the Thames, with one of the riverboat operatives boarding platforms just a little way from the pub entrance, therefore was in a prime location. Flynn had even contacted all the tourist operators making a deal with them to have the pub put onto their tourist destinations due to its historic value, and the cellar was said to be haunted, the place was full of framed smuggling stories and Flynn had spent a fortune finding interesting display items around the pub.

After a long day filming, Bruce intended to grab a quick bite in the hotel bar before heading off to the gym. He received a message from the reception to call his other business partner Jack Mason, Bruce didn't even bother to check the time difference, Jack never seemed to sleep anyway. He asked reception to put in the call for him and said he would be in the bar. Ten minutes later he picked up the call and heard Jacks greeting, 'How is it going out there in Prague, you lucky bastard,' said Jack in his usual no-nonsense manner.

'Really well. Did you get all the designs I sent?'

'Yes, they are looking fantastic, we are going to revolutionize laptops and computer software with your ideas and designs mate, the engineers are working on them now, they should be ready within the next few months for us to launch, don't know how you balance everything you do, thought I was the insomniac,' Jack said laughing.

'Designing is relaxing for me, so it's my way of downtime. How is Jane by the way?'

'History, we finished last week, I can't have a girlfriend named Jane or Jill, sounds too much like a kiddies thing, I'm seeing Louise, I met her at a recent interview, she's a Producer at ITV.'

'Shame, I rather liked Jane - wait, you ended it because of her name?' Bruce asked incredulously.

'No, not just because of her name, she was getting a little … demanding, didn't like it when I turned up late for dates and hinting about Valentines.'

Laughing, Bruce said, 'Jack, mate, neither of those are unreasonable, I don't think any girl would not demand you turn up on time to take them out, and what's wrong with them expecting to be wined and dined on Valentines, you, my friend are the consummate bachelor.'

'Are you implying I have commitment issues? All I have to say is pot, kettle. How is it going with Felicia, heard you two were back together or is that just tabloid?'

'Oh God, don't mention her name, that woman will just not take no for an answer, and she has thoroughly ruined any chance I had with Sara, and now she is with someone else, and we have more intimate scenes to film after she arrives tomorrow, I am dreading them.'

'Don't know how you Actors …' Jack said as in a paraphrasing tone, 'pretend to have sex, I'd be going around with a boner all day.'

'That's precisely what I'm dreading, and I'm not exactly a proper, *Actor*, I got here by default.'

'You mean your looks? say that again when you are holding that Oscar, buddy.'

'Don't remind me, not sure whether I should prepare a speech or wing it, as I'm not expecting to win. Anyway, is everything ok with the designs, and our plans leading up to the launch?'

'Leave it with me, you've done your bit, the rest is my domain, just ring in and let our new assistant Jessica know where you are, just in case I need to get hold of you.'

'Ok, will do, talk soon.'

'Yeah, bye mate.'

Bruce put the phone down, finished his meal and headed out to the gym. It had been such a long day that his workout was not as full-on as usual, therefore he decided to include a run and take in some of the sites of the city on his way back to his hotel. It was easier to avoid recognition in the dark and the Vitava River at night was stunning. Bruce jogged across one of the bridges and returned over the next, stopping halfway, taking a breather and to take in the magnificent views.

He returned to his hotel suite and took a shower, helped himself to the minibar and wandered out onto the terrace to drink it, he thought of Sara and whispered softly into the gentle breeze, 'I wish you were mine, Sara,' he finished his drink returned to the bedroom and collapsed on the bed, immediately falling into a deep sleep.

Fourteen

Davy the Director had left a message for Sara as soon as she checked in, saying he needed to call a meeting with herself and Bruce, and would be arriving at her hotel at 6 pm, they could all have dinner together to discuss the schedule, as there had to be a necessary change and would explain when they met.

Sara went up to her suite and took a shower, then relaxed with a cup of tea on the terrace and finished reading her book, before getting ready to meet Davy and prepare herself coming face to face again with Bruce, it seemed an age since she had seen him, and she wished her heart would stop alternating between a gentle fluttering, and a full out assault and slamming in her chest, every time she thought of him. She had no idea how she was going to get through the next few weeks filming of a wedding, and the intimate wedding night scenes, all of it required extreme close contact, intimate contact.

Preparing for the wedding scenes on the way over in the plane, made her nervous, but at least she had a week working with Bruce again, before the wedding night scenes. It was never easy being virtually naked on a closed set that still comprised of twenty people or more, who were necessary, watching you intensely, in very close proximity and doing the scene over and over again. Touching and simulating intimacy with a man possessing such a sexy and very fit body like Bruce's, was going to require all her experience of being a professional, not to show the effect it was having on her, had in fact, already affected her.

The whole crew had bantered about the chemistry between the leads, from her perspective the attraction was very, very real, no acting required and she hoped to God he didn't think she was a lovesick puppy, making doughy eyes at him, agh … if he did? she would be mortified if she heard that little nugget of gossip going around the set, she hadn't *yet*.

As she entered the restaurant, both Davy and Bruce rose from their seats as she took hers. As usual, Davy came straight to the point, as he handed her a glass of wine. 'The Wedding scenes have been delayed due to technical difficulties with the location at St Vitus Cathedral and will take a few days to sort out, therefore we are going to film the wedding night scenes first, starting tomorrow, the set has been rushed and finished due to the location delay. I just wanted to let you know before tomorrow to allow you both a little time to prep.' Sara's heart slammed in her chest at this news, she thought she had more time.

'Well, there's not too much dialogue to learn. It's mostly action,' Bruce said with a mischievous grin as he glanced at Sara.

Profuse heat, started at her neck and quickly spread across her face, Sara immediately tried to cover up her embarrassment by asking, 'I take it the six-day schedule remains the same for the wedding night scenes or has that changed?' *Please say it has been re-written, deleted even*, Sara prayed.

'No, those will remain the same, we are just switching them around to give the crew setting up, more time to resolve the issues they have for the wedding.'

Sara only just managed to stifle a loud groan. This was going to be sheer torture. Since setting eyes on Bruce again, her decision was definite, she couldn't ask him if he was back with Felicia, she knew the answer she wanted, but what if she got the one, she didn't? How would she react, what could she say – oh good for you, hope you will be very happy – congratulations? No, she will just have to wait until the answer became obvious.

'Let's order dinner and discuss the next few weeks work whilst we are here in Prague, oh, by the way, the Production company are organising a Valentine's Ball, in Austria, and you both have invitations. Without prying Bruce, and with all the recent publicity, I have been told that Felicia will be attending as she is currently in Austria on the European leg of her tour.'

Sara didn't realise that at this, she had stopped breathing, and immediately looked at Bruce as he replied.

'Well, we can hardly let the company down. I take it we are required to attend?'

He smiled and seemed to relax, that was when Sara let out her breath and took short shallow breaths to make up for the lack of oxygen. The expression on Bruce's face was unreadable, was he relieved, genuinely happy or just a very good Actor and not happy. Still no definitive answer to whether Bruce and Felicia were back together.

'It would be too good an opportunity to get early publicity for the film. It will have to be a quick overnight jaunt, Carl will be going with you, to help with coordinating the publicity, then back the following day. Sorry,

I can't release more time, but the schedule has already overrun a little, and we need to finish by the end of March, to fit with the time needed for post-production and scheduling for release.'

For the next few hours, they talked while they dined, as Davy outlined how he would like the wedding night scenes to work out. Sara sat there in a daze, hearing some of what was being said, nodding and smiling, hopefully in the right places, but really, she wasn't taking any of it in, all she kept thinking was *he must be with her*, he hadn't even tried to put Davy straight, he didn't admit it was true, but then he hadn't denied it either. She had hoped he would tell Davy there was no truth to the stories, but he didn't.

Sara didn't want to sit there any longer than was necessary, the mention of Felicia just made her anger flare, and the effort to cover it up was exhausting. She sipped the last of her wine, made her excuses of tiredness and wanting a long soak in the luxurious bath, bade them goodnight and left.

Fifteen

Bruce watched Sara leave the table, his gaze dropped to her cute behind and her swaying hips, my God she looked and smelled good tonight. All day he had been looking forward to seeing her again, he had hoped that Davy would leave and he could have some time with her, just the two of them, and maybe sit out on the terrace with a nightcap. For February it wasn't too cold and they had put some patio burners out there, it had such a stunning view, but it was obviously not to be, *she is with someone else*, chimed that constant, incessant reminder.

Sara was the ultimate professional, Bruce thought, she was graceful, serene, got on with everyone, they all really liked her, from the comments he had overheard from various crew members. She was never late, always prepared and she hardly ever talked about her private life, she was more interested in other people's lives and putting them at ease.

He wanted to know, but he didn't want to hear any details, about how things were with the guy she was with on New Year's Eve, was she still with him? '*You could always just ask her*' he told himself, 'And how would that go – how's it going with you and that fella from New Year's Eve, are you still in love? Only a prize sized moron would say something like that.

He could have kicked Davy for mentioning Felicia's name and her publicity machine, in front of Sara. He was so angry, he had to use all his will power, to refrain from punching Davy in the face, and said the only thing he could trust himself to say, and deferred to not letting the Company down. He really, really, *really*, did not want to attend this Valentine's Ball, knowing Felicia was going to be there.

Davy left soon after Sara, and Bruce went over to the bar and ordered himself a double whiskey straight, one of the barmaids started talking to him, he just wasn't very tired and certainly didn't want to return to his empty room alone this early.

The barmaid was very pretty and very interested, this inner war he was having was nonsensical, his mind wanting to be faithful and his manhood reacting, otherwise. Here he was being flirted with and he was single, he was not cheating on anyone, his brain was not making any sense, and as usual, his manhood won, yet again.

Bruce took his drink over to one of the tables next to a floor to ceiling window, with an excellent view over Prague, all lit up at night time. He was just finishing his drink, when the barmaid came over and asked if he would like another drink, as she was about to finish her shift, he looked up at her and smiled and asked her name, then said that the hotel probably had rules of staff drinking with customers and asked her if she would like to join him for a drink at a place he knew of nearby, she shyly smiled and agreed. He tucked her hand round his arm and they both walked out of the Hotel.

Sixteen

Up before dawn the next morning, and out for a run through the Old Town Square of Prague, watching the breath-taking sunrise as she stood on one of the bridges over the Vitava River, Sara steadied her nerves for the day ahead. Returning to her hotel for a shower and some breakfast, *if her stomach allowed it*, she made her way to the set.

As before when they filmed all the other intimate scenes, there were only necessary members of the crew present. Having undressed and wrapped herself in the robe left for her in her trailer, she made her way to the make-up area and being told by Tania to stop fidgeting, Sara took a deep breath, unfortunately just as she was starting to relax, she heard Bruce and Davy discussing the first scene as they walked across the set, it took all her will power and an argument with Nagy in her mind, to remain seated with her eyes closed to allow Tania to finish.

As Sara expected, disrobing in front of him made her heart beat a fast-staccato rhythm, the goosebumps on her skin had their own goosebumps, and her body was going from overheated to a cold sweat, really attractive!! Sex scenes were definitely not sexy to film.

Sara watched as Bruce disrobed, he had his back to her, she couldn't help but marvel at his broad shoulders, golden skin and how his muscles rippled as he removed the robe, and be mesmerised as the robe slipped lower until his bare backside was revealed.

Sara's mouth went dry and her hands itched to touch, but with an almighty strength of willpower, she refrained from leaning across and cupping his bum cheek, *what is wrong with me, I'm such a letch,* she thought to herself and quickly looked away and concentrated hard on what Davy was saying to her, as Bruce slipped into the bed. The wedding night scenes were not being filmed in sequence, this scene, was her character losing her virginity on her wedding night.

Bruce would whisper encouragement to try and make her feel less uncomfortable and would tease and joke to lighten the mood between takes. He would always find ways to stop her feeling so exposed by pulling the covers up immediately after a take, or handing over her robe whilst they waited for the rushes to be viewed and decision on whether another take was necessary, he would bring her hot drinks and talk to her about anything to take her mind off their next scene, and he would always ask if she was ok, if she wanted to change anything. He was beyond considerate and Sara found she was increasingly drawn to him more and more.

At the end of each day, Bruce would invite her to join him for a drink to wind down, but every day whilst removing her make-up, that little reminder poked her, *he was with her,* and the glow she got from all the intimate contact, she had with Bruce, immediately evaporated and she would refuse.

She would take herself off to the late-night gym, and rigorously work off all her frustration, in the hope, she would return to her hotel completely exhausted, and fall asleep as soon as her head hit the pillow. It worked some of the nights, but not this one, so she phoned her brother Cameron, he always had a way of lifting her spirits, he answered after only two rings.

'Hi Cameron, did I wake you?'

'Hey little sis, how goes it in beautiful Prague?'

'Oh, it's absolutely stunning, I had a run this morning before dawn and saw the sunrise on the bridge of the Vitava River. How are you and what are you up to?' They talked for half an hour, teasing and laughing, then Cameron asked if Sara was ok.

'I'm fine.'

'Sara, it's me you are talking to and I know that when you call me in the middle of the night, you are not fine, what's wrong?'

At this Sara couldn't hold back any longer, she had never confided in her friends, which she usually did about everything, but this was different, she fancied a man who was with someone else and by her own moral standards should have taken him off the grid, no longer available, otherwise engaged, and she should back off and go find someone who was available, maybe that Jake from back home.

Sara took a deep breath and told Cameron everything, he listened without interruption, in the end, Sara just asked if maybe he may have heard anything to confirm that Bruce and Felicia were or were not together.

'Sorry cupcake, same as you, I only know what has been in the press, and Felicia is definitely cashing in on them being together, and I haven't heard any denial reported from Bruce. As you are working with him why don't you ask him?'

'Don't you think I haven't considered that, and how do you think that would sound if he is, with her, and I am interested enough to want confirmation – desperate, that's what.'

'Tell you what, how about I come over for that Valentine's Ball in Austria, give you some moral support, so you don't feel completely alone when Felicia and Bruce are fawning over each other, do you think you can get me an invite?'

'Oh, Cameron, you would do that for me?'

'What, travel to a beautiful city and attend a fully paid for, mass celebrity ball? Umm … let me think, that sounds like such a hardship.'

'Ok, enough, you wind-up merchant,' Sara laughed.

So, is this Ball actually on the 14th?'

'I'll send you all the details – and Cameron? Thank you, this means a lot to me, I was dreading going.'

'No problem, little sis, just notching up the IOU's,' he laughed. 'See you in a couple of days.'

The next few days were the most intimate of all the scenes and Sara had found a way of getting a little more comfortable with being virtually naked, she would not look at Bruce other than when they were filming and concentrate on getting each scene right, hoping to cut down on the number of takes they needed to do. She carried on with her early morning runs and late-night gym visits to avoid uncomfortable interactions with Bruce.

Seventeen

It was the day of the Valentine's Ball and Sara was due to finish the last scene before they were all due to leave and fly over to Austria, Paula, her assistant on the set assured her that one of Sara's favourite designers had delivered the gown Sara would have on loan for the night. She returned to her hotel to pack an overnight bag, as she was about to leave, there was a knock at her door and as she opened it, her heart stuttered and then went into overdrive. There stood Bruce, all showered with tousled dark hair, blue shirt that matched his eyes and black trousers with his jacket slung over his shoulder, which made his arm muscles bulge under the shirt, he looked ... gorgeous.

'Thought we could get a taxi to the airport together?' Bruce said as he leaned his shoulder on the door frame and crossing one foot over the other in a casual pose.

Sara started to get excited at spending time alone with him, maybe she could ask how Felicia was and get a clue if they were together, until he added, 'Carl is downstairs, ready when you are.'

Sara made what she thought was a valiant effort to hide her disappointment until she remembered he was probably looking forward to meeting up with Felicia. That instantly woke up the green-eyed monster and Sara could feel her blood boiling, she needed to calm down and she needed to meet someone new and have sex – real sex. Simulated sex was downright frustrating, harmful even, right now she would take anyone, why not Bruce, after the week they had shared, maybe just a quickie – Lord help her – what was she thinking, I so need an ice-cold shower, she thought to herself *my moral compass is so off*.

As they got to the airport, Carl commented that he had persuaded the Production Company to loan the private jet for the trip, which cut down on travel time. Sara picked a seat and placed her bag on the one next to her, hoping Bruce would sit elsewhere and took out her book and settled down to read, but it may as well have been written in a language she *didn't* understand, for all the concentration she gave it, she noticed Bruce hesitate at her seat, looked at her bag placed there, and moved on to another behind and across from her, good she thought, at least he won't be a distraction for the whole trip, I need to try and get this obsession with him under control, she thought to herself, then Nagy quipped, *'Good luck with that one honey.'* Was she sulking for bringing Carl along and spoiling her snapshot alone time to the airport, she needed to grow up and move on, she was reverting to childlike behaviour, giving up on the book, she reclined her seat and closed her eyes.

Bruce had intended to have some time with Sara, but it was obvious she wanted nothing to do with him, and for some unknown reason, it hurt. He had done his best to make Sara feel comfortable with all the intimate scenes, ensuring she was not unnecessarily exposed or feel awkward, he had teased light-heartedly to help her relax, and it looked to him that she had, but she didn't seem to want to talk to him.

Never looking at him between scenes, leaving as soon as they finished for the day, and was never in her room when he went to invite her for a second time, for a drink, in the hotel bar, where did she spend her evenings. She was even gone first thing in the morning when he called to see if she wanted to travel to the set together, and now, even on this flight, she had put her bag on the next seat in a loud and clear message, that she wanted to be alone.

Bruce took a seat behind and across from her so that he couldn't see her, he needed to get his head straight about Sara and how he was going to react to Felicia, there was going to be a lot of paparazzi. Bruce spent the journey talking to Carl.

Getting ready that night, his black suit had been delivered via his favourite designer, he sprayed himself with the only aftershave he had brought with him, then suddenly noticed it was the one Felicia loved, commenting on it whenever he wore it, he had meant to throw it away, but forgot. The only way to get rid of the scent was to undress and have another shower, he didn't have time for that, it was probably on the suit as well anyway, his strategy would have to be to keep well away from Felicia.

Carl was just about to knock on Bruce's door as he exited, and they went down to the private guest's bar, where they had arranged to meet Sara. They ordered their drinks as they waited. Then the door opened behind them, Bruce was becoming accustomed to this feeling of awareness he had whenever Sara walked into any room, it was like the atmosphere had become electrically static and the hairs on his body became instantly sensitive.

He slowly turned and felt the impact that felt like the air had been vacuumed from his lungs, he couldn't breathe and his heart was pounding. In the doorway, still holding the door open as she scanned the bar with an expression of apprehension or was it fear?

Sara was a vision of sheer stunning beauty. Wearing a bright blood red strapless full length, flowing creation, she looked ravishing with matching lipstick. Her beautiful, glossy blonde hair was pulled over one shoulder, the whole effect was spectacular. Bruce was utterly speechless and couldn't move.

Thank God for Carl, he instantly walked over to Sara and graciously complimented her, as soon as she saw him her expression melted into relief, followed by that full-on dazzling smile. Slowly, Bruce recovered enough to greet Sara taking her hand, and moved in to kiss her on the cheek and whisper, 'You look fantastic this evening,' and was rewarded with a husky, 'Thank you,' as their gazes locked and she smiled at him. Bruce heard Carl clear his throat and offer Sara a drink, had they been staring at each other too long? Bruce had no idea, but taking his eyes off Sara was difficult.

They made their way to the rear of the hotel where two cars were waiting for them, Carl travelled with Sara and Bruce would arrive in the other car. The cars were only travelling round to the front, to fool the paparazzi as to where they were staying, but a necessary subterfuge.

They gave numerous photo calls and interviews, as they walked slowly along the red carpet towards the entrance to the party, but then it was the publicity the Production Company wanted and Bruce and Sara put on the full charm offensive, bantering with each other and deflecting intrusive personal questions.

They were engrossed in answering questions, Sara was talking to a crew from Italy and had switched to answering in Italian. She was completely unaware of Felicia's arrival, and how she quickly got out of the car, and strode straight over to Bruce, hooking her arm in his, even planting a kiss on his cheek, then started flirting with the press about her tour and how relieved she was to be back with Bruce at this event.

Bruce had been publicly ambushed, completely unprepared for this, quickly he was thinking how to get out of this, have a very public row or move Felicia towards the entrance and get her out of sight, she had said quite enough, he would have to leave Sara to make her way in alone and for that, he was extremely angry with Felicia.

When they got inside the foyer, which was crowded, Bruce moved them over to a corner, then he turned to Felicia and through gritted teeth said, 'What the fuck are you playing at Felicia? You know just to imply we are together like you did out there just now will generate a storm of false stories.'

'Darling, are you not glad to see me?' she pouted as she stepped closer and played with the lapels of his jacket.

Bruce grabbed her hands, moved them away from his body and let them go as he said, 'What the hell makes you think I would be? My love for you died long ago when you tried to trap me with a false pregnancy.'

'You. Loved. Me?' Felicia's eyes widened in sheer surprise as she stepped forward again and placed her hand on his chest.

Again, Bruce removed her hand as he said, 'Was it not clear enough on New Year's Eve? Then let me clarify – we are over, finished, done, no more. Do. You. Hear. Me? He turned and walked away.

The evening hadn't even started and Bruce wanted it to end. He made his way into the main party and headed straight for the bar, ordered a drink and sat there for a while to let his temper cool before looking round for Sara.

He spotted Sara through the crowd, and suddenly, the evening had just got worse. Sara was standing next to the same guy that was with her on New Year's Eve, and she had her arms around him and he had just kissed her cheek. She had her palm splayed on his back that was rubbing up and down in a very familiar way, again they looked so relaxed with each other.

Carl appeared next to Bruce and said, 'Felicia has arranged with her tour promoters, for a select few of the press being granted entrance into the venue to watch, as she performs three numbers from her tour, with her dancers and give an interview. As the venue is raising money for a charity and she has suggested inviting you and Sara up onto the stage. The Production Company are excited to be getting this type of publicity before the release of their film.'

'What, when was this arranged?' Bruce asked sceptically.

'Apparently, in the last half hour, since Felicia arrived, and the press is over the moon, she has even contacted the Production Company and got their ok.'

Bruce let out a groan and swore, 'Does Sara know, and how does she feel about it?' he asked.

'Just told her, she's not pleased, but ok about it.'

Bruce went in search of Felicia, finally finding her behind the small stage area the venue had, talking to her dancers, he waited a few minutes for her to finish then walked over to her, 'I need a word with you, Felicia.'

'Sorry Bruce, but we only have a few minutes before we are due on stage, can it wait till after?'

'No, and unless you want to be in the middle of some very unpleasant publicity, you will give me a few minutes - now.'

He didn't wait for an answer, he caught hold of her upper arm and marched her over to a quieter corner then hissed, 'What is this new publicity stunt you've organised for tonight, Felicia?'

'I love the way you say my name, Brucie Baby.'

'Don't call me that, and answer the question.'

'It's just another way to promote the tour, and I thought to help you out with your latest film Darling.'

'As usual, you are trying to get what you want, well it's not going to work, and if you so much as hint at us being together, I will be announcing that I will be giving an exclusive full, no holds barred interview into our relationship,' he paused to allow her to realise what that would include, 'You know how they like exclusives, they will be falling over themselves to get that scoop, and I am sure you don't want that, so you had better behave tonight, do I make myself clear?' he snarled through gritted teeth very close to her face.

Bruce had never been one to scare girls it was abhorrent to him to do it now, even to Felicia, her eyes went wide with fear, and she stammered, 'Y-y-yes Bruce, of course.'

He walked away to find somewhere to calm himself yet again, this was turning into one long nightmare of an evening, and the night was still young.

It was at least a small blessing that the show started, and Felicia didn't announce Bruce and Sara's attendance to the Ball, until after her performance, which gave Bruce a little time to calm and compose himself before going on stage.

The Charity, for the evening, supported children and teenagers who had been abused. Just as Bruce and Sara were announced, one of the Promoters for the event asked Bruce if he could announce the amount that had been raised, and also that an anonymous contributor had donated 25k. They wanted to take advantage of the press present, thanks to Felicia.

Bruce had to bite his tongue not to make a cutting remark that Felicia had not done this out of the kindness of her heart, but for purely selfish reasons, and he did not doubt that given the chance, turn this to her advantage. Bruce had been given the golden opportunity to take the limelight away from Felicia, and shine it on the brilliant cause for the Charity. This lightened his mood and he bounded up the stairs behind Sara and felt honoured to make the requested announcement, which had stopped whatever agenda Felicia had when she organised this show for the press.

As they left the stage, Sara excused herself saying she wanted a word with the Charity's promoter, telling Bruce in a whisper, that she wanted to donate. Bruce couldn't explain why he was so pleased to hear this, maybe because Felicia never made quiet donations, it always had to be done in a blaze of publicity to gain public favour, but there went Sara, quietly, no fuss, no fanfare.

After the show was over and the press left, the evening progressed more sedately, a sumptuous buffet was announced, and the volume and tempo of the music changed, to allow for people to eat and talk without shouting. Unfortunately, as he made his way over to the buffet tables, he saw Sara with her date and instantly, his appetite disappeared. They looked so happy together, while he stood there watching them, he made the decision to wander over and be introduced to the man Sara had fallen in love with, maybe then he could find a way to move on, there were only six weeks of filming left.

As he pushed away from the wall, he had lent his shoulder against, Felicia stepped in front of him, his step faltered and he removed his hands from his pockets and sighed, then rolled his eyes and said, 'What now, Felicia.'

'Darling, I just want to say sorry, I'm really, really sorry, how can I make it up to you.'

'You don't.'

'Please, Bruce,' she pleaded, 'you know how I am? I get a little carried away, and tonight I shouldn't have. Seeing you standing there with Sara, I just got jealous, I'm not proud of that, but I really loved you and because of the way I am – I lost you. Please give me just tonight, for us to say goodbye on good terms, I am willing to do anything, to make it up to you, literally, *anything*,' Felicia said, suggestively fluttering her eyelashes and leaning into him, 'After all, there was no harm done.'

'You're right, no *further,* harm, because you didn't get the chance, but you still hinted to the press we are back together when you arrived tonight, we haven't read the morning papers yet. Will it help get your next single to number one? Your stunt at the airport only hinted and look what happened.'

'Please, Bruce,' she repeated, 'I am trying to walk away from the only man I have ever loved with just an ounce of dignity. Earlier, you told me you loved me once, and I know now how my behaviour ruined that. They are playing a slow dance, please dance with me?'

Bruce hesitated, then looked over towards where Sara was now dancing with Carl, at least it wasn't with her lover, who had made the effort to make the trip here, for Valentine's. Sara got him a ticket to the venue, it was further confirmation that he had missed his chance.

He returned his gaze to Felicia and reluctantly took her outstretched hand, and followed her to the dance floor, for the last dance ever with her, from tomorrow he would start looking for another person to love. His obsession with Sara ends tonight.

As he took Felicia into his arms, he felt her move in very close to him then she said, 'You are wearing that cologne I always loved on you, did you wear it for me?'

'That is so typical of you Felicia, to think this is about you. No, it was the only one I packed for this overnight trip and only realized as I was dressing and ran out of time.'

'Ok, sorry.'

This was just like Felicia. She had a habit of being so nice when she wanted something, and he would always be left confused, as to whether she was being truly sincere or manipulative, to get what she wanted. Their relationship had not been all bad, in fact sometimes, when she was just herself without angling for something, Felicia could be extremely good company, and the physical side had always been … spectacular. As if reading his mind …

'Is there any way, I can interest you in one last night together, I meant it when I said I would do *anything* to make it up to you, I'm willing to do all the things I know you used to like me to do, how about it? I know you have a room here tonight, no-one will take notice of us leaving, if we leave separately.'

How weak was he? A typical man thinking with one part of his anatomy, which had twitched with her suggestive offer, and he was seriously tempted, he knew what she was offering was incredibly pleasurable. Bruce looked over to where Sara had been and couldn't find her, he then looked for her lover and couldn't find him either, with a silent groan, he concluded they must have left together. She must have taken him to her room, and *oh God*, be doing all sorts of things together, he must stop thinking of Sara, it stops tonight, he repeated to himself.

'Well?' Felicia prompted, a little more impatiently.

'Room 505' was all he said as he walked away.

Eighteen

Sara awoke the next morning and her face felt swollen from all the tears from the night before. It felt like the distance was even greater between herself and Bruce. He had abandoned her when they arrived, she had been giving an interview to a reporter from Italy, when she had finished she turned round to see Bruce and Felicia walk into the venue, and when she entered with Carl, they looked really cosy talking in a corner of the foyer.

Bruce had barely spoken a word to her throughout the night, she was so grateful when Cameron turned up as she felt so alone, she always hated these large professional occasions where she had to network with people she didn't know, some she recognised, mostly total strangers. She always braced herself and put on a charm offensive, when all she felt was conspicuous and nervous, no matter that she had virtually been born into this profession, she had never been an overconfident person inside, putting on a false facade, the Felicia's of the world oozed confidence and she envied them. When Cameron arrived and walked over to her, she had never been so relieved, that she just kept hugging him, and didn't want to release him, and repeatedly thanked him for coming over to help her.

Later in the evening when she couldn't find Bruce, she had accepted the offer of a Dance with Carl, as Cameron was talking animatedly with a really good-looking man, and may have found himself a date for the night, she didn't want to spoil things for him.

Then she saw Bruce being led by Felicia onto the dance floor for a slow dance, maybe this was the confirmation she needed, but then it was only a dance and they had history together. After her dance with Carl had finished, Sara decided to go and get herself a drink, as Carl headed over to talk to another Producer, he said he would meet her at the bar. Sara took a seat at the end of the bar that obscured some of the dance floor and provided a little privacy, so she wouldn't look so obvious to be sitting alone as she waited for Carl. As the barman placed her drink in front of her, she saw Bruce leave the dance floor and heading out to the foyer, she was about to jump down from her bar stool and follow him, seeing as they hadn't spoken much all evening, then suddenly, she saw Felicia head out the same way as Bruce.

Sara stood there, unable to move, unable to breathe, then tears sprang to her eyes and she was finding it difficult to stop them from running down her cheeks, all she could think was, *No, oh please no*. She needed to get out of there before she made a complete fool of herself, the barman who served her drink asked, 'Is everything ok, Miss?' Sara came to and said without turning, 'Yes, thank you.' She then quickly walked out to the foyer where Bruce and Felicia had disappeared to, they were not out there and wouldn't have left through the front entrance, as there was still a lot of paparazzi waiting.

Sara made her way to her room, locked her door, undressed before falling on the bed and let the tears fall and allowed herself to cry, which seemed most of the night until she must have fallen asleep through exhaustion.

In the cold light of day, Sara still wanted to believe she had got it wrong and just because they were not in the foyer, doesn't mean they spent the night together. With new hope surfacing, she got out of bed, saw her reflection – ugh … what a fright, she decided to have a long shower and took longer to apply her make-up and look her best, she was going to knock on Bruce's door, to see if he would like to join her for breakfast before they left for the airport.

With a decided spring in her step, Sara knocked on Bruce's door and waited, this was something she would never usually do, but in some way, the innocent invite to breakfast was a way for Sara to find out if her suspicions were right, she was hoping she was wrong, she wanted to lift the confused mood she was in, one way or the other. She knocked on the door again, then she heard footsteps and Sara held her breath as the door opened.

Of all the scenario's that had raced through her mind, it was not to be greeted by Felicia with a bedsheet wrapped around her, the shock was too much and Sara stood there with her mouth open, she just couldn't find any words, it was Felicia who spoke first.

'Good morning Sara, did you want to speak to Bruce, he is just in the shower, do you want to come in and wait for him?' Felicia said sweetly, politely … sarcastically, with a smug satisfied smile, Sara was tempted to slap that expression off her face.

Instead, she said, 'No thank you, just let Bruce know we will be leaving in about an hour and Carl and I will meet him on the plane at the airport.'

Her body felt rooted to the spot, but she managed to walk away with what she hoped was a semblance of decorum.

She was out of tears. She felt empty and numb. Finally, she had her unmitigated proof – now she had to face it and deal with it.

Bruce arrived just in time and only briefly acknowledged her and Carl before he sat down close to the front of the plane. The flight back was the most miserable she had felt in a very long time, similar to when she had lost Matias, and that was ridiculous, Matias had died, and that was far, far worse. Sara tried to make sense of her feelings for Bruce, and if she was comparing this misery equating to the loss of Matias, did that mean she had fallen in love with Bruce, and it had just ended because he had cheated on her, which was ridiculous, they weren't even dating. Oh my God, what was wrong with her. Sara started laughing quietly at her crazy train of thought.

Sara got up and made use of the bathroom facilities, returned and went to sit next to Carl, asking him if it was possible if the schedule would allow for her to have a few days off. To her relief, Carl agreed, he had phoned before leaving, to see if the set was ready for the next scenes. Unfortunately, there had been some unexpected delays, he was working on rearranging the schedules, therefore he agreed for Sara to have the next three days off, and as the jet was making a return flight to London after dropping them back to Prague, if she wanted she could remain on the flight and go directly with the jet. Sara beamed at him and said that would be perfect, she didn't need to pick up anything from the hotel, she could go with what she had, and everything else was at home.

She needed to have a really good girls night out or two and she would phone Jake, see if he was still interested, if not then she was going to chat up any man who took her fancy, take him home and make use of a long night of sexual release, two can play at that game, Mr Bailey. It was a plan, but if she dug deep, it was not the plan she wanted. That ship had sailed.

When they landed, she saw Bruce get up to leave the plane, she heard Carl explain that Sara was returning to London, she smiled and waved at him as he stood at the exit, he paused, turned around and looked at her, then left, what was his problem? Sara puzzled over that as the jet refuelled, then started to taxi and then it took off for London.

Nineteen

Felicia had surpassed her usual bedroom expertise last night, she had been extremely demanding, he hadn't got a wink of sleep. Bruce was feeling relieved that finally, Felicia had accepted their relationship was over and that last night was indeed their last night. When he had returned from the bathroom after his shower, she had been quite sweet by wishing him all the luck with the film, and saying that she really regretted her behaviour, and if things had been different, maybe – they would still be together and it will always be the biggest regret of her life, then she asked for one last kiss, he intended it to be a quick peck on the lips, but as usual, Felicia had other ideas, and with him only in a towel and her with only a bedsheet around her, one thing led to another … he only just made it in time for the flight.

As soon as the flight took off, he must have instantly fallen asleep, the next thing he knew, Carl was waking him up to say Sara was taking a few days off, and as the jet was making a trip to London, she would be remaining on the plane.

Bruce returned to his suite in Prague in a temper that had no justification, Sara had returned to London for a break with her lover, and it was really difficult for him to calm himself, she couldn't wait to be with him again, this was driving him insane.

Over the next few days, Bruce was kept busy finishing scenes of his character spying and gaining information for the British Crown on Napoleon Bonaparte. Davy had spent the time whilst they were away studying the rushes and agreeing with the writers, they needed some extra scenes to give this sequence in the film a bigger impact, they had asked Bruce if he would mind working straight through, he agreed, at least it would give him less time to think about Sara. Although he had promised himself that he would stop this obsession, that was going to be difficult whilst working with her, he may have to delay that thought for when this film was finished.

Sara returned a few days later, and they were ready to film the wedding at the beautiful St Vitus Cathedral and the honeymoon in France that

Prague doubles for. They were long days and had attracted enormous tourist crowds from all the recent publicity that had been generated from the Valentines Ball.

Each scene took twice as long as tourists kept taking pictures, using flashes, or getting in the way or in the shot with their camera, which required more takes. They were repeatedly told not to take them and to stand behind a barrier that had been put up, but they kept leaning so far over or running out and taking a quick picture.

Davy's patience was running out and suggested a solution, he asked Sara and Bruce if they would mind meeting some of the fans to appease them, so they would have the opportunity of taking their pictures then, and refrain from taking them whilst filming. Davy made a loud announcement and the fans eagerly agreed, clearly delighted that they would get close to Bruce and Sara, and get pictures taken *with* them and autographs, this added many hours to their days, but at least they were able to finish the shoot, finally.

For Bruce, the following days passed relatively quickly, and without any major dramas on the set, and they were able to get through many of the more difficult scenes, easier than was expected.

As soon as they finished in Prague, they flew to England and the Stately home Sara had filmed before, which Bruce had not yet seen, his character had been summoned home as his brother, The Duke had died from consumption and the title now fell to Bruce's character. As the schedule had been delayed in Prague, Davy decided to make more use of the Stately home location.

It was now the second week in March, and the whole crew were flying out to America, to finish the film with several locations doubling for England, as their characters toured their various estates, and for Bruce's character to understand the responsibilities he now had. Sara's character was to take on being the mistress of the house.

As the days and weeks passed, Bruce felt like an upspoken truce had been agreed between himself and Sara, he felt they were getting closer, enjoying the friendship and camaraderie again, he had forgotten how much he enjoyed her sense of humour, her teasing, they had finally relaxed in each other's company.

Then Bruce flew out to Hollywood for the Oscars, and although he didn't win, it was still such an honour to have been nominated for Best Actor. He hadn't won the BAFTA either, but again he had been nominated which was still prestigious in itself.

To see Bruce on TV, as he sat there waiting for the winner to be announced, there was no disappointment in his expression when he hadn't won. He hadn't expected to win, she felt he had as much chance as any of the others and he was definitely, better than the Actor who *did* win.

The green-eyed monster reared its ugly head again, Sara watch as a beautiful actress next to him leaned over and kissed him on the cheek, probably in commiserations, but still, Sara felt like screaming 'leave him alone bitch', she needed to do something about this possessiveness, it was becoming a very ugly character trait she was cultivating.

Twenty

It was a week before the film was due to finish and they had arrived in New York, they were in a crowded bar, surrounded by friends from the cast and crew, who had hired the place out for the night. All Bruce could see and hear was Sara, he was entranced by her conversation, the way she smiled, laughed and giggled, her beauty captivated him. He could feel his heart swell, and beat fast in his chest, he had only experienced this once before in his life. They had only been intimate, onset, it wasn't real, but his whole body yearned and ached for it to be *very* real. It was at that exact moment as if he had willed her, Sara finished her conversation and turned her head and looked at him, there was an aura of sexual magnetism between them, that was abruptly severed when her boyfriend walked in.

Bruce swore profusely, under his breath, *he shows up yet again*, he thought to himself and he immediately had to get out, he strode towards the balcony, he stood there with both his hands on the railing and let the soft breeze try and cool his temper, while he endeavoured to reason with himself, of course, he was going to show up, why wouldn't he, they were a couple.

He had no idea how long he was out there, but it was now getting a little chilly, maybe he was a little calmer now and could even meet this man, finally, there was only one more week of filming, and possibly some re-shoots, if Davy felt the need. He would finally, be free of this compulsive, delusional, obsessive infatuation he had for Sara, and it was going to be like a junky trying to wean himself off her, except he was going to have to go cold turkey, a prospect he was not looking forward to.

Bruce went back into the bar and ordered a round of drinks for everyone, and asked the barmaid to deliver them, while he went to the gents. He walked in and decided to use one of the cubicles, he was still stalling for time before going back to the crowd and needed just a few more moments to get his emotions in check and psych himself to be gracious, when he met with her boyfriend.

Just as he was about to leave the cubicle, he heard two men walk in, there was little conversation before there were sounds of kissing and heavy breathing, they fell against his cubicle door, what words he could hear were a definite build-up to sexual interaction, and it was two men.

Bruce had two choices, stay where he was until they had finished – *no fucking way*, he was not staying to listen to this – or, he gets the hell out, now. He unlocked the door hoping to leave without them seeing him, unfortunately, they had chosen to be thoroughly engrossed in each other by the only exit door. The only way to get out was to interrupt them.

As Bruce lifted his head to ask them to move, he was stunned to recognise one of them was Sara's boyfriend, the other was one of the production team, there was no secret that he was gay. Bruce cleared his throat loudly, and they both sprang apart.

'Oh my God, Bruce,' said Sam the Production Assistant, putting both hands to his face and stepping back as far as he could.

'Jesus, Sam, at least check the cubicles next time,' Bruce said.

He reached for the handle of the door, where Sara's boyfriend was still leaning against, as he had no room to retreat.

Bruce stopped and looked up and said, 'Do you mind?' The boyfriend then moved along the wall behind the door, and Bruce was able to exit. As the door swung closed, he heard one say, 'Fuck, that was extremely embarrassing,' which must have been the boyfriend.

'Embarrassing? I have to face him tomorrow,' Bruce recognised as being the voice of Sam.

Bruce went to the bar, ordered a Whiskey, knocked it back and ordered a refill, trying to recover from being caught in that situation, but also because one of them was Sara's boyfriend. So many questions started to tumble through his mind. Did she know her boyfriend was gay or was he bi? Was she into all that? *Oh God*, that had never even entered his head, is she into threesomes, and if he's into men is it a threesome with two men?

Bruce felt like he was going to be sick, not Sara, please, not Sara, had he put her on such a high pedestal, was he being a bloody hypocrite, he had a threesome and not that long ago, but two men together!! and Sara? He had no problem with gay men, he worked with many in the industry, as long as they didn't look at him. He again tried telling himself that whatever they were into, had nothing to do with him. He took a few deep breaths and returned to the main bar area.

Sara was boxed in by friends, in one of the window seats, Bruce joined the circle of actors on the film, then suddenly noticed her boyfriend return, Sara didn't seem to notice and carried on talking with the crowd she was with.

As the night progressed, Bruce started enjoying himself, navigating his way around the room, he loved these smaller, more private events with his work colleagues, no publicity, nobody wanting anything from him, just a relaxing social gathering, and at least now he finally, knew Sara's boyfriends' name was Cameron. Unfortunately, after the incident earlier, the inner argument he was privately having, kept prodding him, and revolving in his mind, as to whether he should say anything to her about her boyfriend vs him minding his own business. What kept niggling him was, what if, by a slim chance, she didn't know, he felt she had a right to know, but still, this would be risky, as she could just tell him that its none of his business, but – curiosity won out.

He hadn't talked to Sara much this evening, and she was making her way over to him, her boyfriend was over the other side of the room, he seemed to be giving Bruce a wide berth. It was now or never, speak now or forever hold your peace. As Sara drew near, she smiled and said, 'Are you avoiding me?'

'Whatever would give you that idea.'

'I'll give you benefit of the doubt, Mr Bailey,' Sara said with a smile and a raised eyebrow.

'Why thank you, Miss Kaye.' This had been the way they had been ribbing each other since they returned to England, as it was the old English way of formal address. Bruce sometimes put the O in front of her surname as he loved finding different inflections when he used it. They were standing over one side of the room next to an old-fashioned fireplace, that had been lit and was adding not only warmth but also a lovely ambience to the room. Bruce thought, *in for a penny*, 'Umm, Sara, not sure how to say this and … well, you may already know …' he inhaled deeply, closed his eyes, slowly opened them and said, 'do you know that Cameron likes … men?'

'Yes,' Sara said, and the expression on her face was not a good sign, it said *so what*. O God, it was the worst of all his scenarios. Then she cut in as he drew breath to speak, 'Do you know how much he has to put up with, just to be who he is, I love him for who he is, a kind loving person, who would do anything for anyone, and so what if he loves another man, love is love, and I love my brother and if you have a problem with that then – just keep it to yourself.'

Bruce was finding it hard to breathe, and Sara was about to stomp away from him. Did she just say, her brother? He stepped in front of her and placed both hands on her shoulders as he said, 'Cameron is your brother?'

'Yes,' Sara said still looking annoyed, then bewildered as Bruce started smiling, then laughing uncontrollably, 'what is so funny?'

'Because … all these months … I've been thinking … he is … your lover.' Bruce said, in between laughing. He felt so elated, immensely relieved, and ecstatically happy, he had to use all his will power, to stop himself from grabbing Sara, kissing her and lifting her in the air, whilst spinning her around.

'What on earth gave you that idea?' Sara said, looking incredulous and trying not to laugh and failing.

'New Year's Eve, the two of you looked good together dancing on the patio before the fireworks, then after, he looked like he was going to kiss you, and as I approached to ask you to dance, I heard, or rather read your lips, as you told him you loved him and he replied the same, I had no idea he was your brother and obviously, came to the wrong conclusion.'

'Why did it matter? You're with Felicia, aren't you?

'No, I. am. not.' Bruce said, emphatically.

'Since when? although she doesn't say it outright, she heavily hints that you are still together.'

'For a very long time now. Felicia doesn't give up easily when she wants something.'

'And she wants you, *still*. Long time being …? – since that Valentine's Ball?

'What do you mean … how do you …?

'The next morning I came knocking at your door to ask if you wanted to join Carl and me for breakfast, Felicia opened the door wrapped in just a sheet, telling me you were in the shower, you never joined us for breakfast and barely made it in time for the plane.'

Just as Bruce was about to explain, Sara put her finger to his lips and said, 'You don't have to say anything, I learn from my mistakes, I have no right to expect any explanation from you – I don't want one.' Bruce held her fingers to his lips and kissed them, then placed her hand in his.

'Felicia never told me you dropped by.'

'Of course, she wouldn't,' Sara said, rolling her eyes, then looking down at their joined hands.

'If I had known, I would definitely have joined you for breakfast.'

When Bruce thought back to all the things he and Felicia had engaged in when he returned from the bathroom that morning, and now knowing that Sara had just left, he felt ashamed, which was a ludicrous thought, it wasn't like he was cheating on Sara, but that was exactly how it felt, just when he thought he could be at peace with Felicia, he felt angry with her all over again.

Did he detect a hint of jealousy in Sara's tone? They stood there silent for a moment, then Bruce's face broke into a mischievous grin, he lifted his hand and placed a finger under her chin and lifted her head to look at him.

'I am going to take a huge risk here,' he took a deep breath, then continued, 'and tell you that I have fancied you for many years, I didn't want to make this film, as it's not my usual genre, and it was my idiotic way of getting out of it, by demanding it be a contractual condition, that you co-lead with me, I never thought you would accept, then when you did, I fell in love with you, that first day at the read-through.'

'You fell in love with me?' she pouted teasingly.

'Did I say love? Sorry, I meant – liked.' What was he thinking, that was a sure way to scare her off, too heavy and way too soon, *although that was how he truly felt, had been feeling, for months,* to quickly cover up his blunder, he asked, 'How come your *brother* is here in New York?'

'He's the Chorographer for our new show *Dance through time*, it has all the dances ever known, did you know that even Cavemen and women danced?

'How on earth does anyone even know that?'

'I read it somewhere that there were pictures discovered in a cave, so it's our big opening sequence, we then go all the way through to the present day – we even include punk rock and get through a lot of bin liners for that one, it's the cheapest and simplest costume I have *ever* had to create,' Sara giggled and he marvelled anew, at how he enjoyed the sound.

'The opening night is the day before we finish filming, would you like to come?'

'I would be honoured, thank you. Tell me how you got involved in owning the shows.'

'When I was sixteen and starred in *Dance around the World*, it was so ... static, I was really bored by the end of the fifteen-month run, it had lost its ... sparkle. I bought the rights to the show. Cameron and I decided to periodically compose new numbers, choreograph and design new costumes, it ensures the show keeps evolving. We encourage the input from the dancers, bringing them in from all over the world, which adds more authenticity and flavour to the show. Initially, we worked on it together, but then I was offered the Lead in that WWII film, that just obliterated everything else I did before, and seemed to catapult my career and won me my Oscar when I was eighteen, therefore Cameron was left to carry the show on his own, I help whenever I can, but it's mainly his baby now.

'That's the show that my brothers and sister took our mum to for her birthday, and the first time I noticed you, we were all amazed by the music, dances and the acrobatics were ... breath-taking, so daring, my mum absolutely loved it', said Bruce.

'Thank you, I'm so glad you all enjoyed it. Six years on, it's still going strong. Later this year we plan to take both shows touring around the world, and in each country audition dancers locally, to continue the tour in that country, while the main show moves to another country and so on. Our ambition is to have each of the shows in each country touring, and hopefully raise money to help charities in each of the cities the shows perform in. We recently expanded into fashion after we started designing the outfits for the shows, it gave us the taste for it. Cameron feels we are good to launch in the next couple of months.'

'Wow, sounds really exciting,' Bruce smiled at Sara, enjoying the excitement in her voice and the animated way she spoke with her hands, as she talked about her brother and their achievements, in everything she said there was no boasting, just stating facts, so different from Felicia. There he went again making comparisons and that would be the last one, he was going to just enjoy the time he had left with Sara, hopefully, it will extend past the end of the film, he certainly hoped so. Suddenly he wanted to be alone with her, the room was too hot, loud and crowded, he asked her, 'Would you like to get out of here?'

'Thought you'd never ask.'

They walked back to her hotel as it was relatively close. It was dark, hopefully, they wouldn't attract any attention. They chatted the whole way and Bruce could feel this was something very special, and he was not going to rush it, even after waiting all these months.

As they walked side by side with their hands brushing together in accidental contact, he felt like a teenager all over again, out on his first date, and an overwhelming need for a more solid touch, he reached down and took hold of her hand, put it in the crook of his arm and laid his other hand over hers, it felt like he was laying his claim to her, *what an old fashioned idea*, working on this period drama was having a profound effect on him. He would never dominate. Growing up, his father had literally, knocked that notion out of him. Sara looked up at him and smiled, then placed her other hand over his, and leaned in close to him, periodically resting her head on his upper arm as they walked along, talking and laughing together, he felt exhilarating joy to the point of light-headedness.

As they approached the entrance to her hotel, Sara turned and asked if he wanted to join her for a nightcap, something he really wanted to do, but he couldn't trust himself that he wouldn't jump at the chance, and persuade her to have that nightcap in her room, and leap on her in the lift. Therefore, he stepped closer, running his hands up her arms and clasped them either side of her face, and felt her arms wrap around his waist, like a lovers embrace, as he said, 'There is nothing I would want to do more, but I would like to take things slowly, I have waited months to have the chance to take you out, to wine and dine you, will you? ... go out with me, to a fantastic restaurant I know of?'

'Yes,' she whispered with a sensual inflection in her voice, as she looked directly into his eyes, her stunning smile spreading across her face.

His heart felt like bursting, this is what he had wanted the whole time working close to her, it had been years since he went to that show and was mesmerised by her from afar, he attempted to tamper his excitement.

'Tomorrow, pick you up at 8?', Sara nodded and Bruce leaned in closer as their lips met, and if he ever believed in all the romantic descriptions of a first kiss, this one blew them out of the water. This was their first *real* kiss, no film crew watching or Davy shouting, action, cut or roll again, this was just the two of them and he could forget everything and lose himself in the moment.

Her lips were soft, she was even a little hesitant at first, and as he caressed her lower lip with his tongue along the seam of her mouth, she then opened to him on a delicate gasp, he deepened the kiss, savouring the quickening of her breath. He plunged his tongue into her mouth, devouring the taste of her and the sweet red wine she had been drinking, he moved one hand to the back of her head, letting his fingers tangle in her silken, golden long hair, as his other hand moved down her back, he drew her closer to him, adding more pressure to their lips, she returned the kiss, moving in perfect sync, meeting and matching his intensity and urgency. It was an intoxicating liquid warmth that was running through his body and he wanted more, he didn't want this heavenly bliss to end.

He was brought abruptly back to reality, by a loud honking of a car horn as it sped by. Bruce slowly released Sara's lips, but not ready to lose the contact he leaned his forehead against hers and whispered, 'That was beyond perfect,' he then gave her a chaste kiss on her lips and whispering again, 'see you tomorrow.'

'Until tomorrow,' she repeated as she disappeared into the Hotel.

Bruce turned and felt like skipping and whooping down the road, but he refrained and walked to his hotel with a wide stupid grin plastered on his face.

Twenty-One

Sara walked away, also with a huge grin on her face, she resisted the urge to turn around as she parted from Bruce, walking into the hotel. She summoned the lift and was glad to have it to herself, as she let go and whooped for joy, dancing a jig around in a circle and punching the air, whilst repeatedly shouting yes louder and louder. Then abruptly stopped and placed her fingers to her mouth as the piquant memory of his lips on hers, she felt a special, almost magical connection with Bruce, when he had held her in his arms.

She closed the door to her suite and wandered over to the music system, put on some romantic music, and started to waltz around the room as if dancing with Bruce, she couldn't remove the constant beaming smile from her aching face. Not ready to go to bed yet, she helped herself to that nightcap from the minibar, and sat on the window seat, staring out over the panoramic vista of New York.

Sara leaned her head back on the window, sipped her drink and relived the evening, allowing the music to evoke pleasurable shivers and thrills to run up and down her spine. She had watched Bruce tonight, circulate around the room displaying confidence and ease, as he talked to everyone, and how they seemed relaxed in his company, her heart wildly fluttering as she gazed in his direction, *she hoped nobody noticed her gawping like that at him.*

Although she relished the chance to just ogle him, she noticed that he had spoken to everyone that evening but appeared to be avoiding her. Taking immediate, decisive action she made a beeline for him and asked him that question, directly, definitely not her usual behaviour, but then Bruce seems to elicit a lot of unusual conduct from her.

Sara wondered – what was it that made Bruce suddenly feel the need to tell her about Cameron being gay tonight. If he was under a misconception of their relationship, did he think maybe she didn't know and had a right to? or and a most shocking thought hit her when Bruce said Cameron 'likes men' did he think they were into threesomes, or that she was open-minded enough for an open relationship. Oh no – not either of them surely! And when, did Bruce find out Cameron was gay? New

Year's? Valentine's? tonight? *Oh my* – it must have been tonight, why else would he have confronted her *tonight* if he had known for months. She was going to have a talk with her brother, *please don't let it be that Cameron hit on Bruce*, she would kill him, although, it did make her temper flare when Bruce mentioned it, after all the problems he now had with their father, she didn't like anyone thinking bad of her brother.

It made Sara laugh and cringe at the same time that Bruce had been under a misunderstanding since New Year's about her relationship with Cameron, and acknowledged it took courage and she thought him brave to confront her as he did.

Still feeling far too awake for bed, Sara ran a bath, topped up her nightcap, undressed and submerged herself in the bubbles, and let the hot aromatic scent lull her senses and laid there till the water cooled to lukewarm. She allowed herself to fantasize about tonight and his admission about the day he fell in love with her, although he changed it to like, but this was *her* fantasy, so love it was.

She got into bed in a relaxed dream-like state, grinning like a Cheshire cat, who finally got the cream. As she laid her head on the pillow, she whispered *I think I can finally let you go Matias, but you will forever be in my heart, I will never forget you.*

Twenty-Two

The next evening, Bruce arrived promptly at 8 pm, smartly dressed in dark blue trousers and shirt with a light grey jacket, and beamed when he saw Sara step out of the lift in a shimmering electric blue, short, fitted dress with her hair flowing freely, again she was stunning and he was so proud when he saw the reaction she was creating, as she walked towards him, he had the honour to be able to lean in and kiss her on the lips in greeting, he was floating on air, as he led her outside, and they climbed into the cab the doorman had hailed for them.

He took her to an Italian restaurant on East 54th Street, as they were seated and the waiter took their drinks order. Bruce lifted his glass and said, 'I would like to propose a toast to us, and our first night free of misunderstandings, you are not with Cameron.'

Sara lifted her glass whilst saying, 'Oh … don't remind me,' and covering her free hand over her flaming cheeks.' After all, this was her brother Bruce had been envisaging she was with.

'And *I* am most definitely not, with Felicia,' they chinked glasses as the waiter arrived to ask if they were ready to order, Sara looked at her menu and ordered in perfect Italian, which garnered a surprised and impressed response from the waiter, then Bruce ordered his, in English. When the waiter left, Sara immediately apologised for what looked like showing off and making him feel uncomfortably excluded, but Bruce said, 'Don't apologise, I have always loved hearing the Italian language spoken, I know you speak many languages, how many is it?'

'Eleven, that's including English, I was asked that question in an interview once and apparently caused controversy as I said ten, then an article said that I was mistaken, and in fact spoke eleven, as I also speak English, I never considered including that one as I am English, but please that makes me sound so conceited.'

'No, it makes you sound clever, never be embarrassed about your accomplishment's when you are stating a fact, there are many people who embellish half-truths and then pretend to own it, that in my book *then* sounds conceited.'

They each talked about their careers, their families and their friends, and the hours passed far too quickly for Bruce, it was approaching midnight and they were the last in the restaurant. As the staff cleared up around them, Bruce finally signalled for the bill, thanked the staff for not rushing them, and left a large tip which even the waiter tried to return, saying it was too much, but Bruce insisted, complimenting them on their restaurant, and saying he would be recommending them to his friends, which received a profuse chorus of gratitude from all the staff.

As they left, Bruce asked Sara if she minded a walk back to her hotel, it was easier at night to be anonymous, Sara readily agreed, he didn't want the evening to end just yet, although they had an early call the next day.

Sara said, 'Very impressive the way you tipped and complimented the restaurant, was it just for show or did you mean it?'

'Do I come across as being superficial, if you are questioning my sincerity?'

'I'm sorry, that was very rude of me.'

'No, it's ok, I suppose there are a lot of insincere people in our industry, and I made a promise not to lose sight of myself and forget what is real and what is fake. I meant every word. I tend to go by the rule of either, say something nice or stay quiet.'

'That's a good rule, I like it, I'll just have to watch you when you go quiet then.'

'Oh, don't worry, if I really hate something or think someone will be hurt, I have no problem letting them know.'

They walked back to Sara's hotel, talking, teasing and laughing. They were about a block away from Sara's hotel when she suddenly asked, 'How did you know Cameron was gay? did one of the crew tell you, he is usually very discreet, and has never felt the need to 'come out', he has always said it is his business and no one else's.'

Bruce stopped and faced Sara and could see, even in this light the flush on her cheeks, but also the determination to protect her brother who was having a tough time with his father, from what Sara had told him last evening, the truth was always best, even if it was unsavoury, and he loathed to tell her what he witnessed. 'I was in the gents at the bar last night.'

Sara covered her face and through her hands, her voice was muffled, 'Please don't say he propositioned you?'

He took hold of both her hands and lowered them, laughing he said, 'No, not me, one of our Production Assistants, I um had to interrupt them to get out.'

'Oh God, and I just said he is usually very discreet.'

'I think they tried to be, unfortunately, they didn't check the cubicles, but they were barring the door so that no-one else could come in.'

'Please don't judge him, he is such a lovely person when you get to know him, he …'

'Hey, Sara,' Bruce cupped her face in his hands and kissed her, 'I don't have a problem with him being gay, his personal life is his business alone. Although, it was rather embarrassing, even if it were any other gender combination.' They both laughed and walked arm in arm together.

Just in case Sara offered a nightcap again, Bruce drew her into his embrace, kissed her softly and gently, then said, 'I would like to give ourselves this week, time to get to know each other, *really* know each other, without any awkwardness at work, I don't want you to regret this, therefore I want to give you time to be sure, this … us … to me, feels too important to rush.'

'Is it to give me time or to give yourself, time.'

'You. I am absolutely, positively, unequivocally, without doubt, certain of what I want. I am giving you the chance to be the same or walk away without guilt or regret.'

'What if I don't need time, what if I am absolutely, positively, unequivocally and without doubt, certain I want the same?'

'Then allow me to wine and dine you, and show you this magical city we are fortunate to be in.'

'I would love that.'

Bruce kissed her slowly at first then losing himself in her softness and almost forgot where he was, so he slowly released her and said, 'I am going to have to stop kissing you outside your hotel or I am going to be arrested for lewd behaviour, see you tomorrow,' he turned and walked away.

Their last week at work passed quickly, and Bruce looked forward to their evenings together, although this was self-induced torture, keeping his hands off her in the evenings and torture every day at work when he had to kiss her and recite words of love to her, as their characters were very passionate in their married life, and although they had already filmed all the intimate scenes, there were still a lot of kissing scenes and the partial removal of their clothes, Bruce found them difficult in covering up the effect they had on him, which led to many fits of giggles between himself and Sara.

It was the night of the opening of the show, 'Dance through Time,' which Sara was excited about, and had given Bruce his ticket, and said she would meet him there, as she would be arriving much earlier to give Cameron support, to ensure all the dancers were ready and for any last-minute problems.

Bruce arrived alone, a massive cheer was heard by the crowd outside, with his name being shouted, and he was being besieged by photographers and reporters. He smiled and waved to all the fans and gave numerous interviews, before entering the foyer, where he was escorted to his seat in one of the boxes, which gave an excellent view of the stage.

Sara arrived in the box, with five other ladies and gentlemen, she introduced Bruce to them, they were Financiers and Promoters from other countries invited to see the show, as Sara explained quickly and quietly to Bruce, as they were hoping to take the show globally, it would also dilute the gossip that they were together, as all eyes seemed to be on their box. Just then the lights dimmed and the show started.

During the interval, Sara invited everyone in the box to join her backstage, as she checked in with Cameron. Bruce was impressed by the performance so far, and when he came face to face with Cameron, he offered his hand and congratulated him on the show, he could see the hesitation, but Cameron shook his hand and quietly said, 'Listen, I am sorry you witnessed what you did the other night, I am not usually so …'

Bruce interrupted, 'No need mate, honestly, no judgement on my part, ok?'

Relief spread across Cameron's face, then he smiled and Bruce could see the resemblance between brother and sister. The bell rang for everyone to take their seats for the second half, as Sara approached, Bruce could see the apprehension in her expression. One of the dancers asked Cameron a question and he turned to answer her. Bruce took Sara's hand and reassured her that all was ok between him and Cameron by telling her,

'I just congratulated him on a brilliant show so far, can't wait to see the rest, shall we?' as he gestured towards the side of the stage to make their way back to their seats, Sara smiled and walked ahead of him.

Twenty-Three

It was the following day and Davy got everyone to gather on-set and announced, 'If all goes well, today will be our last day of filming,' there was a loud cheer that went up from everyone, Davy brought the cheers under control by continuing, 'having viewed all the rushes, I feel this is going to be a fantastic movie. All of you have worked really hard, I just want to give everyone the heads up that there is always a possibility of recalls if deemed necessary during editing, but, as it stands, if all goes well in post-production, cross fingers it will, as the special effects are minimal, compared to other movies I have worked on, the scheduling for release is for November, in time for nominations in Oscar season – hopefully. I would also like to announce that if this film is the success that I am feeling in my bones – then the sequel will get the green light to go ahead, and if that happens, Carl and I will be pulling together the same team, if you are all available, so watch this space.' This was met by an eruption of cheers, hugs and high-fives, Davy had to shout above everyone, 'Let's go to work everyone.' With smiles, all-round everyone dispersed and the day started.

After Davy's speech of the possibility of a sequel, it had resonated in everyone, usually on the last day of filming there was always the feeling of 'the last time', but today it was met with more enthusiasm with the promise of working together again, Davy had certainly lifted everyone's spirits, and the atmosphere was almost a celebration, with lunch being extended and nearly everyone making a toast of thanks for enjoying their time on the set.

In Sara's toast, she had thanked everyone for making her first film with intimate scenes …' there followed a lot of wolf-whistling, Sara commented, 'Yes thank you for that one everybody, I have no secrets left from all of you. As Davy has said, this film feels special, and with a lot of hope and a sprinkle of luck, this will be a successful film, and I very much hope to work with you all again on the sequel, cheers everybody.' Everyone raised their glasses and soon it was time to return to work and finish the day and the film.

The day progressed in almost a party atmosphere after each scene there followed more congratulations and when Davy ok'd each rush, the pace picked up and very soon it was the very last scene and the rush was again confirmed by Davy.

'That's a wrap, it's in the can everybody,' Davy shouted, which was followed by simultaneous cheers, loud whoops and applause, with everyone congratulating each other with handshakes, back slaps, high fives and hugs. Davy announced that a wrap party had been arranged at the Copacabana, the famous Latin themed night club, which received another round of loud raucous whoops and cheers of delight. 'See you all there from 8 pm till the last person drops, well done all of you, it has been both a pleasure and a complete nightmare working with you all,' which was met by a barrage, of good-humoured responses.

'Finally, I can get that lie-in I've been dreaming about – bliss,' said Carl, the Producer.

'Oh no, now, the even harder work begins, I need you with me in the editing of this *wonderful and fabulous project*, isn't that how you pitched it to me?' said Davy with his head cocked to one side and a raised eyebrow.

'Damn, so close to a clean getaway. Ok, see you first thing Monday morning, I plan on a debauched night followed by a weekend of nursing the mother of all hangovers. See you later at the party.'

Sara made her way to her trailer to remove her makeup and change out of her costume, and was looking forward to a long soak in the bath before the party. She had planned on an early night with her favourite book, she knew there would be a Wrap Party, there always was, but had hoped it would be another night, she had been out every single night this week with Bruce, and she had long ago learned that too much of a good thing was tiring.

Having been in this industry from a young age, going out to discos and parties nearly every night, she felt at 23, she was ready for the next chapter in her life. Cripps!!! was she really thinking like that – rewind and scrap those last thoughts – a bath? a book? an early night?!!! *Why not add cocoa, old slippers and a dressing gown to finish off this wonderful look,* chimed in Nagy. You are right, only young once, I love Latin dancing and we are going to show them all how all-night partying is done – but, maybe just that bath – it does sound too good to pass up. Sara was ready fifteen minutes later, hurried out of her trailer to make her way back to the hotel to get ready.

As she lazed in the bath, she couldn't help but think of Bruce, he had occupied nearly every thought she had in the last week. Every time they kissed she wanted it never to end, and for it to lead further, but he was adamant that he wanted this week of dates, maybe wanting the film to be finished and as he said for there to be no guilt or regrets, if either of them wanted to walk away *like that was an option now*, she had tasted his real kisses and she wanted more, much, much more.

Twenty-Four

As Bruce arrived back at the studio, after having finished his last scene with the second unit, filming at a nearby exterior location, he was disappointed to find that nearly everyone had finished, and getting ready to leave to prepare for the party. Jess, the Director of the second unit, told them where it was being held.

He had hoped to catch Sara and ask if she would like to arrive together. What the hell was wrong with him, he had never been *nervous* around women, he hoped he never came across arrogant, reserved maybe, usually he would ask them if they would like a drink, made sure he showed interest in their conversations and one thing would lead to another, he had never specifically asked for a date, it always just seemed to *happen*, but with Sara he always seemed to be anxious, nervous, on guard, on his best behaviour, making sure he didn't swear or blaspheme. Dear God, what was happening to him, what was she doing to him.

Although, he loved, what she was doing to him, making his heart slam in his chest every time he saw her, he looked forward to each day, they had worked together over the last five months. Each morning on waking, he was eager for his early morning workouts with Tom his trainer, vanity rules and he wanted to always look his best. With the numerous carefully choreographed intimate scenes with Sara, which he thoroughly enjoyed, whilst having the devil of a time trying to conceal the evidence, of his enjoyment, not easy when you are standing naked, except for a modesty pouch, in a room of up to twenty people, and that was a closed set!!!

For the past week, Bruce had arrived early each morning, with what felt to him like a stupid grin on his face, that he endeavoured, but probably failed to hide. Watching Sara work whenever he was not in the scene, totally mesmerised by her beauty, her talent, always amazed by her grace, by the way she moved, no doubt due to her dancing and gymnastic career, the way she smiled, the way she laughed, he was completely smitten.

It hit him like a thunderbolt, he had not taken this much interest in another woman, since … *Megan*. He hadn't lived the life of a monk since

Megan passed. He had slept with many women to block out the grief and emptiness he felt. He didn't want to disrespect those women, but they were just to fill in times he felt lost and numb.

He soon realised, he had fooled himself into thinking his recently and finally, ended year-long relationship with Felicia, was a fulfilment of Megan's dying wish, that he lives his life and loves again.

As he changed out of his costume and packed all his things from his trailer, for some reason he thought back to six weeks ago, when Felicia had agreed it was over between them. He finally felt free of her and now realised how wrong they were for each other. She had used all her seductive feminine whiles to try and keep him, Felicia was an extremely sexy and stunningly beautiful woman, with her large clear green eyes and rich, thick auburn red hair. A hugely successful recording artiste, with multiple No1 hits in charts all around the world, he pushed the thought of Felicia's manipulations away.

Felicia was so outrageous in her clothing and outspokenness, her fans loved and adored her, but they only saw her public persona, they had no idea how neurotic and demanding she was, treating people around her with total disrespect, she saw it that they were there to do her bidding, she paid them, therefore, she viewed it as they were honoured to be talking to her. The arguments they had had about the way she spoke to and treated people, especially those who worked for her, shouting at them, demeaning them in front of others, sacking them on a whim, then getting others to reinstate them upon finding she needed them, Bruce often felt either embarrassed, ashamed or both of her behaviour.

Bruce thought there can't be many more bedroom tricks he hadn't tried, but Felicia's sexual appetite was off the scale, and she managed to teach him a few astounding, and intensely pleasurable manoeuvres. She loved to be outrageous and shocking, enjoying sex alfresco, risky, public even. He always thought himself to be uninhibited when it came to sex, but she managed to make him feel almost ... conservative. He never turned her down, what man in his right mind would? but sometimes she would be too demanding and very controlling, her way or no way, it started to get a little bit predictable and sometimes even mechanical, that's when he started to think the relationship was not going anywhere, by then he had started on 'The 2nd Son' *and met Sara ...*

At the time, Felicia was refusing to accept the relationship was over, and constantly bombarded him with phone calls and letters. When that didn't work, she moved on to Aidan, his Agent, and constantly harassed him with visits and phone calls. One of her lowest tricks was demanding Bruce call her very urgently. When he relented and called her, she was very distraught telling him, 'I'm pregnant.' With his heart and mind racing, he felt angry – and trapped. He remembered asking her, 'How? I was *very* careful and always, always wore a condom'

'Well, obviously not careful enough darling,' she replied with a definite tone of glee in her voice, seeming to recover extremely quickly from being upset. Her next comment floored him, and filled him with dread, 'You will have to marry me now, I will not have a child out of wedlock.'

'What? – this is the 1980s not the 1880s Felicia. How late are you?'

'2 weeks and I am *never* late.'

Bruce's mind started to whirl in panic, he told himself to calm down and think, then suddenly, a thought sprang to mind - 'Hold on a minute, the last time we had sex, was in the back of your car as your driver was taking us home from that awards ceremony, with extremely bad timing and in the middle of what we were doing, you casually told me you were on your period, but with a little imagination, there were plenty of other things we could do and we did. That was 2 months ago, which means you have had a period since then if you are only 2 weeks late.' Having worked that out, he was suddenly extremely angry and said, 'You are unbelievable Felicia, but you should have got your maths right first.' And with that, he slammed the phone down, swore profusely, and punched the wall, injuring his fist, which resulted in more loud swearing.

Bruce brought himself back to the present, and put Felicia to the back of his mind, she was no longer his concern. The night ahead was one he intended to enjoy to the fullest, and allow their relationship to progress, no further holding back. Each evening, as they parted, he had found it increasingly difficult to keep his hands off her, and judging from her reactions, she felt the same. Tonight was going to be special. Bruce took a deep breath, closed his eyes, and a broad grin spread across his face. He quickly finished his packing and made his way back to his hotel. He was one of the earliest to arrive at the night club, to be there when Sara arrived.

Bruce positioned himself as close as he could to the front entrance of the club, with a drink in his hand trying to look casual, feeling anything but, he was talking to some of the cast and celebrities who had been invited. He felt it the moment Sara walked into the club. His heart was hammering and he was forgetting to breathe, she looked stunning dressed in an electric purple sweetheart necked bodice style dress, fitted to the waist then flaring out to just above the knee, which showed off all her best assets, her slender shoulders and arms, her synched-in waist and shapely legs. Her beautiful blond hair was loose with perfect natural-looking makeup, the overall effect was just – stunning.

He saw Sara enter the club and greet some people, she turned around and registered him looking at her, and immediately her face lit up as she looked directly at him. Bruce felt like he would never be able to breathe again. The impact of that smile stunned him, and he didn't know if his legs would support him if he walked over to her. Did he detect instant attraction in her eyes? Did she feel the same about him, as he felt for her? Could he be, *that* lucky?

Twenty-Five

Sara had always been excited whenever she had travelled to New York, she had guest-starred in many shows, or attending premiers of her latest films, every time, she intended that this time, she would sample some of the nightlife, but it was always work. Usually chauffeured either to and from her shows, hotels and one interview to another, rarely really seeing or enjoying the sights, the sounds and the smell of the streets and the city.

She had never stayed long enough in this wonderful city, to sample their famous nightclubs, she was excited about tonight. When she left the studios, she was so disappointed that Bruce had not made it back in time from his location filming, she was hoping he would ask to take her here tonight, and was going to be courageous enough to ask him if he didn't. Sara always hated arriving at parties or nightclubs on her own, often asking one or all of her friends to get ready at hers, so they could go together, enjoying a bottle of wine between them, whilst they got ready, she missed her friends, as she had gotten ready tonight alone.

Arriving at the club, Sara felt a little nervous and not sure why, she made sure to arrive a little later than eight, giving others time to arrive first, not because she wanted to make an entrance, but so that she wasn't first to arrive and end up sitting at the bar on her own. As soon as she entered the club, there were a few of the cast who greeted her, she looked around and immediately noticed Bruce standing near the bar surrounded by celebrities and members of the cast, he was never alone and always so popular, Sara envied his confidence, she often felt like she was having to make an effort, but for Bruce, it always seemed effort*less*.

Sara suddenly felt self-conscious, she couldn't stop herself, but react with an immediate smile as soon as she saw Bruce – was it nervousness or just her usual reaction to him, she always seemed to smile whenever she met him or thought about him. Unfortunately, her face always gave away her thoughts and feelings, an affliction her family had always told her she had.

Bruce stood there for a moment, then started to walk in her direction, *My God he looks good,* Sara thought, he was dressed in white jeans and a short-sleeved multi-coloured Hawaiian shirt, with white loafers and no socks, the overall effect was … very sexy. When he beamed that brilliant white smile at her, she felt like everyone else in the crowded night club, no longer existed, it was just the two of them.

Bruce asked if she would like a drink, and Sara asked for her favourite cocktail, a Tequila Sunrise and accompanied Bruce over to the bar, she didn't want anyone else to take his attention.

As they waited at the bar for their drinks, some well-known Actors congratulated them on the finish of the film, Sara took a moment to reflect while the conversation flowed. Looking at Bruce, she thought about Matias, his passing had been so sudden, and only a little over a year ago, was it too soon? Was she betraying his memory? At the time, they had just finished filming 'Completely Ballroom' a very colourful, exciting party look at Ballroom dances, with a thread of romance running through it. Matias never got to see the huge success it became. It was the biggest box office hit of last year and had just been released on video last month, it was already outselling any other video. Filming 'The 2nd Son' and promoting the 'Totally Ballroom' video release, it had been a really hectic and emotionally draining month. She remained in touch with Matias' family, and they were immensely proud of the film. Sara had presented them with a copy of the Video with flowers, a Fortnum and Mason Hamper and Champagne, telling his mother, that this was how Matias had told her he wished to present the film to his family, she had also taken them to the premier when it opened, she felt honoured to fulfil his wish.

She was brought out of her reverie, by Bruce presenting her with her drink and asking, 'Is this your favourite drink?

'*One*, of my favourite cocktails.'

'With so much fruit you are definitely getting a large dose of vitamin C.'

Sara laughed, 'It always reminds me of hot summer holidays, I love all the colours.'

'Would you like to dance? Bruce asked, and led her onto the dance floor.

It had been such a long time since Bruce had enjoyed himself this much at a club or danced so much, Sara was such a good dancer and extremely fit, never seeming out of breath or tired, just watching her smiling, dancing and throwing back her head laughing at things he said to her, how he enjoyed making her laugh, to be the source of her laughter, caused a stirring in his stomach and … his heart.

They had fun learning some moves together that Sara was teaching him, throughout the evening they danced separately or with others, they drank and laughed together. When they were both exhausted, Bruce asked Sara if she would like another drink, and led her over to a sofa booth seating area, where it was a little away from the music, so they could at least hear what they were saying to each other, Bruce signalled to a waitress and ordered their drinks.

Time ebbed away, as they talked about everything, even religion and politics. Bruce was mesmerised by Sara, her gentleness, her honesty, the ease she had with herself. He could just sit there for the rest of the evening and just drown in her deep, chocolate brown eyes. He was enjoying himself in her company so much he forgot to put up a show, a pretence, and now, he didn't want to. She possessed such a warm charm that made him feel … happy. That had not happened in *such* a long time, he felt like his heart would burst. As Sara was animatedly telling him about her transition from a gymnast to dancer, Bruce sent a silent message to Megan, *Hope this is ok with you my Megan, you will always hold that special place in my heart, that will always be just for you, I'll never ever forget you. I think I may even be ready to finally live my life after you, and I'm hoping Sara will be part of it.*

Sara excused herself to go to the ladies. Bruce sat there for a few minutes enjoying the music, when all of a sudden, Felicia planted herself next to him. Occasionally, throughout the night and it seemed, every time Sara moved or danced a little away from him, Felicia was there, each time a little drunker and slurring her words more. This time he could not escape unless he leapt over the table, which he was prepared to do if she didn't leave, *very* soon.

'What do you want, Felicia? Sara will be back any minute, and I don't want her to see you with me,' his voice was dripping with irritation.

'The jealous type, is she? Felicia said, as she moved closer to him, 'I want you back Bruce,' she pouted, moving even closer and placing her hand on his knee, with her fingers moving in little circles, moving her hand higher up his thigh. 'We are really good together, in and out of the bedroom, although, I don't think we used the bedroom as much as everywhere else,' as she leaned ever closer, purposely giving him a closeup view of her low neckline, he could see the tips of her nipples. She whispered seductively in his ear, 'I know what you like and how you like it, haven't I proven that the last time we were together?' she cupped his manhood and said, 'I miss this, I miss us, so much.'

Bruce grabbed her hand, and flung it away from him, in a quick smooth move, placed one hand on the table, the other on the booth and rose, placing one foot on the sofa, the other on the table and took two steps to the end of the table and jumped down. As he turned back to retrieve his and Sara's drinks, he leaned close to Felicia and through clenched teeth snarled, 'We have been through this Felicia, we are finished get that through your head, for a short while there, I had a modicum of respect for you, when I thought you had finally accepted we were through. Now, move on to your next victim and leave me the hell alone.'

He marched over to where Sara had just returned from the ladies and was talking to Carl and Davy. Bruce handed Sara her drink, just as the slow dances started, and he asked her if she would like to dance, to his delight she said yes, he placed his hand on the small of her back as he guided her to the dance floor, depositing their drinks on a table on the way.

Bruce delighted in the way she readily slipped into his arms. She was a perfect fit. Anyone who had a Heart by Luther Vandross began playing, and the night became even more magical. With the music and the lights dimming, he moved his hands slowly up Sara's arms and placed them either side of her face, he looked down into her eyes and tenderly whispered, 'You are so beautiful,' his eyes lowered and he closed the distance until their lips met and he traced his tongue along her lower lip until she opened up to him and he delved into her wet, hot mouth and tasted her. He ran his hands down her back, until he could cup the swell of her behind, and pulled her closer to him, so she could feel the effect she was having on him, he heard a little gasp escape her lips, making his heart sing. He wanted her. Everybody faded into the background, there was only the hypnotic music, the soft lights and an astoundingly beautiful woman in his arms, Bruce felt like this was a dream and hoped he would never wake from it.

Bruce and Sara were so engrossed in each other, that they never noticed Felicia, at the edge of the dance floor watching them, she stood frozen with her fists clenched tight as they joined together for a slow dance, her friend next to her saw where Felicia was staring and said, 'Maybe it's time to leave Felicia, there is nothing here for you, and you are only torturing yourself.'

'How could he do this to me? And in front of me, with her, I love him and he's mine.'

'Without being cruel Felicia, doesn't look like he *is*, anymore, did you ever tell him you loved him?'

'Yes, and thanks to your advice of what was it, *If you love him let him go, it will make him run back to you*, I did that, I told him I was sorry, I said that I wish I had handled things differently, and I asked for one last night to say goodbye to the one man I have ever truly loved. I did everything I know he likes that night and look where that got me,' as she gestured towards the dance floor.

'Felicia, there's a massive difference between love and ... sex, that doesn't make someone love you.'

'If you had seen us, always at it, couldn't keep our hands off each other – both of us.'

'You are describing great sex, not love.'

'Great? It was much, much more than just great – we had *fantastic* sex, I miss it – and him.'

'Come on let's go on to another party.'

Felicia gave another lengthy scowl at Sara, literally stamped her foot and said, 'They are going to fucking pay for humiliating me like this.'

Twenty-Six

Last night had been one of the best nights of her life. Dancing to all her favourite songs, Bruce was quite a good dancer, she remembered showing him some dance moves, and he seemed to pick them up quite quickly and others had joined in, it was like something from a musical movie, as it was very spontaneous, but then nearly everyone at the party was in the movie industry, so maybe not so surprising, helped of course, by copious amounts of alcohol.

When they weren't dancing or laughing uproariously at anything and everything, they would sit in the sofa booth area, and talked for what felt like hours having an intense open, honest and real conversation about themselves. Had they really covered the dangerous subjects of religion and politics, without a major fall out – incredible. She remembered they seemed to agree on so many of the topics and stood together on so many moral platforms.

Could they be so alike? shouldn't opposites attract? She always understood that it made a relationship more exciting and spontaneous – wasn't it? on the other hand, it just sounded like a lot of hard work. Last night they laughed so much, her face hurt and her sides ached.

After leaving the party at 4 am, or was it closer to 5? Bruce hailed a cab, when they got to her hotel Bruce asked the cab driver to wait a moment, jumped out and chivalrously, handed Sara out and escorted her to the front of the hotel, where a smartly uniformed Doorman opened the door for her. On impulse, Sara turned around and faced Bruce, who pulled her close and captured her lips. Sara melted in his arms, and she felt she could keep kissing him forever, Bruce had such lovely soft kissable lips and boy did he know how to kiss. As he started to release her Sara said, 'A gentleman would escort a lady to her front door.'

'Just as well I am a gentleman then, and *you* are most definitely a lady, let me pay the cab and I will escort my lady to her front door.'

They walked arm in arm through the foyer and had the lift to themselves for the first three floors. As soon as the lift doors closed, they could no longer keep their hands off each other, kissing passionately and doing their utmost to feel one another's skin without undressing. Sara had pulled Bruce's shirt from his trousers and had her hands – finally, on his sculpted abs and was moving them up to his chest. Bruce had undone some of the front buttons to Sara's dress and had moved one of his hands to her breast, whilst continuously kissing her, totally oblivious, until the lift stopped on the fourth floor. They were so lost in the moment, it was not until the doors started to open, that Bruce and Sara sprang apart and attempted to straighten their clothing. Two middle-aged couples entered the lift and gave Sara and Bruce a knowing look at their dishevelled appearance. Bruce looked at Sara and he gave her a slow seductive smile, with a mischievous twinkle in his eyes that said, *we are not finished*, Sara returned it with a look that said, *absolutely*.

Sara fumbled for the key, got the door open and Bruce followed her in. They barely made it through the door, when Bruce turned and pushed Sara up against the door, and started kissing her, sweeping his tongue along the seam of her lips, he whispered, 'I want you, you are so beautiful, I want to know what pleasures you, tell me how to pleasure you.'

In a voice she barely recognised as her own she gasped, 'Yes … please yes,' she opened to him, and he seized the opportunity and deepened the kiss, their tongues duelled and fought for supremacy, their desire well matched.

'I want …' she gasped.

'Tell me what you want.'

Instead of telling him, she chose to show him. Slipping his jacket off over his shoulders and throwing it in the direction of a chair, then pulled the rest of his shirt from the waistband of his trousers. Too impatient to undo the buttons, she just pulled his shirt apart and heard buttons ping over the side table and floor, all the while eager for his demanding kisses. Sara tore her lips from his, tilting her head up reaching for air as Bruce feathered kisses down the column of her neck, as his hands continued to undo the buttons at the front of her dress, that he had started in the lift. Pulling, almost ripping, the sweetheart necked bodice style dress apart exposing a barely-there, bra.

Sara suddenly felt her bra loosen, she ached for his touch, desperate to feel his hands on her, then they were. Kneading her breast, rolling her nipples between his thumb and finger, with her hands in his hair as he kissed his way down to take the tip of one hardened nipple into his mouth, letting his lips and tongue work her into a frenzy of need, taking a full mouthful he suckled deeply at one breast, as his hand paid attention to the other, then changing and paying homage to the other breast with his mouth.

Sara let out a throaty gasp, writhing franticly against him producing a deep growl from him, as he returned to kissing her mouth. He pulled her dress and bra down to her waist, over her hips, and let it pool around her feet on the floor, as she stepped out of it and kicked it away, in their mutual desperation to rid the barrier of clothing between them. Sara felt his manhood pulse against her, looked down and noticed the strain in his trousers, she was hot for him, and only had on her tiny black lacy panties, that had matched her bra and stockings, she heard Bruce catch his breath as he looked at her, with half-closed eyes, as she felt the desire for him build, craving and yearning for more, this surpassed any of her fantasies.

Bruce slid to his knees, kissing her flat stomach with his hands on her hips, he started to remove her panties, easing them down over her stay-up lacy black stockings, raising one high heeled foot then the other as she stepped out. He raised one of her legs, kissing his way up the sensitive skin of her inner thigh and placed it over his shoulder, anchoring her against the door. His mouth was so close, his fingers came to her core, he blew on her most sensitive zone, she was open and aching, so wet with need, she was panting, begging, 'Bruce, please, I need …' She was unable to finish.

He knew what she needed, and he gave it to her, he spread her thighs wide, lifting her to him and let his swirling tongue explore, running his tongue through her heat, and closing his lips around her centre, sucking and licking, as his clever mouth sent her wild with need, she was desperate in the way she writhed and laced her fingers in his hair, holding his head where she wanted him to be. As her legs weakened, he supported her, whilst he slipped a finger into her hot haven, her breathing became more rapid as she let out another gasp, and moved her hips in time with the thrusts of his tongue as she rasped, 'Yes, oh God, yes … that feels so good.' Bruce responded with a low growl and increased the intensity of the pleasure he was giving her, with his tongue and fingers.

Sara let out a cry as she reached the peak of her pleasure, with his name on her lips. He held her and persisted worshipping her, as she returned to the moment.

He kissed his way up to her lips, taking her mouth in a demanding kiss saying, 'You are so beautiful, you taste so good.'

He lifted her into his arms and carried her over to the bed, and laid her down, she stretched out dreamily, looking up at him with a seductive gleam in her eyes. Sara felt boneless, as she watched him remove his shoes all the while, never losing eye contact with him. He straightened and moved to the waistband of his trousers and his belt, Sara sat up and let her legs dangle over the edge of the bed, she said, 'Stop.'

Twenty-Seven

Bruce froze and thought she was regretting what was happening between them and didn't want to go further. He would never take anything a woman wasn't prepared to give, he said, 'Do you want to stop?'

'No, I want to do that,' and moved closer to the edge of the bed and pulled him closer to her, so that he stood between her legs.

Relief flooded through him, he would have stopped, and gladly paid the price of having blue balls.

Sara moved his hands to his side and started to unfasten his belt and trousers, looking up and catching the acknowledgement in his eyes, as he guessed what she was about to do.

Bruce reached into the pocket of his trousers and retrieved a pack of condoms, Sara looked up at him with a raised an eyebrow, 'We are going to need quite a few of them,' she said, with a cheeky smile.

'I agree,' he replied, with a challenge in his tone.

She undid the zip of his trousers, reaching around the back, she pulled them down to below his knees, with her feet, she pushed them down to his ankles, whereby Bruce stepped out of them and kicked them behind him.

Sara looked down, raising her hands to do the same with the shorts of his underwear, as she eased them over his hips, his manhood sprang free and stood thick and long, Sara licked her lips and got rid of his underwear the same way his trousers went, and he stood there magnificent and naked.

She looked up as she heard Bruce take a sharp intake of breath, hissing through his teeth, as she wrapped her hand around his shaft, stroking up then down, she leaned forward and took him into her mouth.

Bruce hissed again on a sharp intake of breath through his teeth, tilting his head up to the ceiling, closing his eyes, lost in the overwhelming pleasure Sara was giving him. Slowly he looked down, watching her as she took him deep into her mouth, driving his pleasure with her swirling tongue, her lips and her fingers.

Bruce could feel the pleasure intensifying, and he started losing himself, he wanted them to climb and ride the ultimate moment of pleasure together. He reached down, and gently pulled back her hair from her face and said, 'ah, that feels so good baby, but I need you to stop.'

Sara released him from her mouth, looking up at him and said, 'Why did you stop me?'

He bent down and kissed her urgently and desperately, pushing his tongue into her mouth, revelling in the knowledge that his cock had been there only moments ago, he deepened the kiss, he could taste himself and answered, 'Because you are so beautiful and I want to see you, be with you and lose ourselves, together.'

With that, he pushed her further up the bed, reached over and grabbed a condom and rolled it on in an easy practised movement. He spread her thighs and nestled himself there, all the while moving his lips along her jaw to her earlobe, giving it a gentle nip and soothing it with his tongue, doing the same down the column of her neck, circling his tongue around the place where her pulse throbbed in a fast staccato beat. Moving his head down and taking the hardened tip of one of her breasts, deep into his mouth and heard the sharp intake of breath Sara took, taking pleasure from what he was doing to her. He started to suckle her breast, as he kneaded and rolled the tip of the other, then switching, paying equal attention to each.

'I want you, Sara,' as he took her mouth again.

The only words she could manage to utter were, 'Yes ... Oh, yes.' He stroked and caressed his way down her body over her breasts and stomach, lifting one leg, he spread her thighs and with a fast, deep, hard thrust, he entered her, and through a growl, he said, 'God, Sara you feel so good.' On hearing her gasp he stopped, thinking he may have been too rough in his desperate urgent need to be inside her, he knew he was big, hadn't all his previous girlfriends told him that, which is the reason he always avoided virgins, afraid to be their first, and put them off sex if he didn't do it just right – always too much pressure. He took a gamble that Sara was not a virgin, as she was once engaged and he didn't want to spoil the moment by asking. He looked down at her closed eyes and asked with concern, 'Oh Sara, I'm sorry did I hurt you?' she didn't answer.

'Did I hurt you,' he repeated, more urgently.

'No, don't stop, this feels so good, *you* feel so good.'

The corners of Bruce's lips kicked up, and he bent his head taking her mouth tenderly, running his tongue over her lips, she opened to him on a sigh, and he tasted her as their tongues tentatively explored each other, he started to move again, they moved in sync, driving each other on to move faster, harder, as they panted, and their breaths mingled, they sped towards their ultimate goal. Their senses exploded and they cried out in unison.

They laid there, wrapped around each other, as their breathing calmed, and they returned to the moment. Bruce started to lift himself, concerned that he may be crushing her, but she tightened her grip on him saying, 'Not yet.'

He returned some of his weight, whispering into her ear, 'You are an amazing, beautiful and talented lady.'

'I haven't even begun to show you *how* talented I am,' Sara replied with a cheeky, dreamy smile.

Bruce laughed, raised his head and looked down into her eyes, that were sparkling and full of mischief. They both rolled onto their side without disengaging, her head on his chest, he pulled her close and their legs tangled. They caressed each other as they dreamily drifted between relaxing and kissing.

Sara smiled sleepily and turned towards him, snuggling down in his arms with her head on his chest, as her hand sent shivers through him as she caressed across his chest and down and along his stomach, he was loving the way she tentatively, almost shyly moved her hand down lower and took him in hand again, he was already interested and asked, 'Again? Already?' he murmured.

'Are you up to it or would you like a rest?'

'Careful, I might just have to show you how, *up to it*, I am.'

'Do your worst, stud.'

With that he flipped her onto her stomach so fast, Sara let out a squeal and giggled. Bruce was becoming addicted to hearing that delightful giggle and wanted to spend the rest of his life finding all the different ways to make her giggle and laugh, *where had that thought come from*, he pushed that to the back of his mind, he had other things to concentrate on right now.

They were going to go through these condoms very quickly, at this rate. He grabbed her hips and raised her to her knees, with both hands he stroked her, over her shoulders and down her back to her waist and round her buttocks. Bruce guided himself to her entrance, and could feel how hot, wet and ready she was for him, with all the control he could muster, he gently thrust into her and heard her gasp, 'More,' and he gave it to her, thrusting deeper, grabbing around her waist, raising her higher, wanting to get closer, giving her all he had, thrusting faster, setting a rhythm she was matching, pushing herself back to meet him. Then suddenly he withdrew and flipped her over again, saying, 'I want to watch you', driving into her again.

Sara closed her eyes, threw back her head, clutching on to his shoulders, digging her nails into his back with one hand and the other on his buttock, trying to get more of him, she suddenly cried out his name, as she reached her peak. Bruce pounded into her, while she rode the waves of pleasure, she opened her eyes to watch as he scrunched up his face, and with a deep growl, he was with her in that moment.

Bruce slumped on top of her. It had been such a long time since he had felt such an intense orgasm. It hit him like a sledgehammer – this had not been just sex, it was so much more – he had made *love,* to Sara. Realisation overwhelmed him, he raised himself up and looked down at her, and tenderly stroked down the side of her face, 'I can't get enough of you.'

They made love several more times that night, they ran out of condoms, Sara told him she was on the pill, they were so lost in each other nothing else mattered.

Twenty-Eight

As the light from the early morning dawn sent rays of sunlight into the room, from the gaps in the curtains, Sara opened her eyes to meet amazing blue eyes staring back at her, his hand smoothed back a strand of hair that had fallen over her eyes. 'Good morning, beautiful, I think you might need this,' and he reached over her and retrieved a glass of fresh orange juice, which he handed to her. Sara smiled and said, 'Are you reading my mind, how on earth did you guess I would be thirsty?'

'Well, for one, we totally drained the bar last night, and following our ... *activities* ... call it a guess,' Sara giggled, taking the glass from him and drained it. Bruce took the glass from her, whilst simultaneously kissing her. He pulled back and said, 'I want to take you out, treat you and spoil you, take you wherever your heart desires, I am at your service my lady,' he said, with a grin, rolling his hand round and round, in a mock bow, as best he could manage whilst laying down. 'Last night you told me that on your many visits to New York, you have never been able to see much of it, and as we have only seen some of it by nightfall, what would you like to see in daylight?'

Without any hesitation, Sara replied, 'Coney Island, I have heard so much about it and have never taken the time off to explore it, always working, I want to have some fun.'

'Coney Island it is, my lady. Your carriage awaits.'

They both got up and headed for the bathroom, taking a shower together, standing behind her, Bruce massaged the shampoo into her scalp, and through her long hair, Sara sighed, his fingers felt so good in her hair, he then rinsed it off. Taking the body gel, he worked it into a lather, and spread it across her shoulders, turning her around to face him, he smoothed the lather over her breasts, concentrating on what he was doing, and saying how he loved her body, how tiny she was and how perfect in every way, she wanted him again and she couldn't believe her wanton ways.

Sara took the shower gel and did the same, working the lather into his skin, delighting in his magnificent chest, caressing over his nipples and revelling in his sharp intake of breath, she enjoyed the power she exerted over him and made her plans of what she wanted to do.

'If you continue, we may not make it to Coney Island,' he said on expelling a long-held breath.

'Then, using a woman's prerogative … I've changed my mind. Today, I choose to explore, you, order room service for sustenance, then tomorrow we explore, Coney Island.

'O … Kaye, I like the way your mind works,' he whispered huskily.

'May I proceed, Mr Bailey?'

'By all means, please do.'

Slowly she moved her hands across his chiselled chest, and down his toned muscular abs, over his hips, and lowered herself to her knees, and continued working her hands down his legs, bringing them up on the insides of his thighs, urging him to part his legs as she reached up and took his balls in her hand, and with the other took his, *it seemed*, ever ready, hard and thick shaft and pulled back his foreskin. She relished the idea she had in mind, leaned forward and took him into her mouth, and heard him hiss, and an 'Ahh,' escaped his lips. She felt his hand in her hair, she looked up and took in the magnificent view of him from that position.

'Oh … Sara, this is beyond incredible.' He looked down at her and she felt him pulse in her mouth, and knew he was close and struggling to hold back.

He reached down and placed a finger along the seam of her mouth in an effort to release himself, but she had other ideas, and pushed his hand away, momentarily released him from her mouth as she said, 'You are not stopping me this time,' she grabbed his buttocks to keep him where she wanted him, leaving him in no state to argue.

Sara was enjoying having this towering, striking and impressive man at her mercy, to do with as she chose, relishing the effect she was having on him, she increased her efforts by taking him deeper and faster into her mouth. She licked her middle finger and slipped it into his arse, and heard a loud gasp escape his lips, she felt him grow even bigger and harder in her mouth, if that was possible.

Bruce let out another deep gasp as she slipped another finger into his arse. 'Sara … oh my God,' he had no control left. She could feel the build-up, she was relentless and he was useless, no longer able to fight it. She saw him press his palms against the tiled wall of the shower enclosure to steady himself.

In that moment she felt him let himself go. Sara watched Bruce from her vantage position, mercilessly driving him on faster, harder, tasting him, cherishing and revelling in him and taking everything he had, as he roared his release.

Slowly and evenly his breathing returned to an even pace. Sara circled her tongue around the tip of his cock, released him and licked her lips as she raised herself up from her knees, caressing with her hands and trailing kisses up his body, taking one of his nipples into her mouth, and nipping the tip gently with her teeth, as the water from the shower continued to cascade down their bodies, 'mmm, that was good, I enjoyed that.'

'Nowhere near as much as I did, may I ask where you learned how to do that?' he asked breathlessly, but before she could answer, he took her lips, as he thrust his tongue into her mouth, ran his hands down her back to her buttocks and lifted her, spreading her legs around his waist and walking out of the shower, towards the bedroom.

'I read about it somewhere, I like to keep abreast of interesting, educational facts,' she replied, with a mischievous giggle, and a gleam in her eyes, and squealed with delight as Bruce laughed and lightly slapped her backside, she wrapped her legs tighter around him and threaded her fingers through his wet hair.

'Talking of a breast …' he laid her down on the bed taking one breast in his hand, whilst licking around the tip of the other, then taking it deep into his mouth, he suckled.

Sara emitted a gasp as she felt his mouth drawing at her breast, 'Bruce we are dripping wet, we will soak the bed.'

'I know love,' he held up a towel, he had swiped on his way from the bathroom, 'I intend to dry every part of you.'

He started to work his way down her body, alternating drying her with the towel then kissing, licking and nipping at her skin, when he finished drying her toes he returned to the apex of her thighs, and with his fingers parted her, driving her writhing with his tongue.

'This part I intend to leave wet,' with that he flipped her over onto her stomach, gave the ends of her hair a quick towel dry, as he circled his hips letting her feel the hard ridge of his erection between her buttocks.

Sara should have felt embarrassed to behave so wanton, she always prided herself on having decorum, where had *that* gone. She couldn't believe her bravery with what she had done in the shower and now here she was, spread on the bed completely opened and revealed ... and she was loving it.

She felt Bruce smattering kisses all the way down her spine, which was sending goosebumps to her skin, and he was whispering sweet nothings all the way, telling her how beautiful she was, how he couldn't get enough of her, it was driving her crazy with desire.

Bruce straightened up, he looked down at her, then raised her to her knees, caressing her back and buttocks, slipping a finger into her, Sara took a sharp intake of breath, she felt an uncontrollable need for him and as if he sensed it, he replaced his finger with his cock and thrusted into her, when he was buried deep he stopped and leaned over her, he kissed her on the back of the neck and round to the side taking her earlobe, the sensation was driving her crazy, taking her earlobe into his mouth he whispered, 'I want us to make love together, Sara,' with that he withdrew from her, turned her over again, onto her back.

Sara looked into Bruce's deep blue eyes and smiled, swathed in his arms and savouring his affectionate words, she returned his passionate kisses as their tongues duelled, she could feel his erection prodding her stomach, she reached down and wrapped her hand around his shaft. 'I don't think I can wait much longer for you, I need you,' she said breathlessly and guided him to where she wanted him.

'Thank God, holding back from you is torture, I can't get enough of you or get close enough to you,'

He slowly entered her and they moved slowly and rhythmically together at first, then they were racing each other to the precipice, Sara could hear her heart pounding away in her ears, the intensity increased until she saw an explosion of colours, like fireworks, take place before her closed eyes, letting out a guttural cry, she rode the continuation of shock waves of pleasure, that went on so long, she thought she was going to pass out. She opened her eyes to watch as Bruce followed her.

Later when their breathing returned to normal, and they were enveloped in each other's arms, Bruce reached down and pulled the bedsheet over their cooling bodies, kissed her temple and told her to sleep, Sara murmured, inaudibly and snuggled closer to him. Sara felt a primal reactive need for protection which she couldn't explain. As she started to drift in a sated haze of satisfaction, she heard him whisper, 'You're mine, sweet Sara,' through half-opened eyes she smiled at him, as he caressed the side of her cheek with the back of his fingers. She floated off into a dreamy sleep.

They never did make it out of the hotel room, talking for hours, ordering room service, using imaginative and pleasurable ways to consume the food. Exhausted, they would fall into deep and dreamy slumber, their bodies entangled together in the sheets.

Twenty-Nine

It was early evening, as Sara's eyes drifted open, she felt Bruce idly caressing her back, as she laid in his arms with her head on his chest, she felt something instinctual about trusting him, she didn't know why, but she felt a calming peace permeate through her, as if Matias was with her, urging her to tell him.

Making her decision, she started with, 'Matias died 20 months ago now.' Sara took a deep breath before continuing. 'On the 1st of July 1985 to be precise. It took me a year before I could finish *that* sentence, without breaking down. He had asked me to marry him, we celebrated our engagement a month before, and he took me away on holiday, when we returned it was his birthday, he was 24. He bought himself his very first brand new car, always driving old bangers before that, he was so excited on the phone when he told me, and was on his way over to show me and take me out. It was the last time I would ever speak to him. It was four hours before the police came and told me what had happened. I think I was unable to take in that the accident had been fatal, as I asked them to take me to him. When we got to the hospital, I expected to be taken to a ward, instead, I was taken to the morgue, and asked if I would identify him for them. That's when I completely broke down, as the realisation struck me. They asked if he had any family, and I told them he had, but in Argentina. It had been a head-on collision, the driver of the other car also died, he had been drinking and was speeding on the wrong side of the road. The phone call to his family was the hardest and saddest thing I have ever had to do.' Her voice breaking on that last word, she swallowed and struggled to compose herself.

'If this is too painful Sara ...' she looked up at him, and she could feel he understood.

'I would like to tell you,' there was a silent agreement between them, and she felt her eyes sting whenever saying his name, constantly swallowing to get through telling him, before she would allow the tears to fall.

'He frequently joined me and my friends on our girl's nights out,' Sara was saying, 'and none of them ever told me he was intruding. He always brought joy, fun, spontaneity and every night out with him was special, he was such a fantastic dancer and when we danced together … well, it was magical. We always drew attention and a large crowd, whenever and wherever we danced. We only had eyes for each other, it was as if everyone else in the room ceased to exist. My friends told me we left the audience spellbound by our performance, sounds a little cheesy, doesn't it? Big-headed even.'

'No, not at all, I've seen you both dance, believe it or not, I went to see that film 'Totally Ballroom', spellbound is a pretty accurate description of the effect you both had on the audience. I especially enjoyed the Rumba, very erotic. I don't think there was a person in that auditorium who didn't go home with their partners and at least attempt some of those moves. The other dance that left an impression on me was the Argentine Tango, very dramatic.'

'Really?' Sara was amazed that he had been to see their film and touched that he was admitting to enjoying the dances, so many men wouldn't. She continued, 'Matias was such a perfectionist, we trained for hours, he always said that it should look effortless and seamless.'

Sara sat up, pushed the pillow behind her and her gaze drifted, as she stared out of the window and didn't speak for a while. Sara appreciated Bruce not filling the silence, allowing her however much time she needed. Then she spoke again.

'For a long time after, memories of Matias always made me tearful, that I tried not to think of him too often, then I would feel angry with myself for forgetting him, and guilty for living without him, then the cycle would repeat. For months I was exhausted from crying myself to sleep.'

Bruce pulled Sara gently closer to him and Sara snuggled into him. She continued.

'Five months ago, just after we started filming '2nd Son', I met a World War II veteran, Archie, during rehearsals, when our show 'Dance Through Time' were guests at a special Remembrance Day Tribute at The Royal Albert Hall. Archie started to reminisce about the many friends he lost during the war, and his struggle to change the way he remembered them. At first, he said he was angry, why them not him, then such uncontrollable grief, that he stopped himself from thinking about them. One day, he said, whilst listening to the radio with Vera Lynne singing 'We'll meet again,' a song so popular during the war and one he couldn't bear listening to for a long time, it triggered a memory of his close friend, Monty, singing loudly along to this, with his arm around him at a pub, before they were being shipped out to France, just before the Invasion of Normandy, which is where he lost so many of his friends. For the first time he was able to smile, he told me, even laugh as their faces, voices, personalities and humour came flooding back to life, and the good times they all spent together. It was then, he decided that he would remember them with a smile, and not a tear, because their life deserved to be remembered, not their death.'

A faint smile lifted the corners of her mouth, although her eyes watered and her sight was a little blurred, and a small tear rolled down her cheek, she quickly brushed it away, as she wanted to continue.

'When I got home that night, and for the first time since Matias' accident, I decided to play our special song 'Suddenly' by Billy Ocean. For a long time, I couldn't bear to hear that song, but I took Archie's very wise piece of advice to heart, I got up from the sofa where I had been crying and decided they would be my last tears. Henceforth, I would remember Matias with smiles and laughter. I found our special record, put it on, and it brought the memories of Matias back into my life, and I thanked him for the incredible joy he brought into my life and for knowing him, he was special and made *me* feel special. Matias had such a lovely smile and an infectious laugh, he always seemed to be smiling or laughing at something he found funny. The way he looked at me sometimes, with those heated smouldering eyes of his ...'

Sara abruptly stopped, and her face flushed, 'Sorry that was too much sharing.'

'Don't apologise, Sara, what you had was special and deserves to be remembered.'

'As I snuggled down to listen to our special record, I thanked Archie for sharing his advice and experience, and I raised my glass in a toast, and told Matias, that a piece of my heart will always be only for him, and that his zest and joy for life, will live on through me.'

Sara turned around in Bruce's arms and said, 'Sorry, that was not a very good first - intimate date conversation.'

'You are apologising again, you needn't ever apologise for remembering a very special person in your life, not to me.'

'You sound like you are speaking from experience,' then she flushed, and realised she was asking something very personal, just because she chose to share and confide didn't mean Bruce would, and quickly said, 'Sorry, I didn't mean to pry, you don't have to answer, forget I said anything.'

'It's ok, you're right I understand how you feel from experience, I lost someone I loved, not as recent as yours, and although time does help some of the healing, there are times, I feel the loss like it was last week, not almost 8 years ago now. Your friend's very wise advice is very sound, I often think of Megan and try to remember all the good things of our short time together, and they do make me smile.'

'You don't have to tell me if it's too painful, believe me, I understand.'

'Do you know what? it would make a change to talk of Megan to someone who knows exactly, how it feels. Everyone around me, including my family think that I must be 'over it', since it happened so long ago and we were so young, I know they don't mean to be unkind, but it's hard to understand unless you've been through it. You are still counting his passing in months, I did too, for many years, because the searing ache remained fresh, and I needed to feel she hadn't passed very long ago and was still with me. Slowly, I acknowledged her passing in years, and I had to allow the healing to start, but I wasn't ready to let her go.

Bruce closed his eyes and for a moment didn't say anything, he let out a breath he didn't realise he was holding and began.

Thirty

Suddenly Bruce was transported back to the day he finally, decided to propose to Megan. 'I was 20, Megan was a year younger, I couldn't contemplate a day without having Megan to tell everything to, she always made a bad day good. I remember it was a bright summers day, blue sky, the birds singing, the world and the future just seemed so bright.' Bruce laughed at this absurd description and said so, 'Sounds corny doesn't it?'

'No, it sounds beautiful,' Sara returned his smile, with a light touch to his arm.

'I almost danced along the street, wearing a stupid grin on my face, how my mates would have laughed if they saw me right then. I had just left the jewellers, with the most beautiful ring in the shop, well, in my price range anyway, a cluster of diamonds surrounding a perfect Ruby, Megan's favourite stone. It was Friday night and I had it all planned, I was going to surprise Megan, and take her away for the weekend, and had booked a B&B in Bournemouth. All I told her was to pack a bag, just in case we stayed overnight somewhere, I had already reserved a night in a really lovely hotel in Richmond. That night, was the big event, I was going to 'pop the question'. I made reservations at the Richmond Brasserie, which overlooked the Thames, and very expensive. I had loads of cash, and three credit cards, no expense was to be spared for this weekend. Just to see Megan's beautiful face light up, she had an incredible smile and her eyes sparkled in disbelief when she saw where we were going, I told her this time, I intended to fully wine and dine her in style. The restaurant played 'When I need Love' by Leo Sayer, at the important moment, it was our song.'

Sara snuggled in closer to Bruce, he appreciated the reassurance she was trying to give him, it gave him the strength to continue, and return the trust she had bestowed on him.

'We had been dating for about a year and a half, we often went there, perused the menu, pretending to choose a full meal, and then settle for just a coffee each and a cake between us, as that was all I could afford. Megan never pushed for more, she always said she was content to just be with me, whether that was sitting or walking in the park, with only the expense of an ice cream.'

Bruce was silent for a while, as he remembered the fun and laughter they shared after the waiter left with their small order, Megan telling the waiter, she was not very hungry after having had an early lunch at the Dorchester, with her father, and Bruce would play along, and say that he would keep her company and order the same.

Picking up from where his thoughts had drifted, 'After dropping Megan at her house, I walked home cheerfully whistling one of Megan's favourite songs, 'Best of my Love' by Emotions. She loved going to discos, and would jump up and drag me onto the dance floor whenever they played that song, for an 'upbeat smooch', as she called it, dancing up close and very personal whispering suggestively in my ear of the delights she wanted to do to me, in the car on the way home.'

Bruce cleared his throat and said, 'um sorry, that was too much sharing, and not a very good intimate first date conversation,' repeating Sara's words. Sara looked up at him and they both laughed.

'When I got home, using up most of the hot water for a bath and shave, I wanted to look right that night and spent a long time standing in front of the mirror, trying to get my unruly hair just right, hoping to get out before my father came home from work and spoil the mood. If he saw me in front of the mirror with a hairdryer and brush in hand, he would have started yelling and call me a poofter, for using a hairdryer and smelling like a girl, that night I had my favourite Paco Rabanne on.' Bruce leaned his head back on the headboard with a grin emerging, as he thought of Megan's flirtatious delight in telling him how turned on, she was whenever he wore it, the precise reason he wore it that night.

'Why? That's such a horrible thing to say,' said Sara.

'My father is a horrible person,' Bruce said, in a bitter, angry tone, but he contained the anger and continued. 'At the time, I had an old Hillman Hunter, where the fuses in the headlights kept going, that I had a big bag of mixed fuses in preparation for the inevitable, I couldn't afford to get it fixed, I loved that car and remember parking it outside her parent's house, and walking up to the front door with a decided spring in my step, and rang the doorbell. I felt really good, dressed smartly in new black trousers, a pristine white shirt, and the tie Megan had bought for my birthday.'

'Do you still have that tie?' Sara interrupted.

Bruce gave her a quizzical look, but then smiled, 'Yes, it was the last gift she gave me, I can't bring myself to throw it away, have you kept your engagement ring?'

'Yes, I take it out and wear it when I feel I need to remember him. Sorry, I interrupted, again.'

Bruce continued, 'Mrs Taylor opened the door. Immediately, I could tell something was wrong, she had a tissue crumpled in her fist and her eyes were red from crying, I'd never seen Mrs Taylor cry. I asked what had happened and where Megan was. Mrs Taylor ushered me in and told me Megan was in her room and to go up. I'd never been allowed in her room, my fears quadrupled as this was not … normal, there were no, 'behave yourself, or keep the door open – nothing. I quickly found her room, Megan was lying on the bed curled up, she looked at me and tears were rolling down her cheeks, I asked her what was wrong. I couldn't believe what she told me next …'

Bruce took a deep breath, 'Do you mind if I get a drink? Do you want one?' he asked, as he got out of bed and walked unashamedly naked to the minibar.

'Yes please, anything, I'm easy.'

Bruce heard the intended innuendo, turning around catching her appreciative look at his body, and the flush to her cheeks, the bed sheet she had wrapped around over her breasts, and tucked under her arms still clung to her beautiful curves. Bruce poured the drinks, handed Sara hers, and flung himself on the bed, narrowly escaping spilling his drink on the bed. 'What shall we do now,' he asked with suggestively raised eyebrows.

'You've left me hanging, would it be too painful for you to continue about Megan?'

'No … well yes, but …' Bruce took a minute to remember where he had finished off then continued, 'I laid down on the bed and took her in my arms and let her cry for as long as she needed, handing her tissues. After a long while, her sobs started to subside, I handed her more tissues, and she blew her nose, I said to her, 'Tell me what's happened, sweetheart.' She told me she had a Doctor's appointment that day. For a second I thought she was going to tell me she was pregnant, although we had been very careful, Megan wanted to be a nurse and had recently got a placement at Kingston Hospital, and I had finally saved enough money to go to University and was due to start in September. she told me she had been having tummy pains and backache, initially thinking it was due to her periods, then she felt sick, and panicked that she might be pregnant, then relieved when she got her period, but the symptoms persisted alternating from diarrhoea to constipation. Her mum insisted, she sees the Doctor who took blood, that day the Doctor called her mum and asked she bring Megan to his surgery urgently. When they arrived, he told her he suspected she had Pancreatic Cancer but needed to do more tests for definite confirmation.

Bruce took a deep breath. 'I felt like my whole world had just collapsed, and my heart ripped out, this was my Megan, sweet, beautiful, happy, young and vibrant Megan. I couldn't believe this was happening, my head was whirling, I didn't know what to do or what to say, she was so scared and asked me to just hold her, she was trembling, and I held her tighter as she cried again, kissing her forehead and pushing back her tear-streaked hair from her face. Later, Megan's mum came in and offered tea and sandwiches, no one knew what to do or what to say, we all tiptoed around on eggshells. Megan's father came in later, it was obvious he had been told by Megan's mum, he held his arms out, and Megan collapsed into them, he told her how much he loved her, and they would get through this. We laid together on her narrow, single bed, all night. Two weeks later it was confirmed, Megan had pancreatic cancer, very rare in someone so young, with a poor prognosis, as it was quite advanced, there was no surgery, they could try chemo, but even that had a very low rate of success, for this type of cancer.

Sara snuggled in even closer to him and said, 'Oh Bruce, that is so sad.'

'Megan wanted me with her and her family when she went for that final appointment, to ask how long she had. She had made the decision not to have chemo. As the rate of success was so low, she wanted to enjoy what time she had left, and not be sick, she asked how long she had.' Bruce paused and took a deep breath and a sip of his drink, but it didn't stop the tears that rolled down his cheeks, he brushed them away with his forearms. 'My God, Sara, that has to be the worst question for *anyone*, to ever have to ask.'

Bruce noticed tears escape Sara's eyes, which she quickly wiped away and waited patiently for him to continue.

'She was told she had one, possibly two months. I don't remember that walk back to her house with her parents, there was very little to no conversation, what was there to say. I visited her every day, spending hours with her, watching her get weaker and weaker. Six weeks after that hospital visit, I received a call from Megan's mum saying there was little time left, and I needed to get to the hospital as Megan had been taken in earlier and she was asking for me. As I sat in a chair next to her bed and held her hand, she opened her eyes and looked at me, told me she loved me and made me promise 'to live my life and love again', when she was gone. It was the hardest promise to make, she knew me when I make a promise, I keep it, it was the reason she made me say the words. I took out the Ruby ring and slipped it on her finger and told her that I wanted to marry her, but we ran out of time, telling her to wear it and know she will always hold a piece of my heart that will never be for any other, I told her that I loved her and she was my beautiful Megan. Her face creased up as she groaned, it tore me apart to see her in so much pain. I pushed a stray lock of her hair and whispered to her, 'It's all right, baby. Let go now, and fly free.'

A tear rolled down his cheek and his chin started to tremble, but he continued, 'Megan's funeral was a week later.'

At this, his face crumpled, but he struggled to keep control, he had only ever cried for Megan when he was alone, never feeling the arms of someone around him, comforting him. Not because his mother, brothers and sister didn't try to comfort him, but it was a product of his upbringing, with his father telling him, only sissy's cried.

Sara sat up, facing him and straddled her legs either side of him, putting her arms around him, kissing his cheek she whispered into his ear, 'Don't hold it back Bruce, you never have to pretend with me, crying is not a weakness, it's a release.'

You never have to pretend with me, could he really let himself go with Sara, be himself? All his life he had to be strong, for his mother, for his sister, never cry, when his father beat him or made to watch as his brothers were beaten, everyone wanted him to be … something.

Sara clung to him and he could hear her telling him, she knows how he feels, and she did, she understood, these were not empty words, and he could hear her start to cry as he could sense she was remembering her own loss. 'I still miss her and think about her,' he said in a choked voice.

'I know, I still miss Matias.' He raised his arms and pulled Sara in tight to him as the tears stung his eyes, with the lump in his throat making swallowing difficult, before he realised it he was crying, the way he did when he was alone, but this time, he had someone with him, who was holding him and crying with him.

After a while, Bruce pulled back, looked at Sara's red eyes and using the bed sheet, dried her eyes and used the back of his hands to dry his own. 'You must think me so weak to cry like that, sorry.'

Sara took his face in her hands, looked directly into his eyes and said, 'Grieving is not a weakness, its human, you don't ever have to apologise to me for remembering Megan. I'll make you a deal, you tell me all the lovely memories you have about Megan, I would love to hear about her, and I will tell you all the lovely memories I have of Matias?'

'Deal, I would like that,' and they shook hands. 'You are an incredible person Sara, did you know that you are beautiful, elegant, cute, gorgeous … he said kissing her lips and along her jaw with each word, then moving the sheet lower exposing her breasts.

'Keep talking, I like where this is heading,' Sara smiled and tilted her head back.

'Sexy, hot, sensual, provocative,' Bruce continued saying whilst his lips and tongue, teased her nipples till they were hard, 'I love your breasts,' then, with his hand pushed her breast up, taking it into his mouth and suckled whilst rolling the other nipple between his forefinger and thumb, then moving his mouth to pay homage to the other breast, he heard her gasp and say, 'Yes.'

Sara was writhing, gyrating her hips in a circular motion as she straddled him and could feel his response, 'Oh this feels so good.'

They took their time, making love slowly and tenderly, exploring each other with kisses and caresses, then reaching and riding the wave upon wave of euphoria, together.

Thirty-One

The next morning, Sara woke to the blissful feeling of Bruce making love to her, coaxing shivers that rippled through her and trembles that shook her body, that blossomed and escalated into that euphoric warmth she was getting addicted to. They had made love again in the shower, she couldn't get enough of him and felt like pinching herself that this was happening, and real.

Bruce asked, 'Do you have a bikini with you?'

'Yes, always, I try to fit in some swimming whenever I can – why?'

Bruce told her to pack as they were staying on Coney Island for a few days, as he had a mate who owned a house with a private beach, who was out of town for the next three days, and happy for them to use it. Sara was elated, she had never even been to Coney Island, she felt like a child being given extra sweets.

Sara checked-out and they took a taxi to Bruce's hotel, he collected his things and checked out. They went to reception and collected the picnic basket he had ordered earlier. They made their way down to the hotel car park. Sara gave an appreciative whistle when Bruce walked over to a glossy black Trans Am, that had a Golden Eagle design on the bonnet or *hood*, as they call it here, Bruce put the picnic basket into the boot, *or trunk*, and came around to the passenger side, opening the door for her.

Sara's heart skipped a beat, and she allowed herself an internal squeal, whilst breathing in the very sight of him looking so gorgeous in his black jeans and black leather jacket, with a stark white T-shirt, with his freshly washed and tousled black hair, he looked so sexy, and smelled so good, they had only been out of bed for an hour, but she couldn't stop thinking about their night together and she wanted more, *she wanted him again*. Sara couldn't take her eyes off him, as she got into the car, he closed the door and walked around and jumped into the drivers' side.

Always busy working, she hadn't got around to treating herself to a new car since passing her test four years ago, and because she travelled so much, it was always something she constantly put off. 'Wow, is this yours?'

'No, I just hired it whilst out here, at home I prefer my bike.'

'Oh yes, your now infamous Harley,' Sara said giving him a cheeky grin. 'Those photos of us certainly caught a lot of attention. I've been in this business all my life, but still the workings of the minds of the paparazzi still astound me.'

'Me too, but then it was very early in the morning, and we *were*, leaving a hotel', Bruce said returning her grin with a wink, and started the engine which roared into action.

'Early being the operative word, 5 am early, how were they still around, don't they ever go to bed?'

'Probably not, catching a scoop like that means a lot of money, and with it being their livelihood, they probably don't sleep.'

It was while they were in England, and some of the locations were in Scotland, at the time, they were in Edinburgh. As they were sharing the same hotel, Bruce had offered Sara a lift to the location of the shoot, it was such an early morning start, they gave it no thought, and weren't even aware they had been photographed leaving the hotel, and again, arriving at the film shoot. The article strongly implied they had spent the night together in a secluded hotel, the angle of the photo when Sara had gotten off the bike and was handing the helmet back to Bruce, seemed to capture their eyes meeting and making so much more of it – or had they, there was certainly an attraction, of that there could be no denying. Bruce was sitting astride his bike, with all his tight black leather biking gear, he had just removed his helmet and looked gorgeous, smiling up at her, and Sara was standing facing him and smiling back, she was wearing tight-fitted blue jeans with an ordinary red leather jacket and a white T-shirt. With the early dawn sun rising in the background over stunning scenery that is Scotland, it was quite a scoop and a truly stunning photo.

That particular photo had gone viral, sold to multi-international newspapers, and with features in numerous magazines around the world, all going with similar headlines of, 'An affair between the two main leads of the up and coming film 'The 2nd Son'. Initially, the bosses of the production company were not so pleased to have the location of the film leaked, but when they saw the amount of free publicity this was generating, they started to encourage Bruce and Sara to be seen together, their publicist's went into overdrive with interviews arranged where ever they were on location. Filming locations, leaked more regularly, and fans arriving by the coach load, to watch the film.

'Not that I know anything about bikes, but what Harley is it you have?'

'It's an FLT Tour Glide 1340cc, and my pride and joy. After paying off all my debts from University, I saved like crazy, doing all the jobs I could, modelling which I hated, adverts, which made me feel like I was selling my soul, and it was the only reason I agreed to my first film. Walking into the Harley dealership and buying it outright in cash, it still gives me a buzz when I think of that day.'

'Then you have all the right in the world to be proud of it, you earnt it, literally, all I can say is, it's red which I really like and it's really comfortable. Harleys are the only bikes I like, very recognisable both by sight and sound.'

Bruce beamed and said, 'Many women don't like bikes, and hate the helmet ruining their hair.'

Sara remembered that morning, she hadn't hesitated in putting the helmet on and climbed on behind him, put her arms around him and enjoyed their ride. After a while, she realised, he had taken a detour to extend the trip. It was exhilarating, roaring through the empty streets of Edinburgh watching the beginning of the early sunrise, it was a breathtaking memory. Sara had bought the glossy magazine that made a feature of their alleged story, even framed it, taking pride of place in her bedroom at home, that way, not many people would see it or ask awkward questions.

Sara spent most of the trip, to Coney Island, frequently glancing across at Bruce, and her heart skipped a beat every time, he was so gorgeous in every sense of the word, not just his looks. She felt like she wanted to squeal every time she thought about their time together so far, she had never considered herself so salacious, prurient or lascivious, but remembering what she had done to him in the shower, resulted in heat rising in her face and she wound down the window before Bruce noticed, she was thankful for the sunglasses he was wearing, so he couldn't see how flushed her face was. They were also wearing baseball caps and her hair was tied up in a ponytail, to disguise themselves in case they were recognised. She felt a deep glow of pride to be with him, and surprised he wanted to be with her, she felt blessed and lucky. She leaned her head back on the headrest and enjoyed the sunshine and scenery.

Thirty-Two

It didn't take long to get to Coney Island, Sara whistled appreciatively, when she saw the house, as Bruce pulled into the circular drive. She could hear the crashing waves of the Atlantic Ocean behind the house. The Housekeeper opened the door to them and handed Bruce keys, and indicated the bedroom that had been prepared for them, said the fridge had been stocked, she had even prepared an evening meal for them, it only needed heating up. Bruce thanked her and gave her a tip, which she tried to refuse, Bruce insisted on it, saying he appreciated her waiting for them as they had arrived later than expected. Bruce hadn't been able to keep his hands off Sara, which had delayed their Hotel check-outs, although he didn't tell the Housekeeper that, but he did tell her, he would call her, when they were leaving, she wished them a happy stay, then left.

They took their suitcases to the bedroom the Housekeeper had indicated, changed into beachwear, picked up towels and made their way out the back of the house, with the picnic basket in hand, and walked hand in hand down to the beach.

As Sara laid out the towels preparing herself for some sunbathing, Bruce scooped her into his arms, and ran down the beach, with Sara squealing and threatening him, that if he dunked her in the sea, he was coming with her, as she latched her arms around him tightly. Bruce waded into the sea, and they both fell into the water, laughing and spluttering, then proceeded to alternate between dunking each other, challenging each other to swimming races, and wrapping their arms around each other and kissing.

They finally, returned to their towels, on yet another race challenge, after they finished thwarting each other every which way they could, and collapsed laughing and rolling in each other's arms, Bruce asked, 'Are you hungry?'

'Always.'

'For me or food? Bruce said as he waggled his eyebrows.

Sara threw her head back and laughed, 'You, sir, are insatiable, feed me first.'

They delved into the picnic basket and salivated at the scrumptious food of small meat pies, truffle pate chicken drumsticks, baguettes, salami, kalamata olives, pesto, mozzarella, quiches, and two different salads, there were bottles of water, and a bottle of Champagne, with glasses in one of the new Cool bags that was becoming very popular, ending lukewarm drinks on the beach. There were even mini fruit tartlets, strawberries and grapes. They fed each other, whilst lying in each other's arms.

They laved sun cream on each other, which led to them getting carried away, Bruce picked up one of the towels draping it around Sara's waist, as she sat across his lap facing him, they were on a private beach, but that didn't give complete privacy, and Bruce would never put Sara in a position of potential severe embarrassment, but that didn't stop him from finding ways for them to enjoy themselves.

He started kissing her, and under the towel, her bikini bottoms had ties either side, he untied them and found her most private spot with his thumb, while pushing first one finger, then two into her, he could hear her gasping, with his other hand he held her head against his shoulder, as his fingers thrust into her, he kept whispering into her ear, telling her how good she felt, not to hold back, that he wanted to watch her and feel her shatter in his arms. He loved hearing his name on her lips, and he increased the tempo, as Sara cried out, he slowed his thrusting fingers as she went limp in his arms, with a giggle she kissed his neck and said, 'I can't believe you did that to me, here on the beach, now it's your turn.'

'That's ok you can ...'

He didn't get to finish the sentence, as Sara secured the towel around them, and moved her hand between them, reaching into his shorts, wrapping her hand around his hardened shaft and freed him, then directed his manhood to her entrance and sheathed him in her, then made discreet movements rocking back and forth while holding the towel around them, she pushed herself down so he was buried deep inside her, and he was holding her buttocks underneath the towel, he gasped, Sara kissed him deeply, as she feathered kisses along his jaw, she heard him say, 'Oh, Sara that feels so good,' this time they reached the crescendo together. As they collapsed on the sand, Bruce made sure Sara was covered by the other towel, before succumbing to that intoxicating blissful relaxation state.

As Bruce laid there with Sara in his arms, listening to the hypnotic sound of the waves lapping at the shore, he decided he would do everything he had in his power to make sure this worked. For the first time in a long time he was prepared to do anything it took, it had been so long since he felt like this, he was prepared to change, adapt, all his other girlfriends had to accept him as he was, take it or leave it. With Sara he yearned to learn all the things that would make her smile, reduce her to giggles and make her happy.

That evening they dined, casually dressed at 'home'. The meal the Housekeeper had left them was delicious, they found ice cream in the freezer and found all the different ways they could eat and lick it off each other, collapsing laughing and exhausted in front of the massive TV, and watched a comedy film on video while sipping wine, they took a quick shower together, then leisurely made love before falling into an instantaneous sweet and balmy sleep.

Thirty-Three

The next morning, Sara awoke refreshed, stretching out, she turned and caught her breath as she always seemed to be doing every time she looked at Bruce, he was lying on his back with one arm raised and his head turned to one side nestled in his hand, which made his arm muscles bulge, and the other over his abdomen, with the sheet just partially covering his body below his hips, Sara sat up and looked her fill of him, his face had the shadow of a beard, adding to his breath-taking and rugged handsomeness, yesterday he had woken her by luxuriously making love to her.

She wondered if she dared to do what she had in mind – why not, she answered herself, she slowly pulled back the sheet and marvelled at the magnificence of his body, sinking lower down the bed she cupped his balls with one hand, his manhood into her other and took him into her mouth. He started to move and groan, then slowly he opened his eyes and the corners of his mouth lifted as he said, 'What a wonderful way to be woken up', holding him firmly in place by his hips, she let him know that she was not allowing him to stop her.

As she increased the pressure of her lips and tongue, Bruce growled out her name in a loud roar, she didn't relent as his body relaxed and he was slaked. Sara kissed her way up his stomach and chest then his neck and whispered in his ear, 'Good morning.'

With a gleam in his eyes and a dreamy smile on his lips, he replied, 'Morning, beautiful,' then suddenly flipped her onto her back.

Sara let out a shriek, as Bruce started to feather kisses along her jaw and nuzzle her neck working his way down to her breasts, fondling them with his hands as his tongue and mouth licked and suckled her nipples, which drew a gasp from her, all the while he was murmuring how hot she was, how he couldn't get enough of her and said, 'Sara, you are like the Sahara to me, sooooo … hot,' as he slipped further down her body, parting her legs saying, 'and this is my oasis,' his soft laugh was a warm sensual sound, then his tongue started circling her sensitized spot, sucking and licking, sending Sara into a frenzy, writhing on the bed and grabbing the bedsheets in her fists, until she cried out his name.

As Sara relaxed, Bruce pulled up the bedsheet, laid beside her and pulled her into his arms, Sara felt boneless. When her breathing came under control, she murmured, 'I no longer care, if I see Coney Island, let's just stay here,' and she snuggled closer to Bruce, with a mischievous grin on her face.

Bruce laughed, 'We need sustenance. Breakfast?'

With a groan, Sara said, 'We already had breakfast.'

Bruce laughed again, while he rolled Sara over and swotted her backside as he got up, 'You are incorrigible, come on.'

Sara rolled back and curled up when she made no effort to move, Bruce scooped her up in his arms and strode towards the door, 'You leave me no choice, I will just have to serve you up on the breakfast bar then.' Sara screeched with laughter.

Both still naked, Bruce carried Sara into the breakfast room, and deposited her on one of the bar stools and served her a glass of orange juice. Sara placed her elbows on the counter and thought that she should be feeling embarrassed, as she sat there naked, watching Bruce walk around the kitchen, totally uninhibited by his nakedness, grabbing various breakfast food items from the fridge, pans and plates and proceeded to prepare a full English breakfast, and even brewed her a perfect cup of tea. As they sat down to eat and Sara helped herself to a second cuppa from the teapot, she commented, 'Very impressed, where did you learn to cook and not burn everything?'

'At Uni, you either cook or starve, never had enough money to eat out, you can eat very cheaply, when you make friends with your local supermarket, and buy all the stuff they are about to throw out, but, it does lead to some very weird concoctions, since then, I have never been a very fussy eater – anything will do.'

'Even though now, you can afford to be fussy?'

'There are some things, that once experienced, you never forget.'

'For instance?'

'Waitering in restaurants, low pay, long hours, and little appreciation.'

'You've been a Waiter? – hence, the tipping,' Sara guessed. Bruce nodded.

As soon as they finished eating, they cleared away and washed up the dishes, laughing and flicking water at each other, then chasing each other around the kitchen, till they raced upstairs, taking a quick shower together and finally made it out of the house before noon.

They walked into the main part of Coney Island, along the Broadwalk, talking and laughing. Bruce told her about his friends Dom, Jamie, Max and Flynn, and some of the antics they got up to when they were kids, as they had known each other from school. Sara was laughing and giggling at all the stories, then his face went a little serious, and he stared out to sea, they had stopped at a coffee kiosk and found a picnic bench to sit at, with their coffee and doughnuts.

'What is it?' Sara asked.

'It's nothing, just childhood stuff.' He smiled but was a little quieter.

Sara tentatively said, 'I meant what I said the other night when you told me about Megan, you don't have to pretend with me, you don't have to just tell me the funny times, I'm a pretty good listener.'

'The last story just sparked a memory of something that started as a bit of a lark, in our innocence we thought harmless – it didn't end so well.' Bruce took a deep breath. 'Every morning, we would all meet up and walk to school together, we lived so close to each other, on our way we would go scrumping in the large back garden of this house, that had this enormous apple tree. At first, we would just pick those that hung over the back wall, eat one on the way to school and save another for lunchtime, our parents couldn't afford expensive foods like fruits. As we had picked all the apples from the easy to reach branches, we had to climb further along the tree to get at the others, and took it in turns. This particular morning was Dom's turn, he crawled along the tree, but lost his balance and fell into the garden, just as the owner came out of his house and caught us. Dom couldn't climb up, as there weren't any lower branches, he had to run around the garden to where the wall was lower, and we managed to pull him up. The owner was shouting and swearing at us as we ran off laughing, thinking he wouldn't know who we were, and got away with it, none of us registered that we were in our recognisable school uniforms. He attended our assembly the next morning, and identified us, we each got nine lashings of the Kane, one for each year of our lives. The Headmaster said our parents would be informed. That evening our fathers decided to meat out their own punishments, all except Max, the lucky one, as his father is a real father, never touched him or his brothers, he was just not allowed out for a week. My father, got carried away, I was unable to go to school for a week, unfortunately, he was also off that week having sustained an injury at work, he delivered coal, he said that as I had stolen food I could do without it for a week, and I was not allowed out of my room, the only food I had, was whatever my mother, brothers and sister could smuggle when he slept, he didn't even go down the pub each evening, which made him even more bad-tempered.' Bruce visibly shivered.

Sara didn't need to know anymore, she imagined that week had been one of the worst in his young life. They were here, on a sunny day and he had survived what must have been a sometimes miserable childhood, but she felt there was a saving grace, earlier, whenever he spoke of the rest of his family, it was always with a smile and warmth in his tone, hopefully, it was only his father, who had made his childhood so sad, seemed so similar to her own family dynamics. Sara stood up walked around the bench, and placed herself on his lap and gave him a very passionate kiss, then looked into his eyes and said, 'Race you to the Wheel, last one there buys the drinks,' and she was off before he had a chance to respond.

They spent the day going in all the amusement arcades, and daring each other to go on all the rides, eating hot dogs and ice cream, Sara felt so happy, alive and free, they had donned baseball caps and sunglasses and wore shorts and T-shirts, so that they would blend in and not be noticed, which seemed to be working. It was a bright, clear blue sky, and surprisingly hot for April, and as it was the start of the season, not very crowded.

They walked slowly back to the house along the beach, as the sun was setting. Sara sat out on the terrace as Bruce went in to get a bottle of wine and some glasses, she stared out to sea, watching the sun as it made its last descent before it disappeared, and listening to the evening birdsong, and the sea as it gently lapped at the shore, inhaling deeply and dreamily, as soft music wafted out through the open windows.

'A penny for your thoughts,' Bruce said, as he joined her at the table, placing the glasses down as he poured the wine.

'Wasn't thinking, just feeling ... and right now, right this minute, I am feeling really, really happy, thank you, for showing me Coney Island.'

'My pleasure – strike one off your bucket list, what would you like to do tomorrow?'

'Well I've seen the city by land, how about a flight over the city and a trip on a boat down the Hudson?'

'Your wish is my command, my lady.'

Sara made her way into the kitchen and started to cook the steaks from the fridge, that the Housekeeper had labelled and the marinade smelled delicious, there was a salad that had been prepared, all that was needed was the dressing, which sat next to it, Bruce refilled their glasses and set the table and they talked as they ate.

Sara told him about her family, 'My mother Sofia and grandfather Emiliano are Italian, and my grandmother Athena is Greek. I suppose, that is what started my interest in languages, as Cameron and I could speak Greek and Italian, from a very young age, but our father hated us speaking them around him, he's English and has a foul temper, but whenever he was out, mum spoke both around us, and we were able to speak to both our grandparents when they visited. I used to love all the stories they told us about their lives in their countries when they were young. Our Grandfather, Nonno, told us that he was an orphan during WWI. As he was so young, and they didn't know his name, they gave him the surname of Esposito – it means outsider and would be given to a foundling. During his travels when he got older, he met Nonna whilst he was in Greece, he was not what my great-grandparents wanted for their daughter, so, they eloped intending to just stop off in Italy to collect the money that he had buried, unfortunately, Nonno was forced to do his National Service, then WWII intervened and he was forced to continue his service and fight, they couldn't get out of the country together, Nonna said she learnt Italian very quickly, to enable her to get a job, whilst she waited and prayed for Nonno to return.

'What about all the other languages you speak, how did you learn them?

Sara told him how it was Cameron's idea to learn Spanish alongside French, and threw in German as a challenge, how he turned it into a game, but their father tore down all the pieces of paper with the words in the three languages and told them to speak only English. Whenever our father was out, Cameron turned it into another game, he would share out all the words, then we would race, who would be the fastest to put them all up, and we would check if they were right and score points, as a prize if I won, and as he was taller he could reach the cupboard that had the biscuits in. Cameron was a quick learner. I struggled a little with German. As I grew older, I added the other languages, Russian, Japanese, Chinese Mandarin, a few years ago I started learning Swedish and Portuguese.

'What about the gymnastics, when did you start doing that?'

'I was about four when we started lessons, Cameron was desperate to do gymnastics and me? … well, I copied everything Cameron did, I was his little shadow. As I started school, mum said we could have gymnastic lessons as long as our school work didn't suffer, again it was Cameron who suggested we learn our times' tables in the form of gymnastic sequences, I remember one particular test, I couldn't get one of the answers, I went through the moves in my head, and remembered the answer – it worked.

Bruce laughed, 'Very ingenious, your brother seems very imaginative.'

'He is, nearly all of the most daring and creative things we have in our shows is because of Cameron.

'I'm sure you are just as creative and contribute just as much, don't sell yourself short, you probably bounce ideas off each other.'

'We do and talk daily, sometimes twice a day, if we are not together. Are you close to your siblings?'

'Very, Blake is the eldest, then Brett, then me, and our younger sister Brooke'

'All beginning with B – is there a story there?'

'Well … yes, our mother is called Beatrice, Bea for short, hence the B. Our father is called William, some of his mates call him Bill for short, but mum always refuses to call him that.'

'From what you told me earlier, I can understand that.'

For the remainder of the evening, they chatted and laughed, Sara felt so relaxed in Bruce's company, they cleared away and went up to bed. Bruce made slow, tender, sensuous love to her until she fell into a utopian state of sleep.

Thirty-Four

The next morning, Bruce woke early, while Sara slept on, he went down to the kitchen and made a continental style breakfast of croissants and jam, there was even a fresh fruit salad, and a pot of tea and coffee, taking it up to her, he even added a flower in a vase to the tray, surprising himself with the romantic touch.

Sara stirred, as he placed the tray on the table next to her, and sat on the bed, leaning over her and feathering light kisses to her cheek and along her jaw, then her lips, as she opened her eyes and said, 'Good morning.'

'I've brought you breakfast in bed.'

'Mmmm, what delights do you bear,' she said, with a sultry glow to her eyes and a little giggle.

'Flippant remarks like that, will get you what you're asking for madam, but will *severely*, delay us getting out of the house today.' Bruce couldn't resist the long ardent kiss he gave her, 'And you mentioned wanting to see New York by air and sea, my friend whose house we are in, has his own helicopter and boat with crews, I rang him, and asked if we could borrow them, he made the calls, it's all arranged.'

The sheer joy that spread across her beautiful face, along with the whoops and the excited kisses and cuddles she was showering on him, shot a thrill straight through him, that one simple phone call could elicit such happiness in a person, awakened him from what felt like a long sleep. He remembered the enjoyment he always felt when planning surprises for Megan and the anticipation of the presentation.

Making that phone call, he never expected it to mean so much to Sara, even now she was excitedly listing all the places she would love to view, from the air. As she ate breakfast, which Bruce had to keep feeding her or reminding her the tea was getting cold, with her excitement in telling him, how often she had seen films of all the places in New York, but due to her ever-busy schedule, had never spent the time to see, blaming herself and her own work ethic, and profusely thanking him, as he watched with amused pride to see her so animated.

They showered and dressed, until his phone call, Bruce hadn't noticed the Helipad in the grounds which is where the Helicopter was waiting for them, and the unsuppressed squeal of delight Sara emitted when she saw it, along with the wide beam on her face as they took off.

Bruce was paying more attention to Sara than he did the views, his enjoyment came from watching her happiness. It didn't seem like two hours they had been in the air when they landed, Bruce told her he was taking her for lunch at a Greek Taverna he knew of in New York City, in honour of her Nonna, Sara beamed and said, 'You were paying attention, I'm impressed.'

'Every word.' They got into his car, which one of the staff had delivered, and drove into the City.

When they had finished lunch, they took a walk around times square, again wearing their baseball caps and sunglasses to avoid being recognised, but as it was so crowded and people were busy getting to where they needed to be, Sara and Bruce were pleased to have the peace to blend in, it was their accents that created more attention than the recognition of who they were.

They walked to the dock where Sara was expecting a boat to take them on a trip down the Hudson, she never expected the gargantuan, impressive and luxurious motor yacht that was moored there and then be greeted by a Champagne reception with chocolate and strawberries, by the crew. They took a tour of the yacht and Sara shrieked with delight, when she saw the overnight accommodation and recognised her things in the master en-suite bathroom, she asked with amazement, 'How did my things get here?'

'I arranged it with the Housekeeper, while we took our flying sightseeing tour.' Bruce came up behind her, put his arms around her waist, and nuzzled her neck as he whispered in her ear, 'I thought you might enjoy a night aboard, under the stars and tomorrow a stop off at the Statue of Liberty, it was one of the places you mentioned you wanted to visit whilst here?'

Sara turned around, and lifted her arms, wrapping them around his neck and kissed him saying, 'Thank you, this is unbelievable, I'd love that.'

Half an hour later, they set off for a leisurely trip down the Hudson, as they sipped their drinks, and fed eat other the strawberries, as they gazed out by the railings on one of the top decks, Sara asked, 'What were your original plans for this week after completion of the film?'

'I would probably have flown back to England, oversee and help with the preparations for the launches of various business ventures I'm involved in with friends, how about you? Did you plan a holiday?'

'I never plan a holiday, it's usually Cameron who periodically *orders*, me to take a break, according to him I never know when to rest and he's always fearful, I will keep going until burnout.'

'Is he right?'

'Probably, I had to make some phone calls and delay a few things, Cameron was delighted when I said I was spending some time here in New York … with you, hope you don't mind?'

'Not one bit.'

They spent the afternoon, marvelling at the scenery and sunbathing on the deck, as the yacht toured slowly down one side of the river for two hours, before making a slow turnaround for their return trip, and moored just off Long Island.

A grand table was set for them outside on the main deck, and an opulent and lavish meal was served, as the sunset, and the magical sky, transformed into a midnight, velvety starry night, and the silvery moonlight shone on the water, illuminating the ripples of the tide.

When they had finished, Bruce got up from his seat and walked around the table and asked Sara to dance. They held each other close, as their bodies moulded together, placing her hands on his shoulders as his closed tightly, around her waist. They danced silently, letting the soft music lull them into the peace and tranquillity, that was mirroring the calm of the waters.

The warm balmy breeze loosened her hair, and Bruce pushed the tendril behind her ear, as he looked into her eyes with silent intensity, then he smiled. He thought how beautiful she was, as she looked up at him, her face glistening in the moonlight and again that primal, possessive and protective instinct, rose up in him, *she was his*. He twirled and swirled her around, each time bringing her back close to him, as he nuzzled her neck, she smelt so good and he smiled against her skin, as the music effortlessly, fused into various melodies. Bruce asked her if she would like a cocktail, and they wandered into the bar area.

Sara gasped when she saw the bar, it stretched around two sides in a horseshoe design, and bar stools all around, with bottles of every size, shape and colour, displayed on four tiers of the brightly lit and mirrored glass shelves of the wrap-around bar, Sara asked for her favourite Tequila

Sunrise and Bruce had an Alabama Slammer. Taking their drinks, they decided to stroll around the decks, with the soft romantic music following them, on the speakers all around the yacht. A breeze whipped over the calm waves and brought with it a taste of the salty ocean, as they spoke softly in the stillness and serenity of the night.

They talked about their previous relationships, and Bruce regaled Sara of some of his rather less than cool chat up lines when he first discovered girls, reducing Sara to fits of giggles, the sound enveloped him in warmth. He loved how her face lit up, and her eyes glistened as she struggled and failed to compose herself.

As they sat looking out over the ocean, Sara endeavoured to discreetly yawn, but Bruce notices and takes her drink from her and says, 'I think all this sea air and sunshine has its effect on you.' They stroll back arm in arm to the master suite.

They kiss and undress each other slowly, as Bruce takes Sara in his arms and he lays her on the bed and makes gentle, tender and sensuous love to her, that swiftly becomes urgent and passionate, swivelling his hips, with quick hard thrusts. He looks down at her incredulously, as she pants and gasps and pulses around him, it was stunning to watch, the most delicious and amazing sensations flood him, as it builds and explodes, ecstasy washes over him and he looks down at her again, she can't help the smile, as he collapses on her and her smile broadens, as her hands run through his hair, and they roll on their sides caressing each other as they fall contentedly asleep.

Thirty-Five

The next morning, they awoke in a lazy daze and made love, before showering together in the huge walk-in shower enclosure, and breakfasted on the deck in the bright warm morning sunshine, being waited on by the staff. Bruce told her they would be setting sail within the next half hour and would be taking a wide berth around Long Island to the Statue of Liberty, which would take them a few hours.

There was a wide range of games on the largest deck, a huge connect four board, large wooden Jenga blocks and also shuffleboard. Bruce and Sara challenged each other to races when they took out the aqua scooters, whooping and howling with laughter as they returned and boarded the yacht, each claiming that they had won the last race.

Exhausted, but still laughing and claiming victory, Bruce smothered Sara in sun cream, as they lazed on the sun loungers. They sunbathed and swam in the large swimming pool, then sat in the jacuzzi, only leaving the luxury of the relaxing swirling water, to eat their lunch of finger foods, comprising of small delectable and exquisitely filled sandwiches, devilled eggs, salmon rolled cheese, vol au vents, BBQ spare ribs, green salad and a pasta salad, which were placed on a table set for them to help themselves, with a delicious tropical fruit juice, followed by strawberry and cream filled scones, which Bruce and Sara fed to each other, laughing so much when they made such a mess with the cream.

They were getting close to the statue of liberty, they quickly showered and dressed just in time, as the yacht moored just off the island, and the speed boat was launched to take them ashore. They walked around the island, but didn't climb the statue, as it would have been far too crowded and they would run the risk of being recognised, they bought ice creams and sat on the steps at the bottom of the Statue, relaxing and looking out to sea. They took a tour of the islands, stopping at Ellis Island and the museum, then taking the speed boat back to the yacht which returned to New York.

Later in the afternoon when they moored, Bruce thanked the staff for all their work and tipped each of them individually, he told them the Hotel they would be staying at to arrange their things and his car to be delivered. As he led Sara off the yacht, he told her that he intended to take her out on the town tonight, to experience more of New York at night. A friend of his was having a rooftop engagement party tonight, when his friend invited him, he was unsure if he would still be in New York, and asked Sara if she would like to go, Sara jumped at the idea.

They checked into the hotel, and at the reception, Bruce turned to Sara and asked, 'One or two rooms?' he said, with a cheeky grin on his face.

'What do you think – Stud,' she replied, with a gleam in her eyes, and put her arms around his waist, enjoying the feeling, that she was finally able to stake her claim on him publicly, Bruce laughed and put his arms around her, and they took the lift up to their room.

They ordered room service, delaying delivery for an hour when they saw the enormous bath, urgently stripping each other, in their desperation to get naked and leave nothing between them, sensuously bathing each other, and making love in the luxurious bath, sploshing water over the sides.

They were ravenous when the food arrived, they sat and ate their main meal. Then they talked and laughed, kissed and cuddled in their bathrobes, looking out over the brightly lit panoramic landscape of the New York Skyline, feeding each other the delicious collection of mini desserts.

They finally got ready, Sara wore a short strapless, gold sequin dress, that accentuated her curves, her hair loose, with black strappy high heels. When Bruce turned around from the mirror and saw Sara standing there in the sparkling creation, he caught his breath, she looked stunning, and he felt the pride swell within his chest, he couldn't believe that she was here, with him. Having made love less than an hour ago, he wanted her again, and could feel his manhood pulsing, he felt like he was being swept up in a whirlwind of heady mixed and wonderous emotions. He emitted a slow appreciative wolf whistle, stepping closer to her, he took her hands and softly caressed her arms and pulled her in close to him, nuzzling her neck, as he whispered, 'You look amazing, you are making it very difficult for me to walk out of this room without getting arrested,' Sara laughed and they left for the party.

Thirty-Six

Sara was thoroughly enjoying the party. It was on a rooftop garden of an office building in the heart of New York, the venue and the view were spectacular. She felt a warm glow of happiness and contentment.

Bruce was smiling and charming everyone he spoke to and elicited many flirtatious glances and gestures from women who endeavoured to get his attention, they were touching his arm or shoulder as they spoke to him, it made Sara feel special that whenever they did this, he would hold Sara's hand, place his arm around her shoulder or kiss her, sending them a silent, but clear message of whom he was with that evening, she *almost*, felt sorry for them.

When Bruce went to the bar, Sara congratulated his friend Sam and Fiancée Diana on their engagement again and admired the engagement ring. They told her, that they had met by chance and didn't know they had a mutual friend. Bruce and Diana had previously dated, the split was very amicable, and they had kept in touch. They both still felt uncomfortable, until Sam spoke to Bruce, and asked if this would be too awkward, 'But Bruce was perfectly ok with it, he even gave us his blessing,' said Sam, as he and Diana, gazed at each other, Sam drew Diana close and kissed her.

Unreasonable jealousy shot straight through Sara, she had never before been possessive, but she felt like Bruce was hers. Here was a woman who had history with Bruce, *another* ex, and *another*, who knew him *carnally*. She needed to tamper this emotion down, it was very unattractive, and she needed to cool off, *what was wrong with her*. Sara excused herself by saying she would help Bruce with the drinks, each step as she approached him, lightened her mood, Bruce was with *her* now, and whatever his history was just that, *history*.

She wrapped her arms around his waist, and asked if he needed any help, Bruce placed his hands over hers and looked down at her and smiled, she was never going to tire of seeing his smile, it made her heart skip every time. Tonight, he looked so handsome in black trousers, blood-red shirt and black tie, with his raven hair just touching his collar. Sara scanned the room and decided, that Bruce, was definitely the best-looking man at the party, and he was hers, *there she went again.*

They returned with the drinks, and Sara felt better towards Diana, she sensed she had no cause to worry and tonight, she was going to stop thinking and just enjoy herself, she then asked Bruce if he would like to dance. It was a long time before they left the dance floor.

Dancing, laughing and drinking, Sara felt like she had made new friends that evening, one of them being Diana, there were no difficult atmospheres as Diana never made any comments on her relationship with Bruce, even when they went to the ladies together. The only thing she said was, 'Bruce is a really lovely person, and I'm glad we parted on good terms, able to keep him as a friend, I am so happy with Sam, and I can't wait for our lives to begin together.' Sara ended up even respecting Diana, and laughed at herself for her earlier feelings.

Later, when the slow romantic music was playing and the lights dimmed, Bruce took Sara into his arms and danced up close and *very* personal. Threading his fingers through her hair, as he held her close with one hand on the back of her neck, and the other skimming down her back to her behind, pulling her in so close, she could feel the effect she was having on him, and if she was in any doubt, Bruce told her exactly, what he would like to do when they returned to the hotel later. Sara felt her cheeks burning as she smiled and gyrated her hips, she heard a groan from him.

'Do that again, and I will just have to take you right here, right now in front of this audience.'

Sara giggled as she went on tiptoes and nuzzled his neck, which elicited another groan from him. Sara felt like she was in a dream, which was made even better when Bruce kissed her and sent shivers down her spine as he murmured hot sultry suggestions in her ear.

They didn't leave the party until the early hours, as they were having such a good time. Bruce hailed a cab, even though it was a short journey, it was safer and it had gotten really cold. Sara wanted to get back to the hotel and hold Bruce to doing all the things he had suggested earlier.

They rushed into the hotel, and summoned the empty lift, they couldn't keep their hands off each other. Bruce was repeating all the things he wanted to do to her, and Sara was finding it hard to breathe with the excitement building in her, he had pulled her strapless dress down, fondling her breasts and lowering his head and taking her hardened nipple into his mouth, suckling hard, whilst holding the other, then switching to pay equal homage, raising his head he took her mouth. Sara was finding it hard to be quiet, panting and gasping, urging Bruce on, whilst driving her fingers through his hair.

The lift stopped on their floor, Sara adjusted her dress, as they ran down the hall, quickly opening the door to their suite. Sara removed his tie and ripped open his shirt, 'I am going to have to invest in a lot of shirts,' he said huskily and smiling, as Sara giggled, remembering the first shirt she had ripped off him. She marvelled again at the broad expanse of his sculptured chest. Bruce removed her dress, surprised that she had no panties on, 'If only you had told me you were going, commando, tonight,' he said, with a secretive smile. He didn't remove her stockings or shoes, he laid her on the bed, and told her how beautiful she was, Sara was captivated by the way he was looking at her. He stood up, reaching into his trouser pocket, and withdrawing a handful of individually wrapped chocolates, that Sara recognised from the party, he leaned over her and put them on the bedside table.

'You have a sudden sweet tooth urge?'

'Just think about some of the things I told you I want to do to you tonight,' Bruce said, with a seductive smile and heat in his eyes.

The reminder sent shockwaves of electrifying tingling sensations, through her body, he only needed to look at her to produce this reaction, or do what he was doing now, alternating sultry murmurings and feathering kisses along her jaw and down her neck, which sent hot shivers up and down her spine, producing goosebumps.

He then unwrapped one of the chocolates, and broke it in half, the liquor dribbled out, he allowed the sticky liquid, to trickle down her neck and over her breasts, he then coated each nipple with chocolate, and trailed it down over her flat stomach, then secreting the last of the chocolate in her most secret place, as he looked up into her eyes he said with a provocative smile, 'My reward.'

Sara was gasping with anticipation, as he trailed his tongue along her neck and started to lick the liquor from her body, and the chocolate from her nipples, as he sucked and licked each in turn, which was sending her into a frenzy, as she fisted the bedsheets in her hands. His mouth travelled lower over her stomach, he then stopped and looked up at her and asked her, 'Do you want me to stop?'

Sara was writhing and trying to gulp in air and spluttered, 'What?' incredulously, 'don't you dare.'

She heard him chuckle, as he resumed the torment with his tongue, and dropped to his knees, as he pulled her further down the bed, parting her legs wide, he said, 'Now for my reward,' as he parted her with his thumps and swirled his tongue around her most sensitive spot, then he growled low in his throat, 'Mmmm … you taste so good.'

'Me or the chocolate?' Sara barely managed to ask, as his clever tongue was driving her senseless.

Bruce chuckled, 'Both,' as he returned to what he was doing, increasing the intensity, as he swirled his tongue around her sensitised core, alternating between sucking and licking, until Sara cried out his name and shattered around him, Bruce held her in place, continuing his assault until her body relaxed and her breathing started to regulate.

He kissed her sensitive inner thighs, as he shed the remainder of his clothes and joined Sara, she almost purred as he slipped into her slowly. Sara roused and welcomed him, putting her arms around him as he thrust into her. She placed one hand on his buttocks, urging him deeper and faster, until he let out a loud roar, then collapsed on top of her, she enjoyed the weight and closeness of him.

Sometime later, he stirred, and lifted himself, rolling onto his side, and Sara snuggled into him, 'What are you doing to me Sara?' he kissed her forehead, then her lips and her mouth, as she looked up at him, he rolled her onto her back, 'I can't seem to get enough of you,' he pushed a tendril of hair, that had fallen across her forehead, pushing it behind her ear, as he took her face into his hands, and looked tenderly into her eyes. 'I don't want this to be a holiday fling when we arrive home tomorrow, I want this, us, to continue and let it lead us, wherever it goes. Can I hope that you feel the same?'

Sara had to stifle a squeal, and from doing a bed dance, as she was limited in movement, as Bruce was on top of her, but she couldn't hide the broad stupid grin on her face.

'You don't have to hope Bruce, I most definitely want the same.'

She wanted to tell him that she loved him. She knew she did. Having felt this only once before in her life, she recognised the debilitating symptoms every time she looked at Bruce, she forgot to breathe, thinking about him morning, noon and night. To hear he felt the same was like all her Christmases' and Birthday's had come at once.

He kissed her softly at first, then it grew ardent and fiery as they competed for supremacy and dominance, Sara won, or Bruce let her, as she pushed him onto his back, and straddled him. Caressing his chest, and leaning over him, trailing her tongue over his nipples, taking one into her mouth sucking, and gently nipping with her teeth, she continued her exploration to his neck, and along his strong jaw, finding his mouth and thrusting her tongue in, as it duelled with his.

She sat up and reached between them, taking his long thick shaft in her hand, which produced a growl from Bruce. Sara enjoyed the power it gave her to have him at her mercy. She guided him to her entrance and threw her head back at the rapturous feeling, as he filled and stretched her. Establishing a slow rhythm as she rode him, enjoying his hands as they stroked and fondled her hips and breasts. Enraptured, she increased the tempo as they both climbed and reached the peak together, and cried out in unison, slumping on the bed entangled in each other, smiling and caressing each other, as they drifted into blissful and peaceful oblivion together.

Thirty-Seven

It was the morning of their last day in New York, normally Bruce would have been in a bit more of a sombre mood, the end of a holiday fling or affair, but this time, he felt almost light-headed after last night, and this morning, it felt like a new beginning.

He had woken in the early hours and made slow, sweet love to Sara again, and did some of the things he had whispered to her at the party when they were dancing under the stars and the lights of New York, which looking back now felt like a spellbinding enchantment. Sara was his aphrodisiac, he only had to look at her and his thoughts turned erotic, and with Sara demonstrating her gymnastic talents, he was sure they had invented some new positions, especially in the shower just now.

Room service arrived with their breakfast, and they sat on the terrace in the hotel bathrobes, taking in their last look, *for now*, over the city that never slept, sipping their coffee and making plans for when they got home, and their next projects, and speculating on the success of the 2nd Son and its sequel, Bruce told Sara, that they already had a provisional green light to go ahead with the sequel, as long as the box office figures stacked up.

They chortled about filming the intimate scenes, and Bruce told her that if the sequel goes ahead, he was going to have an even more difficult time covering up the evidence of his desire for her, Sara giggled and teased that maybe they could discreetly, have real sex and not simulated. Bruce told her that it would not be possible for him to concentrate on his lines, and not with the number of takes they had to do, with the constant interruptions of Davy shouting, 'Cut,' all the time, they both uproariously, laughed.

They packed their cases as they dressed, Sara had on a red summer dress, when Bruce saw her in it he wrapped his arms around her waist from behind, and moved her hair to the side over her shoulder, nuzzling her neck, feathering kisses up to her ear lobes and nipping it gently with his teeth, telling her how good she looked, and how her perfume was driving him crazy, he asked, 'Do we have time for a quickie?'

Sara giggled softly and turned in his arms saying, 'You are insatiable, we will miss our flight, but I've always wanted to join the 'mile high club', raising one eyebrow with a smile, and a twinkle in her eyes conveying a promise. He always dressed casually for flights and wore a blue denim shirt over his blue jeans.

They headed to the reception and checked out, Bruce made a quick call to the car rental company, to inform them to pick the car up from JFK Airport, and made their way down to the hotel car park, then set off laughing. Bruce invited Sara, to have a drink at the Scottish pub he co-owned with his friend Flynn, and after dine with him at his joint venture French restaurant, with his friend Max, as soon as they had a chance to recover from the jet lag. Sara gleefully accepted.

Thirty-Eight

New York – April 1986

They joined the Freeway. They didn't notice, two cars had been following them since they left the hotel. They didn't notice the cars split and drive along-side them. They didn't notice, the two cars stay level with them for a few miles. They *did* notice, the guns pointed at them from each car.

In a matter of split seconds, Bruce considered his options, should he speed up, he knew he was driving a very fast and powerful car, but there were two of them in equally powerful cars, all he could acknowledge was that one was black and the other was silver. He checked his rear-view mirror and saw a long break in the traffic behind. Course of action decided, and his heart pounding, he shouted to Sara to put on her seat belt, which she did in seconds. Slamming on the brakes, he executed a handbrake turn at high velocity, just as they heard two single gunshots. He headed, against the flow of traffic, for the exit they had just passed at high speed.

Bruce checked his mirror again, to his horror, he saw that both cars had done the same manoeuvre and were gaining on them. He glanced across at Sara, as she looked at him with sheer terror on her face, she was holding on to the handrail above the door and had placed her feet either side of the footwell, bracing herself, but she hadn't screamed or shrieked or gone into hysterics, in this situation most people would. Instant admiration sawed in his heart.

Concentrating on the road ahead, swerving to miss cars, zig-zagging and weaving in and out of traffic, to try and lose the two cars. Bruce heard sirens and sent up a small prayer of thanks, but in the frequent quick glances he made in the rear-view mirror, he saw the silver car split away, and one of the cop cars followed, but the cops weren't so lucky and hadn't been fast enough to drive between a tanker and bus, as the silver car had, and by braking hard, they skimmed the central barrier and flipped over. No longer in pursuit.

The black car was still behind him, and the other cop car was pursuing both of them, its siren blaring and blazing. Bruce was concentrating hard on missing traffic in front of him. He could hear Sara make a valiant effort not to scream out loud, only occasional stifled shrieks that involuntarily escaped. He swerved around traffic as the tires screeched, he had no option, but to cross the central reservation into oncoming traffic, to escape and avoid the cars that had come to a standstill.

The cop car still in pursuit behind the black car, had hopefully radioed ahead and more cops would soon, *hopefully*, join this chase and bring it to an end. He feared more for Sara then himself, although his breathing and heart rate were in a marathon of their own. Just as he was able to cross back onto the right side of the road, ahead of the accident that had stopped the traffic, he glanced in the rear-view mirror and saw that the black car had slammed on its brakes, and the cop car swerved, as it braked and crashed into the back of the black car, the impact silenced its siren.

Bruce was hoping this would take the black car out, leaving him with only the silver one to contend with, as it had was now tailgating them, he continued to push the car to its top speed to outrun the silver car, but it was relentless and staying on his tail, where the fuck were the cops when you needed them.

Should they turn left or right, this was a part of the City, Bruce had never been to, they were lost. Speeding through the labyrinth of New York streets and narrow alleys. He then made a fatal error – a sharp turn into a dead end.

Thirty-Nine

With no means of escape and the gang right behind, they screeched to a stop. A panicked look behind him, confirmed, they were – trapped.

Hemmed in with no means of escape, he had hoped if he had turned quick enough, they would drive past, no such luck and the only sirens he could hear were too far away, for them to be coming to *their* aid.

He glanced at Sara, she looked at him, her eyes wide with sheer terror. He slammed the car in reverse, maybe push them out. As his car screeched and the engine squealed, there was only a little movement, then at the end of the alley, the black car appeared and blocked the exit across the alley, the back was bashed in, unfortunately, the impact from the cop car had not affected the engine.

As powerful as Bruce's car was, it wouldn't be able to push both cars out of the way, and not enough power whilst in reverse. He searched the alley for a door or a ladder to the upper apartments, there were none, that he could see. Still trying to move the car behind thinking that at least they wouldn't be getting out of their cars, whilst his engine was screaming, he looked all around, suddenly someone was coming out of a back door, he looked at Sara and shouted above the engine noise, 'There's a guy over there just come out of a door,' Sara looked over. 'When I stop the car, get out quick, and run like hell, don't look back.'

She looked at him with panic in her eyes, her voice went brittle as she asked, 'What about you?'

'When you're out, I'm going to reverse the car, surprise them, and cause some damage, then I will be right behind you, ok?' Sara nodded.

Incredible, Bruce thought again, no hysterics, no screaming – that's my girl. He immediately stopped the car, and Sara jumped out and ran towards the open door. Bruce instantly put the car into drive, to move a little forward, then rapidly into reverse, as he completed the manoeuvre, he saw in his rear-view mirror, he had succeeded, they had banged their heads, and were holding their noses, this gave Bruce some vital seconds headway.

The man who had come out of the back door, stood momentarily stunned at all the noise, then quickly retreated back through the door, and it was closing. Bruce could hear Sara screaming at him to hold the door, but it was closing and it was a fire door, no external handles. Bruce shouted to Sara to run faster, but it was too late the door had closed, they banged on the door, and shouted in desperation, for the man to open it, but it remained closed. They were trapped, on the outside.

Bruce heard car doors opening and closing behind him, he saw a man sleeping rough nearby and shouted to him to get out, but the man just raised his head and stared, he was drunk, this early in the day. He turned around to see five men with various weapons, but these were handguns, different to those he glimpsed pointed at them through the car windows on the Freeway. In the background two more men were standing, legs astride, hands in their pockets, no weapons, *non that were visible anyway*, watching, they must be the gang leaders.

Bruce pushed Sara behind him, as the five men started approaching, one of the two leaders shouted, 'You have no means of escape, so you will come quietly.'

They were still a little way off, Bruce whispered to Sara, 'Get behind that large dumpster and hide, there's a small chance I can convince them, you got through that door and there's only me.'

'Bruce ...' she cried in a strangled voice.

'Do it – *do it now*,' he growled, in a restrained whisper. Sara moved behind the dumpster, which was almost as tall as she was.

With Sara hidden, Bruce moved away from the door and around a car, that had partly obscured them from the gang, walking as far forward down the alley as he could away from Sara, he had his hands up in surrender, 'There's only me, if its money you're after, I only have what's in my wallet.'

'The amount of money we want, nobody carries around.'

Bruce's throat went dry, so it was a kidnapping and hostage situation then, he had to do something. The five men in front of the leaders started advancing. He could see one was still in the black car, eight of them in total, he had no chance, but there was no chance he was going to give in, *quietly*.

As they approached him, Bruce lunged at the one on the left of him, punching him hard in the gut with an uppercut to his nose, breaking it as he heard the crack, then as the one on the right went to punch Bruce he fell to one knee and punched him in the nuts and heard him squeal, the other three converged at once, but Bruce managed to get a kick, a punch and a head butt into each of them before the leaders joined in and brought Bruce under control, and had him face down over the hood of his car, with his arms wrenched behind him, and a gun held to his head. The leader then shouted out, 'Sara Kaye, we know you are there, get yourself out here, before I splatter your boyfriend's brains all over this car.'

'She's not here,' Bruce snarled, 'she got away through that door.'

'Do you think we're gonna fucking fall for that, she's behind that dumpster,' he barked, through gritted teeth, close to Bruce's ear.

Bruce saw the leader give a nod, and suddenly three shots rang out, all of them fired into the dumpster, that Sara was hiding behind.

'Noooo,' Bruce yelled, as he struggled to free himself, but was held down more firmly, and the gun was pushed harder to his head, as the leader leaned in closer.

'Didn't think you were alone,' then hit him with the butt of his gun, his vision became blurred, and he could feel wetness run down his head. He heard the gun being cocked. His heart pumped loudly in his ears, and he took short and shallow breaths.

'You have precisely three seconds to come out Sara Kaye,' he spat, 'and we'll have you anyway, but this motherfucker, will be wasted,' he shouted, 'now come out,' he shouted louder.

Forty

It felt like her heart had stopped, then sped into overdrive, when she heard her name being shouted out, how did he know her? There was no escape. There was no way out of the alley, except past them. While Bruce had confronted the gang, Sara had spent her time trying to find a door, a window, in fact, any means of escape. There were none. They had Bruce pinned to the hood of his car with a gun held to his head. As she hesitated, three shots were fired into the dumpster, and they were extremely close to where she was standing. She had no choice, and her whole body was trembling, as she walked around the dumpster with her hands shakily held up.

Could she do anything? What did they want? What were they going to do? What was going to happen? So many questions, all tumbling around in her head. As she moved out into the alley, one of the gang members moved towards her, and grabbed one of her arms, pushing her forward, with her surprise at being manhandled and the amount of force used, she stumbled slightly.

She was pushed again, then pulled to a standstill next to Bruce, and in front of the man, who was still holding the gun to Bruce's head whilst two men were holding Bruce's arms back. The leader locked his menacing gaze on Sara, then with his free hand he grabbed Sara by the throat and through gritted teeth he snarled, 'I've been waiting a long time for this, bitch.' Releasing her throat, he backhanded her across the face, which split her lip, as it caught on one of his rings, and Sara had the salty metal taste of blood in her mouth. Knocked off balance, she was straightened by the gang member behind her, and the leader grabbed her by the throat again and squeezed tighter. She was choking and couldn't breathe, she was grabbing and clawing at him with both her hands to try and release his hand, then just before she felt like she was going to pass out, the leader loosened his grip. She was hacking and gasping for breath.

'Leave her the fuck alone, you bastard,' Bruce desperately gritted out under the hand of one of the men holding him.

'Shut the fuck up,' the leader growled and hit Bruce again with the butt of the gun.

Sara could see blood trickle down Bruce's face. As she started shaking, she could feel her eyes stinging with tears of sheer terror, and fear of what was going to happen next. The leader told the men to tie Bruce up, blindfold and gag him. 'With fucking pleasure, he's broken my fucking nose.' They tied his hands and feet, then threw him into the trunk of the car, Bruce's body was limp as they tied him, unconscious from that second blow to his head, Sara had seen everything from her frequent peeks, from behind the dumpster.

The leader turned to Sara, and without breaking eye contact with her, he told his men to do the same with her, but they didn't tie her feet. There was a debate of where to put her as the black car no longer had a trunk, from being smashed up and should they put her in the trunk with Bruce, the leader decided for her to be put in the back seat of the silver car.

Disorientated and blindfolded, Sara had no idea how long they drove for, it felt like hours, they were no longer in New York. The roads grew quieter, to the point that Sara didn't hear another car pass them for a long while, all she could hear was the wining of the tyres as they drove along a gritty road surface, the gang hardly talked either.

Sara sat quietly, in the middle of the back seat, too terrified to make any noise, and very aware that Bruce was in the trunk, inches away from her. Was he still alive, that thought brought an involuntary whimper to her lips, that escaped around the gag in her mouth, and the leader shouted, 'Shut the fuck up bitch,' Sara suppressed the thoughts of Bruce's demise, and kept hope alive, she just couldn't bear the alternative.

At last, the car made a right turn and then slowed until it stopped and all the men got out, Sara sat there in silence. During the long drive, she had started to relax a little or as much as she could, wedged between two large men, American cars were always wider, but there didn't seem to be very much room. She now started trembling again, where were they and what were they intending to do with them. The door suddenly opened and cold air rushed in, was it still day or night time, she had lost all concept of time. She was pulled out of the car and held by her arms either side, 'Take her inside and tie her to the wall,' she shivered at the coldness in the voice.

All the time, her mind kept wandering back to how Bruce was in the boot of the car. Her hands were still tied behind her, and her shoulders were aching, they didn't remove the gag or the blindfold as they marched her into the building, Sara could barely keep up, and when she faltered, they sharply yanked her up by her arms, she gave a howl deep in her throat that was muted by the gag, the steps she didn't walk, they dragged her. She heard a door being opened and she was pushed inside, then had the feeling of it being a large space, it was no warmer inside, she only had her summer dress on, her shivering was from both the cold and fear. They let her go without warning and she fell to the floor, her hands were untied and she was dragged till her back hit a wall, and her arms were raised and her hands were put into metal cuffs, she was then left alone.

She sat there on the cold concrete floor, it felt like ages before she heard the door again open, but it seemed a long way off and not clear, like it was in another room, angry voices were yelling, 'You've dislocated my fucking shoulder, you fucking bastard, you will pay for that.'

'You can blame your stupid mate here, I was aiming for your fucking neck, then you wouldn't be complaining - you'd be dead.'

Sara was so relieved to hear Bruce's voice, she couldn't keep the smile from her face, she sent up a prayer of thanks, that he was still alive.

There followed a lot of noises of fighting, punches, shouting and swearing, it sounded like a lot of people involved, the sound of the door opening and someone running in, and shouting above everyone else.

'How many of you does it take to subdue this fucker,' there followed the sound of more punches.

'Why the fuck did you untie him?' Sara froze, it was the voice of the leader.

'He was too heavy to pull out of the trunk,' Sara heard another voice say.

'Now tie the bastard up again, and throw him in there with the bitch, she had better be tied to the wall.'

'She is, very securely,' said yet another voice.

In the next moment, another door opened and it was very close, they must have put her in a room. A body was pushed into the room, and it fell against her and rolled next to her, she hoped to God it was Bruce, but he didn't move. Again, she tried to remove her blindfold by moving her arm and shoulder, one side and then the other, but they had secured her blindfold very tightly, and it hadn't budged. After five minutes or was it half an hour, she could hear the gang settling, and nursing their wounds from the comments she could hear.

Sara tentatively started to prod the body next to her, if it was Bruce, she didn't want to cause more injuries. After a while, she could hear him stirring, she still had her gag on, therefore couldn't rouse him by talking to him. Slowly she could feel him start to stir, and it sounded like he was shifting.

Then she heard all at once Bruce's voice, as he was pushed over to her, he fell against her and immediately she felt his hands on her face.

'Oh my God, Sara, I was so afraid they had done something to you.'

He was smattering her face with kisses, as he removed the blindfold and gag, then he was kissing her and repeating over and over, how glad he was she was here and alive. He was kneeling next to her, she suspected they had tied his feet again.

A tear rolled down her cheek and she winced when he kissed her too hard on the lips, because of the cut, he apologised and looked into her eyes and asked if they had done anything else to her, she told him she was ok and only the cut to her lip when she was struck.

She was unable to hug him due to her hands being raised and shackled. Bruce pulled at the chains, but they were set into the concrete. Sara asked how come he was untied. He showed her his hands were still tied, but they were in front of him, he explained that he had been able to move them to the front by lowering his hands down his body from behind, and loop them over his feet, but would have to return them as soon as they hear anyone come back.

'Oh my God, how is your head and your face Bruce, what did they do to you?'

'It's ok, I think they came off worse,' he smiled, 'I pretended to still be unconscious when we arrived, they thought it easier to move me if I was untied, as soon as they did, I removed the blindfold and pulled down the gag and … well, let's just say I didn't make it easy for them out there, and again as soon as they dragged me inside. I couldn't see you anywhere, it terrified me, that they had already got rid of you.'

At this Sara could see his eyes fill with unshed tears, and he cupped her face again and kissed her lips more tenderly.

'I'm so … so scared Bruce, what are they going to do to us?'

'Probably ransom us, we *are* worth a few bob.' He tried to give her an encouraging smile.

Sara could sense he was trying to lighten the mood, but she started shaking again and was trying hard not to cry, there was no telling how long they would be left in this room, or together, and she didn't want to spend the time being weak and crying.

She looked around the room, it was empty, no furniture, no window, only her chains and metal cuffs, hanging from the wall, only one strip light and a CCTV camera, fixed high up. Bruce looked at it and said it wasn't working at the moment, as there would be a red light on the lens when it was on. She had no idea what time it was and asked Bruce, 'Do you have any idea what time it is?'

'No, but it was starting to get dark as they dragged me in, they probably won't make their demands until tomorrow now.'

As he said that, the door was being unlocked and Bruce jumped next to Sara, and quickly slipped his hands over his feet, to put his hands behind him. One of the gang members walked in, he had a brown bag in his hand.

'The boss said you are to be fed – for now,' he added menacingly.

He then walked over and released one of Sara's hands from the metal cuffs, untied Bruce's hands, but put one of his hands into the metal cuff, and left, after tossing the bag at Bruce, returning a short while later with one small bottle of water.

'Well I suppose one hand each is better than none, we'll have to savour the water like it's the most expensive wine,' Bruce said with a smile.

He opened the bag, it was burger and fries each for them, they hadn't eaten since breakfast – was that really, only this morning!!

Bruce and Sara sat hugging each other as best they could, standing when their arms started aching with pins and needles from being raised for so long. They both needed to relieve themselves, Bruce shouted to the gang, until one of them unlocked the door, not at all pleased to be summoned.

'What the fuck do you want?'

'We need to use the toilet, also any chance of more water?'

Ignoring his question he said, 'One of you at a time – you first,' he pointed his finger at Bruce, 'Any more of that punching and kicking crap – she gets it – got it?' he snarled and pointed his finger at Sara.

'Got it,' said Bruce holding the stare.

Bruce was released and a gun was pointed at his back, as he was pushed forward. Then it was Sara's turn as Bruce returned, and the metal cuff was secured around his wrist. She was led out of the room with a gun thrust into her back and her arm held very tightly, she winced at the pain, as she was led across a large expanse of a derelict building, and through the few windows that hadn't been boarded up, she could see it was dark outside.

This must have once been a warehouse, as some huge stacking units reached almost to the ceiling, but some had been pushed over and driven to the sides of the building, as the supports were all bent and buckled as if space had been cleared in a hurry. There were some desks and chairs, where the gang were milling about, even a few old sofas that looked really out of place, there was an office over in one corner, where a few more members of the gang were sitting. The gang leader was on the phone and didn't look very pleased with whomever he was talking to, judging by his facial expressions and body language.

Sara was jostled over to the far side, into a smaller room that had two toilet cubicles, as Sara went to shut the door, the gang member kicked it open, and told her it would remain open, he stood opposite, she would be given no privacy. Sara's face flushed with embarrassment, but her urgency won out and she used the filthy facilities, fortunately, there was some toilet paper. Flushing the toilet, she walked over and washed her hands, there were no towels to dry them, she was again jostled out of the *bathroom*. She received various glares from the gang members, as she was returned to her chains.

As soon as they were locked in, they sat down and Sara leaned her head on Bruce's shoulder, which wasn't all that comfortable with both of them with one arm raised. Bruce gently stroked Sara's face, and tried to reassure her that if they were ransomed, there was a possibility they would be let go. Sara looked up at him, her eyes were glistening, and again she was shaking.

'They haven't even tried to hide their faces. I don't think this is a simple ransom plan.' They both looked up at the camera, the red light was on the lens. They were being watched.

Bruce looked down and in a quiet voice he said, 'I know.' They didn't say another word to each other, what was there to say.

Forty-One

They were woken by the door being unlocked, then it slammed forcefully against the wall. They had endured a long night, neither of them had managed much sleep, sitting up with a glaring strip light on constantly. They took turns leaning their head on each other, sleeping fitfully. They had lost all sense of time, and only presuming it to be the morning when a gang member walked in and tossed them a couple of pastries, 'Ah, morning breakfast, any chance of a cup of tea or coffee maybe?' Bruce asked in his most polite English accent, and with a charming grin, like he was ordering in a restaurant.

The gang member moved closer, towering over them he said, 'You got food, enjoy it while you can,' then dropped another bottle of water into Bruce's lap, and kicked him hard in the side, then walked out and locked the door.

'Are you ok?' Sara asked anxiously.

'Fine,' Bruce answered through gritted teeth, 'do they think we're Houdini or something, they chain us up, but still lock that door.'

'Least it gives us some warning when they are coming – all the good that does,' she muttered despondently.

With no concept of time, it was a while later, a gang member unlocked the door, walked in and released Sara, picking her up abruptly under one arm and pushing her out of the door. Bruce yelled at him to leave her and take him, but he was ignored and the door was once again locked.

Sara was pushed toward the middle of the open space. An old-fashioned wooden chair had been placed on a large expanse of plastic. Seeing this, Sara recoiled in sheer terror, stumbling back into the gang member who just pushed her forward, and grabbed her by her upper arms, marching her towards the chair. Sara was screaming and pleading in terror and panic, plastic meant bloodshed, 'Oh my God, please … please don't do this … what is it you want … please, no.'

She was desperately struggling, when another gang member stepped forward to take hold of her, and firmly deposited her on the chair and held her roughly, while her hands were tied behind her, over the back of the chair. Further ropes were tied tightly around her body and the chair, she could no longer move. The gang leader approached and pulled her head back by her hair, looking menacingly into her eye's, inches from her face and virtually spits his disdain at her. Sara suppressed her revulsion at the smell of his stale breath.

'We are going to make a ransom video. You. Will read off the cards. Understand?'

Sara's mouth went dry, unable to form any words as she started shaking, with her eyes wide and too terrified to even blink. He repeated with increased hostility, 'Un. der. stand?' he enunciated.

'Yes,' she half mouthed and half-whispered.

He violently shoves her head forward, releases her and walks away. With short, sharp and shallow breaths, Sara sat there trembling, waiting, for how long she had no idea. One gang member stood in front of her, watching her, he was the same gang member who brought them their food. She kept her head lowered, too afraid to hold any eye contact, in case it provoked a reaction.

As the waiting lengthened, Sara felt herself relaxing as imminent expectation of danger started to dissipate, and she lifted her head, keeping her eyes lowered, looking through her eyelashes. Her heart was still pounding in her ears, but as it started to regulate and quieten, she started hearing the conversation the gang were having over near the office, two inside the office and two milling outside, with the one standing in front of her that made five of them, then she heard a low moaning sound to her right.

The gang member moved away from in front of her. Sara lifted her eyes and followed his direction and saw a man, lying on an old mattress that looked soaked with blood from a stomach wound. Blood had also seeped through the thick wadding and bandaging.

The gang member leant forward, as he picked up more wadding and placed it on top of the soaked wadding and said, 'Javier, you must stay still, we are getting you a Doctor.' He sounded desperate as he ran his hand through his shoulder-length dark hair.

'I'm not going to make it Jase.'

'Just hold on, Coop and Nate will be back soon with the Doctor,' he repeated.

Gritting his teeth and between gasps, he said, 'Jase … promise me … you'll get my share to my family … I've done nothing but disgrace them … at least I can do this for them … Joe won't think to do that … once I'm gone, he'll move on quickly to another, he's not the loyal or honourable type … I taught him to be like that … the only other person he cares for is his brother.' With an exerted effort, he grabbed Jase by the shirt and pulled him forward and said, 'I spent nearly all my life getting away, now I miss home, I miss Mexico, don't you?' Jase nodded in agreement, he loosened Javier's grip and laid him back down, but Javier grabbed at Jase's shirt again and said, 'You are my cousin, promise me.'

'I promise, take it easy,' Sara saw Javier collapse back again onto the mattress, and didn't say another word, she could see the rise and fall of his chest, he was still alive.

Jase shouted over to the men in the office, 'Where the fuck are Coop and Nate with that Doctor, Javier is bleeding out and it's not stopping, he'll be dead before they get here.' All the men looked over, then they all swiftly walked past Sara to Javier. Sara froze with new heightened fear. If Javier died what would their reaction be?

Jase stood up as the gang circled the mattress, and looked down at Javier, the leader spoke, 'If he dies, they pay.'

'Kill them, Joe? What fucking good would that do? This would have all been for nothing, and I for one am not going home empty-handed, and I just promised Javier I would get his share to his family.'

'Questioning my decisions, are you?' both men squared up to each other. The atmosphere was charged with trepidation and tremulous fear, Sara's breathing quickened.

With Joe's short-cropped dark hair, pallid complexion and close-set, flinty eyes and threatening glare, the malicious malice that radiated from him, he commanded with a tyrannical hold over the other members of the gang. Even being shorter than Jase by a few inches, his muscular build, made up for what he lacked in height. No one crossed him without suffering consequences. Sara gave an involuntary shudder.

With lightning reflexes, Joe punched Jase in the stomach and followed this swiftly with an uppercut to the chin, as Jase fell to the floor, Joe kicked him in the ribs several times, and again punched him repeatedly in the face, till Jase didn't move. Breathing heavily, Joe turned to all the others and asked if they had any questions, which was met by a unison of mutterings that they didn't.

Joe then saw Sara looking and said, 'What the fuck are you looking at Bitch?' he marched over and kicked her chair, which tipped over. He continued his stride towards the office, and shouted over his shoulder, 'Get her up.' Two members righted her in the chair, and Sara grimaced as quietly as she could in pain, the backrest of the chair had landed on her arm, which had been pulled back behind her.

A car swerved and screeched to a sudden stop, the rest of the gang rushed to the windows at the front with their guns pulled and cocked. Joe shouted, 'At fucking last, its Nate and Coop, and that had better be a Doctor with them.' He opened the door and yelled, 'About fucking time.'

There was pandemonium going on outside, then a man was launched through the door and he slid across the floor, he had his hands bound behind him, with a blindfold and gag that had both been dislodged, he tried to get to his feet, but was swiftly shoved back down, and told to stay down. Joe walked back in and over to the man and asked, 'Who do we have here?'

'Dr Jayden Hayes, we got lucky whilst out, we noticed a military base, and thought they would have a Doctor, saved us driving all the way into town, which is miles away.'

'You fucking idiots, I told you to get a hospital Doctor, it would've taken a few days for a missing person to be reported, and the police a bit more time to figure out why they have gone missing, but the fucking Military, will be looking for him, *now*, shit.' He paced, then bit out through clenched teeth, 'Leo, Nick, go move all the cars and cover all tracks.'

Nick had the stereotypical look of an Australian, with his bleach blond hair and brawny build, and when Sara saw Leo, it struck her how odd it was, to have a member of a gang with learning disabilities, Nick spoke differently to him, when he explained more simply, the order Joe had just given them, as they walked out the door.

'We saw how bad Javier was, and knew there was little time, we know what he means to you, Joe. When we saw the Military base, Coop and I thought we had saved a lot of time, and save Javier's life,' said Nate.

Joe glared at Nate, then grabbed him around the back of the neck, pulled him close, resting their foreheads together. They were of the same height, and Sara thought that under different circumstances, she would even consider them good looking, with their mixed-race origin and athletic build, but the way they were handling this poor Doctor, totally negated that impression.

Nate looked apprehensive and winced, as if he was expecting pain, then Joe said, 'It's ok you did good, we just need to be even more careful now, and hope he saves him,' he nodded his head in the direction of Jayden, as he lay on the floor.

Coop walked in, carrying a lot of bags and Sara was struck by the similarities between Nate and Coop, obviously related, 'We told him to pack everything he may need and more,' he said to Joe, then walking over to Javier he said to Nate, 'bring him over here.' He dropped the bag on the floor. The blindfold and gag were removed, and his hands were untied, but a gun was pointed at him, and he was told to do everything to save Javier.

'After you've done what you can for Javier, you can take a look at Jase, he still hasn't moved, weak fucker,' said Joe, 'and I suppose he'd better fix your busted nose Nate and relocate Coop's shoulder,' he then walked back to the office and slammed the door.

'What did Jase do Mel,' Coop asked.

'He questioned my brothers' actions. You can imagine how that went down,' he then strode off towards the office and let himself in.

As they shoved Jayden towards Javier, he looked over and spotted Sara, tied to a chair with the plastic underneath, his eyes widened and he asked with concern, 'What are you going to do to her?'

'None of your business, saving *his* life, *is*,' said Nate, as he strode over and pushed Jayden in the back with his foot, Jayden stumbled and Nate moved the bags closer to him, 'hurry, he's lost a lot of blood.'

Jayden set to work, removing supplies from his bag and checked Javier's vital signs. He constantly looked over at Sara. Nate noticed his distraction and stepped in front, blocking his view of Sara and said, 'Stop looking at *her*, and concentrate on *him*,' he still had his gun in his hands, which Sara saw before he turned his back on her.

After checking Javier and giving him a shot of morphine, Jayden said he needed to try and turn him on his side and see if there was an exit wound or if the bullet was lodged. Nate and Coop rolled him onto his side and Jayden said, 'There is an exit wound at the back.'

'Is that good?' Coop asked.

'Good, that the bullet is not lodged and I won't need to look for it, but bad, as it is higher than the entry at the front, which means, its exited through one of his kidneys, but also his stomach and liver. I can try and operate to see exactly where he is bleeding from most, but I have to warn you, there is only a small chance he is going to survive this. When was he shot?'

'Yesterday,' Nate replied.

'I'm surprised he lasted the night without any help. He's lost a lot of blood and I don't have any with me to replace it.'

'We can all give blood,' Coop said hopefully.

'It's not that easy, I can't give him *anyone's*, blood. Do you all know your blood types? Do you know his? Jayden said pointing to Javier.

'Blood group? No idea,' said Coop.

'This is not an ideal situation to carry out the kind of operation I need to do. Have you at least got a table we can put him on, and I need more light.'

'As a Military Doctor, aren't you experienced in these kinds of situations.' Coop asked, as Nate went looking for a table, and turning on all the lights.

'I qualified six months ago, I haven't served in a war zone, if that's what you're asking.'

When they had chosen this place they found an old generator, which Nick managed to get going, saving them buying one when they were setting up, therefore they had electricity for the camera's, which none of the gang knew why so many were needed, they guessed that a ransom video would be done, that much Joe had told them, but still why so many, and they were all wary of pushing Joe for answers, he could fly into unpredictably quick and savage rages, that only his brother Mel could calm, and then, only if he felt so inclined, their quick-fire tempers were one of the similarities the brothers shared.

Jase started to stir and sat up for a while, before attempting to stand, he then staggered to the door and went outside.

Jayden prepared for surgery on Javier, with Coop and Nate helping him, the operating table was set up over in a corner near the window, to give extra light. The main doors opened and Nick and Leo returned from moving the cars and concealing any tracks, as they opened the door to the office, Sara heard Joe tell Nick to prepare the camera's, he wanted to get the ransom video done, and for it to be posted today.

'Who's gonna do the pickup?' asked Mel.

Nick then said his brother Leo could do it, no one would suspect him. Leo was only a member due to Nick's insistence, Joe relied on Nick for his capabilities with anything technical. Nick was telling Joe that Leo wanted to prove his worth and not be useless.

Joe considered this, and asked Mel what he thought, they then turned to Nick and Leo, agreeing that maybe no-one would suspect Leo, as he had mild Down's Syndrome. As Leo left the office to go and keep an eye on Sara, Joe rose from his chair behind the desk, and stood by the door and asked Nick, 'Are you sure Leo can do this?'

'Give him a chance Joe, he knows he can't do much, he looks up to you, and wants to prove he can do something, I'll go with him and tell him what to do, ok?'

'Ok, it may just work, he looks innocent enough, but don't take your eyes off him.'

'Who are we sending the ransom video to?'

'Detective Ricardo Garcia.'

'What? Why him?' Nick responded incredulously, 'he has history with Javier since they were kids in Mexico, by addressing it to him personally, he will know who we are.'

'Javier wants his revenge, that fucker has been a constant bane in his life.'

'What did he do?'

'You don't need to know. I know and that's enough.'

'What's he intending to do?'

'Draw him out and when he gets the chance, take him out. If he does guess it's Javier, he may or may not connect him to me, but if he knows we are working together, he'll know we mean business, no fucking about, what she tells them in the video, he'll know we'll do, no empty threats. I have a plane on standby, one phone call and we are out of here, once we have the money. Wait 'til you hear the amount I'm asking for, *and* Javier gets his revenge on Garcia and *we* make a clean getaway. It's the reason I picked this place.'

Nick looked a little bewildered, Joe rolled his eyes and continued, 'Coz there's a runway out back for a clean getaway, and we can go *anywhere* we like.' Nick smiled and they left the office laughing.

Forty-Two

Mel was holding placards and stood behind the camera, which Nick placed in front of Sara. Joe went over to Jayden and asked how Javier was doing, Jayden told him that he had been constantly muttering in Spanish, and asked if anyone knew what, 'apenado' meant. as he had been fighting the anaesthetic, Joe told him that none of them spoke Spanish.

When Sara heard this, she started thinking about how she could slip a clue into the video. Joe walked to the side of Sara, and yanked her head back by her hair again, and said close to her ear, 'It's showtime, Bitch, this is very simple, you will read *exactly*, what is written on the placards, ok?'

Sara just nodded, no words would come, and she was not sure she would be able to get through this, she was shaking so much, because as Joe had whispered in her ear, he had held a knife just under her chin, and she could feel the point of the knife.

The placards were held above the camera, she faltered when she read the amount they were demanding, it would take a while for this to be put together, no bank would hold that amount. She faltered again when she read out the time given, five days. What if it took longer? What would they do to them? She faltered and stammered when she read out what would be done to them if this demand was not met.

Sara felt sick and dizzy, the chair was making so much noise on the plastic, due to her uncontrollable tremors. Her apprehension ramped up, when Joe approached her, and again yanked her head back by her hair, and said as he towered over her.

'Now you know. That was just a practice, this time you will read it without stuttering.'

He then turned full circle, and with his fist, punched her, full strength, in the stomach. Sara screamed out, and hurled forward, as much as her bindings allowed her, heaved and threw up. Clamping her mouth shut, trying not to cry and give him the satisfaction of showing her weakness. Joe told Leo to clean it up and her, for *this* video, if their demands were not met, then there would be persuasion, in subsequent videos, and she may not look so pretty.

During this *break*, Joe wandered over to check on Javier again, and asked Jayden if he would live, Jayden answered, 'Only if I can stop the bleeding.'

'Then stop the fucking bleeding.'

'Many organs have been affected by the trajectory of the bullet, I have only managed to stop the bleeding in two areas, with this kind of wound, two Surgeons would be working on him, and he would be receiving blood, I don't think he is going to last much longer with all the blood loss, it's incredible he's lasted *this* long, whilst undergoing major surgery in these conditions.'

'Just do it.' Joe walked back to the camera, scowled at Sara, and told her to read.

Sara took some deep breaths and tried to steady her nerves, to be able to read again, their frightening demands. As hard as she tried, it took two further takes. Sara even managed to utter three words in Spanish, feigning pain, as she uttered the words in little louder than a whisper, hoping that the Police will watch the video very closely, and pick them up.

Joe seemed happy with the last take, and told Nick to send that one, as Nick went to the office with the camera, Leo followed. Joe sauntered menacingly towards Sara, with the knife in one hand and the tip of the knife on the finger of his other hand, twirling it over. Her eyes were wide, her body was shaking and she was pleading and begging, 'Please ... no,' over and over.

Joe walked behind her, grabbed her hair in one fist and said, 'So much beauty in such an ugly place.' She could feel her head being jerked back and forth, as he cut her hair with the knife, ruffling her hair when he was done.

'Not so beautiful anymore. '

He scattered her hair on the plastic in front of her, then strode over to the office. Sara jumped at the sound of the office door, as it slammed shut. She sat there fighting to stop the tears from falling, as she would be unable to wipe them away, no doubt he would be gratified to see them, and she was determined not to give him that satisfaction.

Suddenly, there was pandemonium where Jayden, Nate and Coop were with Javier. Jayden had jumped onto the table and was pumping Javier's chest, and Nate and Coop started shouting for Joe, who came running out the office followed by Mel, Nick and Leo. Jase ran in from outside when he heard all the yelling. Jayden shouted that Javier had stopped breathing, Joe hollered and commanded him to save Javier, all the others joined in, barking a barrage of abuse, for Jayden to save Javier.

It seemed an eternity that Jayden was pumping Javier's chest, then he stopped and said he was gone, but Joe was yelling and swearing at Jayden to continue, joined by the others in their plea to save him, but Jayden repeated that he was gone, there was nothing else he could do.

Joe instantly went into a rage, swearing, shouting, throwing, kicking and breaking everything in sight, only Mel was following him trying to calm him, this only seemed to enrage him even more, so he backed off.

Everyone else stood around the table not knowing what to do with themselves. Then Joe went quiet, he was standing outside the room where Bruce was being held. With renewed rage, he threw back the bolt to the door with such velocity he broke the lock, and the bolt flew across the room.

He shouted to Mel, chest heaving, and through gritted teeth, he said, 'Get that fucking bastard out here.' A few minutes later, Bruce was hauled out of the room with his hands once again tied behind his back, and he was hurled across the room, lost his footing, and sprawled across the concrete floor. Joe did a running kick into Bruce's ribs, following this up by alternating punches and kicks, Bruce had no chance to protect himself with his arms tied behind him, and could only draw his knees up to protect his stomach, as his feet were not tied, was able to retaliate with a few kicks, that threw Joe back off balance, but only added to his rage.

Losing all sense of reason, Joe blamed Bruce for Javier's death, 'If you hadn't done that fucking stupid manoeuvre on the Freeway, that bullet would have been for you, and you would be lying on that fucking table now, not Javier, you bastard.'

Bruce was doing himself no favours, by infuriating him further, saying, 'That's what happens when you bring guns to a fight, you fuckwit,' which earnt him a few more hard kicks to the ribs.

Joe shouted to Mel, 'Finish him off, you wanted a rematch, now's your chance, kill the fucker,' he then ran out of energy and slumped to the floor.

Mel went over and crouched in front of him, spoke quietly, 'Yes, I want a rematch, but not like this, a fair fight, in a ring, there's no glory, if he's tied up and at a disadvantage.' He got Joe to his feet, then told the others to secure Bruce back in the other room.

They walked over to Javier and Joe laid both of Javier's hands over his chest and said, 'Goodbye my friend, your revenge is now mine,' without looking up he said, 'Bury him in the woods outside, no markers,' everyone muttered that they would take care of him. Joe and Mel walked outside. A car was heard driving away.

Sara and Bruce were shackled as before, Bruce had his knees drawn up as he recovered, Jayden was bound by rope to his wrists and looped around his ankles, the door was closed, but they were unable to lock it, but heard metal scrape on the door as a makeshift lock, to keep them in. Then it all went eerily quiet. They had taken Javier out to be buried.

Forty-Three

Bruce tried to move and grimaced in pain, he turned and looked at Sara, she sat rigidly, her face so pale, she was trembling, terror in her eyes. Bruce took a deep breath before he asked, 'What did they do to you out there?' Jayden didn't say a word and sat quietly.

Sara lifted her eyes and looked at him and shakily said, 'I know what they intend to do to us … more specifically - me.'

Slowly, she told them what she was forced to read out, it was so horrific, the details came out jumbled, she was shaking profusely, and tears were rolling down her cheeks, that she quickly wiped away with her arms. When she finished telling them all she could remember, Bruce and Jayden sat there in silence, what could they say, what words of comfort could they give, escaping was the only means to avoid what they had in store, and none of them doubted they would carry it out, or at least they didn't doubt Joe would, he would be even more determined, now Javier was dead.

Bruce looked at Sara and said, 'Well he's wrong about one thing – you are still very beautiful, I like the new hairstyle, it suits you,' he gave her an encouraging smile. Sara wiped her eyes on her arms again and returned a weak smile.

He looked at her in wonder, my God, she was brave, again no hysterics, Bruce thought, where did she manage to muster up the courage to smile, after what she had just told him.

While the gang buried Javier, the three of them got to know each other. Jayden told them, 'I'm twenty-eight, after qualifying as a Doctor in New York six months ago, I was on a one-year secondment from my hospital to the Military, after expressing my interest in A&E, and the Military had just lost their Doctor through ill-health early retirement, it was a mutual benefit experiment. Just my luck - wrong place, wrong time,' he looked up and quickly added, 'No offence.'

'None taken, buddy, we don't want to be here either,' Bruce replied with a smile.

'Both of you are hereby accident, but I think I was targeted. Do you remember when we were cornered in that alley, he didn't just ask me to come out, he used my full name, also they set this place up. I heard Joe, the leader mention, and that they can make a clean getaway after they get the money, as there's a landing strip out the back, they have a plane on standby, and would only take one phone call. In that ransom video, I managed to put in three Spanish words, as I heard them say that Javier has history with Detective Ricardo Garcia, worth seeing if he picks up on them.'

'I was hoping you heard when I asked if any of them spoke Spanish. I recognised you straight away, my girlfriend is a huge fan, so I know you speak many languages. My mother is Spanish, we lived there 'til I was ten, when my father's job brought him back to his native New York. I understood all that Javier was muttering.'

'What did he say?' asked Bruce.

'Basically, an apology to his parents, about bringing shame on them for being gay.'

'By the reaction,' Bruce groaned in pain as he tried to move again, 'Easy to guess who his lover was.'

'Doesn't this make you think? All the things you took for granted, now become an integral part of you, I was just on the cusp of asking my girlfriend, Layla, to marry me, and maybe getting cold feet at the magnitude of the commitment. Now, I can't stop thinking of her, and would give anything to have her in my arms right now, asking her to be with me for the rest of my life.'

'That's so beautiful,' said Sara.

Bruce and Sara looked at each other, and a silent secret smile passed between them, that didn't go unnoticed by Jayden, who was lying bound on the floor in front of them, he asked, 'I take it that's happened to the both of you, judging by those smiles?'

The three of them spent the evening talking, telling each other about their careers. Bruce and Sara told Jayden about their amazing week in New York, even finding things to laugh about. A pleasant evening, *if it were anywhere else.*

When the gang returned, Jayden was taken out and returned a while later. Bruce asked what they wanted, Jayden said with a smile, 'I had to reset a nose that you broke, and realign a shoulder you dislocated,' Sara looked at Bruce in amazement and smiled.

There was no food for them that night, not even water, and when they shouted to get attention to ask for some, all they got was a lot of loud banging on the door to, 'Shut the fuck up.'

Forty-Four

Detective Ricardo Garcia, woke up and rubbed his eyes, still feeling tired after yet another long shift, a late night and an early start again this morning. He leaned over and caressed the cheek of his girlfriend, Elise, kissing her cheek, she stirred and turned onto her back, looked up at him and smiled as she said, 'Good morning, handsome,' he returned her smile, leaned in and kissed her lips, she put both her arms around him deepening the kiss, not giving him the chance to get up just yet. He had hardly seen her lately, he worked long hours, but he loved waking every morning before she did, and making love to her in her sleepy state, leaving her content to return to a dreamy slumber.

He got up, turned around and gazed at the beautiful creature in his bed, and a slow smile crept across his face as Elise snuggled down to sleep, with a sated grin on her beautiful face, and her light brown curly hair spread across the pillow, with the rays of the light coming through the window catching the golden tresses in her hair. Ric felt a burst of such pride swell in his chest and couldn't believe his luck when she agreed to move in with him two months ago, after knowing each other for less than a year. They met through work, she was a Social Worker, dealing with teenage and special needs kids.

They complimented and balanced each other in their personalities, he always regarded himself as serious, dark and moody, a product of his peasant upbringing, whereas Elise, was always sunshine to his night, laughter to his seriousness, and she had made him start to even laugh at himself when he was being surly, she had a way of looking at him that resulted in both of them laughing.

He was now always eager to come home, whereas before he would work all the hours, hating the quiet and loneliness when he got home. He had built a reputation at work, for being the first one in, and last to leave. Not so in the last few months, and his partner, Cade, whom he'd worked with for the last ten years, commented on his recent lighter moods. They had joined the force on the same day and got promoted to Detective together. The team had nicked named them the opposites, with Ric's

Mexican looks, Cade was blonde with deep blue eyes, it was also their temperaments, Ric was a little more serious whereas Cade was always the joker.

Elise got on well with Cade's wife Natalie, in fact, it was being Best Man at their wedding, and during the reception, Ric finally gathered up the courage to ask Elise to move in with him. She was such a brilliant cook, and spoiled him with all her delicious dishes, packing him off to work each day with scrumptious sandwiches or wraps, Cade was so jealous, she started packing enough for him as well, it was always the first thing he asked each morning, 'What have we got for lunch today,' which always made them laugh.

Ric wandered into the bathroom, showered and shaved, groaning at his appearance, all these long hours were taking their toll, and he was starting to look older than his thirty-one years.

Growing up in Mexico City, there was just him and his mother, no siblings, and he never knew his father. His mother would evade the issue every time he asked. As he got older, he asked if his father was white, which would explain why he was not as dark as all his friends, it was the only time he gained a clue about him, 'He lives in New York,' was all she said. Eventually, he stopped asking.

On her death bed, she told him that the family she had taken him to, were her parents, his Grandparents. He remembered those visits every Sunday, his mother would knock on the door, as soon as it was answered, the door would be closed, and his mother would try to cover up being upset. He asked why they kept going there, she told him, 'One day, we will be invited in, when we are, I will tell you everything.' That day never came.

As his mother lay dying, she gave him a letter, and told him to read it after she was gone, he took the letter with tears rolling down his cheeks. They spent the evening reminiscing, laughing and crying together. She told him how much she loved him, and how proud she was of the man he had grown into, and that he was like his father. That night she passed away.

He read the letter, it told how she fell in love with his father, but because he wasn't Mexican, her parents wouldn't accept him, and even drove him away at gunpoint, with the threat that she would suffer if he ever returned, he never knew she was pregnant, and when her parents found out, they disowned her and threw her out. Ric was so angry, and he unashamedly cried for the life his mother was forced to live, who desperately wanted her family back. The long hours she worked to keep them fed, and how she could only afford a really small room for them to live in, the injustice of it.

The letter went on to explain that she was given a choice by her family, give the child up and she could return home, but she couldn't do it, he never doubted her love, however hard her life was because of keeping him. The reactions of contempt and cold-shouldering given to his mother, because of how different Ric looked, compared to his friends, and the bullying he endured from some of the boys, but he also had many friends.

The worst bully was Javier, two years older, and a foot taller than Ric at the time, everyone was afraid of him and his gang. It was widely rumoured that Javier preferred younger boys. Walking into the toilets one day, Ric witnessed a younger boy being sexually abused by Javier. He punched Javier hard in each kidney and got the younger boy out of there, but the next day, they all learned that the boy had taken his own life, and the priest had refused the family, his burial in Holy ground, as he had committed suicide. Javier showed no remorse.

When Javier turned his sights on Ric, he fought hard, severely injuring Javier again. The next day he endured a severe retaliation beating from the gang, as Javier looked on. During the beating, through a closing eye, Ric saw the Headmaster run out of the school because of the noise, Ric decided to expose Javier, shouting out how he liked young boys, and how it was his fault, Carlos had taken his life, the Headmaster broke the fight up and questioned the accusations, Javier's father was called. Javier never returned to school. Unfortunately, it didn't mean he moved out of the area, and Ric became his target every day after school, some days he managed to escape, some days, he didn't.

Ric turned eighteen one month after his mother died, he decided to move to New York, and trace his father if he could, now he had his name from his mother's letter. Before he left, he made one last visit to the house his mother took him to, he knocked on the door, it was answered by an elderly lady, he asked for her by name, when she confirmed who she was, he told her that her daughter Maria had died, that he was her grandson. There was no reaction, he said, 'Just thought you ought to know,' he turned around and left without a backward glance. She didn't call after him.

Shaking the sad memory, he washed and dried his face and went into the kitchen, Elise was there and handed him a mug of steaming coffee and lunch for him and Cade. He finished his coffee, drew her into his arms, and kissed her thoroughly, before leaving for the station on the Upper West Side of Manhattan. Before he left, Elise reminded him of the family meal, if he could *try*, and not be late.

He loved his family, the day he turned up on his father's doorstep, he will never forget, immediately his father threw his arms around him and cried, actually cried with happiness, he cried again later with sadness to hear that Maria had passed. It was weird to be glad, that someone else cried over his mother's passing, and sad that it brought sorrow to another person. Even his stepmother wholeheartedly welcomed him, she knew all about Maria, but they didn't know about him. They gave him a home and siblings, he had a half-brother, half-sister, brother-in-law and a nephew he doted on.

As he walked in and went to his desk, Cade told him that the Captain wanted to see them both as soon as he got in. The Captain walked in just after them and told them to sit down, as he closed the door, it was serious then, he never shut the door, normally preferring the ball everyone out who entered his office, for all to hear.

'A down and out drunk walked into the station in the early hours, and reported a kidnapping of a couple by a gang, in one of the dead-end delivery alleys behind shops in Manhattan Valley, although we don't always take what they say seriously, we sent a patrol car to do a drive-by to check it out, they found a black Trans Am, damage to the rear, abandoned with blood on the hood, and three bullet holes in one of the dumpsters. A team have been there for a few hours now retrieving the bullets and securing the area. The car was a rental, paperwork found in the car gave us the name of the company, when contacting them this morning, they told us it was rented to the British Celebrity, Bruce Bailey.'

Ric and Cade raised their eyebrows in recognition at this.

'He called the company yesterday morning, to tell them to pick the car up at JFK Airport, he never made his flight, neither did fellow Brit Celebrity, Sara Kaye. Take a look into it, interview all the shop owners and staff, they may have heard or seen something.'

'When did the kidnapping happen?' Asked Ric.

'Apparently, yesterday morning.'

No need to ask why it took this drunk so long to report it!'

'He said he thought he had hallucinated it, 'til he woke up and saw the car still there, he said a guy shouted at him to get out, he tried to get up, but fell over and passed out.'

'Who's looking into the disappearance of the Military Doctor?' asked Cade.

'What's this?' asked Ric.

'I'll tell you on the way out,' said Cade.

'Jones and Delaware, are taking that one, let me know what you hear, get something before I have to inform the British Embassy, and before the news breaks to the media, they will be all over this, considering they are such huge celebrities,' said the Captain.

As they walked out, Cade told Ric, 'We suspect a Military Doctor has been taken, the medical supplies room was ransacked at the Military base, and large supplies of nearly everything taken, along with many drugs. The Doctor hasn't been with them long, on secondment from Bellevue Hospital. They are not sure if he took the stuff, or if he's been kidnapped, they are looking into his background now.'

'I'd have preferred that assignment, these two are British *and* Celebrities, translated means – long hours and diplomacy, dealing with the British Embassy,' said Ric.

They grabbed their coats and made their way to the scene. As they arrived, the team brought them up to speed on their discoveries, they had taken scrapings of silver paintwork from the back of the Trans Am, and samples of the blood from the hood, but there wasn't as much as they were expecting, considering guns were involved, and the bullets had been retrieved from the dumpster, one had gone through and was embedded in the wall behind, they surmised someone was hiding behind it and it was to scare them, as the bullets were not concentrated in one area, as a target.

Ric and Cade went to the shops first, that had back doors out into the alley, they probed harder, when one owner of an electrical shop acted like he didn't want to be questioned, glancing at some of the equipment through the door to the back, Ric told him, officers would be arriving soon, to take a look at some of the equipment he could see outback, the owner soon admitted that his son had gone out the back yesterday, and came back visibly shaken, but wouldn't tell him what had happened. Ric asked to question his son, only to be told he was at college, after getting the name of the college they were on their way again.

The young boy was only seventeen, and obviously really nervous to be questioned, he told them, he went outside to get rid of box packaging and saw the black Trans Am with its wheels screaming, whilst in reverse to try and force a silver car back, and he also saw another black car blocking the alley further down. He told them that a girl with blond hair was running towards him, he panicked, went back inside and let the door shut, and was too scared, when he then heard a man's voice and a woman, hammering at the door to be opened.

'Did you hear or see anything else?' asked Cade.

'I went upstairs and saw them take hold of the guy, they held a gun to his head on the hood, I think they bashed his head with the gun.'

'Can you give us a description of the gang or at least the guy with the gun?'

'Not from the angle I was to them.'

'Anything else?'

'I then heard, the gunshots, and the girl came out from behind the dumpster.'

'You didn't think to report this?' asked Ric.

'I think you've seen the equipment in my Dad's shop, didn't want to get him into trouble with Police crawling over everything.'

His nervousness, dissolved suddenly, and he appeared more arrogant, did he have more than stolen electrical equipment, and was it he or his Dad running that little racket. They gave the son a ride back to the shop for the team to look into. They returned to the station to update their Captain on what they found so far.

'That little shit could have saved them if he had opened that door,' Ric said exasperated, as they helped themselves to coffee.

'Exactly my thinking,' agreed Cade.

As they sat down, the Captain came out, and they were appraised of details that were now being linked together.

'Traffic reported a car chase on the Freeway yesterday morning, involving a black Trans Am, a silver Chevrolet Camaro and black Dodge Charger, that according to the report, had significant damage to the trunk, following a manoeuvre that took out one of the police pursuit cars. The other patrol flipped over in another daring stunt, the cars disappeared and sightings were lost, before others could apprehend them, the number plates we have were stolen. The cops are in hospital, fortunately, they were not critical and will be able to go home later today.'

Ric and Cade spent the rest of the day reading various reports from other eyewitnesses from the apartments above, piecing together exactly what happened in the alley. Ric started having a little more respect for Bruce Bailey, he had tried to save the girl, but was simply outnumbered. The British Embassy was informed and they were given a direct contact to keep them up to date of their progress, they asked this be kept out of the papers and news for as long as was possible, something they agreed on, once the media were involved it always got more difficult.

The next morning when Ric and Cade arrived, they were informed there was a briefing starting in the next ten minutes. Before Ric moved to go into the briefing, he was stopped by a delivery, marked, *extremely urgent*. When he opened it, there was a scrawled note addressed to him and two names, Bruce & Sara. An icy chill went down Ric's spine, this was not good, and the British Embassy was not going to like this. He went directly into the briefing, as there were a TV and video that was permanently set up, showed this to the Captain and addressed everyone, informing them that it had just arrived, personally addressed to him.

The whole team gasped as the video started, all of them recognised the very beautiful and extremely talented Sara Kaye, tied to a chair, they could see the plastic, and they could hear the total fear in her voice and on her face. When it finished, Ric immediately stood up and asked if he could watch the video again. He told the Captain he heard something, but needed to check it out first.

The Captain outlined to everyone, how they were going to move forward, with the ransom demand, it was an enormous amount of money and impossible to raise in the time given, therefore they would operate a sting and apprehend whoever picks up the money.

Both Ric and Cade objected, saying this would put Bruce and Sara in too much danger. Piecing together what happened in the alley, it was clearly a gang, and they would only send one or two of them to pick up the money, and it would definitely not be the leader.

'It's a chance we will have to take, we cannot raise the kind of money they're demanding, in the time given and to leave less will be just as dangerous, we also don't know who we are dealing with,' the Captain explained.

Ric knew they had no other option. He played the video a few more times, and this time he was sure he heard what he suspected from the first time. Sara had given them clues, feigning pain on three occasions, she had said 'almacen', 'fuera' and 'ciudad'. 'You brilliant, clever girl,' he said under his breath.

He quickly announced over the various conversations, 'She gave us clues in the video, as to where they are being held, a warehouse outside the city. I know this is a little vague, there will be many and we don't know which direction, but obviously, it will be a disused one, which eliminates some, it's a start.' Everyone immediately dispersed to start their search.

'How did she give the clues, the Captain asked, I didn't hear any?'

'She said them in Spanish, obviously none of the gang speak it, and it was subtle, I had to play it a few times to be sure.'

Forty-Five

They were left alone for the next few days, spent mostly shackled, released only to be taken to relieve themselves, food in brown bags thrown to them from the door. They left Jayden's hands tied behind his back in a way that prohibited him from passing them through to his front, and his feet were still bound, but at least the rope that bound his hands and feet together was severed, and he was able to sit up, but it meant that Bruce or Sara had to feed him.

They guessed the gang were waiting for the ransom demand deadline. Five days was what she read out in the ransom video, but they quickly lost perspective of time and started finding games they could play to occupy themselves.

Again guessing, it must be the fifth day, as there was a commotion in the main area, muffled shouting, they only heard some of the words. Those going would be gone overnight, they later found out it was Nick and Leo that were doing the pick-up, they didn't see or hear Joe or Mel, it was either Nate, Coop or Jase they saw who brought them food, when they remembered!

The following day, there was more commotion in the main area as Nick returned, without Leo. He slammed into the warehouse, shouting and swearing. Joe rushed out of the office.

'The fucking police were waiting, course they would be, he had to climb into the fucking dumpster to the get the money, Leo was caught and arrested as he climbed out, that was a fucking stupid idea instructing them to …

Before he could finish the sentence, Joe punched him hard across the face, sending him off balance, he staggered and fell, blood was dripping from his mouth. Nick was surprised and all the gang were standing around apprehensively, waiting to see what would happen next.

Nick didn't get up, just pushed himself to his elbows as he said, 'They've got my little brother Joe, he's never been without me,' he said pleadingly, 'I could only watch as they pushed him against their car, frisked him and handcuffed him, he looked over at me with such fear on his face, then they took him away, he will be so frightened.'

'Will he say anything to the cops?' Joe asked.

'No, I have told him to never give his name to anyone wearing a badge. What are we going to do?'

'Let me think, but don't you ever ... question my decisions again,' he said through gritted teeth and pointing his finger at Nick.

'Ok Joe,' he then cautiously got up and walked away, wiping his lip with the back of his hand and sat on one of the sofas. The rest of the gang gingerly went over and joined him, one of them handed Nick a drink, they all sat there subdued, smoking and drinking.

Joe was in the office with Mel, 'Just as well I have a fall-back plan to get money, it will take longer, but just as lucrative, maybe even more so,' Joe said.

'What's that then?'

'A Snuff movie,' he paused, leaned back in his chair to allow that to sink in, 'think about who we have in there, went after one and got two into the bargain, double the money.'

'Is that why we have so many camera's?'

'Bright boy,' Joe said proudly, 'I had a feeling that the pick-up may not work, they were not going to just give us that money, and I didn't fancy walking around with masks on, those two and the Doctor were never going to be walking out of here. Not only that, one or other of that lot out there were going to let slip our names. That's why I agreed to Leo doing the pick-up, he has difficulty remembering names, the only one will be Nick's, and let's face it, Nick is already their main suspect, being his brother an all.'

'You planned this from the beginning? Why didn't you tell me?'

'Well, if we got the ransom, I may not have bothered with the Snuff movie, too much trouble, it was just back-up insurance.'

'When I looked into this, adding a child ...' but before Joe could finish.

'You sick fucker. The fuck you will harm a child Joe, I won't have it and neither will they,' he pointed to the gang through the office window.

'I'm not going to do anything with the child, but it will make those three … a little more pliant, and will make good screen time, if they *think*, we will do something to the child. Sometimes a threat is more effective than the deed.'

'Wait a minute, a snuff movie is murdering them at the end, that's a whole different level to what everyone signed up for, they may not go for it. And what happens to the child, you going to kill the child too?'

'No, I promise you, we will drop the child off near a hospital, after just frightening them a little, not to reveal who we are, they'll grow out of it, after all, they will be quite young, maybe five or six, no older.'

'Why not just leave a child out of this, there isn't any need Joe?'

Joe didn't answer, and distracted Mel by saying, 'That rematch, no reason not to rig up that ring right here, film it if you like? After all, he's the reason your career ended, he deserves to pay for that, and Javier's death'

Forty-Six

Ric and Cade were in the viewing room with the Captain. Handcuffed and looking frightened, he hadn't said a word.

'We need to be more relaxed when questioning him, I propose bringing in Elise, she specializes in kids with learning disabilities. By treating him gently, he may be more forthcoming with information, if he doesn't feel threatened.' The Captain agreed, and Ric went to make the phone call.

They moved him into another less hostile room by the time Elise arrived, and she had now been talking to him for the past hour, had managed to get his name, Leo. Using friendly language and calm questioning had also ascertained his brother's name, Nick, but he wouldn't say his surname. Food was ordered and Elise sat with him and talked about his favourite foods, but no further names were forthcoming, and it was difficult for him to remember his address.

Elise came out of the room and suggested that they take him on a road trip, and to play it down as to what they were doing, let him tell them things that looked familiar, and for Ric to hide his badge, before he was introduced to him.

They drove around notorious places in Manhattan, asking Leo about his family, and how worried they would be about him. They got nothing.

Suddenly, Leo got excited, and pointed to a diner on a corner, they thought he was hungry again, so they parked up, and went in. Leo was greeted very familiarly by three of the waitresses, they asked how he was and where was Nick, then looked at Ric and Elise suspiciously, as Leo bounded into the diner and sat at one of the tables. Elise said quietly that she was a cousin from out of town, and wanted to treat Leo, asking them what was his favourite. They readily believed that and were pleased that Leo was being given his favourite treat, and went and got his order of chocolate and banana pancakes and a vanilla milkshake. Ric and Elise just ordered coffee.

They wandered over to the table, Elise sat opposite Leo, and Ric took the seat next to her. One of the other waitresses brought the order and started talking to Leo, asking him where his buddies were, Leo put his finger to his lips and made a 'ssh' noise, Elise gently said in a soft friendly tone, 'Oh its ok Leo, you can say who your friends are, everybody needs friends, what are their names?'

The waitress told her in a hushed voice, while Leo was distracted, tucking into his pancakes and milkshake and looking out the window, that he had problems remembering names, then turning to Leo said, 'Where are Joe and Javier, Leo, they are usually with you when you come in here. Again, Leo put his finger to his lips and made a 'ssh' noise.

Ric lost all colour in his face, his eyes went wide, and his whole body stiffened. Elise didn't notice straight away, as her attention was on Leo, as she asked if he lived far from here. Leo shook his head, but said, 'Around the corner, we eat here often, I like the waitresses, they always talk to me, while Nick argues with Joe and Javier. I don't like it when they argued, I want them to be nice to each other, Joe doesn't like me around all the time, but I don't like being on my own, Nick takes me with him. I love my brother. He looks after me.'

Ric sat rigidly still holding onto the end of the table, trying to bring his breathing under control, he then asked, 'Is your name Leo Miller?'

Leo looked up, smiled and said, 'Do you know my brother Nick?'

Ric tampered down his anger and returned a restrained smile and said, 'Yes, do you know where he is? I would love to pay him a visit and say hi.'

'Are you a good friend?'

'I'm a *very,* good friend.'

Leo gave a large goofy grin, and said that Nick was working with Joe and his brother, but couldn't remember his name, but thinks it starts with an M, Ric took another deep breath and said, 'Is that Mel?'

'Yes,' Leo said grinning even more widely, and getting excited by banging his hands on the table, 'You are a very good friend if you know Joe and Mel, but they scare me sometimes.'

Straining to control his tone of voice, Ric asked, 'Where are they today Leo?'

'I have problems with names, and Nick is really smart, he taught me a way to remember things, it has something to do with a cut,' he looked a little pensive, looking up as if he was trying hard to remember, then he suddenly got excited again, and shouted, 'I remember – connect a cut.'

While Elise congratulated Leo on remembering, Ric excused himself to make a call to the team, to centre their attention on Connecticut and disused warehouses, it was still a huge area, and they would have to plan either to start at the centre and work outwards or on the periphery and work their way inwards. Ric returned to the table and asked Leo, if there was anything else, he could remember.

Leo was quiet for a while, he then said, 'Javier was hurt bad and bleeding, everywhere, Coop and Nate brought a Doctor, he was pushing on his chest for a long time. He died. Nick told me what that means, it's the same thing that happened to our mam. Joe was *really* angry.'

'Do you remember the name of the Doctor, Leo.'

'No, but I think it began with a J. Does that help?' Leo's face lit up.

Ric returned a tight strained smile, and said, 'Yes, thank you, Leo. One more thing, do the names Bruce and Sara, sound familiar to you?'

'I think so, but Joe didn't like them at all, and when Javier, died, he *really*, didn't like that man and beat him. When he did that, Nick took me outside, I don't like seeing people get hurt.'

Ric raised his eyes to the ceiling and let out a silent exasperated sigh, as Leo turned to look out of the window again, as he finished his milkshake.

They returned to the station, and Elise made arrangements for Leo to be looked after at one the secure centres for troubled teenagers until decisions were made of what was to happen to him.

They convened a briefing. Ric had called Jones and Delaware to be present, as they were leading a team looking into the kidnapping of the Military Doctor, Jayden Hayes. They now had something to go on, even though it came from a young lad with learning disabilities, and was not completely reliable to connect the two cases, at least it narrowed the search area, of a Military base and a disused warehouse close to each other.

Forty-Seven

Bruce, Sara and Jayden had no idea of days or nights, they had been left in the room and were sick of eating greasy cold takeaways, and never given enough water, that they had rationed it. Jayden's bindings were relaxed enough, that he could bring his hands to his front over his feet as Bruce taught him, and quickly back again when any gang member periodically removed the makeshift lock, to throw them their food and water.

They stopped counting the days by their food deliveries, as these were never regular but noticed the difference in the gang's movements, louder during the day and quieter at night. As Jayden had a little more freedom to move around the room, he found a stone and started making faint markings on the wall for each day. By their combined reckoning, it was now day seven since Bruce and Sara had been taken, and day six for Jayden.

Suddenly, they heard a lot of busy movement in the warehouse area, and the sound of cars outside, they all apprehensively looked at each other, voices from outside got louder and angrier.

The makeshift lock scraped, and the door was flung open, Jayden had no time to return his arms behind him, and none of the gang members, Jase, Coop and Nate seemed to notice, instead, they bound him tightly around his body and untied his feet and pushed him towards the door. Bruce and Sara were unshackled and bound the same way, and taken roughly, out of the room and pushed to the ground. The loud angry shouting they heard earlier was continuing between Joe and Nick, with Mel looking on.

'It's too risky to stay here now, your brother will say something, and give our whereabouts away,' Joe said.

'How can he? he has no fucking sense of direction, can't remember names of people, let alone fucking places, and it was a long fucking drive, from here to New York. There is no way he will be able to direct them here.'

'I ain't taking the fucking chance, the ransom was fucked up, so I have another plan to get us our money. Now take down all the cameras, as I told you to do and stop wasting fucking time. Unbolt those chains and cuffs, Javier fashioned them, they're hard to get hold of,' Joe said getting really close up in Nick's face, they glared at each other for a while, before Nick backed away and did as Joe said and removed the cameras.

'Where are we going?' asked Mel.

'New Jersey. Javier bought some land a few years back and had a massive wood cabin built in the middle of the woods, very secluded, has its own generator, all mod cons. It's near a stream, beautiful it is and a hell of a lot more comfortable than an empty warehouse. There's a large barn, where you can have your rematch, and another to hide all the cars, a great place to hide out for a while, no neighbours close by.'

Their shocked silence, and mutual understanding of hearing so much detailed information from the gang, without any guarded words or secrecy, was a really bad sign, a really frightening one.

Sara froze, then started to visibly shake, and she looked at Bruce with such fear in her eyes, if only he could do something, but his ropes were so tight, they were cutting into him, and he couldn't even get close enough to give some comforting reassurance to her, what could he give her.

This gang didn't mean for them to live through this, they wore no masks, called each other by name and now, giving so much information of where they were moving to.

Once again, all three of them were blindfolded and gagged, then thrown into the trunk of separate cars and the journey felt as infinitely long as the first. Being jostled around in the trunk, Bruce let out strangled groans and shouts, from the pain to his ribs from the ropes. Sharp turns and sudden braking was almost beyond his tolerance, Bruce was glad when he lost consciousness, giving him some peaceful bliss, only to be abruptly awakened by yet another sharp turn, which slammed him against the wheel arch, awakening him with an explosion of pain, with his relaxed body taking the full impact.

Finally, they came to an abrupt stop, the wheels skidding on a gravelly surface and Bruce was jostled around, letting out grunts, as pain shot through his body. The other cars did the same and stones hit the side of the car he was in. He braced himself for the trunk to open, but it didn't, he heard all the car doors open and slam shut and still the trunk remained closed. There followed a lot of activity and raised voices to get the barn organised. It was a long time he lay there, suffering cramps in his legs and arms, he tried to change his position, but due to the restricted space, it was very limited and didn't ease the cramps.

His thoughts wandered to Sara, she was in one of the other cars, he couldn't even call out to reassure her, he just hoped and prayed she was holding up. As time ticked by and still no movement from outside, he started to think about all the time he had spent with Sara, they were even more precious now, as they may be all they would ever have.

Anxious questions clogged his mind, he was finding it increasingly difficult to turn them off – after the ransom failure, were their plans unchanged for what was in store for them? Were their plans worse after what happened to Javier? Could they escape? The chilling fact remained – the gang had never disguised their faces or names. *Joe was not intending for them to live through this.*

White-hot anger and rage surged through him, he kicked at the catch of the trunk over and over, letting out grunts and growls from behind his gag, he caused some dents, but still, the catch held and slowly, after a while his energy waned, he had made no progress, the ropes were too tight for him to get a proper kick at the catch, and all he was doing was exhausting himself and incurring more injuries. All he could do was lay there in the silence and wait.

Bruce let his mind wander to more pleasant thoughts, of his family. His mother would be really anxious, but it was comforting to know that he could rely on his brothers and sister, to be with her and comfort her. He then thought of Sara, her face, her smile, laughter and giggles, each tinged with sadness that he may never see them again, he had to find a way to escape. He started planning, if this was log cabins and barns, from what he overheard from Joe and Mel, there may be possibilities of digging their way out, but with what with and how, if they were kept constantly bound.

Eventually, he could hear voices coming closer and he heard the trunk open, Bruce had no idea if it was day or night. His blindfold and gag weren't removed, as he was forcibly and roughly lifted from the trunk and rolled a few times in the dirt, instead of standing him up, two of them grabbed him by his rope bindings and lifted him. The pain that seared through him took his breath away, he felt sick and dizzy but tried to concentrate his mind by thinking of Sara.

With the gag in his mouth and being carried part of the way then dropped to the ground and rolled, if he were to be sick, he was most likely to choke on his vomit, he concentrated all his efforts on *not* being sick.

Eventually, he was hauled into a sitting position, and he felt his back hit a rough uneven wall, the ropes around him were cut giving him instant relief, his hands were bound separately, and he heard chains as his hands were raised and secured with rope. His blindfold and gag were removed, and a bottle of water was thrust through his lips and water gushed into his mouth, and although desperately welcomed, it made him choke, cough and splutter. The remainder of the water was poured over his face and head, he shook his head and licked around his mouth, to savour what water he could, he didn't get to drink as much as he badly needed.

Bruce looked up to see his hands bound in rope, and looped through chains, they had placed him in the corner of a huge barn, massive double doors at one end, with a smaller door within one of the doors. It was a thick log structure, and a high roof with a ladder up to an empty hayloft, straw was strewn across the hardened dirt ground, there were six horse stalls to one side, with what looked like more half-finished.

Then with sheer horror, he looked at all the cameras that had been placed all around the barn, what the fuck were they for? A really cold chill rippled through his body and he shivered, they were going to film all the things they were going to do to them, the sick fucker.

He then noticed two more sets of chains like his, spaced out either side of the corner he was in, only one of them had the metal cuffs from the warehouse, he had a gnawing feeling of dread, those were going to be for Sara. His face drained of all colour, how was he going to get her out of here, with ropes he may stand a chance, but how could he get the cuffs off her without a key or cutting tools.

Suddenly one of the barn doors opened, and Jayden was thrown in, bound, blindfolded and gagged. He let out a gasp of air, as he hit the ground, and one of the gang rolled him over with his foot, then two of them picked him up under his arms, and dragged him over to one of the sets of chains, and did the same to Jayden as they did to Bruce, untied him, removed his gag and blindfold, rebound his hands in rope and looped them through the chains and gave him water forcefully, Jayden choked and spluttered, but endeavoured to take as much water as he could.

Before departing Nate and Coop administered a swift and crippling punch to the stomach, rendering them breathless and doubled over in pain. Coop snarled, 'That was for Javier,' they both then administered a further kick each to Bruce, saying, 'that's for his nose and my shoulder.' Bruce endeavoured to catch his breath, as the barn door slammed shut and they were left alone.

Taking a moment to recover, Bruce asked, 'Did you hear anything of Sara?'

'No, as soon as they opened the trunk, they grabbed me and threw me in here.'

Bruce started getting very worried, what was taking so long for them to bring her in here, so he could see how she was, he was desperate to see her. Minutes ticked by, and still, the barn doors remained shut, Bruce strained to hear any movement from outside, the barn was so large and the doors were a long way from them, he heard nothing.

They both started looking around for means of escape, the barn was very well built, the ground was extremely hard, and there were no tools or implements of any kind within their immediate area, they both stood up to see if they could do anything with the ropes, but they were bound tight and the knots were intricate, they were spaced too far apart to help each other. For a long time, they endeavoured with the ropes, but made no headway, they sat down again, and Bruce leaned his head back, and looked up at the roof, and worried about Sara. There was nothing he could do.

Forty-Eight

Sara laid in the dark, petrified, her breathing was short and shallow, each time she heard one of the car doors open and close, she thought she would be next. She was extremely panicked by what they were going to do to her. She tried to roll onto her back, but the rope knots dug into her skin, so she rolled onto her other side, this made her nervous, as she would be facing away from the opening when they came for her, so she only laid on that side for a little while.

After all the commotion of their arrival and the gang getting themselves organised, there was eery silence, for so long, she thought they had forgotten her. Then she heard kicking from one then the other car and guessed that Bruce and Jayden were trying to dislodge the catch, she tried to do the same, she had always been strong in her legs but to no avail. She heard Bruce, then Jayden being taken from the other cars, then more silence.

It felt like an eternity lying there in the dark and the silence, with no idea of what was in store for them, had changed, and be far worse now. Please God – no, Sara pleaded. This cold chilling thought flooded Sara's system with adrenaline, her heart pumps and beats so fast, like it's trying to escape or explode, she squeezes her eyes shut behind her blindfold, as the adrenaline surges so fast, it makes her almost vomit, and beads of sweat trickle down her brow. She tries to calm herself by taking deep breaths, through her nose in, to a count of five, and out to a count of five, and thought of Bruce. He was the only thing that made her feel safe, which made no sense in this situation, but Sara grasped whatever comfort she could.

Slowly, she was aware of footsteps, as they crunch in the gravel and she hears the trunk open, she is grabbed and hauled out. Fear barrels through her whole being, and Sara frantically shrieks behind her gag, as she is half carried and half dragged. They don't say a word to her, and she feels her legs graze on steps, they didn't bother to lift her or tell her, she lets out a strangled cry. She hears a door open and is aware of more voices, they must all be together, then she hears Joe's voice, 'Put that bitch over there.'

As she's dragged further she hears plastic crinkle under her feet, she's then dumped roughly on a chair, they didn't bother to remove the ropes around her, they just added more, by tying her to the chair, her arms are pulled tighter around the back of the chair, which made her shoulders ache.

She heard footsteps approach over the plastic, her blindfold was whipped off, and her gag was forced down over her chin, reeling back in shock to see Joe bent over her, with his face so close to hers, she could smell his putrid breath.

He snarls through gritted teeth, 'You have no idea how much I hate you, but let me give you a demonstration,' he gave her a sharp hard backhander, which snapped her head to the side, followed by a punch that sent her head the other way.

Sara let out a scream at the searing pain in her jaw, and felt like a back tooth had loosened, she felt sick with fear. Indecision warred within her as to whether she should ask why he hated her so much, for now, she stayed quiet. Joe had walked away and as she caught her breath, and the pain subsided, she looked around the room, it was a large log cabin with comfy sofa's in a lounge area, an open plan fitted kitchen, the area she was sitting, the dining area. Her chair was on plastic, as she had suspected, and there was a wooden dining table close to her, with two large windows front and back, looking out onto densely wooded grounds.

Joe returned holding a knife with a six-inch blade in his hand, Sara froze when she saw it and began trembling, her eyes were wide and her chin quivering, tears fell as she started pleading and begging, asking why he hated her? What had she done?

'That's exactly what I used to ask, I was five years old, and do you know what she did? – She laughed.'

Sara was bewildered, 'Who?' was the only shaky word she could muster.

'You look very much like her. I hated her, I hate you, and all your kind.'

He walked behind her and cut the rope that bound her hands, walking a full circle around the chair he pulled the table closer and raised Sara's left hand and slammed it flat on the table, with a quick movement, he stabbed the knife through her hand, skewering it to the table.

Sara let out a high-pitched scream, she was finding it hard to breathe, and had never experienced such intense searing pain. Then she was breathing fast and hard, tears were rolling down her cheeks as she sobbed so hard through the pain. Without any reprieve, Joe turned and slapped her across the face and told her to, 'Shut the fuck up.' Sara clamped her lips together, but small whimpers escaped, she tried to stifle them. She was so afraid to look at her hand, the pain was making her feel sick, and if she looked, she may not be able to contain it, and that will only infuriate him even more.

Sara forced herself to take deep, slow breaths in, to a count of five and out to a count of five, after a while, the pain subsided to a constant throbbing sensation, she could feel herself perspiring profusely, with sweat trickling down her brow, her back and chest, she had to calm herself, or she was going to vomit, she leaned her head against the table until she got her breathing and heart rate under control.

Then slowly lifted her head, her hair was in her eyes, through the strands she surveyed the gang, they were sitting around and all had their eyes on her, a few with a surprised expression, maybe some didn't know he had that planned, but none of them said anything, Joe was very much in command of them all. He was seated across from her, maintaining a hard stare, without looking away from her, he told Jase and Nick to, 'Go get the boyfriend,' he then gave her a smile that had the undertones of a sneer. Sara rested her head on her good hand on the table.

Forty-Nine

Bruce was frog marched into the cabin, his hands bound behind him, with a gun jabbed into his ribs. Immediately he saw Sara, he is pushed forward when his steps faltered, his face drained of colour, his jaw goes slack as his brain stutters, trying to take in the scene before him. He couldn't believe what they had done to her. He felt like it was playing out in slow motion.

Sara was sitting there with her head resting on her hand on the table, a serrated knife plunged through her other hand and blood, what else had they done, she wasn't moving, he made an urgent move forward towards her, but was held back, and the gun jammed harder into his ribs, which made him wince.

'You fucking coward,' Bruce shouted as he locked eyes with Joe, he lunged forward again, only to be held back and jabbed hard in the kidneys with the gun. It felt like all the air had been knocked out of his lungs as the burning pain lanced through his entire body, and he dropped to his knees. Joe produced a gun and held it to Sara's head and said, 'Sit the fuck down. Another move and I'll take the safety off.'

Bruce was lifted under his arms and slung into the seat to Sara's left side, he looked at her face that was turned towards him and gently said her name. Her eyes opened, then she squeezed them shut as she took a breath in, on a gasp, struggling with the pain, she raised her head, he then saw redness forming on her jaw.

Joe moved around the table and sat opposite Bruce, keeping the gun trained on Sara. Bruce felt the rage burn within him, 'You really are the lowest kind of coward to do this to a woman.'

'Oh, a woman is capable of doing far worse than this *and* enjoy it whilst doing it.'

'Is that what this is? A woman hurt you? or is it mummy issues.'

'Shut the fuck up.' Joe leapt from his seat, rounded the table and hit Bruce's head, with the butt of the gun, which sent him flying off balance, with his seat crashing to the floor, he was seeing stars, he concentrated on not losing consciousness.

The rest of the gang were still seated, a few rose out of their seats, unsure what to do. 'Get him up,' Joe said, looking around at the gang, as he returned to his seat opposite Bruce, he then pushed Sara's head back down on the table, and held the gun to her temple, looked at Bruce and said, 'Now remove the knife.'

Sara's eyes flew open wide with fear and sheer terror, he could see her shaking and tears were rolling onto the table. This was tearing him apart to see her like this, he desperately wanted to take her pain, her fear and her terror away, but all he could do was hold her gaze, and try to transmit silent reassurance.

'Do it,' Joe snarled, through gritted teeth, he nodded to one of the gang and his hands were cut free, 'And if you think of doing anything with that knife …' He didn't finish the sentence, instead cocked the gun he was holding against Sara's head.

'You fucking bastard,' Bruce said, his voice cracking and his eyes glistening, fighting to keep any tears falling, this was the hardest thing in his whole life that he had ever been asked to do.

Struggling to get his emotions under control, he looked back at Sara and whispered, 'Take some deep breaths, concentrate on your breathing and your heart rate, I'm with you, it's you and me, just keep looking at me, ok?' Sara nodded against the table, and he heard her exhale.

Bruce took a silent deep breath, he knew that to warn Sara, when he was going to do it, would make her tense, best she didn't know the exact moment. With a quick movement, he grabbed hold of the knife and simultaneously pulled it out. Sara let out a massive scream and was sobbing and trembling.

Joe leaned over her and whispered in her ear, 'Now that wasn't so bad, was it?' he shoved her head forward, got up and walked away.

As soon as the knife was out, Bruce threw it across the room, it embedded itself in the log wall opposite, he quickly grabbed Sara's hand to try and stem the bleeding. Joe casually strolled away. Bruce was out of his seat in an instant, leaving one hand on Sara's hand, he wrapped the other around her shoulders as she slumped in the chair, he was whispering encouragement to her, telling her he was with her. He looked around for anything to wrap around her hand, and saw some cotton napkins on the table, and quickly took one, shook it out and made a bandage around her hand, tying a tight knot to try and stem the blood flow.

He wanted to soothe her and say he loved her, but not here, not now, not in the midst of all this ugliness, he wanted her to hear him, know that he meant it. He had to find a way out, a way to escape, then he would tell her, love her and spend the rest of his life with her, he had felt this before they had been taken. This grotesque situation had not in any way made his decision and he would spend the rest of his days convincing her of that. They were not going to perish here, not like this, of that he was determined. It was the only thing that was giving him hope.

He looked into her beautiful face, that was so pale and glistening, he kissed her forehead as he whispered, 'Please stay with me, my love, I can't lose you,' her head rolled to the side, she had lost consciousness.

'Take them back to the barn – and clean that mess up,' he heard Joe say, as he slammed out of the cabin, then shortly after, heard a car roar away, and the sound of gravel spraying everywhere.

Nate and Coop came around to cut Sara's ropes, Bruce refused to move away, and growled through his teeth, 'I will carry her back, no one else,' he threw them a challenging glare, neither of them argued. He gently nestled her injured hand in her lap, and tenderly picked her up into his arms.

They walked through the barn, with Nate and Coop trailing behind, both with guns in their hands, trained on Bruce's back.

They reached the back of the barn, Bruce lowered Sara to the floor in front of Jayden, then turned to Nate and Coop and said, 'Jayden needs to take a look at her, did you bring those medical supplies? he could use them – please? he pleaded. Nate and Coop looked uncertainly at each other, and then back at the barn doors, Bruce said, 'Please, she is losing so much blood.'

'Alright, but one false move and your efforts will be in vain, she gets it.'

'No false moves,' Bruce assured, as he looked at Jayden, who nodded his agreement.

Nate went to get the medical supplies, as Coop kept his gun in sight. When Nate returned and threw the supplies to the side of Jayden, he then untied him. Jayden set to work organising what he needed after he had examined Sara's hand that Bruce was holding, and wouldn't let go.

'The good news is the knife was small and where it's gone through, hasn't hit any major tendons, let me clean it up first, it may need stitches and I have antibiotics I can give her, its good she's out.'

Jayden worked quickly, cleaning and stitching the wound both sides and then bandaged it up. As soon as he was finished, Nate and Coop didn't waste time tying them up again, even Sara. Bruce pleaded with them to let her recover lying down, but they wouldn't listen, they said they couldn't take the chance, Joe would be really angry if she was not secured.

Bruce couldn't sleep, he worried about Sara all night long, Jayden offered to take shifts, but Bruce said he wouldn't be able to sleep anyway, and told Jayden to rest, he may be needed tomorrow when Sara woke if, they allowed him to check her.

It was a very long night, he noticed the periodic activation of the red lights on the cameras, they must have a live feed, or it was time programmed to record. Bruce warred with the temptation to react and shout obscenities, or to stay still and make it very boring to watch, he chose the latter, and not give Joe the satisfaction, Bruce wasn't sure if there was sound, and him shouting at the camera without sound would only make him look like a lunatic.

Sara stirred a few times, and Bruce spoke quietly to her, reassuring her and she went back to sleep, as uncomfortable as it was sitting up, with her head hung forward, she was going to have a creek in her neck and there was not a damn thing he could do to make her more comfortable.

In the still of the night and when the cameras were not working, Bruce whispered, 'I'm so sorry I couldn't protect you Sara and save you from this, but I will do all I can to get us out of here.'

'I'm with you on that one buddy,' Jayden whispered. Bruce had not been aware that Jayden was awake. 'I want to see my girl and make her my wife, and I'll be damned if I'll let this lot take that away from me.'

Fifty

Ric and Cade had spent the past three weeks putting together a file on Joe and Mel Forbes, Javier Rodriguez, Nick and Leo Miller. Due to Joe and Mel having been under the protection of Social Services they had been able to piece together substantial information on their childhood.

They convened a briefing to outline the reports they had, and the information they still needed on the rest of the gang. Reports had been coming in from people whose apartments overlooked the alley, and they now knew there were eight in the gang and they only had five names, they still needed to find out who the other three were.

Ric started to brief the team with what they had. 'Joe Forbes, we believe he is the leader, 32 years of age, 5'9" in height, black hair, his last photo showed he sported a moustache, he has a prominent beak-like nose, dark brown eyes and stocky build. Sexually and physically abused by his mother from a very young age, the father left the family after Mel, the brother was born. Mel Forbes 29 years of age, 5'10" in height, light brown hair, amber coloured eyes with a similar stocky build to his brothers. Social Services had been involved, but each time they got close, the mother upped and moved to another state. Working with Social Services and Police Precincts in various States, we have managed to piece together what happened in their childhood. Joe endured the abuse but snapped and killed the mother when he found out she was now turning her sights on the brother Mel, from four years of age.' Ric paused to let that information sink in, then continued.

'After extensive court actions, it was deemed more beneficial for both the boys to be put into foster care. They were so young, there was the hope that with love and care they could have grown to be well-adjusted boys and the memories would fade. Joe was very protective over his brother and insisted that they not be parted, wherever it was possible they were placed together, but as they grew into teenagers, darker behaviour started to manifest in Joe, he was cruel to insects and animals, he received extensive therapy, but the behaviour became more frequent and got more gruesome, many foster carers found him difficult to handle, they were moved around from foster home to foster home for a while.'

Cade took over, 'When the abuse started for Mel, being so much younger and possibly with the protection he received from Joe, he didn't seem so affected and was much easier to handle, therefore it was decided to separate the brothers, which sent Joe over the edge, he started stealing from the foster families. Small items at first, that didn't get noticed, i.e. jewellery, then got more confident and sold larger items. When they were unable to find foster families that would take him, he spent many spells in more secure children's homes, committing crimes that were difficult to prove, but Joe was their suspect, every time. As he got older and given 'privileges' for periods of *good behaviour*, the crimes became more serious, he was very clever and although known to the Police, each crime where they suspected Joe, they couldn't gather enough evidence to convict him. Instead of moving around, he stayed in the same State. As you know Social Services would endeavour to keep Mel safe from Joe's unstable influence, but Joe found out where Mel was staying and secretly kept in contact with his brother.'

Ric continued, 'When Mel was eighteen and no longer under the protection of Social Services, Joe and Mel teamed up. Mel had adjusted quite well, he graduated from school and was into sports, kick-boxing in particular and entered international championships. A year later both Mel and Bruce Bailey were matched for a fight, Mel lost his temper and ignored the strict rules of conduct, the match had finished, Bruce was declared Champion, Mel took this really badly, committed an illegal move causing Bruce a serious knee injury which ended his Kick-Boxing career, Mel was subsequently disqualified, bringing *his* career to an end in the sport.

'Do we have any information on the others?' one of the Detectives asked.

Ric answered this, 'Leo Miller has learning disabilities and he has a brother Nick, I am pretty sure he would have been looking on when we arrested Leo as he attempted to collect the ransom, we found their address, had a warrant to search their premises, we didn't find much, minimal drugs. It was obvious they had packed, there was very little clothing left and neighbours said they hadn't seen them for a while. We learned from Leo that Javier died, we don't know how or exactly when. I knew Javier Rodriguez when I was growing up in Mexico, he was a particularly vicious and nasty person with psychopathic tendencies, he never showed any remorse for the things he did. With what we know about Joe and that he and Javier know each other, I can only tell you this is really *not* good news for Bruce and Sara.'

Cade continued, 'We know there were eight gang members in that alley, therefore we need the names of the other three. Look into all the people Joe, Mel, Nick, Leo and Javier know, talk to neighbours, friends, places they frequented, anything and everything, we need to know who we are dealing with. We are also still searching all empty warehouses close to military bases in Connecticut.'

'Are we now linking the kidnapping of the Military Doctor Jayden Hayes, with the same gang that kidnapped Bruce Bailey and Sara Kaye?'

'Yes, we are for now, with the information given in code by Sara in the video, and with what Leo has told us, we cannot discount it, Jones and Delaware are leading on that investigation.'

He was interrupted by noisy activity outside the briefing room, and Ric could hear his name being hailed, Ric went to the door as a Patrol Officer came rushing towards him, saying he had been sent to inform him that the derelict warehouse they had been searching for, had been located, Ric asked, 'What's the situation there?'

'It's empty sir, they've left.'

'How do we know it was the right one if it's empty?' Ric was running for his coat, followed closely by Cade.

'There was a camera with a cassette in it, left in one of the smaller offices and forensics are looking at it now, I was told before coming here that they have identified Sara and Bruce and there is another captive, possibly Jayden Hayes on the recording.'

'How careless of them to leave that piece of evidence, but a very welcome boon for us,' Ric shouted, over his shoulder to Cade as they ran out to their car to get to the warehouse.

Fifty-One

When they arrived, forensics were everywhere. Ric and Cade were updated that there was a table soaked in blood like there had been an operation, there was also a small amount of blood on the plastic where the chair was, samples have been taken. There was also a lot of long blond hair on the plastic, like it had been hacked off. Ric felt a cold shiver, *an operation*, dear God, please don't say they had tortured the captives? no - wait, Leo said that Javier was injured, it was most likely his blood on the table and the blood on the plastic would most likely be Sara's, Joe wasn't above hitting a female. 'Check the grounds for any disturbed ground, they must have buried Javier somewhere.' Ric called out to the team.

'Yes sir', one of them replied.

He had been interrupted at the briefing and hadn't got round to telling the team, that he and Cade had found out that Joe was married, they managed to get an address for his wife Hailey, two sons, Joe Jnr aged twelve, Ryan aged ten and daughter Ruby aged eight. She told them she had no idea where he was, hadn't seen him for three months, she had moved several times to try and escape him, but each time he had found them, last time he had threatened that if she moved again and he found her, she would pay severely, that was the only reason she had stayed put.

She told them, he only turned up when he felt like it to see the kids or for sex, which was just to control and humiliate her and he was lousy at it, could only perform if it was perverted and violent, there had never been any love in the relationship and she was sure he was more into men. She had no idea what he did when he left and she didn't see him for weeks on end, he had no interest at all in his daughter. Whatever he had done this time, she hoped they would throw away the key on him, his influence was really bad on the boys, especially the eldest. Every time he came round, there was always problems getting Joe Jnr to settle again, he wanted to be with his father, only his father didn't want him, he just liked stirring trouble, and didn't really have time for them.

After seeing all there was to see at the warehouse and knowing the team had taken all the evidence, Ric told them to keep him informed when they found Javier's grave. He and Cade headed back to pay a visit to the Forensics Department to see the video. Matt who had been scrutinizing the video, told them that Jones and Delaware had identified the other captive in the video was indeed, Jayden Hayes. Ric asked if there were signs of any of them being tortured, Matt said there was none on the video, but they were definitely being beaten, Sara returned at one time with a cut lip and her hair had been cut, Bruce had also returned beaten, Jayden had been pushed and shoved into and out of the room, but from the video, there were no evident injuries.

'You may want to watch some of this, it's worrying that they install a camera, but don't even attempt to cover or even hide their faces. I hear you still have three of the gang to identify, do you know any of these? Matt asked.

As they watched the video, Ric and Cade had no trouble identifying the other three members. 'That's Jason Taylor, Nate and Cooper Wilson, cousins,' Ric said looking anxiously at Cade, 'this is a really bad mix.'

'Damn it,' Ric said with frustration, as they returned to their offices via the coffee station. Sipping their coffees, before they faced the Captain to update him. 'He is not going to like this, not one little bit, and we have no idea where they are, they could be anywhere, we don't have a clue where to look and no idea what their next move will be, why the camera?'

As they wandered over to the crime chart, Cade looked at the photos they had, then exclaimed, 'Oh my God.'

'What?' Ric said.

'Look at the picture of the mother, Joe and Mel's mother, now look at the picture of Sara, notice the similarities? Both have long blond hair and didn't they say, Sara's hair had been cut or more precisely, hacked? The abuse Joe and Mel, particularly Joe, when they were young, is enough to affect anyone.'

'Fuck – you're right, didn't one of the witnesses say in their statement that they heard Sara's full name being called out – they targeted her, this was no opportune kidnapping, it was planned, but why the camera?

'We don't know if that was the only one or if there were more.'

'Let's get the team to take another look around and see if there is evidence of other camera's having been taken down,' said Ric.

'I'll make that call, you need to update the Captain, he is really not going to like the fact that we can only wait for their next move, and the

British Embassy are on our backs for information, this is not going to go down well.'

'Oh no, you don't get out of it that easy buddy,' Ric said smiling, 'I need to check on a detail, will meet you in his office.'

'So close – damn, ok see you in five,' Cade laughed as he walked away.

Fifteen minutes later they meet in the Captain's office, to appraise him of the situation and all the information they have gathered.

Cade started, 'Various members of the gang are wanted in other States for crimes including, drugs, armed robbery, and the recent kidnapping in Ohio of a young woman in her early twenties, the main suspect is Joe Forbes, the investigating officer is on his way, to update us and help. In this case, the young woman managed to escape, but is traumatised, and hasn't been able to speak of the event, as yet and is receiving treatment for her injuries.'

'We are not going to be able to keep this out of the press much longer, they are going to go crazy when this breaks,' Ric said.

'I'll deal with the British Embassy. Can you both meet with this Detective … Logan Brody? he should be arriving in the next few hours.'

'Will do Captain.' They both left his office and made their way back to their desks, Ric's phone was ringing, he answered and asked, 'How many? … How sure are you that it was recent?' … Ok, thanks, Frank.' Ric replaced the receiver and looked at Cade, 'They think there were at least nine other cameras, the same amount of screw holes as the camera that was left, and all recent.'

Cade's face suddenly contorted, his upper lips curled and the corners dropped as he said in a low disgusted tone, 'He's making a snuff movie. You don't need that many cameras to keep an eye on someone, look at who they have. There's a market for them, full of low life's who'd pay a premium for them. Would also explain why they didn't disguise or cover their faces – they have no intentions of letting them go.'

Ric looked at him with his mouth gaping and wide-open eyes, his hand came up to cover his mouth which slid through his hair as he looked down and said, 'Fuck – we need to talk to this Logan Brody, as soon as he gets here.'

'Did I hear my name?'

Ric and Cade spun round to see a well-built young man standing at over six feet with blond wavy hair and green eyes, about their age, they had been expecting an older Detective. As he walked closer the three of them drew eye level.

'Logan Brody, I take it?' Ric said, they shook hands and Cade did the same.

'Pleased to meet you, wish it were under other circumstances though.'

'Your accent, are you British?' asked Cade.

'Yes, I am. Been working over here for the last five years, girlfriend is American.'

'Well, you may be just the person to help us, considering we are investigating the kidnapping of two Brits. The British Embassy is already involved and awaiting more information.'

'Shit, damn him,' Logan said through gritted teeth as he stepped back, looked down and putting one hand in his trouser pocket and rubbing the back of his neck with the other in an agitated motion, 'I was hurriedly briefed when I left and told only to share and gather information on recent activities of Joe Forbes, who did he kidnap?'

Ric and Cade went through everything they knew so far and witnessed Logan's face go through a kaleidoscope of expressions at the magnitude of the situation.

'Both are huge celebrities in Britain. If you have no further clues as to where they can be, you do realise we will have to call a press conference? usually, I hate the media, but in these circumstances, they and the public may be able to help, if nothing else, the gang will know, that we know who they are, and sightings will give us an idea of where to look for them.'

'Hate to agree with you on that one, can't see we have any other option,' said Ric.

'What about the young lady who escaped, what can you tell us about her?' asked Cade.

'Her name is Katherine Tamaro, a twenty-four-year-old Med student from Italian immigrant parents, her family are with her, but she is so traumatised, she hasn't spoken yet. From her injuries, I can tell you, she was tortured.'

At this, all three of them expressed their imprecations. 'She has or *had*, long blond hair, which was the same as Joe and Mel's mothers and we believe, in his sick, twisted and distorted mind, is his way of revenge for what his mother did to them.

'Well that explains – why he targeted Sara, the blond hair the celebrity status, a bonus, in his own mind, I figure Bruce just happened to be with her and why he was taken, but we don't believe he was targeted, but considering the history between Bruce and Mel, there will probably be a rematch,' said Cade.

'Do you know how Katherine escaped?' Cade asked Logan,

'Until she starts talking, we won't know for sure, she had severe rope marks around her wrists and must have somehow, slipped them and dug her way out from somewhere, her fingers and nails were in a really bad state, how she did that with her injuries … she was picked up limping and staggering along a highway by one of our Officers. She was so petrified, she kept looking behind her and would only sit in the footwell of the car as he brought her back. She was taken to hospital where they sedated her, initially. Since then she refuses to say a word.'

'Ok, I will get the press conference set up, Logan can you deal with the British Embassy?' Logan nodded and left to make the calls. 'I'll also update the Captain. Cade can you go over the video again and see if there is anything else we can gather from it, liaise with forensics.'

'Will do.' They all separated.

Fifty-Two

It was early evening, and the whole gang were sitting together in the cabin after Nick and Jase had returned from replenishing the supplies. Nate and Coop had checked their captives, ensuring they were secure for the night, having given them their meagre meal.

They were now in the log cabin. Jase was the cook amongst them, and they had just finished their meal and had the TV on, although none were paying attention to it, Nate and Coop were playing cards, Jase was clearing up the kitchen, Nick was quietly strumming on his guitar, Joe and Mel were playing a game of darts, they were all drinking beer. The news came on and a special press conference was announced. As their names were revealed one by one with a short description of them, a list of their crimes, locations and dates committed, their police photographs were displayed on the screen.

There was instant silence, the gang were all transfixed on the TV now. Joe recognised Ricardo Garcia, Javier's adversary since childhood who was making the announcement. Sara Kaye and Bruce Bailey and also a Military Doctor Jayden Hayes had been kidnapped, giving the dates they had been taken, that the British Embassy and the FBI were involved and asked the public to be vigilant, but not to approach as they were all very dangerous. They were reporting that this was being linked to the kidnapping of a twenty-four-year-old Medical Student in Ohio, who had survived and that Joe Forbes was their main suspect in this case.

As the first part of the conference came to an end, the press wasted no time and went into overdrive firing questions.

Joe exploded and went ballistic, kicking the TV over which shorted out, he followed this by throwing everything in sight at it, yelling and shouting, 'How the fuck do they know all of us,' he then stopped suddenly and looked at Nick. 'Did you leave a fucking camera behind?'

'Not sure, I didn't count them and you wanted to leave in such a hurry, I may have missed one.'

'Not sure? You put the fucking things up, and we have been here for three fucking weeks, did you not bother counting in all that time, when you got the fucking barn ready, did you not notice?'

'No. Different buildings and why the fuck do we need so many cameras anyway, what are they for? And why are we not wearing masks? Maybe if we had we wouldn't have been recognised.'

In two strides, Joe reached Nick, without warning, punched him in the face, followed by a volley of punches, while shouting a stream of obscenities, Nick didn't retaliate he was just guarding himself and rolling on the floor to avoid punches in the same place, eventually, Mel stepped in, pulled Joe back and told him they needed Nick.

Joe was breathing hard, shook Mel off him and told Nick to find somewhere else to be for the night, Joe continued, saying, 'Between you and your idiot brother …' before he could finish the sentence, Nick turned around and landed one punch that knocked Joe off his feet and he went sprawling across the dining table.

'Say one more word about my brother and it will be your last, you hear?' He didn't bother to wait for a reply, slung open the front door, lurched through it and didn't bother closing it.

Joe stood up, grabbed the car keys and left the cabin, Mel followed him.

Jase who had stayed seated at the breakfast bar throughout said, 'I for one would like answers to those questions Nick asked. Joe keeps things to himself and only tells us what he thinks we need to know, now we're all in this, he owes us a full explanation. Three weeks and we have just been sitting here, there's only so much fishing I can stomach,' Nate and Coop grunted their agreement.

Fifty-Three

Bruce was blown away by the courage Sara had been displaying since Joe had injured her hand, he admired her stoic approach, there were no tears or hysterics, only a little wincing and gritting her teeth during some of the dressing changes, Jayden had been allowed to tend to her wound daily, thankfully no infection had set in. Bruce got angry each time her hand was put into the metal cuffs.

Jayden had been discretely marking the passing of the days as they had windows in the barn, after he found a stone and hid it when he did a dressing and was marking one of the logs, therefore they knew it had been four weeks since they had been taken, three weeks since arriving at the Cabin.

The days were long and the nights even longer, they had long given up on trying to work out why they had been taken or what their intentions were, every time one of them came to the barn it was only to allow them to relieve themselves or unlock one hand so they could eat and drink.

Until one day about two weeks ago they started to erect a partition in wood logs, with a door in the middle that was locked, they were thankful that there was a window so that it wasn't totally dark and they still had awareness of the passing days, although they debated whether this was a good or bad thing.

They each talked about their lives, their families, they laughed by telling each other silly jokes, playing silly word games, but always kept the hope that they would live through this and see their friends and families again.

Joe had made several appearances, each time he scowled at Sara with such hatred and had reopened her wound on one occasion by squeezing her hand so tightly, Sara had screamed, cried and pleaded for him to stop, it only seemed to incite his actions further. Bruce could see blood dripping through his grip, he had shouted and tried to kick out, Jayden had done the same, it was totally futile, Joe stood too far away, it was clear he was not going to stop until he was satisfied he had incurred sufficient damage.

He released her hand and wiped the blood on a handful of straw from the floor, discarded it and walked out.

Sara sat there with tears rolling down her cheeks trying to stifle her cries. It wasn't till Nate and Coop had brought their food, hours later that Jayden was released and could tend her wound again, and give her some pain relief and comfort her, they refused to release Bruce. He felt frustrated and inadequate.

That night she hardly slept, waking and bravely trying not to call out as the pain relief wore off, they weren't checked on until the morning, by this time Sara was finally sleeping, Bruce's request that her food be left for her to eat later was ignored, and Nate kicked Sara awake with his boot, saying if she didn't eat now, she could go hungry.

Sara stirred and screeched in pain when her injured hand was released instead of her other hand for her to eat, Bruce and Jayden argued that her injured hand was useless to be able to grip the food, again they were ignored and Nate just walked out without another word.

Sara endeavoured bravely to eat, but her appetite had depleted, but if she didn't eat, there would be less delivered later. The little food they were given, was always accompanied by the threat that there may not be any later, therefore they rationed their food and water hiding it behind them.

The only relief they had from sitting was standing, the chains were not very long, but they found ingenious ways to exercise with the limited movement they had, to keep up their strength in case they needed to fight their way out, Jayden and Bruce kept trying to outdo each other, which reduced Sara to fits of giggles, Bruce loved the sound and played to his audience.

The second injury was now healing nicely, and Joe had left them relatively alone in the last week, but not enough that they forgot the danger and uncertainty they were in. Suddenly there was lots of movement outside their little room, in the main barn area, all of them were out there, then there were all sorts of hammering and drilling going on with instructions to pull the ropes tight.

When they heard the word, 'ropes' all three of them looked at each other too fearful to voice their thoughts, they sat in rigid silence, taking shallow fast breaths, listening.

Bruce closed his eyes and tried to calm his breathing, he didn't want to express his biggest fear that they were rigging up a platform with nooses for their execution by hanging, and cameras to film it. He knew what snuff movies were, and was praying this was not the plan, *please God don't let it be that* he prayed.

The door to their little room was flung open, and Joe walked in followed by the others and all three of them were simultaneously released. Sara and Jayden were bound with their hands tied behind them and taken out, then tied to the posts at the end of the horse stalls facing a boxing ring. This was what they had been rigging up and thankfully, not what they had each been fearing.

There was a slightly raised wooden platform, wooden posts in each corner with three holes drilled with the ropes threaded through. There were metal spikes spaced between each post with the ropes passed through the top to give them extra support, and pulled tight.

Bruce was then frog-marched out by Jase and Nick, boxing gloves were forced onto his hands and secured, the ropes were held up for him and he was told to enter, when he hesitated, Joe appeared next to him and pointed a gun in Sara's direction, he then leaned close and in a low voice, only Bruce heard, 'You even think of killing my brother in there with one of your fancy moves - I kill her,' he said thrusting the gun in Sara's direction, then told him to get in the ring. Bruce moved forward and was shoved through the ropes.

Mel entered the barn, dressed in long shorts, t-shirt and trainers, Bruce was still in the clothes he had been wearing when they were taken, Mel entered the ring and walked straight up to Bruce and snarled in his face, 'A long-awaited rematch, that title should have been mine, you took *it*, and my career.'

Bruce was taller than Mel by several inches and bigger in build. Sara and Jayden looked at each other guessing that this was going to be a vicious fight, the atmosphere was thickly charged with tension.

Through gritted teeth Bruce hissed back, 'The way I remember it, you lost control and *you* got *yourself* disqualified, for an illegal move which ended my career, look in the mirror if you want someone to blame.'

With that, Mel pushed hard with both hands to Bruce's chest, but Bruce must have anticipated it and sharply raised his hands in a circular movement coming up on the insides of Mel's arms, which weakened Mel's hold, Bruce followed this with a jab-cross hook uppercut move, so quick, Mel wasn't prepared for, it threw him off balance, as soon as he recovered he quickly advanced with a jab-cross slip, which Bruce countered, with a sweep squat kick, that knocked Mel on his backside, the fight progressed and became faster and more vicious, there were no rules, and no referee.

Bruce was getting the better of Mel, which was infuriating him even more. To Sara's untrained eye, he seemed to be fighting more with temper than skill, whereas Bruce seemed to be a lot calmer and his moves were quick and decisive, he had obviously been training.

Watching Bruce fight, sent such a peculiar shiver down Sara's spine, with a mixed bag of conflicting emotions. Anger, fear, disgust and contempt, that he was forced to fight, rivalling, excitement, surprise, happiness and pride at the *way* Bruce was fighting. Every time Bruce got hit, it was like feeling it herself, she was willing him on quietly, she didn't want to call out and distract him, he needed to have all his concentration on his opponent.

Sara found she was unable to take her eyes from Bruce, he looked so in control, so fast and lethal, Mel was not fairing very well, no wonder Bruce won the title, and she couldn't keep the prideful smile from her face, forgetting that Joe was watching her, until he walked up to her and slapped the smile off her face, she tasted blood and spat out a mouthful of it. Joe had his back to the fight, therefore obscuring her from the ring, Bruce wouldn't be able to see what was going on, but Jayden was directly opposite, he swore at Joe telling him to leave her alone, which only resulted in Joe striding across and punching Jayden in the stomach, so hard it made him vomit.

Sara was trembling, there didn't seem to be an end in sight to this constant roller coaster ride of fear, apprehension and uncertainty. Joe got distracted with the fight in the ring as Mel was now seriously flagging, he was battered, one of his eyes was swollen, he was bleeding from his lip with reddish marks over his body that will turn into a lot of bruising. Bruce looked like he was fairing much better, he too had reddish marks on his body, but not as many, as he had blocked many of Mel's punches.

Joe brought the fight to an end, announcing that this was just the beginning of a marathon of fights, which would see Mel as the victor and prove that Bruce should never have won the title, this was met by a rowdy cheer from the others. Sara and Jayden looked at each other with incredulous looks with the silently agreed message that they were all deluded, it was clear that Bruce was the much better fighter.

Bruce left the ring, Nate untied his gloves and quietly said, 'You might want to consider letting Mel win.'

'Why? coz he's such a wimp?'

'Suit yourself, but it won't be you, who pays the price, will it?'

Bruce flinched at this, realising he would have to lose the next fight. He was taken back and his hands were once again tied to the chains, he slumped and put his head back and wondered what they were accomplishing by having these fights, was it just for Mel to prove a point, he had gotten very sluggish over the years and had not been training. Bruce had, with his trainer each day, he enjoyed the workouts and although he could never compete again, it was good to be able to do the sport he enjoyed, and it kept him fit both in body and mind as the sport demanded respect.

A short while later Sara was brought into the room and shackled, as usual, he noticed straightway her cut lip and asked what happened as soon as Coop left the room. Sara looked up and smiled, 'You were beating his arse out there, I was fearful for you, but also really proud, you looked really good, *he* looked pathetic. Which was exactly what I was thinking and not noticing Joe looking at me, he slapped the smile off my face, but he couldn't slap the truth, that you were beating that pillock's arse,' she repeated and smiled.

My God, he loved this girl, he thought, in the middle of all this, she showed resilience and managed to find a way to lift his spirits and make him smile, he couldn't help letting out a laugh, he really wished he could reach for her, he wanted to kiss her, taste her, but all he could do was look at her with wonder and again, hope they would get out of this alive.

Jayden was returned a short while later and once they were alone, Jayden said he was forced to tend to Mel's wounds, 'You did a pretty good job on him, he was whimpering as I cleaned his wounds, so pathetic. How are you?'

Bruce shrugged his shoulders and said, 'Fine, few bruises, that's all.'

That night Mel brought their food, but before giving it to them he knelt in front of Bruce and said, 'You know I would have won that fight.' Bruce just stared hard at him, 'I would have won.' Mel hissed in Bruce's face, 'Joe called a halt to it far too soon, we *will* have a rematch and you will see.'

'Keep telling yourself that, if you like.'

Mel stood up, his face contorted and he started kicking and punching Bruce, repeating over and over that he would win next time, Bruce curled up as best he could to protect himself. When Mel ran out of energy, breathing heavily he walked over to the doorway.

Through gritted teeth and taking deep breaths, Bruce said, 'You are nothing but a fucking coward, the only way *you* are going to win is if big brother rigs it,' Mel turned sharply at the door and lobbed their food at them, he left them tied, Jayden shouted for them to be untied, but it was ignored, they looked at the food, they could only reach it with their feet.

Sara comes up with the idea that she may be able to get hold of their food if they stood up and she throws it to them with her feet, 'Comes in handy being a gymnast sometimes,' she says with a smile.

'I am so sick of burgers,' said Jayden.

They both looked in amazement as Sara managed with her feet and toes to unwrap the burger and with some careful positioning, was able to feed herself with her feet, Bruce and Jayden stood there gaping.

'There's no end to my talents,' Sara said with another smile and suggestively waggling her eyebrows at Bruce. Bruce laughed.

'They need to give me a separate room,' Jayden said smiling whilst shaking his head.

Fifty-Four

That night as Mel lay on the bed next to Joe, not an ideal arrangement, but there were only two bedrooms, Nate and Coop, being cousins, shared the other bedroom, Nick and Jase slept in the lounge area. Mel kept groaning whenever he moved and it was getting to Joe, 'Stop being such a fucking baby, you've gone soft over the years, he was beating the shit out of you. It was getting embarrassing.'

'Then why don't you have a go with him, if you think it so easy?'

'All that work to set the ring up and that happens, if you don't beat him, the others will have no respect for you.'

'Tomorrow I will do better, he is not getting away with this.'

'Tomorrow? Look at you moaning and groaning like a girl, worse than a girl, that bitch made less noise than you with a knife through her hand. Get your shit together, or this lot will take over and all your talk that the title should have been yours, will make you a laughing-stock among them.'

Mel rolled over away from Joe and stifled a groan, he was going to show them all, that he should have taken that title. Begrudgingly, he had to agree, that he had let himself go too soft.

Joe also rolled away from Mel in disgust, he knew he had to do something to enable Mel to win, after tonight's fight he could see Bruce was the better fighter, but he couldn't let this go without Mel winning the next fight.

Joe waited for everyone to fall asleep. He got up and went over to the barn and looked through the medical supplies and found exactly what he needed, left the barn and returned to bed. Mel would get his victory.

The next morning after breakfast, Joe told Jase and Nick to get rid of the cars and *obtain* a less conspicuous vehicle.

'A van will be useful to pick up supplies, we need to lie low for a while, get your mates to get our supplies,' he said to Nate and Coop, 'This is a good place for us to sit it out, the cops will soon move onto another crime and use fewer resources, and the press will move onto another story, we need to be patient.'

'And what do we do for money in the meantime,' asked Coop.

'Well, these mates of yours need to earn money, I take it? Nate and Coop nodded, 'We plan it, they execute it, and we split the bounty,' there were smiles all round.

They were all getting bored, there had been constant bickering, arguments, and fights had been breaking out between them.

'Mel and I will scout each job in Javier's car that he left here, as it won't be recognised. Nick and Jase, get rid of the cars and get that van. You two,' pointing to Nate and Coop, 'talk to your mates and get the supplies we need.'

They were just about to leave to do his bidding when Jase asked about the captives and his plans for them.

Joe said, 'Before we leave, Jase, go check they are bound tightly. They won't know we have all gone, let's get what we need and get back here, I will then explain everything, ok?'

Jase nodded and left with Nick, then Nate and Coop left together.

Fifty-Five

Jase walked in and checked they were secure, but no breakfast had been brought to them, and no answer when Bruce asked. They heard the cars leave, they looked at each other, wondering if they had been abandoned. Jayden and Bruce looked at each other, stood up and started working on the ropes which Jase had tightened.

For the whole morning they worked on them, the knots were intricate, the rope weaved and knotted up and around their arms to their elbows and tied very tight, it was difficult to work them with just one hand. Jayden managed to free one hand, Bruce managed the same, if they were a little closer together, they could have helped each other with their second hands in a combined effort. They continued with the ropes, there was no lunch for them and the water was finished even with rationing it. They doubled their efforts, as they would have to find something to free Sara from the metal handcuffs, maybe there would be something in the main barn area left from them erecting the ring if they couldn't get out through the door, as they weren't sure if it was locked, but there was the window.

Triumph - they both got free, they tried the door, it *was* locked, the window it was then. No opener, they would have to smash it, there were four panes of glass set in a wooden inner frame surrounding each pane. They looked around the room for anything, there was nothing, Bruce removed his shirt and wrapped it around his arm and smashed the glass, pushing the central wooden frame out. Jayden climbed through the window.

Bruce bent down and gave Sara the kiss he had been dreaming of doing for such a long time, it felt good to have her in his arms, as he released her, she said, 'I must stink, sorry.'

'Same - I think we cancel out the effect on each other, but you will always, in every way, be nothing but beautiful to me.'

'Charmer,' she replied with a smile. They had only been given the use of a horse trough filled with freezing cold water and a single bar of soap, each of them had been taken out individually to use twice a day to relieve themselves, using a bucket in one of the empty horse stalls, then at gunpoint, taken outside to dig a hole and empty the contents.

Bruce put his shirt back on and climbed through the window. Jayden and Bruce ran round to the front of the barn and entered through the smaller door, they looked around for anything they could use to remove Sara's handcuffs, ideally a bolt cutter, but a drill, even a screwdriver to remove the chains would suffice.

All tools had been removed, but there were a few of the metal spikes that had been used for rigging the fight ring. They looked at the door to the room that had been holding them and saw a large padlock, with no tools and only a spike, Bruce told Jayden to see if he could try it while he went in search around the cabin.

Bruce exited the barn and took a look around, there was another slightly smaller barn next to them, there were no vehicles in sight. Bruce looked in the smaller barn first, it was empty, no tools. He went to the cabin, fortunately, it was unlocked, he went in and found the tools he needed before he left, he found some bread and ham, he spotted a jug and filled it with water and took it with him.

He returned to the barn, the spike had been useless, while Bruce ate, Jayden drilled to remove the lock to the smaller room. Entering the room, Sara was standing, he handed her the bread, ham and jug of water, Jayden took his share and started to eat. They figured the best way to remove the handcuffs was to drill through the chains near to Sara's wrists as the cuffs were a tight fit and the drill could slip, these could be removed later. Bruce asked Sara to hold her wrist to the log walls as he drilled.

The cuffs had triple links, he drilled through the first and second, both had been fairly difficult as the drill slipped a few times, he was now working on the third link on the cuff holding Sara's injured hand. They heard a van pull up outside the barn and other vehicles further away, Bruce was doing the drilling, Sara was to keep an eye on Jayden who was being lookout on the barn door, if there was any movement he would motion to Sara and she would alert Bruce.

The small door to the barn began to open, Jayden immediately motioned to Sara for Bruce to stop and for them all to be quiet, with any luck they would only be dropping things off and would go back to the cabin. They were in luck and they left, the barn door closed. Bruce continued drilling through the last link. Suddenly one hand was free, Bruce and Sara smiled at each other, they were going to escape.

Jayden kept watch on the barn doors, again they opened, he motioned to Sara for Bruce to stop, this time it was all of the gang and they were joined by many others he had not seen before, there were also a few women and they had all been drinking and some had beers in their hands. Jayden looked at Bruce and they frantically tried to pull the last chain holding Sara, but there was no give from the log walls.

The smaller door started to open, they had split seconds, they looked around, there was nothing except one spike, Bruce gave this to Jayden, they posed a fight stance facing the door knowing they had only a slim to no chance of getting out.

Mel and Joe were through the door first noting the broken lock, saw Bruce and Jayden free and the smashed window behind them. They yelled to the others, fighting and shouting followed as Jayden and Bruce fought hard, but they were outnumbered, overpowered and eventually, subdued, held to the ground with their arms held behind their backs. Joe stepped forward and gave a swinging kick to Bruce and then Jayden, through his seething anger hissed, 'So you thought to escape, did you,' then delivered a single punch to each of them in the kidney, as they were held down. They were then hauled up onto their feet and taken out to the main barn area, shoved into the middle of the ring and forced to their knees, Nate held a gun to Bruce's head, Coop held a gun to Jayden's head.

Joe brought Sara out, once again she was tied to the post of one of the horse stalls. Joe stepped into the middle of the ring and announced like he was a circus ringmaster and shouted, 'Do you want to see a real fight? There were about twenty people, in addition to the gang, mostly men, and five women. Sara looked around and wondered how these women could be part of this, but as she looked on, she noticed that the women were worse than the men, it was them, who were shouting, 'Fight. Fight,' the loudest.

Joe looked over and caught Sara's eye and repeated louder, 'You want to see a fight?' This was met with a rowdy cheer, gesturing towards Bruce and Jayden, he asked who they would like to see first.

Jayden was chosen for the first fight, receiving the loudest cheers, his opponent was one of the newcomers. The ring was cleared except for Jayden, Bruce was held between Jase and Nick to the side of the ring, with a gun visibly held to his back. Sara had gotten to know Jayden over the last month, he was such a lovely person, and she so wanted him to get through this alive and return to marry his girlfriend Layla, he was tall and obviously worked out as he was told to remove his shirt by the women, with his curling dark brown hair and piecing clear green eyes, Sara could appreciate the attraction some of the women were showing towards him, which some of the men clearly didn't like. His opponent entered the ring and was introduced by Joe as Eric, he was smaller in height and build to Jayden, he also removed his shirt.

Joe produced a bell and rang it for the fight to begin, Jayden and Eric circled the ring sizing each other up, Eric moved in and grabbed Jayden, but with a flash quick movement, Jayden turned full circle within Eric's grasp and Eric was caught from behind around the waist and flung to the ground, Jayden followed this in quick succession with a bombardment of punches that Eric had no chance of avoiding, or able to protect himself. Eric frenziedly tried to scramble to the ropes and get out of the ring, shouting that he gave up, one of his mates jumped into the ring and pulled Jayden off him, delivering a few punches of his own, Jayden retaliated, both of the men scrambled from the ring and Joe sounded the bell.

There were many shouts from the crowd that Jayden was a lunatic. Joe asked if there was anyone else who wanted to challenge him, two more jumped at the challenge, but Jayden made quick work of both of them, there were boos and cheers from the crowd. Jayden was removed and tied to the opposite post to Sara. When he had recovered his breath, he looked at Sara, she smiled at him and mouthed, 'Amazing.' He shrugged his shoulders and smiled back.

Joe left the ring. Bruce was forced to remove his shirt and it was flung into the little room. Sara's mouth went dry at the sight of his body, it was magnificent, although she was ogling him, she was also really afraid for him, forced to fight *again*. The crowd had disbursed from around the ring to replenish their drinks, no one was looking at Joe and Bruce, but Sara hadn't taken her eyes away from Bruce.

Joe was standing behind him, suddenly Bruce lurched to his right and he keeled over, was finding it hard to get up, Joe hauled him to his feet, whispered in his ear and shoved him towards the ring, Bruce staggered and fell against the ropes, Nick and Jase picked him up and pushed him through into the ring, Joe entered and held Bruce up. Sara was instantly anxious, what had Joe done to him.

Joe announced that the next fight would be with Bruce and asked if there were any opponents, from the back of the barn, Mel shouted that he would fight him, there were cheers from the crowd, the ropes were held for him as he entered the ring.

Something was wrong with Bruce, he was holding his side and finding it hard to stand if Joe wasn't holding him up. Rousing the crowd that the fight was about to begin, he nodded to Nate who sounded the bell for the fight to begin.

Joe stepped away from Bruce, who staggered to try and stay on his feet, moving away from Mel who lunged at him, using a jab-cross uppercut movement, Bruce was able to block some of the moves, he wasn't fighting as he did yesterday. Mel advanced again with a sweep squat kick, Bruce had tried to use a jab and uppercut, with his right arm, a weak movement as he was clearly having problems, Mel followed his move with a forward kick, that sent Bruce to the floor, he only managed to get to his knees, unable to get to his feet and holding his right side, Mel advanced, turned and gave Bruce a back kick, which sent him sprawling to the floor, he didn't get up.

Joe entered the ring having sounded the bell to mark the end of the fight and raised Mel's arm, announcing him the winner, which was met with a resounding cheer from all around the ring. As the crowd disbursed, Joe gave Bruce a swift kick to his right side as he lay motionless on the ground, before leaving the ring.

It was a pathetically short fight and how anyone deemed it a victory for Mel, they must all be high, drunk or delusional, Sara thought. Joe had done something to Bruce, Sara was convinced of that, also really afraid and worried for him. Jase and Nick entered the ring, each taking one of Bruce's arms and dragged him out of the ring under the ropes and into the room at the back. Jayden was released next, Sara didn't want to ask Jayden to look at Bruce, just in case by her asking, they would do the opposite, but a silent glance of acknowledgement passed between them.

Sara was eventually released and placed back in the room, and her injured hand was placed in the single handcuff. Bruce was lying on the floor with his hands and feet tied together behind him, he was lying on his side and still unconscious. As soon as they were left alone, Sara asked Jayden if he had been able to take a look at Bruce.

'They allowed me only a quick look at him, I checked his right side, I noticed that he kept holding and his staggering gait veered to his right, Joe did something to him. I saw a pinprick near his kidney, I think Joe stabbed him with a needle before the fight, as they brought me in here I also saw a syringe on the ground near the ring, it's possible, that it was from one of the crowd, they all seem *too* high for it to be from drink, although, I suspect it's what Joe used.'

'That bastard,' Sara spat the word, 'Mel is still a complete loser.' Looking at Bruce she asked, 'How is he? Will he be alright?'

'Yes, he may be out for a while, and be in pain when he comes round, but he should be ok.'

'Will this damage his kidney?'

'Not permanently, it's similar to a kidney biopsy, an injection needle is thinner and not as long as the biopsy needles, we use. He will be very sore, but ok,' he reassured her.

Sara let the tears fall that she was unable to hold back, she apologised to Jayden, she hated being weak. 'You don't need to ever apologise Sara, I've seen how brave you are, crying is a release, think of it as a valve on a pressure cooker, it's definitely, *not* a weakness.'

'Thank you,' she whispered hoarsely.

That night it was particularly cold, the wind blew in through the broken window. Bruce stirred and groaned in pain, but there was not a single thing she or Jayden could do, soothing words seemed so ineffectual. Sara was closest to the broken window and sat shivering most of the night, but Bruce had no shirt on to even give him that warmth, it was out of her and Jayden's reach, where it had been flung earlier. The next day the window was boarded up, making the room dark.

Fifty-Six

Over the next week the party nights continued, Bruce and Jayden were expected to fight and wagers were placed, the gang wanted to make money on the fights. When Bruce refused to fight anymore, Joe devised an incentive. Only if they won, would Sara be given food and water, if they lost, she went without. They couldn't even give her theirs, they were forced to eat and drink, before being taken back to the room.

The fights were getting more frequent, Jayden and Bruce were getting fatigued and they were starting to lose, which meant that Sara was now going without food and water, sometimes she would get water, but no food, they were keeping her alive, just. Every time they lost, they were both racked with guilt that Sara went hungry and extremely angry with themselves, they were continually forced to eat and forced to fight.

Some days later, the women were getting bored with the constant fights, when Jayden and Bruce were brought out on yet another evening of fights, and Sara was tied to her usual post to watch, all five of the women entered the ring and demanded a different sort of entertainment, at this the men started to cheer.

Standing between Jayden and Bruce just outside the room, and forced to their knees, with their hands tied behind their backs, Joe shouted, 'What kind of entertainment do you have in mind?'

'Bring them into the ring, don't untie them,' all the women started to walk around the ring and the men were cheering as they started to remove some of their clothing until they were quite scantily clad. Each of the women went over to their partners and whispered to them, they left the barn, only to return shortly after with an old fashioned ornamental wagon wheel, that was found in the other barn, it was nailed onto the wall close to the ring and tested to see if it spun freely, paper was brought out, an arrow was drawn on one and placed at the top above the wheel. The women went around the crowd of men for suggestions and wrote them on the paper, these were then stuck to the spokes of the wheel.

Bruce and Jayden were shoved into the ring. The women surrounded them, then faced the crowd and one of them said, 'Are you up for a different kind of entertainment, with these fine, prime specimens?' one of the women drooled, as she stood between them, and trailed her hands down Jayden and Bruce's bare chests. There followed an uproarious chorus of cheers and whoops from the men, as the women crowded round Bruce and Jayden, running their hands all over them.

Apprehension coursed through Bruce's body, he looked over at Jayden, who returned the same shocked look when they read the papers on the wheel. He then glanced at Sara with a look of pleading and apology in his eyes, for what was to follow, Sara looked back, closed her eyes with a slight nod, as if to say, *I understand, none of this is your fault*. From the angle of the wheel and where Sara had been tied, he doubted she had been able to read the suggestions on the wheel, but would undoubtedly know it was not good.

Many bottles of alcohol were arranged on the top of a storage unit, an assortment of drugs was arranged on another. Joe appeared next to Sara and placed a gun under her chin, forcing her to raise her head, he then looked over at Bruce and shouted, 'Do we have your full compliance tonight?' neither of them answered, Joe cocked the gun and Bruce and Jayden reluctantly nodded. 'Good,' said Joe as he lowered the gun and walked over to the ring.

One of the women remained between Bruce and Jayden and the others formed a circle. An empty bottle had been placed in the middle of their circle on a board within the ring and was spun, as it stopped the bottom of the bottle was facing Jayden, the other end pointed to one of the women. There were whoops and cheers, one of the men spun the wagon wheel fast, it started to slow, then it stopped – oral sex, was written on the paper. It seemed the ringleader of the women, who instigated the game, stepped forward and announced, 'Well Kitty, dear, *you* have to perform oral sex on this gorgeous specimen, are you game? And is your man, game to watch?'

Jayden looked down in total disgust. With his mind reeling, he thought of Layla. He'd been dating for the last year and as he had admitted to Sara and Bruce, he was on the cusp of asking her to marry him. He had met her on her first day at Bellevue, she had recently transferred from Surgical at another hospital and started in A&E. He noticed her straight away, with her short and silky blonde hair, with the most beautiful clear ocean blue eyes, thick eyelashes and her beautiful gentle smile. She had a competent natural way with the patients, that galvanised their confidence in her, he was drawn to her like a magnet, and he thanked his lucky stars, she felt the same way.

He had never dated anyone so calm, undemanding in their manner, that made him feel he wanted to give her the world. He fell in love with her overnight, but he held back as this was such unchartered territory for him, he wanted to be sure, he also wanted to give her time and not have her running. Just when he was sure, all of this happened, and now he regretted waiting. If only he hadn't taken that secondment to the Military Base, if only he had asked her to marry him, would things be different? on and on it went in his head each night since he had been taken, but always he imagined her smiling face and the way she loved him, it was this last thought each night that enabled him to sleep.

Brought back to the present, he endeavoured to think of anything other than beautiful Layla, it would spark an aroused reaction, he didn't want that, he turned his mind to things that would make him sick and ill and decided that *this*, being made to do this, was all he needed to concentrate on, these girls were lowest of the low, and he endeavoured to separate his mind from his body, although medically, he knew his body would react to stimuli and react accordingly against his will.

One of the men called out, 'Damn right, she's got the hottest, wettest, filthiest mouth and talented tongue around,' which was met with a massive cheer.

Kitty sauntered over to Jayden and fell to her knees, undid his trousers, took his member out and set her mouth to work on him. Jayden stood still with his head down and his eyes squeezed shut, his fists clenched behind him, he was trying to blot out the raucous noise around him, but she had managed to arouse him and he sent a silent apology to Layla. The noise was getting louder in their encouragement and Kitty was taking him deeper into her mouth and sucking harder and faster. He stifled his climax as much as he could, but Kitty let it be known he had indeed come, as she licked her lips, and rose to her feet, there was another cheer as she put him back in his trouser.

The bottle was spun again, this time it was two of the girls, the wagon wheel was spun, it was a drinking competition, two glasses were filled and they had to drink it back as quick as possible to see who would finish first. The next turn was Jayden again and another of the girls, this time it was that they had to take a drug, one in each hand and they had to choose a hand, not knowing the drug they would be taking. Jayden tried to refuse, but two men stepped into the ring, he was forced to his knees and the white pill was dropped into his forced open mouth and water gushed down his throat, they checked that he had taken the drug, he was left on his knees.

The next round was Bruce and one of the women, the wagon wheel was spun hard, when it stopped – it read – intercourse. Bruce swore under his breath, closed his eyes and gritted his teeth, the girl strutted over to him and backed him into one of the corners of the ring and told him to sit down, Bruce was reluctant and two men pushed him down from over the ropes.

One of the men who pushed Bruce down must have been the boyfriend as he said, 'Go on, Suzie Darlin, capture him with those sweet pussy lips.'

He tossed her a condom as she kicked Bruce's legs apart and knelt between them, undid his trousers, took his member in her hands and massaged him, then slipped the condom on, removed her panties and straddled him as she placed him inside her and started to ride him, to a chorus of whoops and cheers from the audience.

Bruce tried to disassociate himself from what was happening and as much as he tried, his dick was performing, as the saying goes, 'A hard dick has no conscience.' She rode him hard, and the crowd were cheering her on. He could feel himself climbing the summit, he desperately grappled with different thoughts, anything, trying not to comply, he willed himself not to think of Sara, who was being forced to watch. He stifled his climax, but Suzie announced that he had come, the evidence was in the condom, which was whipped off him and paraded around the ring, to his disgust. She returned and tucked him into his trouser and whispered in his ear, 'I enjoyed that, you felt really good.' Bruce just closed his eyes and looked away from her.

The wheel was spun again and Bruce was forced, the same way they had with Jayden, to take an unknown drug, they forced an alcoholic drink down his throat to ensure he swallowed it, initially it made him feel, alert and wired and all the noise from the crowd was more intense.

As the evening went on and the alcohol flowed, more drugs were forced on them both. With more spins of the wheel, they were both forced to perform oral sex at the same time on two of the girls, by this time they were both high and very drunk.

Sara didn't want to look, but Joe was forcing her, every time she looked away, he gripped her hard under the chin forced her head up and told her to watch, she wanted to scream at Joe. These two men were decent human beings being forced to perform in this way was disgusting, degenerative and immoral, but these people had no moral compass.

A call went up that Joe should bring Sara into the ring, as the men could do with some participation, Joe yelled back that sex was pleasure, and she would be given no pleasure, they chorused that he was keeping her for himself, or was the boyfriend more to his taste, they all laughed and Joe retorted, 'Now that is not a bad idea.'

This made Sara flinch, Joe noticed and whispered in her ear, that it could be arranged, but he wasn't into public displays of sexual depravity, he preferred a more private, intimate session. She couldn't control her need to heave and Joe just laughed and said, 'Don't worry sweetheart, they're right, you're not my type. Now, your boyfriend … mmm, very good looking and that body …'

'No … Please no, he's not …' She stopped herself, but he had got her meaning and gave her a sick smirk.

'Exactly, think what that would do to him?' his lips broadened and curled into a sick smug smile as he walked away to watch the - *entertainment*.

Oh my God, Sara thought, had she just given him that idea, what they were being forced to do right now was bad enough, but to be raped by a man, how would Bruce come back from that, *if they survived*. Sara looked over to the ring as girls straightened, adjusted their clothing and lowered their skirts and walked away, informing them just how good that had felt.

The evening eventually and gradually came to an end, the crowd had gotten so drunk and taken so many drugs, half were sitting around, stoned and passed out.

The week progressed and settled into a degrading and humiliating repetitive pattern, each night they would change the papers on the wheel as new suggestions were added. During the day Sara heard the movement of several vehicles leave for the day, and return later for the evening, *entertainments*. Bruce and Jayden were being paraded each evening, forced to fight to win food and water for Sara, then coerced into performing depraved sexual acts.

They spent most of the day recovering from the drug effects, and the rest of the time they were becoming more and more subdued as the week wore on.

Bruce found it difficult to look Sara straight in the eyes, he told her he felt ashamed, she reassured him the best she could, but what could she say, they knew it would be happening again that evening and the next. On the sixth evening, as Sara and Jayden were removed by Nick and Jase, Joe approached the small room, Sara looked back and saw Joe resting his shoulder on the door frame, then he closed the door. Her step faltered, she resisted and protested.

'Please, bring Bruce out here, he needs to be out here,' she was yelling, attracting attention from the crowd, but not one of them was bothered and turned back to their drinks and conversations. Two evils, equal to each other, out here and whatever was happening in that small room.

'Eager to watch your boyfriend perform, are you?' Nick taunted as he moved away and shoved Jayden into the ring.

Sara was tied to her usual post, she was hungry, Jayden and Bruce had lost the fight last night and she had not eaten since … she couldn't remember, she was feeling weak, but she was given some water as Jase finished tying her to the post.

Fifty-Seven

Joe stood in the doorway, leant his shoulder on the door frame and crossed his arms over his chest and looked at Bruce for a few moments, then he walked in and closed the door, walked across the room and stood over Bruce with his legs either side of Bruce's outstretched and bound limbs. Bruce shifted uncomfortably against the wall, but there was nowhere for him to go. Joe lowered himself to his knees, using his weight on Bruce's legs to keep them in place. Bruce who was sitting up, his hands were bound as usual to the chains above him and the ropes around his wrists were tighter.

Joe looked appreciatively at Bruce, with a seductive smile his gaze moved down the length of Bruce's body and slowly back up again, meeting the hard stare Bruce was giving him, 'Have you been enjoying yourself?' Bruce didn't answer. 'No?' he asked with a raised eyebrow, 'maybe you would enjoy an alternative taste,' as he reached out and took Bruce's chin in one hand forcing his head back, 'you really are a *very* attractive man,' he said provocatively.

His fingers trailed down Bruce's neck, then started unbuttoning his shirt slowly, when it was fully undone, Joe flicked the ends open, using both hands he fondled Bruce's chest, and gently tweaked one of his nipples, then ran one hand down over his stomach.

'Mmmm,' he murmured, 'you keep yourself in really good shape, you must work out – *hard.*'

Bruce did the only thing he could do – he spat in Joe's face and said, 'You. Sick. Depraved. Degenerate,' he sneered. Bruce was feeling nauseous, this could *not* be happening, he had to think quickly to put this sick twisted bastard off him.

Joe wiped his face with the back of his sleeve and stood up, splayed his legs either side of Bruce's, and rubbed his crotch area, then started to undo his trousers, as he looked down at Bruce with a gleaming smile.

The corners of Bruce's mouth were pulled down and his brows were drawn in close, without looking up, Bruce said, 'Put anything of yours in my mouth, and I'll bite the fucking thing off,' Bruce slowly looked up and glared at Joe.

Joe faltered, his hands stilled and there was a flash of fear in his eyes. Joe refastened his trouser and Bruce breathed a silent sigh of relief, endeavouring to bring his breathing back under control. Joe walked away, then turned around and said, 'The guys out there were asking for me to take that bitch into the ring for some entertainment, but how about we take you? Have the boys hold you down as we take turns with *you* instead? some of them are as depraved as you say I am.'

Bruce's heart pounded faster in his chest and his breathing accelerated rapidly, which he was struggling to control, determined not to let Joe see the effect this was having on him. Bruce learned from a very young age with his father, not to show fear. Cowardly bullies were, all the same, the look of fear from their victims, it gave them control, it empowered them, it fired them up and drove them on. In a calm voice and maintaining eye contact, Bruce said, 'You'd better make sure I don't get up from that, if I do, your exertions will be the last breaths you take.'

Joe recoiled at Bruce's cold, calm demeanour, 'You think you can get out of those again?' he motioned to the chains and new ropes.

Holding his glare steady and unwavering, even though his heart was slamming in his chest, his lips thinned and through gritted teeth, he said, 'Did it once when you weren't expecting it.'

Joe looked at him and that flash of fear was again in his eyes, 'We'll see.' He stepped towards the door, opened it and left.

Bruce sat there, now able to breathe freely, he took deep gulps of air as he tried to control his trembling and suppress the fear, he felt for himself and Sara. He sent up a silent prayer, 'Please, give me the strength to see this night through and find a way out of here for all of us.'

A moment later, the door slammed open, Bruce jumped, it was Nick and Jase, they untied him and marched him out, each holding one of his arms behind his back. His fear escalated and intensified as he saw Sara by the ring, not tied to the usual post, Joe was next to her holding her head back by her hair and a gun pointed under her chin. Bruce was launched into the ring, he landed sprawled on the floor beside Jayden. The crowd quickly quietened, eager for the announcement for the nights' proceedings to commence, Joe raised his voice and said, 'The other night, you - gentlemen, well men, not so much gentle,' this garnered a rowdy, raucous response. Joe brought the crowd under control and continued, 'Requested more participation,' again this was met with a loud chorus of cheers, whoops and whistles.

Bruce went into a distraught and panic like state, he had to find a way out of this, not waiting to see if it was he or Sara that would be this night's show. He desperately, frantically, looked around, he couldn't rush Joe, not with the gun in his hand pointed at Sara, he then saw Mel standing near the ropes. Before he could even formulate a plan, he launched himself through the ropes and lunged at Mel, took him with him as he rolled, he instantaneously grabbed him around the neck and had him in a headlock, the movement was so fast no one had time to react, Bruce quickly checked that no one was behind him, then facing Joe he said, 'One quick movement and I break his fucking neck, put the gun down.'

The crowd fell silent, 'You think I am just going to do as you say, look around, look how many of us there are.'

'Well, that depends on how much you love your brother, doesn't it?'

To make his point, he tightened his grip and Mel started to make choking noises, he grabbed Bruce's arm, trying to loosen the grip.

Joe immediately put the gun down and spread his hands wide, as he released Sara. Bruce told her, 'Move over here behind me, you too Jayden.' They both moved behind him and the crowd watched as Bruce started to make his move around the ring, telling Joe's friends to back up as they made their way towards the barn doors.

The smaller door opened, Nate and Coop entered. They weren't alone.

Fifty-Eight

Nate entered first, holding the hand of a little girl who was crying, he was towing her as she was frightened and afraid, Coop followed and gently pushed the girl forward. Bruce had his back to Nate and Coop, still holding Mel in the headlock, with his concentration on Joe, he didn't initially, take in the shift in the situation, Jayden tapped him on the shoulder as he and Sara gaped open-mouthed and wide-eyed at what they were seeing, Bruce turned and couldn't believe that they would take a little girl.

Joe stepped confidently forward, Bruce stepped back a little, still holding Mel. Joe announced to everyone that this, motioning to the little girl, was their newest guest who would be joining Sara, Bruce and Jayden. There was an instant chorus of disapproval from the crowd, shouts of Joe being a total sick bastard and how they would not be part of this.

Joe was for an instant, a little hesitant, but he then shouted above the crowd, assuring them that he had no intention of harming the child, explaining that it was just an insurance policy that Bruce and Jayden complied, this pacified them slightly, but many of them were saying they were leaving, as each person walked out of the barn, more joined the exodus, until there was only the original gang of Joe, Mel, Jase, Nick, Nate and Coop left.

Joe stalked out quickly trying to reason and reassure them that no harm would be done to the child, all to no avail, there followed the sounds of car doors opening and closing and vehicles leaving.

Bruce went to make a move, still holding Mel, but Nate held up his joined hand with the little girl, as a reminder and Coop stepped back and discreetly held up his gun, out of the sight of the little girl, *his* reminder of what they could do. It was a standoff.

Joe kicked open the door to the barn, stormed in swearing, 'Well you have just single-handedly, broken up my fucking party, and, lost me a very lucrative business. Those fuckers will not deal with me now. All because of you,' he pointed to Bruce.

Bruce looked at the very pretty and very petrified little girl, she had gorgeous long red curly hair with the most amazing large green eyes, she was crying and asking for her mummy, Nate bent down whispered to her and she immediately stifled her crying, but looked even more frightened. Bruce swore under his breath, whatever he whispered, it was evident it only *scared* her into silence.

Bruce looked at Joe incredulously, 'Even your low life friends have a line they won't cross.'

'Your little display fucked up my plans of introducing her,' he jabbed his pointed finger in the little girls' direction, 'they would have come round, I could have persuaded them. I lost Javier, because of *you*, I lost a lucrative business, because of *you*.' Joe stepped behind the little girl and produced his gun and aimed it at the little girls head, Coop lowered his gun and stood there watching, Joe said, 'Release my brother. Now,' he bellowed, which made the little girl jump and she started to cry again.

For the first time, Mel spoke, 'Seems you have no choice, fucker.'

Bruce hesitated and Joe said, 'Would you prefer a demonstration of what I will do if you don't co-operate?' he stepped closer and cocked his gun, the little girl cowered, was visibly shaking, Bruce looked down as a pool of liquid appeared round her feet.

Bruce felt powerless, empty, defeated. He'd failed, *again*. He muttered quietly, a stream of profanities as he closed his eyes for a moment, looked down and slowly released Mel. The instant he was out of Bruce's grip, Mel spun around and using all his strength, enraged and infuriated by his humiliation, delivered a punch to Bruce's face, followed by an onslaught of rapid punches and kicks to the chest and stomach as Bruce went down.

Bruce laid there, not bothering to get up. He knew what was to come.

Joe said, 'Mel, take her back to the cabin,' he motioned to the little girl. 'You four, tie these two *very* securely to the posts.'

As the others moved away, Joe crouched down over Bruce and said in a low voice, 'You and I, are going to finish our conversation.' The others returned after having secured Sara and Jayden, Joe told them to take Bruce back to the room and secure him, then to stand guard outside the barn.

Bruce sat in the little darkened room, with one light, that Nick had installed when they had erected the partition, and the camera that he had forgotten about, he hung his head, it would all be filmed.

He concentrated on his breathing, taking in deep steady streams of oxygen, trying to calm his galloping heart. His mind was racing, jumping around, what should he be thinking of right now, not on what was to come, Joe was vicious, vile, warped and perverted.

Bruce had gay mates, it had never bothered him what their sexual preference was, they were good people, good mates and that was all that mattered to him, they knew and accepted his preference was with women and they never pushed or tried to persuade, they would join in with the usual banter, and there were numerous innuendo's relating to their relationships, but Bruce never judged them, but the thought of sex with a man, made him shudder.

He finally managed to focus his whirling mind on all the training Jim had given him when he was young, how he had taught him to concentrate and channel his mind. In that frightening void, where he would be waiting for his father and the beating to follow, where the fear escalated, becoming acute and he felt he was about to lose control, Jim told him to meditate and fixate on regulating his breathing and his heart rate, to block out everything around him, to centralize all his focus, to anticipate, formulate a plan, hold steady, engage and block if he could.

He had been able to do all of these things when training for a fight, but this was not a fight, this was capitulation, submission, yielding. To resist, to fight, would potentially put that little girl and Sara in danger, of that he had no doubt and was not about to risk testing the theory, how was he to fight anyway, bound as he was, the inevitable was about to happen.

His only strategy in this situation was to accept it and try to block out all thoughts, to take his mind elsewhere, to be present in body, absent in mind. Bruce tightly squeezed his already closed eyes, took deep breaths and started to channel his mind.

Bruce had no idea how long he had been left alone, he heard the door open, then close, his breathing accelerated and his heart slammed in his chest. Bruce looked up in total disgust, 'You are a sick bastard, taking a little girl, are you that fucking low. You're beyond depraved.'

'My tastes may be beyond the *norm*, but children have never appealed to me, in *that* way. However, her safety is entirely in your hands.'

Bruce recognised the pungent, acrid, offensive unwashed body odour from earlier, as Joe crouched close to him, and in a low menacing voice he said, 'Any biting, let me tell you what will happen.'

He took his time to explain in avid and fanatical detail all the things that he had lined up for Sara and the little girl if he showed any resistance or didn't comply. He then smirked at Bruce's bewildered expression he said, 'Do you understand?'

Bruce glared rigidly at Joe, but didn't respond, 'Un-der-stand?' Joe enunciated bringing his face closer. His foul breath was a fetid odour of hours old cigarettes and garlic, Bruce had to stifle his urge to heave and just nodded. 'Good.'

Bruce hung his head as Joe stood and started to undo his trousers. Joe looked down and said with a wide grin, 'Ready?'

Joe passed Sara, as he swaggered across to the little room, at the doorway, he paused, looked back at her and gave her a leering smile as he closed the door. She could taste bile in her mouth and spat it out.

The gang were outside with the smaller barn door open, talking and laughing, she didn't pay attention to the conversations.

Sara and Jayden were left alone. Sara lowered her head, Jayden said, 'Look at me, Sara,' she raised her head, 'We *will* live through this, and you and I will help him recover, ok?' Sara nodded, with her whole being, she would help Bruce.

They fell into an awkward silence, neither of them knew what more to say or where to look, they both closed their eyes and hung their heads, lost in their own thoughts, wishing they could cover their ears as they heard movement, grunts, groans and repetitive slaps coming from the room.

When Sara heard a pained and strangled roar over and over that she knew was from Bruce, she squeezed her eyes tight shut, it was then she found it impossible to hold back the tears any longer, they fell onto the ground in front of her, pained with the misery she felt for what Bruce was being subjected to, right now, in that little room.

Hope was all she had left, that they would come through this, alive as Jayden had said. She focused her mind on images of Bruce being funny, fun-loving, caring, smiling, laughing, gorgeous, her Brucie, he was *hers* and no one else's.

She let the memories of their wonderful week in New York flood her mind, so long ago now, another lifetime ago. She closed her eyes and made a vow and prayed. *Please, God, let us all live through this and give me the strength, patience and know-how to bring Bruce back from this, I vow I will spend the rest of my days loving him, make him happy again, please don't let this be the end, I love him so much*, with that her composure collapsed and she allowed herself to let the tears flow freely but stifling the sound of her crying.

Fifty-Nine

Ric and Cade sat at their desks on an unusually and decidedly chilly morning for the end of May, and they had gotten nowhere, in moving forward in the investigations into the kidnappings of Sara Kaye, Bruce Bailey and Jayden Hayes. The gang had gone to ground and were sitting it out till the attention died down.

What they couldn't work out was why there weren't any sightings from the public, that was extremely unusual if you discount the usual bunch of cranks, who call claiming to have sighted whoever was in the current news. They were joined by Logan who was looking very grim-faced as he got off the phone from the British Embassy.

'Apparently, the media are going into overdrive in Britain, pushing for more information on their whereabouts, and we are not looking very competent. In fact, they have called us very, *incompetent*.'

'Great,' said Ric as he roughly pushed his hand through his hair. 'We still have nothing, no sightings, no demands and no clue where they have moved to, they could have travelled to the other side of America, crossed into Mexico, or be hiding out just around the corner. No damn idea.'

'I suggest we push harder on those friends of the gang, we recently interviewed, I got the distinct impression they had just returned from somewhere,' said Logan.

'What gave you that impression?' Cade asked.

'Not anything said, just by observation, I saw some bags that looked half unpacked. When I spoke to them, I'm afraid being British, they were not very forthcoming, maybe if either of you have a crack at them and leans a little harder!?'

Ric said, 'We'll do it, right now, anything to get the British Embassy off our backs, by giving them something – anything.'

❖

When they arrived at the first address it was in a run-down area of Brooklyn, narrow hallways, graffiti everywhere and a known drugs warren. Ric knocked on the door, identified themselves only as, 'Police,' when asked from behind the closed door, then there was a delay before the door was opened.

A woman appeared in the doorway, there were three men and another woman in the room, the air was thick with the smell of marijuana and other substances, probably the cause of the delay in opening the door. Their line of enquiry was more important than the personal consumption of illegal drugs, but if their questions didn't get the answers they required, they would then use it and call it in, have the place searched, it would give them a reason to arrest and detain them for questioning.

Ric asked for their names and ID. The first was Eric Johnson, Susan (Suzie) Whittaker, James (Jimmy) Watson, Katrina (Kitty) Kuznetsova and Miguel (Mick), Rivera, they quickly established that Suzie and Jimmy were an item, and same went for Kitty and Mick, the couples were draped over each other and caressing each other in very suggestive ways in an attempt to make Cade and Ric uncomfortable Ten years on the force each, they had seen enough, that this little show had no effect.

The instant Ric saw Mick's ID his face drained of colour, his mouth went dry, and he quickly turned away from everyone to gain a few moments to compose himself, to school his face and get his breathing and heart rate under control.

Miguel Alejandro Rivera was one of Javier's gang members and participant in an incident growing up in Mexico, when he was a child, that he had no intention of jogging his memory by revealing his name, therefore skipped the introductions, Cade looked across at him when he didn't identify themselves formally and kept quiet, the gang didn't seem to notice or ask for their names and their badges were only flashed at them when they came in through the door, which the girl, now known as Kitty, didn't scrutinize, probably too high on lots of different drugs, not just marijuana.

Ric and Cade asked them a few questions about their whereabouts recently, as there had been no answer when they had first called about a week ago, an untruth, to observe their reactions, both the girls looked at their respective boyfriends, who returned a steady glare and a slight, almost missed if not looking for, shake of the head, an obvious, 'stay silent' message.

Eric looked down at his hands and avoided eye contact. Ric reeled off all the names of the gangs and asked if they had seen them recently, the girls denied knowing any of them, the men said they vaguely knew them, but hadn't seen them. Ric and Cade looked at each other, instinct told them this was an obvious lie, the number of drugs they had taken had rendered them incapable of remembering their lies, they contradicted themselves and slipped up when Cade asked the same questions in a different way.

Ric reiterated that he suspected that they *did,* know all of the members of this particular gang and they *had,* seen them recently, if they didn't want to be arrested on drug-related charges, then to tell them the information they needed. When they remained silent, Ric asked if he could take a look around, one of them asked if he had a warrant, Ric said no, he wouldn't need one as this would be a drugs bust, where he had acted on a tip-off and needed to act instantly, ergo, no warrant needed.

He switched his Dictaphone to record, and discreetly placed it on the sideboard in front of him, tipped his head at Cade, and they both went into the next room, Cade whispered, 'Why have we both left the room, that's not usual procedure?'

Ric put his finger over his lips to be quiet, pointed into the room and mimicked talking with his hand and pointed back at the room, Cade nodded and they listened. Sure enough, they were whispering loudly and Suzie said, 'What about the little girl they took, you agreed with me, Joe had gone too far this time and that you would do something about it, I don't like it.'

'I did and I will sugar, but not to the cops, ok? Joe has friends in places you don't wanna know about.'

Ric and Cade looked at each other – what little girl? their mutual looks and unspoken words said.

They returned to the room, Ric went and retrieved his Dictaphone without them noticing, and told them that as they had persisted in remaining silent, it left him no choice, but to read them their rights and take them in, sighting evidence of drugs found in the next room, another lie, but sure back up would find some when they arrive to search.

As they left, after backup arrived, Ric hoped the recording would be of sufficient quality to confront them of Suzie's admission, that a little girl had been taken, and knowing Joe. Cade asked why he hadn't introduced themselves, Ric explained that he knew Miguel from growing up in Mexico, he was one of Javier's gang and didn't want to detract from the investigation and left it at that. In truth, Ric didn't want to explain to Cade the details of the incident, it was far too personal, and not relevant to the case.

They got back to the station and Cade immediately made enquiries with the FBI if they were investigating a possible kidnapping of a young girl, in New York or any neighbouring state, as they were hoping that the gang were not too far away if they had been in contact with local lowlifes like Eric, Jimmy and Mick, there were possibly others involved.

They placed each of them in separate interview rooms, one of the officers working vice, enquired why they had Susan Whittaker and Katrina Kuznetsova in custody, as they were well-known prostitutes, Ric offered them a short explanation and said it was not on prostitution charges, *this* time, but any information they had on them, would be helpful to their investigation.

Starting with Suzie, Cade did the interviewing and fully introduced himself and put the tape on the table, played it and scrutinized her reaction, he turned the tape off when it finished, then said, 'What little girl?' Suzie shifted in her seat, was fidgeting with the bottom of one of her shirt sleeves which covered half her hands, and pulling at a cotton strand that had come loose, 'What. Little. Girl?' Cade repeated, louder as he thumped the table, hard, making Suzie jump, he then leaned in closer across the table. 'Tell me, Suzie.'

'They will do horrible things to me if they know I've talked.'

'Not as horrible as the things some of my Officers will do if a little girl gets harmed and you say nothing,' he shouted, and thumped the table again on the last word, again Suzie jumped, 'Now talk.'

'I can't,' she whispered, as tears rolled down her cheeks and she started trembling, 'They will know it's me who talked, you've no idea how evil they are, I'm not saying another word.'

Cade sat back in his seat and glared at her, she glanced up only once, then refused to look at him or answer when he asked her more questions. He left the room and joined Ric in the viewing room.

'Maybe the FBI will have some success, did you call them?'

'Yes, they're on their way,' said Ric.

Sixty

Ric was informed the moment the two FBI agents arrived, they introduced themselves as Special Agent Morgan Murphy and Special Agent Carlos Sanchez. They wasted no time in updating each other on their respective cases.

Ric told them the names of those they were holding on drug-related charges, for the moment, and that the women were well known by their Vice Division. Logan gave an update on the contact they had with the British Embassy and the frenzy that the British media were in over this, due to the interest generated by all the pre-publicity of the up and coming film that Sara and Bruce had just finished, 'The 2nd Son' along with Bruce's connection with the International Superstar Felicia Bianci.

Morgan and Carlos showed particular interest in the male names of those being held and the names of the members of the gang holding Sara, Bruce and Jayden. They explained the Bureau has been investigating them for some time now, and there had been a significant increase in armed robberies recently, which had the same characteristics of the bigger gang.

'I'm beginning to get the feeling, with everything you have told us so far, these are all connected and if we lean on those currently in custody, we may be able to get the names of those we don't have,' said Morgan.

'What about the little girl,' Ric asked, the feeling of dread he had since he heard about them having a little girl was overwhelming, from all the information they had gathered on Joe, he knew he had no morals or empathy with anything or anyone, other than his brother. He prayed he hadn't descended even lower than he already had.

Carlos said, 'Unfortunately, we have two little girls missing that we're investigating, one in Philadelphia and the other in Pennsylvania, have you been able to get a description of the little girl being held?'

'No, they are all using the same Lawyer, and exercising their right to silence, we've not been able to get any more information.' Ric played the recording but said that it would be inadmissible in court due to the nature in which he had obtained it.

'What are the names of the little girls, and can you give us their descriptions,' Ric asked.

'We have their photos,' he handed these over to Cade and Ric, 'anything you can give us will be much appreciated. We have several leads on the little girl taken from Pennsylvania, which we are looking into, but the one taken in Philadelphia … nothing, her name is Ava Heughan, five years old, it's her sixth birthday in two weeks. Her very distinctive hair colour and large green eyes is not a child you can miss or suddenly pass off as your own, and no one saw her being taken. She was with her parents and ran off to fetch the ball she and her younger brother had been playing with, the ball was found in some bushes, as you can imagine the parents are extremely distraught. There hasn't been a single sighting of her or whoever took her,' said Morgan.

Suddenly, an officer rushed in and announced that Ric and Cade were urgently needed in one of the interview rooms, informing them on the way that Suzie had severely injured herself.

'What? how the fuck did that happen?' said Cade as he and Ric, with Morgan and Carlos following, set off running towards the interview room, 'wasn't anyone watching her?'

'Yes, but nothing was noticed until blood started dripping on the floor, she had been just sitting there with her head bowed, most of the blood got absorbed by her clothing.'

'What the hell did she use, surely she was properly searched when we brought her in?' asked Ric.

'She was, she used one of her false nails, she's made a right job of her wrists, EMS are on their way.'

They crowded into the interview room, Suzie had been laid on the floor and her wrists had been tightly wrapped in bandages, she looked very pale, her clothes were soaked in blood.

The EMS arrived and checked all her vital signs and got her on a stretcher quickly and whisked her off to the hospital. Ric and Cade followed.

When they arrived in the ER, they were told Suzie had died in the ambulance on the way over, they attempted resuscitation, but she had lost too much blood. 'Fuck,' was all Cade said.

'Such was her fear of the gang, to do this and in the way, she did it, Jesus.'

'Well let's go see how the boyfriend reacts and the other girl – Kitty was it?'

They made their way back to the Precinct and were summoned by the Captain to update him. Death in Police custody involved a lot of paperwork and an investigation, which created a distraction from the case they were originally working on, and bad publicity for the Police. Cade and Ric made calls to their respective wife and girlfriend, letting them know they would be home *very* late tonight.

Morgan and Carlos offered their services to interview Suzie's boyfriend Jimmy and the girl, Kitty. Ric and Cade watched the interviews from the viewing rooms. Jimmy's reaction was instant, he was shouting and calling the police all the names he could think of, threw the table and chairs at the toughened glass mirror, hitting the officers as they quickly overpowered him, handcuffed him and took him to a more secure cell to cool off.

Kitty absorbed the information more quietly, hung her head and started to cry, saying that Suzie had always looked out for her. Carlos placed his knuckles on the table and leaned over and told her that her visa had long expired, she would be spending a good part of her life here in prison or deported back to her own country.

She looked up at him with tears streaming from her eyes and said, 'And if I talk, I will be dead.' She fell silent again. He then placed the photograph of Ava Heughen in front of her and watched her reaction, at first she remained very guarded, then Carlos asked, 'If you say nothing else, please just tell us, if this is the little girl Joe Forbes abducted or had abducted,' he appealed to her, 'help us save a little girl who is only five years old.' Kitty looked at the photo and nodded.

There was relief that at least they now knew that Ava was alive, but they still had to be cautious in what was released to the media and not endanger her life. Ric and Cade immediately updated the Captain and Ava Heughan's parents were informed. They were cautiously elated and agreed to keep this from the media for the time being.

They could see Kitty wanted to say more, but she remained silent. Mick and Eric also refused to say anything, after their initial anger at the Police, that was similar to Jimmy's, which was anticipated and contained. They had hoped that Mick would give them something when informed that Kitty could be deported, but they all stayed resolutely silent. They were getting nowhere.

Susan Whittaker's death in Police custody with all its implications and associations were going to the Press and would make the news thereafter within minutes. Their Lawyer must have arranged the sudden interest and was poised for an announcement and interview on the front steps. This was all about to explode and get very ugly.

They needed to urgently re-strategize their investigation, and if the press were going to go into a feeding frenzy for information, they needed to use it, they needed to find where Sara, Bruce, Jayden and little Ava were being held.

Morgan and Carlos wasted no time in contacting their offices and instructing them to raid all the addresses they had on file, and detain all the members they knew about before this hit the news and the gang scattered.

Sixty-One

Returning from replenishing their supplies, Nick set up the new TV, after Joe had smashed the one in the cabin when they first arrived. The other gang members, told them that the publicity was still intense and they would need to lay low a little longer, Nick had found out that his brother was in a secure unit, but not prison, that eased his mind, a little.

Joe had been informed that the pilot and plane he had on standby when they were at the warehouse, had returned to Mexico, and wasn't returning, he had said that for him, it had become, 'too hot' for his liking and wanted nothing more to do with it. The coward.

Their get-away had got away. Joe asked about getting a helicopter, given their current hideout and lack of airstrip it would be easier to land, their friends said they would make enquiries for them and to call them in a few days.

They had a new daily routine and a new enterprise, watching Mel put in a warm-up session with Jayden, before he challenged, or rather forced Bruce to a fight, his incentive being a meal for Sara still. Each day they left the little girl in the room in the barn with Sara, Bruce and Jayden, in the afternoon when they watched the training, they locked her in one of the cabin bedrooms.

Their new idea to make money, was for Mel to get in optimum fighting shape, then arrange a big fight night, here. Encouraging lots of matches and rounds, with large wagers, the ultimate fight being between Mel and Bruce, a fight Joe would force Bruce to lose to ensure Mel won not only the title, be it unofficial, but also all the money. They were also forcing Jayden and Bruce to eat, to keep them in good shape to ensure the ultimate fight was believable. Winning this fight, be it a fixed fight, was the only thing Joe could give to Mel. To ensure he never found out, Joe would only tell Bruce at the last moment, having that bitch and little girl's life in his hands would ensure his co-operation.

Before they went out to the barn, they settled around the table and breakfast bar to eat, Nick turned the TV on. The news flashed up with breaking news, there had been a death of a twenty-seven-year-old woman, Susan Whittaker, a Prostitute in Police custody, her picture was flashed up on the screen.

'Isn't that one of the women who were here – Suzie?' Jase said.

They all gaped at the TV, each expressing their preferred stream of profanity. The report switched to their Lawyer giving an interview on the steps outside the Police Station blaming the Police for her death. Next was the turn of the Police, Captain Neil Ridings said that it was with much regret, that Susan Whittaker, had taken her own life. There followed many questions from the reporters, but he said there was no more he could say, as there will be a full investigation into the incident.

The news continued, detailing that Eric Johnson, James Watson, Miguel Rivera and Katrina Kuznetsova had also been arrested on drug charges, and were part of or known, to a gang that the FBI had led a raid on, at several addresses, and all were wanted for a string of recent armed robberies around New York, their names and photos were shown.

They all stared in a frozen state, at the TV, as their photos and names were shown as another link connected to the bigger gang.

Instantly Joe went into a rage, Nick moved to save the TV, they needed it as the only link to the outside world, which had instantly shrunk further for them. The table went flying and so did some of the chairs that had been repaired from the last time.

'There goes our only chance of *flying* out of here, they were making enquiries into getting us a helicopter and pilot, to get the fuck out of here,' he was pacing and kicking everything in his way, 'those fuckers in there did this,' he shouted very loudly whilst pointing to the barn. 'It's because of who they are that's done this.'

'Isn't that *precisely*, the reason we took 'em?' said Coop. In a flash Joe punched him hard with a right hook followed by a left uppercut, Nate moved in to defend his cousin and Mel joined in to protect his brother, it was down to Jase and Nick to break up the fighting.

Joe was seething, breathing hard through his clenched teeth, he shook off the hold Jase had on him. 'Fuck, they have all of them, that's wiped out the fights we had planned and if one of them mention where we are …'

'None of them will talk, you know that Joe, no one likes a grass, inside,' Mel said.

'They are going to pay for this, literally, and they only have themselves to blame for what is about to happen to them.'

'What do you mean?' chorused in unison by a few of them, with a quizzical look from the others.

'The camera's – you asked why we needed so many Nick, you will be playing an important part in this. A snuff movie,' he stood up and straightened his clothes, he gave them a moment, as that information sunk in, 'I need you to edit the footage from all the camera's, disguise our faces and make it into a movie we can sell, there's a huge market out there for it.'

'You had this planned from the start, didn't you? And timed it to tell us, so we had no choice,' Nick said.

'An insurance policy, if all else failed. Look around, everything else *has* failed, and it's their fault,' he glared at Nick for a moment. 'Don't play the moralistic prick, you've killed people with no hesitation.'

'So, you plan to march over there and kill them, now, tonight, we cut a film and sell it, how and to who?'

'No, I intend to get maximum footage out of them, toy with them, torture them – and then I plan to get out of here and yes, sell it to a contact I have.'

'You are not fucking torturing that little girl,' Nick exploded.

'Take it easy,' Joe quickly said with his hands up in a surrender gesture, 'Not the little girl, I already promised you all, the little girl will be left alone, unharmed and won't even witness any of it.'

Sixty-Two

The additional gang members had left and in the many days that followed, they hadn't returned. Since then, Joe and his gang had introduced a new gruelling routine. The day began around lunchtime after they had slept off the effects of the night before, there was a lot of drinking and drug-taking. Sometimes, they would force Jayden and Bruce to take the drugs, they found the following days difficult, as their thirst from the after-effects from the drugs, left them with extreme thirst, but no water was ever left for them.

They left the little girl with them each day. Then the gang would disappear, they didn't know where they went. Ava ate her meals with Bruce and Jayden who would then be forced to train with Mel in the afternoons, they would take Ava away during practice and returned her later, in between they would be locked in the backroom, thankfully they never restrained Ava.

Sara was left, tied, in the backroom all day. Ava would then be taken back to the cabin and locked into one of the bedrooms for the night, she told them, she was allowed to visit the bathroom once before being left for the night, which frightened her. Sara suggested that when she was in that room alone and felt frightened, to think of her family and have conversations with them, if she wished hard enough, they would hear her.

They had gotten to know little Ava really well during this time, they played word games and I spy with her to try and occupy her mind and reassure her, Bruce, Jayden and Sara took turns to cuddle Ava at times when she missed her mummy and daddy the most, at least they never tied her up, she told them all about her family and her little brother Caelan.

Sara was feeling weak, she was never given enough food or water, some days she would get more and others not enough or nothing. One time to entertain himself, he tied both of Sara's hands tight above her head, she was too weak to stand and left her like that all day, in the evening before the fights, he placed a bowl of food within her reach, then suddenly released her hands, as the blood painfully rushes down her arms, rendering them useless. He shouted at her to eat before he took it away, she was so hungry but so weak to do anything, but slump over and eat like a dog from a bowl, Joe would laugh so hard he leaned forward holding his tummy, forgetting how close to Bruce he was. Bruce kicked him full in the face that propelled him across the room into the wall. Joe was so mad he punched and kicked Bruce repeatedly, as a result, there were no fights that night.

At least Ava was fed well, she was the only spark of happiness in their dull and fearful day.

Bruce noticed that Ava was never searched when she was left with them each day, he gently asked, 'Do those men, ever ask if you have anything in your pockets when they bring you in here, sweetheart?' Ava shook her head, he then asked her if she would share her food with Sara. Sara started to argue, she couldn't take food from a child. Bruce continued, 'You know every evening when you sit with us out there, whilst we eat, Jayden and I can give you some of ours, coz they are not giving much food to Sara, do you think you could do that.'

Ava looked at Sara and her little face beamed. She nodded and said, 'Yes, those horrible men are really mean.'

Bruce looked up at Sara, gave her a weary smile and said, 'I wish I could do more, love.'

'I know, thank you,' she gave him a weak smile, it was all she could muster, she was choked with emotion, with all he had to contend with, he was still thinking of her, putting her first, it humbled her.

Jayden and Bruce were forced to spar and fight with Mel, the others started joining in, to get rid of some of 'their pent up energy', as they put it, although when it came to Bruce, there would be two against one. The battering's they endured each evening, were taking its toll on their bodies which were covered in multi-coloured bruises and their faces never seemed to recover either, from being bruised and swollen.

Food for Sara continued to be their incentive to fight, she was tied to her usual post to watch. Ava was taken back to the cabin before the fights, Sara was brought out to watch the warm-up with Jayden, after which he was tied to his post and Bruce was forced to fight for Sara's supper. Sara noticed a pattern start to emerge, whenever Joe had a word with Bruce before a fight, he would lose, he would look over at her and drop his head – she knew, there would be no food for her tonight.

Every night after the fights finished, the same thing would happen, the gang would leave and return to the cabin, Mel and Joe would return Bruce to the back room, only Mel would leave and close the door, walk passed Sara and Jayden without looking at them, leaving them tied to the posts.

Later, Joe would leave. One evening, as Joe passed Sara he paused, and said, 'Your boyfriend is rather quite talented, isn't he?' and waggling his eyebrows and laughed as he walked out, his smugness and callousness, made her want to heave.

Some nights they would be forgotten and left tied to the posts all night. On the nights they *were* returned, later in the evening, by a member of the gang, Bruce would not look at them, did not say anything, he would sit with his head hung low, probably with his eyes closed. The smell in that small darkened and enclosed room was evidence of what had taken place. No words could be offered that would be adequate, appropriate or give any alleviation.

Sixty-Three

They heard the smaller barn door crash open, immediately Ava was frightened, she ran over to Bruce for protection, something Sara had noticed happening lately, but if she felt she needed to talk about her mummy or her family, then she would snuggle up to Sara, if she felt a little unwell or her tummy ached, it was Jayden she went to.

The door to the back room was unlocked with sudden force, Ava screamed and huddled up to Bruce even closer. Joe strode into the room followed by the others, he told Mel to lock the little girl up in her room. He then released Sara and dragged her into the barn area. Bruce expected he and Jayden to follow, but the door was closed, he started shouting, joined by Jayden, they called and hollered to leave her alone, to take them. The door suddenly opened, Coop and Nate walked in and gagged both of them, then left the room.

Bruce will never forget the screams, the begging and pleading he heard from Sara, they both jumped to their feet and were pulling at the chains, trying to untie the ropes, but there was no give in the chains and the ropes were too tight and the knots difficult to reach.

Sara's screams continued for what felt like an eternity to Bruce, for the longest time he heard her pleading again followed by more strangled screams and groans, then the door opened and Bruce was released and frog-marched out to the barn area by Nate and Coop, what he saw made him reel in horror, he struggled to escape the stronghold they had on him.

Sara was lying on the ground in the middle of the wide walkway in between the horse stalls, she was being held down by Nick, Jase and Mel, Joe had a knife in his hand which was dripping with blood, her face was bright red and he could see the start of swelling on her cheeks. Her right knee was covered in blood and there was another smaller knife still embedded in her inner right thigh, so much blood from both wounds. Sara was crying and trying to hold back her cries of pain, through clenched teeth.

Joe sat back on his hunches, took out a cloth and started to wipe the blood from the knife in his hand, looked up at Bruce and said, 'Would you mind removing that knife,' he pointed to the one in Sara's leg, 'release him, I don't think he'll do anything stupid, far too concerned for *her*,' he said to Nate and Coop. To Bruce he said, 'Remember we have the little girl, now get over here and remove the knife, I rather like it.' The others released Sara and moved away from her.

They released Bruce and removed his gag, he ran and skidded to his knees beside Sara, 'You fucking sick, cruel bastards – why?'

'Why *not*. We have just had yet another set-back, *this* ...' he motioned towards Sara, 'and the cameras are part of our new venture. Remove. The. Fucking. Knife,' he menacingly hissed through his teeth while glaring at Bruce.

Bruce looked into Sara's distraught, tear-stained face, gently caressed her cheek, then looked at the knife in her leg, another blade he was forced to pull out of her, he felt sick at having to cause her pain and hoped to God he could pull it out straight, to not shake and cause more damage to her perfect, beautiful leg. He looked at the knife again, it looked like a large penknife, the blade was about an inch in width judging by the wound, but it hadn't gone through, therefore was not a long blade.

'Get on with it,' said Joe impatiently as he rose to his feet.

Bruce turned to Sara, 'Keep looking at me ok?' Sara bravely nodded as perspiration beaded on her forehead. He had his hand on the knife and without further warning, he quickly pulled it out. Sara screamed, and fresh tears rolled down her cheeks, as she scrunched her face in agony, and tightened her lips to muffle any further screams, then passed out.

Bruce threw the knife at Joe, who jumped out of the way, swore loudly and profusely, picked it up and wiped it with the same care he did the other knife. Bruce clamped his hand over the wound.

'Get them back to the room, let the other one patch her up – for now,' Joe added and shot Bruce a sneering look of contempt.

Bruce swiftly picked Sara up in his arms and rushed back to the room and shouted for the medical supplies to be brought in. Jase fetched them and tossed them in from the doorway, Bruce quickly remarked that Jayden was hardly able to, 'patch her up' if he remained tied. Jase told him to back up away from the door, Bruce gently laid Sara on the floor and moved back, Nick appeared in the doorway, they were both obviously weary when Bruce wasn't restrained.

As soon as Jayden was released, he was beside Sara, assessing the damage to her knee and the knife wound, he quickly took out a wad bandage and told Bruce to wind it around the thigh wound, as it was the less serious of the two injuries, while he checked her vital signs and her knee.

After Jayden had time to assess the damage, he said, 'They forced a knife through her kneecap between femur and tibia, causing possible ligament and cartilage damage, the good news is, the knife didn't go all the way through the knee.'

'Oh God – what can you do,' Bruce asked desperately. He looked at Sara's face, she was very pale.

Jayden rummaged in the only bag given to him. 'They didn't bring all the supplies from the warehouse, I have only basic first aid, I can only tend the wound, clean it and suture it, I won't be able to fix the damage they've caused, she would need an operation for that. At least I have antibiotics, to ward off any infection.'

'Please, do everything you can,' Bruce pleaded.

'They took all the Lignocaine, it was in this bag, I remember hurriedly packing it when they took me. I'll have to work quickly and hope she doesn't wake, keep an eye on her and hold her if she does.'

Bruce prayed that she would not, they had held her down and tortured her, he dreaded her waking, and it be him, holding her down, while Jayden had to inflict more pain to help her.

He raised her gently and cradled her head and shoulders against him, brushing her hair from her face and caressing her cheeks, whispering that he was with her, and silently begged that she didn't wake while Jayden cleaned the wound, fortunately, he had sachets of sterile saline to do this, they had no water.

He stitched first her knee and bandaged it, then unwrapped the wound to her thigh and did the same, cleaned and stitched it and then gave her the antibiotics. The gang didn't return that night which Bruce was thankful for.

For the first time in weeks, he laid next to Sara, he didn't get much sleep, he kept watching her, fearful her condition would worsen, Jayden didn't have tetanus to give her and the knife, would not have been clean, God only knows what it had been used for.

The night was long, Sara fretted most of the night, in pain and hot to the touch, all he could do was mop her brow with a bandage, there was no water to soothe or cool her, Jayden checked her constantly, gave her another dose of antibiotics. Bruce could see the contusions forming under her skin, on her cheeks and one eye, there was swelling and bruising forming on her beautiful face.

Throughout the night Bruce had constantly whispered to her, he brought alive the memories of their time together, the things they laughed at, the things they loved about New York, he thought that if she could hear him, he would make her think of good things, he told her they would get through this and return home, she would see her family and friends again, he told her to embrace those thoughts and hold on to them, tight.

Eventually, morning came or was it the afternoon in the room with no window, their concept of time was lost.

Sixty-Four

Three weeks of trying to locate the kidnapper's new hideout, Ric and Cade were under enormous pressure and extremely frustrated at their lack of progress and their line of enquiries getting nowhere. Those they had arrested either continued to keep silent or sent them on wild goose chases, they had run out of time and either had to arrest them or let them go, therefore they were arrested on drug charges, better that than to let them go free.

More and more cranks and weirdos, were crawling out of the woodwork, making up stories of sightings or suddenly remembering seeing the little girl on the day she disappeared, and who took her, none were consistent enough to add any credible leads, a few were even genuinely convinced they were helping with their false sightings.

Every line of enquiry was amounting to a big, fat nothing. The American media, the British Embassy and the British Media, were getting impatient and they couldn't blame them, there was a child involved now, not to mention two high profile celebrities and a Military Doctor.

Little Ava's sixth birthday had been celebrated by her heartbroken family and the nation - without her. The parents, Connor and Alana were finding it difficult to continually fool the media with their many questions about their missing little girl and not let it slip that they knew she was alive, but didn't know where. The Police emphasised that to let it slip who had her, would endanger her life, therefore they took over answering any questions and moved the family to a safe house, the Police let it be known that the family were taking a break, siting the stress and strain on their family of their missing little girl. Her father Connor agreed to give a heart-warming interview about his little girl. A re-enactment had been shown on all the TV channels across America.

The Captain reassigned Ric and Cade's caseloads to other Officer's, to enable them to concentrate solely, on this case, an incident room was set up with a team of Officers to help collate all the information. They were able to follow up other leads, primarily on the gang holding the kidnapped victims.

Ric and Cade were in New Jersey, following up on a lead, not sure how reliable the informant was, it was another drunk, who staggered into a station saying he remembered a conversation in a bar many months ago, with a man called Javier Rodriguez, the land was near a stream, the fuzzy bit, *as he put it*, was that he couldn't remember if it was New Jersey or New Hampshire, but it wasn't New York, that much he was sure of. When asked why it had taken him so long to come forward, he shrugged his shoulders and said that the conversation in the bar was many months ago, and admitted that his hold on reality, wavered, but the name suddenly crystallized when he saw the news last night.

They were given an office in one of the Precincts and spent a week trying to find a needle in a haystack, there were so many Real Estates in both States, and that was only if Javier had bought it legally, and whether it was in his own name or a false name, or possibly his parent's names. That thought led Ric to making numerous phone calls to Mexico, to locate Javier's parents, in a country with a popular tradition of naming children after the parents and grandparents, there were many couples with his parent's names and Rodriguez was also a very popular name.

'Eureka,' Ric jumped up and shouted as he came off the phone, 'I have found them and they have a son called Javier, born in the right year for it to be them.' As a child in Mexico, Ric never really knew Javier's parents and as it had been many years, they had moved. They spent the rest of the day and the next re-calling all the Real Estates, then suddenly the puzzle fell into place.

Javier had bought a piece of land in his parent's names, and it was near a stream, and it was local which saved repeating the work if they had to travel to New Hampshire.

Ric made a call to their incident room, everyone was listening on extensions and an almighty cheer went up, when he explained its location, everyone felt it was a perfect place to hold up and lay low. The team told them that through their collaborative efforts with the FBI, they had put together their supposition that the arrested branch of the gang did most of the work, storing supplies, carrying out the armed robberies and probably masterminded by the kidnapping gang, in particular Joe Forbes.

Although the team wanted to be there to be part of finding the little girl, they realised that time was of the essence and that Ric and Cade would have to take a back-up team from the Precinct they had been working from, but to keep them updated.

Sixty-Five

Sara lay on the floor in the little room, she felt so weak, dizzy and sometimes delirious, the only food she got was what Ava managed to smuggle in, or from the fights Joe allowed Bruce to win against Mel, she was given water only twice a day, they didn't bother to handcuff her, there was no need anymore. Bruce and Jayden were often left unrestrained, Joe sniggered from the door, to, 'Patch her up.'

Every day Bruce and Jayden would *'train'* with Mel, after, they would take her out to the main barn area, initially, tying her to a chair. As she grew weaker, and toppling sideways and falling to the ground taking the chair with her, they would just drag her out and drop her on the floor in the middle of the barn between the horse stalls, ensuring she was conscious to watch them all eat their lunch and dinners. Joe taking great pleasure watching her desperate look at the food, and attempting to lick her dry lips.

They forced Bruce and Jayden to eat *all* their food to, 'Keep up their strength.' Joe found this amusing as he winked at Bruce, who looked away with a look of disgust on his face, finding it difficult to finish his food, which delighted Joe to goad him even more.

Sara could see they found it difficult to eat, knowing she was slowly starving. One day before they brought Ava into the barn, Bruce refused to eat unless Sara was given food, Joe walked over and leaned down close into Bruce's face and said, 'If you don't eat then you will lose strength, then our *special,* little meetings will be very disappointing for me,' as he said this he seductively ran his finger down Bruce's cheek and throat. Bruce visibly shuddered and moved back away from his caress. Joe continued, 'And I won't have your training with Mel interrupted, so eat your fucking food, now,' he bellowed in Bruce's face. He then turned and kicked Sara in the stomach.

'Leave her alone,' Bruce shouted.

'Up to you, are you going to eat your food like a good boy, or shall I bring the little girl in here?'

Bruce placed a piece of bread in his mouth while holding his glare at Joe, feeling like he could choke on it.

It was a blessing that Ava wasn't brought into the barn after that, they kept her in the cabin, at least they spared her watching their cruelty and only spent mealtimes with Bruce and Jayden.

Joe liked to torment Sara with a knife whenever he felt like it, on this occasion he threatened to cut out her tongue, holding her head and placing the knife in her mouth, with a quick sharp movement, instead, he severely cut the left side of her mouth.

It required many stitches and without lignocaine, Joe told Jayden he had loads of it in the cabin, but she would get none of it. As Jayden prepared to stitch her, Sara asked him if he was good at embroidery and not to give her a Joker smile, from the Batman series. She had made him laugh. Bruce whispered, 'You can still make a joke of this? You're incredible,' but she had made him smile too.

Joe particularly enjoyed watching this, Sara took some deep breaths and focused her mind on repeating in her head a mantra, *this doesn't hurt, there is no pain, it will heal,* over and over. Bruce was cradling her head in his lap, it was awkward for Jayden, but there was no table, not one they would give him anyway. She didn't make much noise as this was being done, and Joe got exasperated asking, 'Why isn't she making any noise? she should be screaming – or something,' as he kicked her bad leg.

Was she getting used to the pain? or had her leg lost all feeling, she didn't feel the kick and continued to concentrate on repeating her mantra. Joe walked out in disgust. She had deprived him of his entertainment.

When Jayden had finished stitching, he gave her a dose of antibiotic. It was the last he had, Bruce and Jayden looked at each other in despair. That night as Bruce lay beside Sara, Jayden sat over in a corner to give them the only privacy he could in such a confined space.

Sara looked at Bruce and whispered, 'You know, none of us is leaving here alive, don't you?'

He stubbornly refused to believe that, every day he had been looking for a way, a time where they relaxed their guard, but they hadn't, and always the threat towards Sara or Ava, there had to be a way out, Sara needed to reserve her energy, 'You need to rest, love.'

'Not yet, I will have a long time to rest, soon enough.'

Bruce closed his eyes. Dear God, please not that, never that. When he opened them, the tears escaped. 'Please don't say that.'

Sara raised her hands and caressed his face and ran her fingers through his hair, 'You have to listen to me. You need to get Ava out of here, I'm not going to make it.'

Bruce put both his hands tenderly to Sara's face, 'This can't be the end.'

'Not, while I am breathing, but after … he is not going to leave witnesses, you know that. I can't bear to have the death of a child being my fault, you have to get her back to her parents.'

'Oh Sara, my beautiful Sara, I didn't want to say this to you here, in all this ugliness. I. Love. You. Not because of all this, I fell in love with you the first day we met, you had my heart with that first smile.'

'I love you too, also not because of this,' they both smiled at each other, 'I felt it that first moment we met. Thank you for helping me to love again, I didn't think that would be possible, not in the complete way I love you.'

They laid there for a few moments, absorbed in staring deeply, into each other's eyes, which said everything, they didn't need words. Bruce wanted to kiss her, but her lips were so swollen, and he didn't want to cause her more pain, he feathered kisses across her cheek, her nose and her chin, and told her all the things he loved about her.

Sara took a deep breath and called Jayden over, he sat by Sara's side opposite Bruce, who didn't get up, he wanted to stay close to her. 'You both have to listen carefully, and please don't interrupt, I don't have the strength to argue.' When she got a nod from them both, she continued, 'Tomorrow, when you both sit and eat with Ava, as soon as you have finished, I will use all the strength I have left, to cause a distraction, that is when you pick Ava up and both of you run like hell, you *don't* hesitate and you *don't* look back.'

'I can carry you and Jayden can carry Ava,' Bruce said desperately.

'No,' Sara said sharper than she meant to, she closed her eyes and took a breath, it took too much energy to talk for too long. 'You can't run with me and get away from six men, you know that, in your *head*, you know that. I can't do this anymore, and each day I'm getting weaker. Soon, I won't be able to cause the distraction to help you both get away, and when I'm gone, he will …' She couldn't finish the sentence before a tear trickled down her cheek, and she closed her eyes, she took a deep breath and steeled herself to continue, 'They never close the barn doors at lunchtime, when you are eating anymore. It's the perfect time. The only time, and it has to be tomorrow.'

'There must be another way, Sara, I can't bear to leave you here, when one of us can try and get you out of here,' Jayden said.

'If we try and fail, there will be no second chance, my weakening is the only reason they have not been so careful lately. My knee will not bend, and it will be impossible to carry me through what is likely to be woods out there. No, you both need to get Ava out of here, promise me,' they both looked down, but nodded their agreement and promised.

Sara took Jayden's hand and said, 'Get back to Layla, marry her and have a full life together.'

'I will never forget you, Sara, Ava's parents will know what you have done to save their little girl,' he bent down and kissed her on the forehead, then got up and returned to the corner to allow Bruce and Sara to say their private goodbyes. Silently, he let the tears fall, he admired her bravery and will forever honour her sacrifice.

Sara looked deep into Bruce's eyes, 'Before we met, I thought you would be a little arrogant, a man's man, trying to prove you were the world's greatest lover, seducing every female.'

'You trying to break it to me that I'm not, the world's greatest lover?' he mocked with a weak smile and raised eyebrow.

Sara smiled, 'Always the greatest lover to me. As I got to know you, I was privileged to see the man you *are*, a kind, caring man, I could see the way your sister, your brothers and your friends react around you and others gravitate towards you, you are a genuine person. Don't let all this change you Bruce, stay true to yourself.'

'I want you with me, I can't …' a tear rolled down his cheek followed by another and another, Sara kissed each tear away.

'Do you believe in life after?'

Bruce cleared his throat, 'I believe there is – something, not sure what, just don't believe *this*, is all there is.'

'*If* there *is* life after, and there's a way, I will find you and visit you in your dreams.'

They laid in each other's arms, they were saying goodbye to each other in every stroke and every caress. Eventually, Sara fell asleep. Bruce tried to stay awake, he didn't want to miss a single moment of the time he had left with her, he laid there caressing her face, stroking her hair and whispering sweet nothings to her, telling her there will never be another to replace her in his heart, he told her he wouldn't be able to honour one of the promises she asked of him, and that was to find love again, she smiled as she told him that third time *would* be lucky, she promised, as she would put a word in for him on the other side. That was when he told her in a choked whisper to sleep, and he let the tears flow as he cradled her in his arms, for what would be the last time.

As much as he wanted to stay awake, he must have drifted off at some point, because he had a dream that he had walked out of here, carrying Sara asleep in his arms, he was then in New York, walking down one of the streets with her in his arms to safety. He woke and for a few seconds imagined that they were safe, the dream was so real, until he looked around and sudden realisation kicked in, and the day Sara had outlined was about to begin and unfold.

Sixty-Six

The day started when Nate opened the door and threw a bottle of water at Jayden and Bruce, they always shared this with Sara. Then Bruce and Jayden were taken out to spar with Mel, they found it difficult to fight and Mel kept throwing harder and quicker punches, thinking that he was getting better and was able to out-wit Bruce, he kept taunting him that he was weak and slow. Bruce's heart and body felt like lead, he found it hard to concentrate.

Sara was adamant her plan was the only way, throughout the morning he and Jayden came up with alternative suggestions, each one Sara countered with the flaws in their plans, and it always came back to one fact - Ava had to be reunited with her parents.

As lunchtime drew near and Ava was brought out to the barn, Sara was dragged out by Jase and Nick and dropped to the floor in the middle of the barn as usual. Joe laid a piece of bread on the dusty, filthy ground and a small cup of water close to her, but just out of her reach, he stood over her, looked around checking the cameras and said, 'Are you hungry? are you thirsty? Bitch.' It was another one of his torments, a play for the cameras.

Bruce and Jayden were sitting with Ava on a pile of timbers, in the clearing past the horse stalls and closer to the barn doors, Sara noticed and thought it was perfect for them to get away, Nate and Coop stood off to the side, Mel was just leaving the ring which was at the opposite end of the barn, just outside the room they had been kept in.

Sara didn't immediately react, this was her chance to create the diversion, he was expecting her to move slowly, to crawl, he would not expect her to do anything, it was now or never. She took some deep breaths and concentrated her mind, she let him come closer to her and he would, he was baiting her. If she held off for a moment, even though her attention was fixated on the bread, something so bland had never looked so delicious.

Joe stepped forward, grabbed her and pulled her head back by her hair, in the same movement using the momentum of him lifting her head, Sara turned over in the small confines between his spread legs and took advantage that he was bent over her. With all her strength, she punched him hard between the legs, before he could react, she swiftly followed it with a kick using her good leg to the same area, he immediately let out a loud roar and dropped her, as he crumbled sideways to the floor holding himself.

Sara looked over and saw Bruce pick Ava up and paused, for just an instant, a split second. He looked at her, time stopped for them both in that moment. Then he was gone, and she whispered, 'Goodbye, my love.'

Sixty-Eight

Jase and Nick dashed after Bruce through the barn doors. Sara saw that Nate and Coop had gotten hold of Jayden, as he was closest to them, and had one of the spikes in their hands, and were pushing him back against the log walls of the barn, he was fighting with all his strength, but they managed to pin him to the wall and both of them were delivering punches, suddenly Joe hollered for them to go after Bruce and the girl, then yelled at Mel to see to Jayden.

Mel ran down to the front of the barn, Sara heard a lot of punches and scuffling, then an almighty cry followed by a gunshot. Joe was immediately on his feet and ran at full speed from where he was, Sara raised her head, looking for Jayden, he was sitting up at the end of the barn by the doors with a gun in his hand, he pointed it at Joe, pulled the trigger, but there were no more bullets, the spike was protruding through his left side at waist level, he was conscious, just. He looked over at Sara, then his head slowly slumped forward.

Mel lay at Jayden's feet and Joe was crouching over him, he dropped to his knees and immediately was trying to stem the flow of blood from Mel's left arm, Joe pressed hard against the wound, he took off his belt and strapped it around his arm as a tourniquet, 'Shot by your own fucking gun, you're getting sloppy,' he then dragged Mel up and sat him next to Jayden. 'At least you got one of the fuckers,' as he pointed to Jayden.

Joe had his back to Sara. She couldn't hear and she didn't care what they were talking about, her energy was spent. Then she heard Joe's raised voice, as he tried to rouse Mel, he kept shouting, 'Mel don't you die on me, you hear, don't you dare die on me.' It went quiet for a while, then Joe got up, turned around, paused and stared at Sara with a murderous look in his eyes, and started towards her.

Bruce was running as fast as he could with Ava in his arms, he concentrated his mind on his training to try and maximise his breathing, and control his heart rate, to gain maximum speed and not tire fast. Ava was being such a brave little girl, her arms and legs were clinging tight around him, and she wasn't crying, just kept her head buried between his neck and shoulder.

He could hear two of them right behind him, he had to keep ahead of them, he had no idea where they were, or what he was running to, just logic or hope, that eventually he must come across something, a road, a house, anything.

He heard shouts and the voices were very close. They were shouting to Nate and Coop to spread out, who were shouting back to Jase and Nick to do the same, he had four of them after him. Just before he left, he saw Nate and Coop go for Jayden, if they were now after him, Jayden hadn't made it, he sent up a silent sorry, and thanked him for everything he had done.

He was not going to be able to outrun them, and he was aware of the noise he was making as he crunched over dry leaves and twigs, they only needed to stop for a second and listen, the woods were getting thicker and denser, and the noise was echoing through the quietness that enveloped the forest. If he stopped and hid, he may have a chance to take a few of them out of the chase.

He spotted a clump of trees that were unusually close together, more so than the others and headed for them, there was one tree, that looked like it had split in a storm or been struck by lightning, and there was another that created a hiding place for a very small person, perfect to hide Ava. He put her down and explained that he needed to stop the men from chasing them, and if she stayed curled up and didn't make a sound, she would be safe until he came back and got her, and would get her back to her parents, she promised to stay still and quiet.

Bruce picked a spot a safe distance away from Ava, but close enough if he needed to get to her. He waited and planned his strategy, let them get very close, be fast, break a leg and render them unconscious, he knew how to do that from his training, in competition they were illegal moves, this was survival therefore permittable, at least in his books. Muffle the noise or it will give his position away to the others, his heart was hammering loud and fast in his chest, praying he could take them out, one at a time. It wasn't long before he saw the first one, it was Nate.

Nate had his gun in one hand, and he was cautiously moving forward, but looking all around him, Bruce saw him approaching, he looked to see if Coop was anywhere, as these two tended to always be together, there was no sign of him. Bruce reacted quickly, grabbed Nate's wrist and with a quick twist disarmed him, he followed swiftly with a downward flat handed chop to his neck which rendered him immediately unconscious, he dropped him to the ground and stomped hard on the back of his leg and heard the crack, that took him out of the chase, as there was no telling how long he would remain unconscious, he emptied the gun of all the bullets and threw them in one direction and the gun in another.

Bruce hated guns, had never fired one and even if he took it, he was sure he wouldn't use it, maybe it was being British or maybe it was from his training in kickboxing and mixed martial arts, and the spiritual respect the sport stands for, but he would prefer to disable them one by one, if he could.

One down three to go.

Bruce crouched down and listened, he was no longer running from them, he was hunting them.

He glanced towards the area that held Ava and moved to another position and heard another of them approaching, it was Coop with a flick knife in his hand. Bruce stepped into his direct path, with a fast movement he put one hand on the inside of Coop's wrist, with the other, delivered a fast tap to the outside of his wrist, which opened the hand and knocked the knife out, Bruce spun around behind Coop and had him in a headlock with his arm around his neck and a hand over his mouth, he squeezed until he lost consciousness, as he dropped him to the floor, he stomped on his leg and heard the crack, he then threw the knife into the woods.

Two down, two to go.

Listening again, Bruce had to move further away from Ava, he looked around memorising the layout of the trees and the unusual clump hiding Ava, to ensure he made it back to her.

Again, he listened, he heard a movement further ahead, Bruce followed.

He spotted the back of Jase as he climbed over the large root of a tree and looked back, Bruce darted behind a tree. Bruce crouched low and fast as he came up behind Jase, and grabbed him, unfortunately, he let out a yelp, Bruce delivered his blow to the neck, but it wasn't as hard as he wanted it to be, Jase wouldn't be out for long, the blow had been hindered by Nick who had come up behind Bruce and stabbed him with a knife to the shoulder blade, Bruce felt searing hot pain to his left shoulder, he spun around and deflected another swipe of the blade by moving to the side out of its path, he quickly looked around and saw a thick fallen branch, he picked it up to defend himself and the adrenaline helped to disguise some of the pain from his shoulder.

Bruce deflected another swipe with the knife from Nick and he lunged with the branch, directly to the throat, Nick went down. By this time Jase had recovered and was getting up and the first Bruce knew of it, was when he felt a hard punch to the small of his back, as he spun around and fell to one knee, he noticed Jase had a knuckle duster on, the punch winded Bruce and made him cough. Jase gave him no time to recover, he moved in to land another punch, but Bruce quickly rolled away and came up on his feet to the side of Jase, he grabbed his arm, bent it back and heard the crack, Jase screamed out and fell to the ground. Bruce delivered a blow to his neck, there was no further movement, Bruce broke his leg, removed the knuckle duster and threw it into the woods. He walked over to Nick and picked up the knife with his blood on it and threw that too into the undergrowth, stomped on Nick's leg and heard the crack.

Suddenly the pain in his shoulder returned. He leant against the nearest tree and allowed a moment for his breathing to settle and for his heart rate to calm, he removed his shirt and ripped the right sleeve off, then tied it tightly around his injured shoulder and put his shirt back on.

He checked both Jase and Nick for any further weapons and threw two further knives he found far into the woods. He retraced his steps and checked Coop then Nate of any further weapons, only Nate had a further hidden gun in his boot, he emptied it and threw the bullets and gun in opposite directions.

He staggered further and leant against another tree to steady himself and wipe the sweat from his brow before he went to get Ava. As he got close to the tree she was huddled in, Bruce softly called out her name and told her it was he, who was approaching so as not to scare her, she lifted her head and immediately jumped out of the tree and ran to him and hugged him tightly, he winced and groaned at the pain to his shoulder, he eased her grip, 'Sorry, did the bad men hurt you?' as a tear rolled down her cheek.

'A little.'

'Are they still after us?' she asked as she anxiously looked behind him.

'Not for a while, but we need to move quickly, are you ok to walk?'

Ava nodded. Such a brave little girl, concern for him and no crying. They set off and soon the woods started thinning out and weren't as dense, Bruce looked back to gain his bearings and started to break branches to mark his path.

He was coming back for Sara.

They started running. A little while later, they spotted a farm up ahead. Bruce ran up the front porch steps with Ava beside him and knocked on the door loudly. Bruce took one step back as the door was opened by a young man, in the background, Bruce saw a middle-aged-women, who had the look of a friendly kind and homely person, behind her was another man of similar age to the woman, a couple and son maybe?

Bruce quickly introduced himself, the little girl and what had happened, the young man introduced himself as Sergeant Tyrone Lawrence and his parents Tom and Maisie.

'Please come in, we've been hearing all about what has happened, I'm stationed at the base Dr Jayden Hayes was taken from, I'm home on leave.'

'I don't have time to come in, I must get back to Sara, God only knows what he is doing to her. Can you please call the police, and take care of Ava and get her back to her parents?

Maisie immediately moved forward and crouched down in front of the little girl and confirmed that she would indeed get her back to her mummy and daddy, went to take her inside, but Ava didn't want to let go of Bruce's hand.

Bruce knelt down and gently said to her, 'I have to go back and deal with those bad and mean men to bring Sara home.' He didn't add, *'dead or alive'*. He couldn't bear to think of his beautiful, vibrant Sara gone from this earth, he was praying she was alive and he could get back to her in time.

If not, then to take her away from that dark, evil, ugly place.

'You have been such a brave little girl, and I want to get you back to your mummy, daddy and your little brother, Caelan, they have been missing you so much, go with this lady, she will see you are safe.'

'Will I see you again?' she asked, and a tear slipped down her cheek.

'Definitely,' he kissed her cheek and wiped away the tear with his thumb, winked at her, she smiled and went into the house.

Tyrone came out of the house with his gun over his shoulder and told Bruce he was coming with him, Bruce didn't argue, he could use the help.

They set off at a run, obviously, Tyrone easily kept up, they entered the woods, Bruce recognised the markers he had left and it was easy for a while, he then slowed. For one moment Bruce felt a sudden panic as he lost his bearings, he looked around, they had passed the tree he hid Ava in, but from this point on he lost his direction, as he had been running with Ava in his arms and hadn't had the time or thought to make markers.

He stood and turned in a circle, at a sudden total loss, as to which direction to go in, Tyrone asked, 'Do you know what type of building you were held in?'

'It was a large barn, there was another smaller barn next to it and a large log cabin.'

'Oh my God – that's where you've been held all this time? I know it – this way.' They started at a run.

'How come you know of it?'

'All the locals know it. It's owned by that nasty piece of work, Javier something, sick bastard, some of the things he's known to have done, bragged about it. Made a pass at me in the toilets of a bar one time, my fists and boot made quick work of showing him how *un*interested I was, he never looked at me again.

On their way through the woods, Bruce briefed Tyrone on what he had done, and said he needed to check they were still unconscious, 'You broke a leg on each one of them? – impressive and good thinking. I brought rope, let's make sure they are bound, just in case they wake up.'

Sixty-Nine

Joe was approaching her and Sara knew this was the end, she looked at Jayden with his head slumped, she said a silent thank you to him for everything and felt a sadness that he didn't make it back to Layla. She prayed that Bruce had gotten little Ava to safety and return her to her parents, she could meet whatever happened now, if Bruce and Ava got away.

Without warning, Joe picked Sara up by her hair, and dragged her towards the back of the barn and flung her against the wall opposite the ring. As she lay there catching her breath and rubbing her head where he had ripped out a clump of her hair, she watched as he quickly dismantled the ring and went round twisting all the cameras to point towards her.

He turned around and went back towards the front of the barn, collected Mel and walked him slowly towards Sara. Mel slumped against the wall opposite Sara and took out his flick knife, Joe turned around, looked at Sara as his face took on a malicious scowl, a vile smirk and a venomous sneer as he walked towards her. Sara closed her eyes and prayed that whatever was to come would be quick, she wouldn't be fighting the inevitable, there was no saving her, Bruce was gone, thank God, Jayden was dead and she would soon be joining him.

Sara laid curled up on the filthy cold floor of the barn, in excruciating pain. Concentrating on her breathing until the pain subsided again. She had no idea where she was or how long she had been there, the only thing clear, was that it would all end soon. Her plan had worked, Bruce and little Ava had gotten out, they had escaped.

Sara reflected on her life. She had packed so much into her 23 short years. All her hopes, her plans and her dreams for the future were to be snatched away, violently.

A sharp sting, sprang to her eyes and a huge lump rose in her throat, making swallowing difficult. She refused to let any tears fall, that would show weakness and she would not leave this world and give that evil bastard, any satisfaction.

This was but a short reprieve between the savage beatings, just long enough for him to knock back another whiskey and get his breath back. Her fears were magnified as she realised, she was staring directly into the face of her own mortality.

'Please God, let me peacefully slip away before he returns,' she pleaded.

She let her mind drift and thought of Bruce, the night of the Wrap Party, the very special nights in her hotel, and all the ways they found to love each other, and their very understated visit to Coney Island, just the two of them. How long ago was that? It seemed like time had slowed down and the world had disappeared.

Life was so cruel. To have experienced such a life-altering connection with love once in a lifetime, but to be given that chance twice, and have it end tragically short both times, made her belief in fate a mockery, and a far greater suffering than the physical pain she was enduring.

Her mind drifted on to thoughts of her parents and she sent them a heartfelt farewell:

Mum, you were always there for me with a loving smile and staunch encouragement for Cameron and me to do better and succeed. I am so sorry to leave first.

Dad, forever the Jekyll & Hyde, the generous sole one moment, and nasty the next, with a vicious temper, I hope one day you will acknowledge your depression and seek help, please give mum the support she will need in the coming days and weeks.

Cameron, my wonderful big brother, I would never have achieved all that I did without you, always by my side, guiding me and sharing my hopes and dreams, thank you. For the love you have for me, please give Bruce the support I know you are so good at giving.

I carry all your love in my heart and I send you mine, please take care of each other, until we meet again. I'll be waiting.

Last but by no means least, Bruce. We had such a short time together, but what an incredible time it was. I take all those wonderful memories with me. Even in these darkest moments, the thought of you makes me smile, thank you for showing me how to love again. I love you and it hurts so much to never know what might have been, remember me with a smile, you carry the remainder of my heart with you.

Her mind drifted again in a kaleidoscopic haze of wonderful memories, especially the day she first met Bruce …

Joe flicked his hair back, took a deep breath and with a large nail and a hammer in his hand he approached her, Sara squeezed her eyes shut. Joe reached above her and hammered in the nail, then bent down and picked up her wrists and bound them, Sara clenched her teeth to stifle a scream from the pain she had everywhere, she couldn't tell where it hurt the most, he then hung her hands over the nail, she had no strength to support herself on her good leg, it seemed to hurt just as much and it didn't seem to matter she realised, as she was hanging a little higher than her height, but the pain in her arms and shoulders was excruciating.

Joe stood in front of her, grabbing her around the throat with one hand and squeezed, while he held a gun to her forehead, Sara started seeing black spots in front of her eyes, before passing out, he eased his grip, but didn't let go, she was gasping and gulping for air, then he leered close to her face, she could smell his stale breath, making her feel sick, then she heard the cocking of the gun as he lowered the barrel and held it between her eyes, then he said, 'Your boyfriend was more to my liking and I had a good time with him, but Mel may take a turn with you before you … expire, you do realise you're going to die, don't you?'

'It will be a release from looking at your fuck ugly face,' Sara managed in little more than a strained whisper.

He stepped back and Mel walked forward with a lustful, salacious smile on his face as his eyes lowered to her breasts, with the very last of her energy, Sara swung her foot and kicked Mel in the groin as hard as she could manage, he instantly fell to his knees cupping himself. In a flash of movement, Joe bent and picked up the flick knife Mel had dropped and pulled out his own, he paused and slowly pushed both knives simultaneously into either side of her abdomen, Sara sucked in her breath, gulped and her eyes widened, 'These wounds will not kill you, just yet,' Joe said, as he pulled out both knives together.

Sara let out a strangled scream, her throat hurt and she was trying to control the pain through her breathing, and failing. As hard as she tried to stop them, tears rolled down her face, she wiped them on her arms, as she gritted her teeth, the pain pulsated through her whole body, as he cut the ropes holding her and she fell to the floor.

She was losing the battle to manage the pain, then she felt a punch to the face, the room started dimming, the pain was subsiding and voices were fading, until, at last, there was only blissful blackness.

Seventy

Bruce and Tyrone arrived in the clearing close to the barn, Bruce was eager to get inside to, *God willing*, rescue Sara. Tyrone said, 'We need to agree our plan, if we go rushing into the front doors, who knows what we are facing. How many of them are there?'

'Two. Brothers Mel and Joe, who is the sick twisted son-of-a-bitch leader.'

'Where is Javier?'

'Dead. Shot, with a bullet, probably meant for me, when they took us.'

'Couldn't have happened to a nicer guy,' Tyrone said sarcastically, 'Let's find another way in.'

'There's a window we smashed to the rear of the barn. When Jayden and I tried to escape, it was hurriedly boarded up, it's the room we were held in.'

'Let's go.'

They made short work of removing the nailed boarding as quietly as they could and climbed in, they moved towards the door, Bruce peeked out and reeled in horror.

Sara was slumped with her back on the log wall and Joe was standing over her, pointing a gun at her head and had just cocked the gun, taking aim. Without further thought, Bruce darted out of the door and aimed a dropkick on Joe, just as the gun discharged.

Bruce landed on top of Joe, he quickly rolled away and came up on his feet fast, kicked away the dropped gun, Joe recovered, but not as fast, and staggered to his feet. Bruce grabbed hold of Joe's head pulled it down as he used a knee strike to hit him in the face. As Joe staggered back, Bruce followed this with a hard kick to the outer thigh, Joe screamed and was finding it hard to know where to protect himself as Bruce was so fast. An uppercut punch to Joe's chin, followed immediately by a throat punch which sent Joe to his knees, Bruce dived on top of him and had his hands around his throat with his knuckles pressing into his Adam's apple, Joe was kicking out, but it was ineffectual as Bruce had him incapacitated and snarling all the insults he could think of in his face, as he increased the pressure.

Tyrone dashed out of the room, straight behind Bruce and dealt with Mel, diving in low, aiming his gun and disarmed Mel with fast moves, brought him to the ground and had him in a headlock, choking him till he was unconscious. He looked over at Bruce, saw what he was doing, shoved Mel away from him and immediately jumped to his feet and pulled Bruce off, telling him the scum will get his comeuppance, and how he wouldn't want to be tried for his murder, let the police take care of him.

Bruce was breathing heavy, his heart was drumming hard in his chest, slowly he returned to reason and instantly sprinted over to Sara, 'Oh my God, she's been shot in the head, that bastard killed her,' he looked her over, 'He's also stabbed her twice, that fucking bastard. I wasn't in time, Sara oh Sara, I'm so sorry. I should have been faster, acted quicker.' Sara lay in his arms and he was rocking her back and forth, inconsolably distraught.

Tyrone spotted the bag of medical supplies and fetched them, he crouched beside Sara, checked her vital signs, first her wrist, but felt nothing, then her neck, after a short while he could feel a very faint pulse, looked up and smiled at Bruce, 'She's alive.'

'What? How?' Bruce couldn't believe it.

'Tyrone looked at her head wound first, 'It's serious, but not life-threatening,' he looked at Bruce, 'you *did* save her buddy, you changed the trajectory of the bullet, he was aiming for the centre of her head, you were quick enough to knock it off course,' he handed him a wadded bandage and told him to tie it tight around her head wound to stem the flow of blood.

'What about the stab wounds?'

Tyrone went to lift Sara's dress to inspect her wounds, he hesitated for a second, but Bruce quickly said, 'It's ok you need to look at her wounds.'

'They are deep, there is no telling which organs are damaged until they get her into surgery.'

He was already unwrapping more wadded bandages and pressing them to the wounds, replacing them with clean ones then tightly wrapped it around her hips and secured the ends.

'Where is Dr Hayes.' Bruce looked up crestfallen, and pointed to the other end of the barn, 'He was over near the doors the last I saw him. I don't think he made it.'

'I'll check on him on my way out, I'll run and get help.'

Tyrone found Jayden close to the door, slumped forward, with a spike in his side, as he was checking to confirm he was dead, he pondered on all the violence that had gone on here, he saw all the bruising on Bruce's face, and he was looking at the bruises on Jayden's face, not to mention all the bruises everywhere on Sara, such a small delicate creature, how could anyone be so callous and inflict so many injuries, he was amazed that she was still alive. All of a sudden Tyrone felt a weak pulse, and Jayden gave a small feeble grunt, Tyrone shouted, 'He's alive, Dr Hayes is alive.'

Bruce very gently picked Sara up into his arms, she weighed next to nothing, it was like carrying a doll. He walked towards Tyrone and laid Sara reverently, on the ground, there was nothing to place under her head, he took his shirt off, rolled it up and tenderly lifted her head.

Bruce moved over to Jayden and placed hands either side of his face and slowly lifted his head and said, 'Hey, Jayden, mate, I thought you were a goner.'

Jayden grimaced, then opened his eyes and asked, 'Did we get them?'

'All of them, this is Sergeant Tyrone Lawrence, he's stationed at the same base you are.

Before Tyrone could say anything, Jayden groaned loudly and slumped his head forward, Bruce checked for a pulse and sighed with relief, 'He's passed out again.'

'We can't release him, if we pull that spike out, he could bleed to death,' you ok to stay here whilst I run back and get the police, mum will have called them by now, and I can direct them here using the road, to get the ambulances in. While I'm gone, tie those bastards up, just in case they wake, use the rope from … What the hell was that over there?' He pointed to the dismantled ring.

'A fight Ring. They forced us to fight.'

'Poetic justice then, tying them up with their own ropes,' they both smiled. Tyrone swiftly rose to his feet and was gone.

In one of the scenes in his film, he remembered being taught different knots to tie a person up, that if they moved excessively, they would slowly tighten their own ropes. With a smile, he trussed Mel up and tied it around one of the stakes still in place from the ring, but with Joe he laid him on his front, and bound his legs and arms together, looping the rope around his neck, and thought, now this truly is, Poetic Justice, when he finished, he kicked Joe.

He went back to Sara and Jayden, checked their breathing and wounds, they both looked really pale and he prayed Tyrone was a fast runner, it seemed like an eternity waiting for the Ambulance and Police.

Joe started stirring, and Bruce had the satisfaction of hearing him choke, he said, 'Struggle and you will slowly choke yourself, so be my guest and keep struggling.'

'What the fuck, take this off me.'

'I think you are through, giving orders.' He walked back over to Joe, removed the neckerchief Joe was wearing and gagged him, 'How does that feel? Uncomfortable? - Good!' Joe struggled and Bruce had the satisfaction of hearing him choke a little more. 'Keep it up Joe,' as he walked away. Joe stopped struggling and laid there quietly.

Seventy-One

Ric and Cade were on their way with a back-up team following, the FBI would meet them there, although they had no idea if there was any building on the land, from their checks, no permission had been granted, they were searching blind.

As they neared the area, there was a message from despatch, 'The missing girl, Ava Heughan has been found.' Ric and Cade looked at each other in disbelief. As Cade was driving, Ric responded and got more information. They had received a call from a Mrs Maisie Lawrence and they gave her address, as Cade put the sirens on and sped up, despatch continued. Bruce Bailey had come knocking on her door with the little girl, and asked her to call the Police to get her reunited with her parents, then took off running back into the woods, their son Sergeant Tyrone Lawrence, who was home on leave, went with him. Ric told despatch to notify the FBI and the Ambulances.

Within minutes they were all converging together outside Mr and Mrs Lawrence's house, the FBI arrived in a helicopter landing in a field. At the same time, Tyrone came running out of the woods as the ambulances arrived. Tyrone asked who was in charge, and there was confusion as to whether it was the FBI, Morgan Murphy and Carlos Sanchez or NYPD Ric and Cade, it was very quickly agreed to treat it as a combined co-ordination, and not to waste time arguing.

Tyrone quickly told them of the serious injuries Sara and Jayden had. They all jumped back into their vehicles. Ric and Cade led the way, with Tyrone directing them and the FBI following overhead.

All of a sudden Bruce could hear lots of sirens and a helicopter, it was the sweetest music to his ears, they came screeching to a halt and gravel sprayed everywhere. Bruce opened the large barn doors, the Emergency Medical Services entered the barn and were quickly attending Sara, an

Intravenous line was set up very fast when Bruce told them she was seriously dehydrated and had been starved, they next tended her head wound and quickly reassured Bruce that although it was serious, it was not life-threatening, as the bullet had not imbedded, the most serious wounds were the stab wounds, and they were quickly cleaning them up and applying fresh dressings and bandages. They left her knee as it looked really well dress and Bruce explained that Jayden had tended it but it would need urgent surgery.

The other EMS team were attending Jayden, they called out that they needed bolt cutters to break the spike that was embedded into the log wall, it would take too long to get the Fire team out, some of the Officers searched both barns, no bolt cutters, but a crowbar was found in the next barn and the spike was dug out, and Jayden was quickly released from the wall and laid on his side. His wounds were checked, Jayden didn't wake up and it was just as well, an intravenous line was put in and they whisked him off to the Ambulance and hospital.

Tyrone was explaining to Ric and Cade, that there were four of the gang tied in the woods and they *may*, have broken legs, Ric raised an eyebrow, Tyrone shrugged his shoulders and said with a smile, 'No idea how that happened, they *must* have tripped, those woods are very dangerous you know. I will admit to tying them up, though, to stop them from escaping.'

Bruce informed them that their weapons were spread around the woods close to where they were. Ric and Cade directed the team into the woods, to round up the rest of the gang and the weapons.

Morgan and Carlos were searching the barn, Ric and Cade joined them, Morgan said, 'All these,' pointing to all the cameras, 'has made our job easier, we won't need a confession to get a conviction.'

Ric walked over to where Bruce was kneeling close to Sara, as the EMS were still working on her, and said, 'How are you holding up?'

Bruce was looking at Sara with tears glistening in his eyes, he didn't take his eyes off her as he answered, 'I just find it hard to comprehend the level of hatred and brutality they showed her. She is so small and delicate, she didn't stand a chance against them, why did they do all this to her?'

'I've been in the Police force for many years now, seen so many things, and *I*, am still mystified at human behaviour, but I have also seen some brilliant things that people will do for each other, and I have to remind myself of that, when I see *this*, happen to such a beautiful person, if I didn't, I don't think I could keep doing my job. When this all starts sinking in, you will find that a lot of people will want to offer, all of you, help and support, focus on that, and not on these lowlifes, they don't deserve your time or consideration. You saved that little girl, her parents have her back, believe me, *that*, doesn't always happen. You also foiled their plan and saved Sara, when you start blaming yourself for what you *didn't* do, think about everything you *did* do.'

Ric looked at Bruce and new admiration for the man rose in his eyes, Tyrone had told them some, of what had happened on their way here and right now, Bruce wasn't thinking of himself, he was thinking of Sara, everything he had read about him had given the impression that he was focused on himself, self-progression and getting rich. Ric knew first-hand though, that the media didn't always care about the truth, even the truth they did get was sometimes twisted, they just wanted sensational stories and scandal.

'We need to take a look at your injury,' one of the EMS crew, said to Bruce.

'That can wait till we get to the hospital, please, just look after Sara, I'm ok, honest.'

'Obviously, I will need to talk to you, but that can wait till later, I will catch up with you at the hospital,' Ric said.

They had Sara on a trolley and were about to leave, Bruce walked alongside the trolley and a blanket was thrown over his shoulders.

Ric joined Cade who was looking over Joe, they were impressed by the intricate rope knotting, noticing how, as Joe struggled, the rope was tightening and he immediately stilled. They looked at each other and smiled, 'This is better than handcuffs, it would keep many of the perps we capture *very* still, do you think the Captain would go for this?' said Cade.

'Not officially, unfortunately,' they laughed and set about untying Joe, handcuffing and putting him in the back of their car, Mel would need his wounds tending and go in an ambulance, which the team attended to. Before leaving, they liaised with Morgan and Carlos, asking if they could have a look at all the tapes first. After a little consideration, they agreed they could hold off for no more than two days, or their own bosses would be grilling them.

Morgan said he and Carlos would ensure all was detailed from the scene and would see them back at their offices in New York, the others would be processed locally first, but Ric was keen to get Joe back for interrogation, or *questioning* being its official phrase, but this lowlife had threatened the life of a little girl, and the injuries he saw on Sara made him sick, she had been tortured.

Seventy-Two

The EMS crew introduced themselves as Luke and Ashley, who was driving, they set off at great speed with sirens blaring. Bruce sat in the back of the ambulance looking bewildered as he gazed at Sara, her face was so swollen with a bandage around her head. She looked so small and delicate, but was so brave, she had survived all they had done to her. He wanted to hold her, to soothe and comfort her, but he couldn't even hold her hand, as it was the left one that was closest to him, and it was the one that had been skewered to the table. Luke had told him that her left arm had also been broken in more than one place. Bruce shuddered at the scale of their cruelty. Luke was checking her vitals, hooking her up to a heart monitor, which was like a soothing balm to his soul, to hear it beeping away, *she was alive*, her blood pressure was being checked.

Suddenly Luke looked worried and shouted to Ashley to put his foot down, the monitor wasn't beeping, 'We need to get her to the hospital. Now,' he shouted and then started resuscitation on Sara, he was pumping her chest, put an airbag over her mouth and asked Bruce to press when he told him to, then shouted, 'Clear,' for Bruce to lean back as he shocked her heart. Bruce silently prayed, *'Please God, don't take her now, she's gone through so much, she deserves a life, I will do anything to give that to her.'* Then the monitor resumed its constant rhythmic beeping, and Bruce let out a, *'Thank you,'* on a huge sigh of relief.

Then, Ashley shouted over his shoulder, that they were pulling into the hospital. As soon as they stopped, the rear doors immediately opened, and there was a team of Doctors and Nurses waiting. Sara's trolley was pulled out and rushed into the hospital. He followed the team through A&E and was told to wait in the reception area as they rushed Sara through a corridor, straight to Theatre. As the doors and all the commotion faded away, Bruce was left alone.

In the silence of the corridor, everything that had happened started to feel so surreal, he had no idea if Sara would make it or not, the vacuum of silence, felt like life and time had been suspended.

He heard a door open behind him, and a Doctor came up to him and said they needed to take a look at his injury and get some details from him. He was taken into a side room, and he sat on the examining bench, the blanket was removed from around his shoulders, and his makeshift shirt sleeve bandage was untied and removed by a nurse. It seemed so long ago, was it only earlier today that his shoulder was injured, so much had happened.

The sleeve had stuck as the blood had dried, and the nurse said she would use warm water to remove it, Bruce didn't care, all he could think about was what Sara was going through right now, he closed his eyes and conjured up the image of her stunning smiling face, and the sound of her laughter. He made a silent vow to her, *If you make it back to me, my sweet beautiful Sara, I will spend the rest of my days finding ways to keep you smiling and laughing, I swear, just come back to me.'*

The Doctor sensed Bruce's need for quiet contemplation and respectfully, she quickly cleaned the wound, stitched it up with only necessary comments. Finishing the bandaging, she handed him the cup of tea the nurse had brought in, then closed the door and left him alone in the little examining room, to give him a little privacy.

Bruce closed his eyes and appreciated the quiet, calm way the Doctor dealt with his shoulder, he couldn't manage to talk, and he knew he had a long wait to hear anything of Sara's condition, *if*, she survived, 'Please God, let her survive,' he whispered, and let the tears slowly fall, unashamedly.

Slowly, he became aware of familiar voices outside, quietly the door opened, and he saw first his eldest brother Blake, Brett was behind him and then Brooke pushed past them, but gently put her arms around him, 'Oh Bruce, I am so glad you are alive, I love you so much, and was so scared of losing you.' Bruce hugged her with his good arm, and breathed in the essence of his little sister, so glad to see her again, and hating the gang for making his family worry.

He noticed the expressions of shock and concern on his brother's faces, which warned him that he must look a real sight, he looked down as Brooke stepped back, and noticed all the bruising over his body, they would fade, so too, would the bruised ribs, a few felt like they were probably cracked.

'How did you get here so quickly?' Bruce asked amazed that they were here, with him.

'We all took a sabbatical from our jobs within days of your disappearance, they could see we were useless at work while we awaited news about you, and have all been living in an apartment in New York, as soon as you were found, Detective Ricardo Garcia notified us, Brett drove like a madman getting us here,' Brooke said.

'You have no idea how good it is to see you all,' Bruce smiled and felt his heart swell in his chest to hear what they had done, to be closer to him. 'Blake, could you find out if there is any news on Jayden?'

'Of course.' He quickly left the room.

'How is mum?' he asked and noticed the looks pass between his siblings, 'What's happened, tell me.'

Brett answered, 'Since you were taken, the media in Britain has been unbelievable, in their frenzy for information. You and Sara have been in every newspaper, magazine, in the news, even the government have been involved, putting pressure on the American Embassy back home, and liaising with the British Embassy here, especially since that poor little girl was kidnapped, and the Military Doctor. The story has been huge.'

'What's happened to mum,' Bruce repeated with panic in his voice.

'She is fine, but the media got carried away, they were following her every time she left home and pestering her for an exclusive on you. Two weeks ago, when the media were still going crazy after the gang were arrested, and it was linked to your disappearance, mum had walked over to the park opposite her for some fresh air, she immediately decided to return home, when approached by three journalists. Whilst crossing the road, she was hit by a car and her leg was broken.'

Before Bruce could interject, Brett continued, 'She's ok,' he reassured him, 'if it weren't for all our Aunties and Uncles converging on her to keep her company and at home, you know she would have been here with us, she asked if you could give her a call as soon as you are able.'

'I'll call her once I know about Sara.'

'Mum was crying down the phone, at the relief that you're alive, as are we,' Brooke said.

Blake returned and was followed into the room by a pretty young woman with short blonde hair and large beautiful clear blue eyes, she introduced herself as Layla Burns, Jayden's girlfriend.

'I met your brother outside asking after Jayden, apologies for the intrusion, but I just wanted to say a huge, thank you, the Police told me briefly, what had happened, that you escaped, but went back, I honestly don't think he would be here if you hadn't.' Her eyes were red-rimmed, and she looked like she was struggling to hold back the tears.

Bruce felt just as emotional and she was on her own, he opened his arms and she stepped into a hug as he whispered into her hair, 'You don't need to thank me, it is I, who would like to say a massive thank you, to Jayden, he is an amazing person and Doctor, everything he did was incredible, and he was really brave, I couldn't have got through this without him. Have you heard how he is doing?'

Bruce relaxed his hug and she stepped back and said, 'No, he is still in surgery. Have you had any more news on Sara?'

Blake answered, 'It's the same, she is still in surgery.'

'At the moment, I am just holding onto the fact that no news, means she is still alive.'

'Same for me, I'm an A&E nurse at the Bellevue Hospital where Jayden was before his secondment to the Military base, I have some friends who work in Theatre here, while I ask for news on Jayden, I will ask about Sara as well.'

'Really appreciate that Layla, thank you. You are more than welcome to join us, while we wait for them to come out of surgery,' said Bruce.

'I'd like that, I'm here alone, thank you. I'll go and see if I can get any more information and then come back.'

As the time passed, Bruce told his siblings a few details of the ordeal, they were shocked, he wasn't ready to tell all, if ever he would be, and who would he tell, it was far too personal, and at the moment, he was still so wired with turbulent emotions.

They had nearly lost their brother and at a time like this, they were not ashamed to show or tell him how much they loved him, Blake, Brett and Brooke each whispered into his ear as they hugged him, how they had been feeling, whilst he had been captured and their joy and relief that he was alive.

He was finding it hard to hold back his emotions, Brooke saw it and moved in to hug him again, that's when the dam opened and he broke down again. Bruce was not ashamed to cry in front of his brothers and sister, not after all they had been through in their childhood. His brothers moved in and they all gently hugged him again and were just there for him.

Bruce brought himself under control, 'Sorry, what a cry baby,' he said wiping his eyes, Brooke grabbed some paper towels and handed them to him.

'You don't ever need to apologise to us, Bruce,' said Brooke, with tears of her own rolling down her cheeks.

'What's the date?' Bruce asked, 'We lost all concept of time.'

'It's Monday 30th June, you've been gone exactly twelve weeks.'

'My God, that long, although weirdly, it feels more like twelve months.'

As the hours ticked by, Bruce went and made an emotional call to his mother, he couldn't bear for her to suffer any more anguish, and wanted her to hear from him, that he was fine. She cried down the phone, and apologised for not being there with him, they told each other that they loved one another, he promised to call again soon, but he needed to check on Sara.

She asked, 'Are the reports true, Brucie, that you and Sara are together?'

'Yes, for once the papers have got it right. I love her mum.'

'We will pray for her full recovery, such a beautiful girl, call me again as soon as you are able, I love you, my Brucie.'

'I will and I Love you too, mum.' He ended the call, as he turned around, he saw Cameron approaching.

As soon as Cameron saw Bruce, he strode straight over to him and with a strained look, his eyes red and brimming with tears he said, 'The Police were in the reception area and told me some of what happened. I can't thank you enough or find the words to adequately convey how grateful I am for what you did. You went back for her, whatever happens, I will always be indebted to you for that, I came close to losing my little sister, I can't imagine my life without her in it.' He held out his hand, Bruce took it, Cameron placed his other hand over the handshake and said, 'Thank you.' They held the handshake as they hugged.

Seventy-Three

They were given a larger, separate room where they could all wait together, they sat or paced in front of the large windows that overlooked the park to the rear of the hospital. The door opened and the Surgeon walked in, all of them rose to their feet as one, and took a deep breath. The Surgeon took off his cap and approached Bruce.

'She is in recovery and stable, for now. During the surgery, her heart stopped again, we had to revive her, she had lost so much blood. In all my years in surgery, I have never operated on anyone with so many separate injuries, that's what took us so long, she is no-where near out of the woods ...'

Bruce stifled a smile at his unfortunate turn of phrase, for him, she was well out of the woods, but understood his meaning, and didn't waste the time to correct him, and allowed him to continue.

'She is being taken to a private suite. As soon as they have settled her, you can go and see her, a nurse will come and get you.'

'How is Jayden?' Bruce asked.

'He is also in recovery and stable, he will be transferred to a ward very soon, we will come and get you when he is transferred.'

'Please, take him to a private suite, I will pay all his medical bills.' Bruce said.

'Oh my God, I don't know what to say, except, thank you, thank you so much,' Layla said as tears brimmed her eyes and rolled down her cheeks. She stepped forward and gave Bruce another hug.

Bruce now smiled with sheer relief and accepted the whiskey in a plastic cup from his brothers for a toast to Sara and Jayden, even his sister and Layla joined them, even though they didn't like whiskey.

Later, Bruce walked into Sara's hospital suite, he pulled up the large comfortable cushioned chair that was in the corner by the big window, that overlooked the gardens opposite, and drew back the blinds to let in the beautiful sunshine, they had been in the darkness for too long, and he wanted Sara to feel the rays of sunshine on her face. He also opened the small windows to their full capacity on their safety catches, and a cool gentle breeze drifted in.

He placed the chair next to Sara's bed and sat down. His brothers had gone out and got him toiletries and new clothes, he had been able to take a shower, which felt really good, although it had been difficult whilst keeping his shoulder dressings dry. All the new bruises had come out along with all the aches and pains, but how dare he grumble, when he now looked at Sara.

Before coming up to the room, the Doctor appraised him of all the injuries, there were a load he didn't know about, he was shocked with disbelief at the brutality she endured after he had left. The Doctor told him about the surgery she had undergone, her jaw had been broken and two back teeth were so loose, they had to remove them, her arm had been broken in three places, he also warned that the bullet to her head may affect her hearing, her sight and even her memory, they will know more when she wakes up. Bruce appreciated his phrasing of *when*, not *if*. Her head had been shaved, as they discovered numerous cuts and so much blood had matted against her scalp, it was difficult to tend all the cuts, also clumps of her hair had been pulled from their roots. He warned him that her stab wounds were very close to her womb and only time would tell if this would result in any lasting effects. They had also spent a long time in repairing her knee and said she will need extensive physio.

Bruce asked, 'Does this mean she may never have children?'

The Doctor replied, 'It's a possibility, but given time these may heal, it's too difficult to answer with any certainty, at the moment.' Bruce absorbed this and made his decision, that whatever happened, he would be beside her, no matter what.

He sat to the right of her, as her left arm was plastered and her hand was bandaged, there were tubes everywhere, going into her and coming out of her, a monitor was beeping away and a nurse was checking all the machinery around her.

In the middle of all this was his precious Sara, she looked so tiny, he carefully took her hand, with the intravenous drip feed, and looked at her beautiful face, although more swollen than the last time he saw her, with all the different colours of bruising, she was still and always would be beautiful to him. There was a bandage around her head and under her jaw, she had a nasogastric tube going into her nose and an oxygen tube. There were drains from her surgical sites hanging around the edge of the bed.

He lifted her hand and kissed it reverently, the nurse turned around and told him that she was stable and would leave them to have some privacy, the monitor would alert them at the nurse's station, but to call if he had any concerns. He thanked her and she quietly shut the door.

There was just the two of them, together, and free.

He moved closer and started whispering to her. 'After talking to the Doctor, I am not sure if you can hear me and maybe this is just for my benefit, but if you *can* hear me, know this, my sweet Sara, I am never leaving you alone again, if you want to be rid of me, then you will have to wake up, open those beautiful chocolate brown eyes, and tell me yourself.'

He decided to talk about all the wonderful memories he has of their precious time together in New York before all this happened, he told her how he treasured them and was the only thing that kept him going throughout this ordeal, and how he wanted to create many more magical moments with her, however, she wanted to interpret that, she could do so at her own prerogative, at this he let out a cheeky laugh.

He talked on into the night caressing parts of her face not covered in bandages, with his finger-tips, gently kissing her hand, telling her all the local news, and how there were now thousands, if not millions of people around the world, praying for her recovery.

He got up to get himself a glass of water and saw the early morning dawn starting to break through, he realised he had been talking all night. He gazed at the park opposite, as the sun rose and cast its stunning kaleidoscope of colours across the sky, and took in the panoramic view, yawned and stretched, as much as his body and shoulder would allow, then turned around and returned to his chair, took Sara's hand in his and rested his head on the bed. For the first time in months, he slowly drifted gently off to sleep.

Sara had been hearing low husky murmurings for a while, now she could see pinpricks of brightness in the engulfing and all-consuming darkness. As the light got brighter, she realised she had opened her eyes, grimacing through pain, she could feel her hand being held and looked down with her eyes and saw Bruce's tousled hair and his face turned towards her, asleep.

Was she dreaming or was she alive and Bruce was with her, she moved her fingers and could feel the warmth of his hand covering hers, she was alive.

With the ghost of a smile on her lips, she drifted back to peaceful oblivion.

Acknowledgements

To my Husband Allen for listening to each chapter and grateful for all your suggestions and feedback, also for keeping the house and me fed whilst I concentrated on my writing every day.

To my Daughter and Son, Leanne & Aaron for their patience while I talked about my book and for their feedback.

To my friend and Published Author, Hazel Reed for her advice and for introducing me to MTP.

To Keith & Karolina at MTP for their patience, guidance & advice while I finished my manuscript and for the brilliant book cover.

About Lynne Hunter

I first fell in love with writing at school when my English teacher would set me a task of writing a story based around one single word and I enjoyed exploring different angles rather than the obvious.

Life got in the way and I tried various career avenues, undertaking Nurse training in Surrey where I met my Husband and we started our family.

I qualified as a TESOL Teacher and accommodated students from around the world and taught them English.

My Husband and I set up our own Company and business in the Care Industry. After 13 years, we closed the business and converted the property into private houses to sell.

Our children have now grown up and left home and we recently welcomed the arrival of our Granddaughter. I am an Estate Manager for a large retirement Development in West Sussex and decided the time was right to return to my first love of writing.

More from me at:

@LynneHunter0

www.facebook.com/lynne.hunter.96343

Books in the Resilience Series

Resilience in Love (Book 1)

Sara Kaye and Bruce Bailey are the leads in an epic romantic period drama movie. Experiencing a potent attraction to each other on set, they spend an idyllic week enjoying the sights of New York and falling in love.

A gang kidnap them, and events spiral into a series of sinister situations, that forces Sara to sacrifice her life, to save a five-year-old girl.

Bruce was powerless to protect them, but can he find a way to save them?

Resilience in Life (Book 2)

Sara's physical recovery is excruciatingly painful. Bruce is fearful she will give up and slip away, and it's tearing him apart. He pleads with his brother Blake, who is a Doctor, to find a way to help.

Bruce endures a Police investigation as the gang await trial. Desperate to start a family, Sara faces heart-breaking news.

Having survived their horrific kidnapping ordeal, they now face a new ordeal, finding ways to help each other with more than just their physical recovery. Will their love be strong enough?

Resilience in Life *again* (Book 3)

They have endured incredible highs and unbelievable lows in their life together. Throughout all the heady heights of their careers and the depths of their nightmares, they have treasured the love of their family and their circle of formidable friends.

Many years have passed since their kidnapping, Bruce and Sara have raised their family and are looking forward to the next chapter in their lives. Until the son, of an old enemy endeavours to finish what his father started. Sara once again faces her own mortality. Will Bruce be able to save her?

*Available worldwide online
and from all good bookstores*

---

www.mtp.agency

@mtp_agency

www.facebook.com/mtp.agency

Michael Terence Publishing

www.ingramcontent.com/pod-product-compliance
Lightning Source LLC
LaVergne TN
LVHW091531060526
838200LV00036B/559